D1671612

THE HAUNTING OF EDGEFIELD MANOR

KIM POOVEY

Copyright © 2022 by Kim Poovey

All rights reserved.

No part of this book may be reproduced in any form or by any electronic or
mechanical means, including information storage and retrieval systems,
without written permission from the author, except for the use of brief
quotations in a book review.

Cover design by Rena Violet.

Photo of Magnolia Dale by Alyssa Krob of Wildscriber Marketing.

Dickens Ghost Publishing, LLC

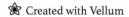 Created with Vellum

Dedicated to God, my rock and my salvation.

THE HAUNTING OF EDGEFIELD MANOR

1

A chill skittered down Sarah's back as she padded along the dull wood floors in the corridor of an unfamiliar building. Books lined floor to ceiling shelves on either side of her with artifacts cluttering the top ledges. She continued through the darkened space despite her inability to see clearly and her inner voice clamoring for her to run. Her heart pounded harder with each step as if something waited in the shadows. When she got to the back wall, she stood in front of an old door. Reaching for the knob, Sarah swallowed her trepidation as her hair stood on end. The icy brass knob stung the palm of her hand as she rotated it. A screeching sound pierced her ear drums as the door creaked open and an eyeless woman stood before her, the right side of her head smashed in.

An ear-shattering scream jolted Sarah from her temporary slumber on the couch, causing her to knock over her empty wine glass. Scooping up the glass, Sarah glanced about the darkened space of her parlor. Danni sat nearby, wide-eyed with her mouth gaping open as she stared at her best friend.

"How can you sleep through this? It's one of the most terrifying films ever made," Danni said, pausing the movie.

"What can I say? I was tired," Sarah croaked, rubbing her forehead.

"Not many people could sleep with this kinda horror on the screen."

"Pfft. I've seen worse in my dreams," Sarah responded, raising her eyebrows and trudging to the kitchen to put her wine glass in the sink.

As she rinsed the glass, a misshapen aura reflected from the window, sending a frosty blast through her veins. She blinked a few times, the foggy image disappearing as quickly as it had materialized. *Probably just my mind wandering after the horror flick.* Returning to the front parlor, Sarah's muscles constricted as another ear shattering scream echoed from the TV.

It was Danni's idea to have a scary movie sleepover since they were set to head to Edgefield first thing in the morning. Now Sarah was questioning why she'd let her best friend talk her into something so crazy. Sarah had enough difficulty sleeping with the lifelike visions of the dead haunting her slumbering hours without adding spooky stimulation from the television.

It had been a year since she discovered a lifetime of haunted dreams and the occasional ghoulish vision were a gift she'd inherited from her biological mother, Edie Monroe. As a dreamist, Sarah was able to help the dead with unresolved issues, move onto a peaceful afterlife through her dreams. Of course, being an antiques estate dealer made for some interesting ghostly experiences when cleaning out old houses or handling period pieces. At least now she understood the strange encounters were part of her dreamist abilities and not some form of insanity.

When the movie finally ended, Danni bid goodnight and headed for bed while Sarah cleaned the dishes. Once everything was in the drying rack, Sarah climbed the stairs, her rankled nerves weighting her limbs. She changed into her nightshirt and crawled into bed. Despite a crazy evening of frightening films and a disturbing dream, Sarah rested her head against the pillow and quickly drifted off.

THE STALE SCENT of weathered books and air freshener stung Sarah's nose as she wandered through the shadowy space. A sense of déjà vu permeated her soul. She recognized this place. It was the same one from her dream when she'd dozed off in the parlor while Danni watched scary movies. As she padded through the dreamscape, Sarah exhaled, relieved this wasn't one of her haunted nightmares but merely a replay of a previous dream.

Surprised by her self-awareness in this vision, she continued down the long corridor to the door at the end of it. The air grew colder as she reached for the knob when a wintry draft ruffled her hair and a sense of unease ignited her apprehension.

Staring at the wooden door, she heard steps on the other side and watched the knob rattle. *Don't trust him*, hissed as the door screeched open and the eyeless figure flew toward her, its sinewy hands reaching in her direction. Sarah tried to run but terror paralyzed her legs as the creature's fingers scraped at her throat...

Sarah bolted upright in bed, her body quivering and her skin sticky from fright. She switched on the night table lamp, wrapped her arms about her knees, and rocked back and forth, trying to chase the horrific image from her head. She hadn't had a dream this grotesque in over a year.

Filling her lungs with air, Sarah held it for a count of five and released, just like she'd learned in therapy decades earlier. As the tension began to melt from her shoulders, she stared around the room. *Why was this happening now?*

In an effort to calm her racing heart, she trudged to the

bathroom and splashed cold water on her face. She needed to get some sleep. They were supposed to be on the road at eight the next morning. Blotting the droplets from her face, she stared at her reflection. Wisdom and hard work were beginning to crease her skin. She drew closer, examining the lines parading from the corners of her eyes when the ghastly visage from her nightmare flashed in the mirror, sending her stumbling backwards. She rubbed her eyes with the palms of her hands and looked in the mirror again. Nothing. No doubt, her mind was playing tricks on her after the vivid images in the dreams. At least that's what she told herself to quiet the blood rushing through her veins with the force of white-water rapids.

Hanging the towel on the rack, she hurried from the bathroom. Momentarily, she considered waking Danni but thought better of it. Her friend was cranky enough when she'd gotten plenty of sleep. Bothering her in the middle of the night wouldn't be pretty.

No point trying to sleep now. Experience had taught Sarah these kinds of dreams would linger in her mind. The only thing to do was fix a cup of tea and try to relax. She walked down the hall as a translucent hand reached for her neck, vanishing as she flipped on the light.

2

Danni's Mercedes whizzed down the back roads towards Edgefield, the hot summer air swirling through the car. It was a three-hour drive to the small town situated between Aiken and North Augusta. Sarah's hair whipped against her cheeks as she sang along to *Hungry Like the Wolf* by Duran Duran. How Danni had convinced her to take on this project was beyond her. Ever since Sarah inherited the multi-million-dollar Monroe estate, her life had altered considerably. Of course, it wasn't the money, or the discovery of her adoption that had made the difference in her day-to-day life but learning her haunted dreams were an ancestral trait. It was a much better prospect than believing she was crazy.

Nevertheless, her best friend, Danni, had stood by her and helped her hone her dreamist skills. Now she was returning the favor by helping one of Danni's college friends, Brady Anderson, with a family crisis.

"Any more news on Brady's cousin?" Sarah asked when an ad for Bardwell's tires sounded from the radio.

"Last I heard, he was being arraigned this week. Brady is adamant his cousin is innocent," Danni said, the open window thrashing her sandy-brown hair about her face like the arms of those tall blow-up creatures at used car lots. Danni had been practicing law for over a decade and had developed a solid reputation across the state. It was no wonder her former college friend had asked for her help.

Sarah huffed. "Of course, he claims he's innocent, it's his cousin. Most people don't want to believe a family member could commit such a heinous crime."

"Aren't we skeptical?" Danni replied, as Michael Jackson's *Beat It* started blaring from the speakers.

Sarah reached over and turned the knob, hushing the music.

"The man bludgeoned his wife to death with a fireplace poker he made in his own forge! He didn't call the police when she failed to come home, and he doesn't have an alibi. I know you want to support your friend, but the case seems pretty solid to me."

"It's all circumstantial. Besides, I have a talent for weaving a tale. All I need is reasonable doubt, and Dusty walks away a free man."

"And what if he *is* guilty?"

Danni furrowed her brow. "I'm his attorney; I need to believe in his innocence."

"Suit yourself, but I suspect there's more to this story than what Brady told you."

Sarah stared out the window as the landscape blurred past. A whistle blew out a warning as a train chugged along the tracks running parallel with the road. Sarah watched as the conductor on the train smiled and waved before the train leapt from the tracks, crashing to the ground like a tower of blocks. The conductor rose from the wreckage, his face crushed and his eyes hanging from the sockets. Sucking in a breath, Sarah blinked several times before realizing the tracks had been unused for years and she was the only one who'd seen the accident.

"You OK?" Danni asked.

"Yeah, just caught a chill," she replied, not wanting to discuss what she'd just witnessed.

"Did you see something?" Danni queried, glancing at her friend.

"Yes," Sarah muttered, wanting to wipe the grisly image of the bloody train conductor from her mind.

"Want to tell me about it?"

"Not really," Sarah muttered, her skin still crawling from the experience.

"We need to learn how to control these visions," Danni said. "I've almost got the next chapter figured out."

Sarah exhaled. She was thankful Danni was helping her interpret the *Dreamist* book which was a manual to her haunted dreams. Still, it didn't make the visions or the creepy dreamscapes any easier.

As if sensing her unease, Danni changed the subject. "Where are your parents now?"

"Africa. Mom wanted to go on Safari and Dad has always been captivated by Egypt."

"How many countries does that make for them?" Danni asked.

"It's easier to list the places they haven't visited," Sarah chuckled. "Tell me more about Edgefield. The only thing I've ever heard is that it produced ten governors."

Danni gave a sly grin. "You won't believe this place. It's got more shootouts in its history than the OK Corral."

"Is it safe?" Sarah asked, her eyes widening. Her dreams were grisly enough without having to worry about being shot.

"Of course, it is," Danni replied. "There's very little violence in town now."

"How's that?"

"Everyone's packing."

"Great," Sarah said, rolling her eyes. Something told her this was going to be an experience she'd not likely forget.

GRAVEL CRACKLED BENEATH THE MERCEDES' tires as Danni pulled down a curved drive to a two-story white house a couple blocks from the main drag of Edgefield. Crumbling shutters framed its windows and paint flaked from the wooden siding like the bark of a birch tree. Danni put the car in park and got out with a stretch.

Sarah stood, her legs and back stiff from hours of travel. Walking around the car, she stared at the old house, her scalp prickling as something shifted in one of the upstairs windows. She took in a deep breath and convinced herself it was probably just a tree branch reflecting from the glass.

"Looks like this place could use a good overhaul," Sarah said, scrutinizing the overgrown gardens and unkempt lawn.

"Brady's aunt doesn't live here but keeps the place since it's the family homestead," she said with a grimace. "But you're right. It could use a serious make-over from one of those HGTV shows."

"Is it even inhabitable?" Sarah queried.

"Hope so or we'll be looking for a hotel room."

Sarah shivered at the thought. She hated hotels. There was always some sort of entity drifting about or entering her dreams. Hotels seemed to house a lot of spirits of those who'd once slept there. It creeped her out.

A red Mercedes was parked beneath a sprawling oak at the side of the house.

"Looks like Brady's already here," Dani announced. "I'm surprised at his new ride. He was always a Beamer guy."

"What is it with lawyers and fancy cars?" Sarah asked with a sly smile.

"What's with antique dealers and rusted out pickups?" Danni retorted.

"They're affordable to maintain and you can use duct tape to repair any holes in the body," Sarah replied, raising her nose in the air.

Shaking her head, Danni walked up to the front porch and knocked.

The door opened and a tall gentleman with waves of flaxen hair and eyes the shade of the ocean stepped out, pulling Danni into an embrace. "Danni, thanks so much for coming."

Brady was the cliché of a southern attorney dressed in a linen suit with a starched white shirt and yellow bow tie. His charm permeated the air with the power of a strong cologne. Stepping back, he offered his hand to Sarah. "You must be the infamous Sarah I've heard Danni prattle on about for so many years."

"And you must be Brady. It's nice to finally meet you," Sarah replied, returning the handshake.

Funny, she'd heard about their college hijinks from Danni and yet they'd never crossed paths before now. It wasn't like Sarah and Danni hadn't seen each other while Danni was in law school. They'd hang out on weekends when Sarah didn't have to work on the renos at her grandfather's mercantile or clear out an estate. Danni was one of those brainy types who didn't have to study, giving her time on the weekends for a little fun with her best friend. She always hated that aspect of Danni. Sarah had to study intensely while Danni could hear the information once and pass a test without having to crack open a book or reread her notes. It was disgusting.

"Come inside, I just opened a bottle of scotch," Brady offered.

"Sounds good to me," Danni said, following her law school friend into the foyer of the old house.

Sarah closed her eyes and inhaled, taking in the musty

scent of aging plaster, mildew, and old wood. The smell of an old house was ambrosia to an antiques dealer.

Something in Danni's gaze caught Sarah's attention, something she hadn't seen in years. There was a flush to her cheek and a twinkle in her eye when she looked at Brady. Sarah's eyes drifted to his left hand. No ring. Hmm, perhaps something latent was brewing.

They entered the front parlor with its outdated 1980s attempt at Victorian style. Washed-out swags of floral cotton draperies framed the windows with a mishmash of antique furnishings filling the room. A 19th century Jacobean tea cart functioned as a bar. Brady tipped a crystal decanter of amber liquid and filled two glasses before turning to Sarah.

"Would you like a drink?" he asked, flashing a dazzling smile. There was an allure about him that put Sarah at ease, not at all what she'd expected. According to Danni, Brady was known as the Shark due to his aggressive nature in the courtroom. Needless to say, aside from the expensive sportscar parked outside, he seemed as down to earth as they came.

Not wanting to seem unappreciative, Sarah nodded her ascent even though it was only late morning. He poured a shot and handed it to her.

Brady raised his glass. "To proving my cousin's innocence," he said as Danni and Sarah repeated the phrase and clinked glasses.

The scotch was smooth as it warmed Sarah's throat. Danni and Brady chatted while Sarah roamed, surveying the antique pieces and artwork. The collection wasn't as valuable as the Monroe estate but would still bring a decent amount of money.

"What do you think, Sarah?" Brady asked, pouring himself another drink. "Will you be able to make some money with this stuff?"

Sarah nodded. "Your aunt has some nice pieces. I'll know

more once I get a chance to go through it all. Hopefully, it will bring enough to cover Dusty's legal fees."

"I hope so. She's overwrought with worry. No one has lived in this place for years, but she refuses to sell. Says she can't let go of the family homestead," he said, shrugging his shoulders.

"It's hard to let go of family heirlooms," Sarah replied still looking around. "It's sad she has to liquidate the contents to pay for her son's legal expenses. At least she can keep the house."

"It's prime real estate and would provide enough money for her to retire and enjoy her golden years," he said. "This house is on the National Registry of Historic Places."

"You know I'm giving you the friends and family discount," Danni said with a smile. "Maybe she won't need to get rid of everything in the house."

"I appreciate it Danni, but I don't think you realize the complexities of this case. Even though the evidence seems circumstantial, Dusty will still have a difficult time explaining away the manner of Tara's death, not to mention the fact he failed to contact the police when she didn't return home that night. The argument they had at the genealogical library is the nail in his legal coffin."

Danni slapped his arm. "Apparently, you've forgotten who you've hired to defend him. If you recall, I have a knack for the seemingly impossible cases."

"Which is why I asked you to represent my cousin. If anyone can prove his innocence, it's you."

Brady's phone chimed. Pulling it from his pocket, his brows furrowed as he gazed at the screen. "Excuse me, I need to take this." He walked from the room with the phone to his ear, leaving Danni and Sarah alone.

"Tell me again why you're defending Dusty instead of Brady?" Sarah queried.

"It's his cousin. Anything he said would be suspect because of the family connection."

"I suppose."

"Do you really think you can get any money for this stuff?" Danni asked, looking around.

With a nod, Sarah smiled. "If the items in the other rooms are like these pieces, we should be able to raise some funds. I'm going to check things out, if that's OK."

"Go for it," Danni said, plopping onto the settee.

Sarah traipsed back to the entryway and studied the five-foot-long Persian rug and the ornate gilded mirror on the far wall. Several pastoral oil paintings graced the walls along with an Eastlake-style hall tree and a pair of velvet covered parlor chairs. A towering grandfather clock held court over the space.

Following the hall to the back rooms, Sarah was surprised to find a fully stocked library, formal dining room, and eat-in kitchen. She climbed the back stairs to the second floor and stepped into one of four bedrooms where stacks of boxes lined the opposite wall. Thankfully, this bedchamber housed high-end furnishings, mostly from the Regency period, with what appeared to be an exquisitely hand-woven lace coverlet and canopy. Fingering the lace bedspread, Sarah was astounded at the delicate workmanship. All of a sudden, a shock of electricity surged up her arm, stealing the breath from her lungs.

Immediately releasing the coverlet, she shook her head trying to dispel the tiny stars blinking across her sightline. When Sarah refocused, she noticed a shadow ruffle the curtains before dissipating. Taking in a deep breath, she backed out of the room, her eyes fixed on the area where she'd observed the movement.

Now wasn't the time for eerie visions or creepy encounters. She was here to help Danni and she wasn't about to let ghostly guests interfere. While Danni accepted and supported her strange dreamist abilities, others would likely deem her as crazy. She'd come too far in the past year to succumb to the shame and self-doubt she'd lived with her entire life.

Sarah closed the bedroom door when a chill fingered her spine and a hand grabbed her shoulder, squeezing a scream from her lips as she whirled around ready to bolt.

"What's going on?" Danni asked, her head cocked, and eyebrows raised. "Don't tell me you're seeing ghosts already."

"Not exactly," Sarah mumbled. She hadn't *seen* a ghost per se, just movement.

"Do me a favor, let's keep the dreamist stuff quiet around Brady. I don't want to dispel his confidence in my abilities. I'm not sure he's the type to buy into the supernatural stuff."

"You know me, I'm not one to advertise my odd abilities. My secret is safe," Sarah said, running her hand across her lips as if zipping them shut.

IT WAS rare for Sarah to witness Danni in all her glory within the confines of a courtroom. Danni wore her signature navy blue suit, Prada heels, and a crisp white blouse with her hair tucked neatly into a bun. Her approach to defending a client was a combination of drama and strategy to prove his or her innocence.

Brady perched on the bench next to Sarah, his back stiff with his hands clutched in his lap as he watched the proceedings unfold. Brady's cousin, Dusty, sat in the chair next to Danni, his shoulders slumped, and his countenance subdued. He wore a brown suit with his long hair pulled neatly into a ponytail. His defeated stature actually made Sarah believe in his innocence.

"Your honor, my client has been judged unfairly based on circumstantial evidence and jailed during a time of shock and grief over his wife's death. I move he be granted bail and allowed to return to his daily activities so he can earn a living and take comfort in the love of his family," Danni articulated firmly, her stature tall and shoulders squared.

"If you consider being incarcerated after his wife was found viciously beaten to death with a weapon he created to be unfair, Miss Cook, then I suppose this court is the most unjust in the county. Bail denied."

The gavel landed with a thwack that echoed through the room, causing Sarah to jump. Dusty turned toward Danni as the bailiff led him away, a pleading expression clouding his face. Sarah sensed the fury brewing in her friend by the tension in her shoulders and the rigidness of her jawline. Danni snapped her briefcase shut and snatched it from the table before marching over to where they sat.

"Sorry, Brady," she said angrily. "Is this judge always such a jerk? He didn't even give me a chance to present all the facts."

"This is a small town," he shrugged. "It's difficult to silence the rumor mill, especially when the judge is vying for higher ambitions."

"I don't buy that for a minute. This is about the evidence, not some pool hall conversation over a few beers."

Raising one eyebrow, Brady gave a sly smile. "In this town, if you can't get satisfaction in court, just take it outside."

"What are you saying?" Danni asked, her brows furrowed.

"Sorry," he chuckled. "It's an old saying I heard when I was a kid. This place has a colorful past when it comes to justice."

"I don't understand."

"Let's grab a bite to eat at Edgefield Deli and I'll fill you in on some of the more notable aspects of the town's judicial history."

3
_____

They took their seats at a worn pine table in the sandwich shop across the town square from the courthouse. The place had an old-fashioned décor with floor to ceiling shelves holding a hodgepodge of canned goods, vintage advertising boxes, antique toys, and a host of other nostalgic items. A waitress dressed in black leggings, an apron, and a blue t-shirt sporting the deli logo, sauntered over and placed menus on the table along with silverware rolled in paper napkins.

"What'll you have to drink?" Her porcelain skin glowed beneath a silky head of ebony hair streaked with pink.

"Sweet tea," Brady answered.

"Same for me," Sarah said.

"Got anything stronger?" Danni asked.

"Gotta go to the distillery for that," the waitress responded with a smile.

"Make mine a sweet tea," Danni muttered, slumping back against the chair.

As the waitress walked away, they opened their menus to look over the selections.

Without looking up, Danni grumbled, "After we finish lunch, I may need to go across the street for a shot of something."

Sarah stared at her friend. "Maybe you ought to keep your head clear so you can come up with a defense for your client."

"Alcohol clears my head," Danni said with a sideways glance and a smirk.

"Good to know some things never change," Brady chuckled.

"Hey, I was on point in that law class and not at all tipsy, just a bit influenced from the night before."

"Ha! So influenced the professor nearly threw you out of class."

"Stop with all the drama. Professor Jenkins shouldn't have scheduled the debate on a Monday morning after the Super-bowl. I couldn't help it if I had a few too many the night before. Who would've thought alcohol could linger that long in a person's body?"

Danni's question was rhetorical yet classically her. She could argue her way out of a paper sack and defend her behaviors while still making the accusing party believe it was their fault for her actions. It's what made her so successful as an attorney.

"You hate football," Sarah said.

"Sure do, but not the food and libations that accompany the Superbowl."

A laugh erupted from Sarah's lips as the waitress returned to take their orders.

"What do you recommend?" Sarah asked.

"The grilled gouda with poblano pepper on pumpernickel is a favorite," she replied. "You can get a cup of spicy tomato soup with it."

Sarah smiled. This was comfort food for her.

After a filling lunch, they headed back to the courthouse.

"I'm going to the jail to speak with my client," Danni said.

"No shot from the distillery?" Sarah asked, mockingly.

"Maybe later when I don't have to limit my consumption."

"I'm going back to the house to start the inventory."

"Want me to drive you?" Brady asked.

"Nah. It's a nice day and I could use the exercise," Sarah replied.

"Get used to it Brady. She's one of those health freaks, except for the occasional foodie indulgence."

Sarah stuck out her tongue and started down the sidewalk. "See you later," she called over her shoulder.

Meandering along the sun-drenched main drag of Edgefield, Sarah admired the variety of architectural styles and colors of the old homes. Summer heat moistened her skin as she gazed upon blooming gardens and sprawling picket fences. As she neared Edgefield Manor, Sarah noticed a good-looking man on the opposite side of the street running with a Jack Russell. He flashed her a smile and a wink and continued on his way. A flush spread across her face as her eyes followed him down the road.

Was he real or was this another one of her visions, she thought, her heart pounding. If he was a ghost, he was the best looking one she'd ever encountered. When she realized there wasn't anything ethereal about him, not to mention a dog running alongside him, she accepted he was probably real. Too bad she didn't have time for romance. Granted, it would be nearly impossible to find a guy who could deal with her haunted dreams, thus why she'd remained single.

Wiping the idea from her mind, she continued on her way and climbed the brick steps to the verandah of Edgefield Manor. Birdsong filtered through the trees as a soft breeze fluttered Sarah's ponytail. She gazed at the once beautiful garden with its unkempt azalea bushes and crawling ivy when a chill rattled her body. The hair on her sweat-soaked neck stood on end, alerting her to something otherworldly. She gulped down the fear lingering in her throat and turned slowly to find nothing more than a rocker swaying back and forth. She glanced around trying to figure out what had caused the chilling reaction in 90-degree heat. When nothing material-ized, she blew out a breath and stepped into the house.

Sarah inhaled the musty scent of a home long since occu-pied. The place was in shambles, its once elegant interiors dulled by neglect and an army of dust.

"I'll bet this place was something in its day," Sarah muttered to herself.

BAM!

A loud crash emanated from the second floor, startling her. Without thinking, she raced up the stairs looking for the source of the noise. Sarah crept to the first door on the left and turned the knob. Hinges creaked in protest as the stale scent of old linens and furniture polish tickled her nose. The room was a soft lavender with chenille spreads on each of two twin iron beds. Sheer white curtains shaded the two windows over-looking the front yard. Her body shuddered. The far right window was where she'd noticed the shadowy figure when they'd first arrived.

A large oval rug was centered below the outdated white ceiling fan, its brass fittings gleaming. Despite the stagnant odor of the room, it appeared to have been recently cleaned. Nothing was disturbed that could have caused the crash she'd heard from downstairs.

Sarah checked the next two rooms only to find them filled with old furnishings and stacks of boxes. In the last room on the right, the one she'd looked in earlier, she noticed one of the boxes on its side, obviously having tumbled from the stack. Relieved to have found the source of the noise, she padded over to the carton and lifted it from the floor. Inside were several scrapbooks and photo albums that appeared to be from the sixties and seventies. Sarah's propensity for perusing old albums and photos was a problem. She'd often get distracted by these things, thus putting her in a crunch to meet deadlines. But this time was different. She didn't want to hinder Danni's case by delving into Dusty's family history. Refolding the flaps, she placed the box back on top before leaving the room.

It was her understanding she and Danni would be staying at the house. Since the only inhabitable bedroom was the one with twin beds, she assumed they'd be bunking there. Danni was going to freak out when she discovered they had to share a room and sleep in twin beds. Even though her friend was helping to interpret the *Dreamist* book, Danni still wasn't comfortable with the actual haunted portion that went along with it. Knowing her, she'd string cloves of garlic around her bed to keep any of Sarah's ghostly acquaintances from crossing to her side of the room.

Trudging down the stairs, Sarah gathered her tools: a multi-colored pen, journal, and tape recorder. She needed to get to work and stay focused if she was going to run an estate sale in time to help Dusty's mom, Melinda, raise money for his legal fees. Danni was cutting them a break on the price, but with Dusty unable to work and his wife's salary no longer available, he needed money to maintain his home and business during his absence. The legal fees only added to the financial cyclone swirling through his life.

SEVERAL HOURS LATER, Sarah startled when the Batman theme bellowed from her cell phone. Danni's obsession with all things Batman had prompted her to program Sarah's phone with the Batman theme as her ringtone. With Sarah's proclivity for ghosts, Danni programmed the Dracula theme for Sarah on her own phone.

"Hey, Danni."

"How's it going?"

"It's going," Sarah sighed. "I've been able to get through the front parlor, but this stuff won't bring as much money as I'd hoped. It's pretty typical mid to late Victorian furniture. Sadly, this style isn't highly sought after right now."

"Not everything can be as valuable as the Monroe estate," Danni replied teasingly.

"That's not what I meant. By the way, did you see the room we're sleeping in?"

"We?"

"Yup, we're sharing a room like the good ole high school days, except this one is equipped with twin beds."

Silence.

"You're kidding me, right?" Danni responded, her voice tense.

"Nope. Looks like the sleep over from my house has been extended," Sarah announced, a grin spreading across her face.

"Maybe I'll get a hotel room."

"Hey, you make it sound like you don't want to be around me," Sarah whined.

"It's not you, it's your spirited friends."

"Like I haven't heard that one before. *It's not you babe, it's the glowing specters floating about your room. Sorry, but I have to end things before I get possessed or something,*" Sarah said in a mocking tone. "At least that's what I imagine a guy would say."

"Please, you haven't had a boyfriend since 5th grade. How do you know what a guy would say about the haunted thing?"

Sarah rolled her eyes. "Nonetheless, we're bunking together whether you like it or not."

"That's fine, just keep your ghostly visions on your side of the room. I need to be well-rested if I'm going to prove Dusty's innocence." Hopelessness saturated her voice.

"Is it that bad?" Sarah queried.

"From what I've learned so far, this is going to be my toughest case yet."

"Sorry to hear it."

"Anyway, Brady asked us to join him at Corner Pocket for supper. Says it's the best burger in town."

"Sounds good. What time?"

"Pick you up in an hour."

"I'll be ready."

Sarah slid the phone into her pocket and started up the stairs to wash off the sweat and dust cocooning her skin.

After a hot shower, Sarah braided her dark hair and slipped on a fuchsia tank and khaki shorts. She dabbed on some concealer and headed downstairs as the front door opened and Danni stepped inside.

"You ready?" she called.

"Aren't you going to change? You're still in your suit and heels."

"I'm already acclimated to it. Might as well finish out the night in it."

Sarah raised her eyebrows. Danni never opted for what she referred to as her 'Batman attire.' She considered a suit and heels to be the most uncomfortable clothing ever invented and preferred jeans and a t-shirt. Whatever Danni's inexplicable reason, Sarah was famished and ready for some food.

They drove to a nondescript white brick building at the other end of the square, a few doors down from the courthouse. Walking inside, they were greeted by 90s music intermingling with the crack of cue balls making contact. Swags of twinkling Christmas lights, some sections not working, hovered over walls displaying local sports memorabilia. In the far corner, a good-looking guy threw darts. Sarah focused on his sleek build, broad shoulders, and auburn hair. Her stomach fluttered. This was the guy she'd seen running earlier with his dog, the same one now sitting near his owner. *So, he is real.*

"Danni, Sarah," Brady called out from the bar, breaking Sarah's concentration from the dart player.

"Hey," they answered in unison.

Brady sauntered over and planted a kiss on Danni's cheek, before leading them to a booth at the back of the room. He slid in next to Danni and smiled.

"How are things going?" he asked.

"Slow but steady," Danni said as a waitress approached.

"Hey Brady, heard you were back in town," she said, her hazel eyes sparkling from beneath a coif of platinum blond hair.

"I'm only here to see my cousin exonerated and then I'll head back home." His response was surprisingly curt, leading Sarah to suspect there was a history between them.

"Maybe we can have a drink before you leave," she said seductively.

"Probably won't be any time, Stella. Danni and I have a lot of things to cover." He looked at Danni with a glimmer in his eye and a slow smile.

Stella seemed to take the hint, the animated expression fading from her face. "What'll it be tonight?"

Once the orders were placed, the previous discussion resumed. While Danni went on about the day's events, Sarah's attention drifted back to the guy at the dart board when a shadowy figure misted behind him. Decomposing skin hung from the creature's bones, sending a shiver through Sarah's body. Her breath caught as the entity glided seamlessly across the floor, its clouded eyes meeting her gaze as its decaying hands reached for her. Part of its skull was missing. A scream hovered at Sarah's lips. Without warning, the gorgeous guy's dog leapt into her lap, snarling at the now empty space. As soon as the dog landed, Sarah's scream erupted like lava from a volcano as she simultaneously tipped over her wine glass.

Danni grabbed a stack of napkins and started sopping up the wine as Sarah righted the glass with the dog still planted firmly in her lap. Instantly, the dog's owner was at her side, lifting his canine companion while issuing a series of apologies and a promise to buy her another drink. Thankfully, the mess was contained to the tabletop and hadn't made it to her clothes.

"I'm so sorry, I don't know what got into him. He usually doesn't leave my side," he said.

Sarah scanned the man's deep green eyes and well-trimmed beard and mustache, momentarily silencing her until she felt the sharp toe of Danni's stiletto slam into her shin under the table. The jab loosened Sarah's tongue and brought her back to reality.

"It's not a problem," she said with a halfhearted smile. "Does your dog always jump into the laps of strangers and growl at the people sitting across from them?"

"Only if there's a ghost around," he replied, with a sheepish grin.

"Your dog sees ghosts?" Sarah gasped.

"Don't be ridiculous," he chuckled. "He doesn't see them, he senses them."

"Like there's a difference," Danni snorted.

"Actually, there's a huge difference," he responded confidently.

Danni's lips scrunched as she looked at Sarah.

"I'm Garrett Duncan," he said, offering his hand.

"Sarah Holden," she replied, returning the handshake. His grip was firm yet soft. "This is Danni Cook and her friend Brady Anderson."

"Brady and I know each other well," Garrett said.

"We used to play together when he'd visit his grandmother during summer breaks," Brady responded.

Garrett flagged down the waitress and ordered another glass of wine for Sarah.

"I'm sorry about Dallas. I'll make sure he doesn't bother you again."

"It's really not a big deal," Sarah said with her brightest

smile, shocked at the way her skin tingled and her cheeks warmed.

Garrett strode away, a confident swagger to his step as Dallas trotted alongside him.

"He seems nice enough," Sarah said when he was out of earshot.

"Garrett's a good guy. He lives in his grandmother's old house a couple of blocks from here."

Sarah nodded at Brady's statement even though her attention was fixed on Garrett as he sat at the bar and ordered a beer. The waitress placed a fresh wine glass in front of Sarah, breaking her concentration. Her hands were so sweaty the glass nearly slipped from her fingers as she raised it to her lips. *Must be nerves from the fright of the grisly creature and the dog jumping into her lap,* she thought. What was it Garrett had said? The dog sensed ghosts? There was truth to his statement, making her ponder how he came to know such a thing from an animal who didn't speak English.

A short time later, the waitress placed three plates piled high with fries and some of the best-looking burgers Sarah had seen in a while on the table. She dipped one of the fries in ranch dressing and closed her eyes as she popped it in her mouth, savoring the flavor.

"Didn't realize I was this hungry," she said, eating another fry.

"Probably because you burned off a thousand calories walking across town earlier," Danni replied with a snort.

"Ah yes, the one thing Danni finds most offensive, exercise," Brady said with a chuckle.

"You know her too well," Sarah responded.

"If you two are going to badger me about my activity impaired lifestyle, I'm going to take my burger and join hunky man and his little dog over there," she said, with a nod in Garrett's direction.

"You think he's good looking?" Brady asked, turning to look at his old friend.

"Uh, yeah," Danni replied, her brow furrowed. "It's OK to admit when another guy is handsome. It doesn't take away from your masculinity."

Brady straightened in his chair. "I'll have you know I'm quite secure with my masculinity, but I've never scrutinized the *hunkiness* of my friends before."

Sarah giggled at their exchange. She'd not seen anyone who could handle her friend this well since Danni's ex-husband, Scott.

"If nothing else, he's caught Sarah's eye," she teased.

"Hey, don't drag me into this lust fest," Sarah declared. "I'm just here for the food."

"And the view," Danni mumbled.

Sarah flicked a French fry at her friend while kicking her under the table. From that point forward, Sarah was careful not to look in the direction of the bar area where Garrett sat with Dallas curled at his feet. Relief washed over her when Brady paid the bill and started for the door. As they crossed the room, Garrett gave a nod and a quick smile at Sarah before she stepped into the balmy night air.

"See you tomorrow?" Danni asked Brady, her eyes glinting.

"Maybe in the afternoon. I have some things to take care of at the old homestead."

"Homestead?" Sarah asked. "I thought you lived in Columbia?"

"My family's home is on the outskirts of Edgefield. I lived here until I went off to college. Ever since my mother passed several years ago, I come back when I can and check on the old place."

"I'm surprised you don't live here and practice law," Sarah said, curious as to why he wouldn't reside in his familial residence.

"It's a rather large peach farm. I have a guy who tends the orchards, but the main house has been closed up since mama died," Brady said. "Spent enough time as a child helping with the orchards and all the other things my parents grew. Of course, I'd never get rid of the property. It's been in our family for generations."

Sarah smiled. "I can understand that. Even though I recently inherited my family home, I kept my small cottage. After all the work I put into it, I couldn't bear to part with the place."

"Sarah has an affinity for old houses," Danni added.

"You'd like this one," Brady said. "It's an old Victorian style farmhouse complete with a ghost."

A shudder rankled Sarah's frame at the mention of a ghost, the strange figure she'd seen earlier in the restaurant flashing through her mind.

"Don't tell me you're afraid of ghosts?" Brady taunted.

"Not at all," Sarah replied, forcing a smile. "I'd love to see the house sometime."

"Once Dusty is cleared of his wife's murder, I'll take you two out there."

"Speaking of Dusty, I need to get back to the house and do some work," Danni said.

"See you tomorrow," he smiled, kissing Danni's cheek, his lips lingering for a moment. "Goodnight, Sarah."

"Goodnight, Brady."

Sarah and Danni got into the car as Brady walked across the street to the hotel.

"Why is he staying in a hotel if he has a house just outside of town?" Sarah asked.

"He keeps the place out of loyalty to his mother, but I've always gotten the feeling he wasn't overly fond of it."

"How much do you know about his childhood?"

"Not much except it was pretty normal. Typical kid growing

up on a peach farm, working in the orchards, breaking bones, and getting stitches, that sort of thing," Danni said, pulling onto the road. "I think Brady had his heart set on big city living but only made it as far as Columbia."

"Columbia is a big city," Sarah replied.

"It's not Atlanta or New York."

"Why didn't he go there if that's what he wanted?" Sarah asked, perplexed Brady hadn't tried harder to achieve his dreams. From everything Danni had told her about him, he was top of their graduating class from law school with a host of offers.

"His mother's health was beginning to wane and although he couldn't stand the idea of coming home to practice, he wanted to be nearby in case she needed anything. Columbia is only an hour from here. Close enough yet far enough away."

"Wow, that's dedication. He must've had a strong bond with his mother."

"I think he felt obligated to care for her. His younger brother, Thomas, disappeared while we were in law school."

"They never found him?"

"Nope. Thomas was eighteen and had just graduated from high school. Some believed he committed suicide while others feared he'd been murdered. According to Brady, that was the beginning of his mother's health issues."

Sarah gasped. "That's terrible."

"Said his brother adored his mother and would never have run off without staying in touch. Brady took it pretty hard but not hard enough that he'd return to Edgefield to practice law. I think his brother's disappearance is the main reason he avoids his hometown. Shortly after Brady graduated, he met Sofia, got married, and settled in Columbia," Danni added.

"Sounds like he did the next best thing by staying fairly close."

They pulled down the curved drive of Edgefield Manor and

parked under a large oak. The winds picked up and a flash of lightning snaked across the sky as the clouds opened up in a deluge of rain.

"Let's make a run for it!" Danni hollered as she leapt from the car and dashed to the front porch with Sarah right behind her.

Rain peppered the porch as Danni fumbled with the key. While Sarah waited for Danni to unlock the front door, a frosty finger traced the back of her neck, sending bumps across her skin.

Turning slowly, Sarah scanned the area for whatever had touched her. Nothing was there. The wind created mini cyclones out of grass and leaves when another thunderous boom, accompanied by a blaze of lightning, sent both women scurrying inside. They closed the door as rain pelted the windows and roof. It sounded like golf balls were falling from the heavens.

"Phew, got here just in time," Danni said as she made her way to the bar in the front parlor.

Sarah nodded, her insides quivering. Something wasn't right. Her stomach curdled like it did after one of her dreams.

Danni poured a shot of Scotch and a double shot of bourbon which she handed to her friend.

"Here, you look like you could use this," Danni said, handing her the cut crystal glass.

"Thanks," Sarah replied, taking a long draw.

Danni walked into the dining room where her briefcase and laptop rested on the Duncan Fyfe table. Kicking off her stilettos, Danni plunked onto one of the Chippendale dining chairs and started tapping on the computer keys.

Sarah wanted to get some work done too but was distracted by whatever was niggling at her nerves. Another clap of thunder, followed by a bright flare of light, made her jump as the electricity blinked.

"Crap!" Danni hollered. "I do not need to lose electricity! My computer hardly has any charge left."

"I'll check the kitchen for candles and flashlights in case we lose power."

Sarah rushed to the outdated kitchen and flipped the switch, sending the overhead florescent light flickering to life. Rummaging through the worn oak cabinets with brass hardware, she searched for anything that could provide light should the storm knock out the electricity. After sifting through several drawers, another thunderous crack sounded, and everything went dark.

Frozen in place, Sarah waited for her eyes to adjust to the darkness when she felt something skitter down her neck. A loud thumping reverberated in her ears as a voice whispered, *he took it.* Her breath caught so that her lungs felt as if they might explode. A scream erupted from Sarah's lips when a hand grabbed her shoulder.

Danni let out a howl in response and stumbled backwards against the cabinet.

"What the heck, Sarah? You scared me half to death!"

"I scared you? I'm not the one groping shoulders in the dark! Make a noise next time!" Sarah retorted, her entire body quaking.

Rain drummed against the roof and cascaded in torrents down the windows.

"We need some light," Danni said, her voice beginning to strain, telling Sarah she wasn't comfortable in the dark.

"Where's your cell? We can use the flashlight on it to finish looking through the cabinets."

"Blasted," Danni said, patting her skirt pocket. "Left it in the car. What about yours?"

Sarah searched her pockets. "Same."

"Seriously?" Danni screeched.

"I'll go get them," Sarah offered.

"I can go."

"In your stocking feet? Don't think so. I can sprint out there faster than you can anyway."

"See, lack of exercise can be a good thing," Danni snorted.

Sarah could hear the sly smile in Danni's words.

"Where are the keys?"

"It's not locked."

Sarah made her way through the darkened parlor to the front door and onto the porch where the rain was blowing sideways. In all her years, she never remembered rain so fierce, and that was saying a lot being from the Lowcountry where the wind and rain could be deadly.

Darkness engulfed her as she sprinted from the porch into what felt like an abyss. She ran along the walkway toward the car when her toe caught on a loose brick, catapulting her into a puddle. Soaked and muddy, she looked up when a bolt of lightning shot horizontally across the sky temporarily illuminating the yard. A shadowy figure stood near Danni's car, its arms like bat wings reaching for the sky.

Sarah's shriek was drowned out by the pounding rain and rumbling of thunder. Paralyzed, all she could do was watch until another flash of light revealed the creature moving toward her. Swallowing hard, she willed her body to respond but all it did was shiver. Obviously, Danni hadn't heard her scream due to the deafening noise from the storm. She opened her mouth to yell once again when a shrouded hand reached from the darkness, gripping her arm. Her lungs constricted as she screeched. The entity pulled her to her feet and wrapped its cloaked arm around her.

"Let's get you inside," a voice shouted over the pelting rain.

"Brady?" Sarah managed to mutter as he guided her to the porch.

"Who'd you think it was?" he asked, helping her up the stairs.

"Not sure," Sarah replied, slumping over and resting her hands on her knees as she gulped in air.

Danni stepped out as the front porch light flickered to life. *Thank goodness,* Sarah thought, *the power is back on.*

"Brady?" Danni said. "When did you get here?"

"Just now. I'm afraid I may have scared poor Sarah."

Sarah stood upright, revealing a mud-stained tank and shorts, her sneakers completely saturated.

"I tripped in the dark. When the lightning flashed, I saw a figure," Sarah said breathlessly.

The rain subsided to a pitter-patter as Danni howled with laughter, triggering a giggle from Sarah that quickly turned into a gut-wrenching laugh. Tears sprouted from Sarah's eyes mixing with the rain dripping from her hair as her gaze met Danni's, the two women laughing hysterically.

"What on earth has gotten into you two?" Brady asked, removing his poncho and draping it on one of the rockers.

"Sarah looks like a drowned rat," she chortled. "What the heck did you do to make her fall?"

"I didn't do anything," he replied, his face flushing. "All I did was help her up."

Sarah swiped the tears from the corners of her eyes. "I tripped on a brick and fell down. When I looked up, I saw something resembling a demented Batman."

Danni's head tilted back, releasing another squeal of laughter. Brady shook his head, the right corner of his mouth rising.

"I don't know about you two, but I'm wet and in need of a drink."

"What are you doing here?" Danni queried. "I thought you were going back to the hotel."

"Changed my mind. I haven't seen you in years, so I decided to come over. I texted that I was on my way."

"Phone is in the car," Danni said.

He walked past them both and into the house as Danni draped her arm around Sarah's shoulders.

"I believe a couple of drinks are in order."

"Let me grab our phones first," Sarah said, scooting across the yard.

The rain had stopped, leaving a muggy atmosphere in its wake. Grabbing the phones, Sarah sloshed across the puddled grass, darted in the front door, and plunked the phones on the coffee table.

"Poured you a drink," Danni smiled, pointing to a highball glass.

"After I change out of these clothes, I'll happily partake of a libation," Sarah replied, bolting up the stairs and into their room.

Her muscles ached and her skin felt like a wet rag. She grabbed a change of clothes and dashed into the bathroom. After washing her face, she stared into the mirror and chuckled again. The terror that had cemented her body to the ground, mixed with the image of Brady as some sort of mystical creature, was humorous in the bright light of the bathroom. At the time it had been terrifying.

One thing was certain, she needed to get a grip on her imagination before she drove herself mad. They'd be in this place for a few weeks and the last thing Sarah needed was to start envisioning things that weren't actually there, even though Brady had been real, but not as a crazed bat creature. Her real visions were creepy enough without inventing ones to join the fray.

For a split second, her mind drifted to Garrett and his little dog, making her insides quiver. Dismissing the image, Sarah inhaled, content to be clean and dry in her favorite pajamas. Unbeknownst to her, a shadowy figure reached for her hair as she flipped off the light and scurried down the stairs, the words *he's not what you think* dissipating into the darkness.

4

Danni and Brady were huddled on the settee, chuckling like a couple of teenagers in the back wing of the school library. Sarah grabbed her glass of bourbon and curled up on the wing chair.

"Wanna let me in on the secret?" she asked playfully.

Danni straightened up and put on her 'you're being silly' expression. "There's no secret, we were just laughing about the time we had snow on campus and Brady and some of his friends got a bit *creative* with their snow sculpture."

"You mean a snowman?"

Danni's laugh echoed through the room. "Oh, it was a snowman alright, complete with all the anatomically correct parts."

Sarah's eyes widened as she glanced at Brady. A flush colored his cheeks as he shrugged one shoulder.

"Me and the guys in my dorm were bored."

Shaking her head, Sarah smiled at the image forming in her brain. "And I thought Danni was the crazy one."

"Don't let her fool you. She had her share of antics," Brady grunted.

Danni stood up and walked to the bar for another drink. "I plead the fifth!" she exclaimed. "Besides, I never did anything quite as scandalous as building a snowman with an erection on the campus lawn."

"But you did fill the fountain with soap powder. It looked like a giant washing machine exploded in front of the library."

"That's nothing," Danni said with a wave of her hand as she sat back down. "Lots of people did that."

"There was the time you played that prank on Jessica, Dr. Seigel's intern."

"Well, she shouldn't have stuck toothpaste in my dorm room lock and squirted baby powder under my door. Took me forever to get that stuff up! Talc sticks to wood like powdered sugar to a donut."

Intrigued, Sarah leaned forward. "What did you do?"

Danni grinned as she started into a dramatic rendition of her practical joke. "Jessica was a prankster and got me several times with her witty little antics. One weekend, she went home to visit her fiancée and left her room key with me so I could spritz her ferns. The girl was seriously obsessed with her plants," Danni smirked. "Anyway, I decided to pay her back for all of her tricks. I started with three different alarm clocks."

"Oh no, this can't be good," Sarah groaned, taking a sip of her drink.

"I knew she had Monday off, so she'd probably be getting in late the night before and sleeping in. I hid the first clock in her closet and set it for 1:00 AM. I hid another under her bed and set it for 2:00 AM. I hid the third one in the cabinet of her kitchenette and set it for three."

"Danni, that's terrible!" Sarah declared.

"It was great! At about eight o'clock the next morning, she was banging on my door. Said she didn't get in until midnight and had just fallen asleep when the first alarm sounded. Took her twenty minutes to find it and get it turned off. She crawled back into bed and fell asleep when the second one started. After finding that one and turning it off, she went back to bed only to be awakened at three o'clock. By then she figured it had to be me and swore vengeance."

"What did she do to top that?" Sarah queried.

Brady started laughing. "This is where Danni's superior arbitration skills kick in."

Sarah's eyebrows arched as she waited to hear what happened.

"I negotiated a truce," Danni replied nonchalantly.

"So, she never got revenge?"

"Nope. I think she realized things could only get worse and felt it was best to put the pranks to rest before one of us got kicked out of law school."

Another round of laughter filled the room as they each downed the rest of their drinks.

"I think we've had enough excitement and laughs for one evening. I know Danni still has a ton of work to do," Brady said, grabbing his keys from the table. "I'll say my goodbyes and head out."

"Thanks for checking on us Brady," Danni said with a smile.

"And for scaring me half to death," Sarah added.

"Glad I could be of service," he winked, leaning over to kiss Danni, except this time his lips brushed hers. "See you ladies tomorrow."

Brady strode across the room and out the door. Sarah looked at Danni with a head tilt.

"That was an *affectionate* farewell," Sarah said.

"Stop it. Brady is a good friend. It was only a peck, not a Romeo and Juliet scene," Danni replied, heading for the dining room to resume her work.

Sarah knew her best friend well enough to know the subject was closed. With a yawn, Sarah decided to turn in.

"I'm going to bed," she announced. "I'll leave the bedside lamp on for you."

"Ugh, I forgot about the sleeping arrangements," Danni sighed. "We need to clean out one of those other rooms. I haven't slept in a twin bed since kindergarten."

"Afraid you'll roll out?" Sarah asked, stopping in the doorway.

"More afraid the monsters under the bed will have easier access," she chuckled.

"Well, if you have monsters under your bed, keep them to yourself."

"Agreed, so long as you keep the ghosts on your side of the room."

Sarah shuddered. "I'll do my best," she said, forcing a smile.

Trudging up the steps, Sarah's skin began to crawl, making her wonder what secrets the house would reveal in her dreams. So far, she'd not encountered anything too frightening, except for the misty shadow at Corner Pocket and the not-so-haunted Brady in his rain poncho. Yet something disconcerting niggled at her nerves.

Sarah had come to accept most of her haunted encounters; however, being in an unfamiliar house with specters of its own was a bit unnerving. Somehow it was easier to deal with the ghosts she'd come to know versus the mysterious ones. At least this job wasn't too stressful.

Brady and Danni's recitation of their law school hijinks had gone a long way to relieving Sarah's jitters. She'd also noticed the furtive glances between them and wondered if there might be something brewing. It would be nice to see Danni in love again.

Sarah changed for bed and slipped beneath the cottony sheets. She left the windows open, allowing the fresh summer breezes to waft through the room. There was nothing better than the scent of clean air following a rainstorm to sooth a frazzled soul. Resting her head on the pillow, Sarah closed her eyes and thought about the good-looking guy she'd met at Corner Pocket. Too bad she didn't have time for a relationship or the fortitude to explain her unique dreamist abilities. Her heart sank. Even if she didn't have a haunted secret, she'd only be here for a few weeks before returning to her home in Beaufort nearly three hours away, so a relationship was out of the question. Sarah sighed. Why was she even thinking about this? It's not like Garrett had shown any interest.

Exhaustion finally took hold, escorting her to dreamland where gorgeous men and their quirky little dogs warded off shadowy mystical figures.

TOWERING bookcases cluttered with dozens of leather-bound tomes, lined the walls as Sarah walked along the darkened space. Displays of antique pottery interspersed with architectural artifacts topped the shelves.

As she approached the door at the end of the corridor, a cold chill rankled Sarah's body as she reached for the knob. The palm of her hand sizzled when she wrapped her fingers around the ornately molded brass, a voice whispering in her ear, *don't trust him.*

Sarah turned to see a slender woman with auburn hair, sculpted cheeks, and a gaunt expression, staring at her with empty sockets. Blood trickled down the side of her head and her mouth formed a thin line as if it had been sewn shut. Her translucent hand reached for Sarah, forcing a scream from her lips...

Sarah jolted upright and looked around the shadowy space not recognizing where she was until her mind's fog began to dissipate. She was at Edgefield Manor. Rubbing her eyes, she glanced at the clock on the nightstand which read 12:30. Sarah scanned the room, her gaze resting on her suitcase at the foot of the bed with her running shoes next to it. Danni's luggage was in the corner. That's when she realized Danni's bed was untouched. *She must still be downstairs working.*

Sliding back down onto the mattress, Sarah tried to make sense of the dream. It had been so realistic; she could actually smell the musty scent of old books and feel the angst of the eyeless figure, the same one from previous dreams. The woman seemed to be tormented by something, of that Sarah was certain. But who was she and what was she trying to communicate? Sarah blew out a breath. It didn't matter how disconcerting the images, if there was a spirit who wanted to communicate with her, she had no choice but to listen.

Sarah closed her eyes and took several deep breaths until the tension melted from her muscles. Her breathing slowed as she finally drifted off to sleep. Moments later, a hand grabbed her shoulder, wrenching a shriek from her lips.

Sarah gasped for air as she sat up and stared at her bleary-eyed best friend.

"Sorry, didn't mean to scare you," Danni muttered, "but I was wondering if you heard that noise."

"The only noise I can hear is the pounding of my heart in my ears!" Sarah hissed, trying to steady her breathing. "What noise?"

"Like a scratching or something."

"You scared me awake because you heard a scratching noise?"

"Now that you mention it, maybe it wasn't such a big deal," Danni said, her shoulders slumping. "I figured if it was a ghost then you oughta know about it."

Sarah closed her eyes and inhaled. She needed to be more tolerant of Danni's nervousness. Even though Danni was helping her with her dreamist skills, dark, unfamiliar houses purported to have ghosts were probably unnerving for her.

"I'm sorry Danni," Sarah muttered. "I'm sure it's nothing more than a mouse or something."

Danni shivered. "Eww...not helping," she replied, looking down at her feet before sprinting to her bed.

Slipping between the sheets, Danni switched off the lamp. "Goodnight, Sarah."

"G'night."

DANNI LEFT EARLY to interview several people affiliated with Dusty and his late wife, Tara. Sarah grabbed her CD player, ledger, post-it notes, and multi-colored ink pen, and went to the dining room in search of treasures. Dusty's mother, Melinda, had given her permission to inventory anything she deemed of worth. Once the list was made, Melinda would remove any items of sentimental value, although she felt certain everything of personal significance had already been taken by family members.

Sarah grabbed a bottle of water from the kitchen, popped in a Benny Goodman CD, and started working. While the furnishings weren't overly exquisite, the china, crystal, and silver were highly collectible. There was a partial set of Queen Victoria by Herend and a 12-piece place setting of Blue Fluted by Royal Copenhagen. She also found Waterford crystal flutes, wine, and water glasses as well as a full set of Rogers silver flatware in the Crown pattern.

"Wow," Sarah mumbled. If she could find the right buyers, these pieces could bring a lot of cash. However, an estate sale would see most of the items walk away for a pittance of their true worth. In most cases, estate sales were nothing more than high-end yard sales. Maybe she could talk Melinda into letting her sell the more valuable pieces at auction. She scribbled a note reminding her to discuss it when they met.

Benny Goodman's *Moon Glow* swept through the room as

Sarah made notations of each piece of china, crystal, and silver. The A/C window unit blasted cold air through the space as Sarah continued rummaging through the buffet draws when she realized the music had stopped. If she remembered correctly, *Moon Glow* was only the third song out of about twenty on this particular CD.

Rising to her feet, she walked across the room to check the CD player and was surprised to find it turned off. She pressed each button. Nothing happened. As she inspected the back of the CD player, Sarah noticed the end of the cord was laying on the floor. A chill slithered across her skin, making the hair on her arms stand up.

She jumped when, *In a Sentimental Mood* blared from the speaker. Sarah stumbled backwards, covering her ears. The music was so loud, she felt certain it could be heard all the way to the courthouse. She tried pushing buttons and when that didn't work, she attempted to pull the CD cover open. It wouldn't budge. Her eardrums began to pulse as if they might explode from the deafening sound. Snatching the CD player, Sarah ran for the front door to toss it outside.

She rotated and tugged the doorknob, but it wouldn't open. Her head was beginning to ache from the noise and her heart was racing. With all her might, she raised the CD player over her head to throw it to the floor. Before she could smash it, the music stopped, and everything went silent. Paralyzed, she stood for a moment, her ears ringing. Sarah lowered her quivering arms and stared at the machine as the knob on the front door jiggled and opened. An icy breeze drifted through the space, swirled around her body, up her neck, and whispered in her ear, *don't trust him.*

Sarah dropped the CD player, bolted out the door, and down the porch stairs to the front lawn. Bending over, she heaved out the breath she'd been holding. *What was happening?* she thought as she stood up. She knew it had something to do with her dreamist abilities; however, being in a strange place made interpreting the visions and ominous declarations more perplexing.

Pulling the cell phone from her pocket, she started to call Danni but thought better of it. Danni was trying to save a man's life and didn't need to be burdened with her ghost-a-pades. Instead, Sarah took in a deep breath, held it for a count of five, and released it slowly like she'd learned in therapy when she was a kid. Dreamist abilities or not, she might need therapy when all was said and done, and possibly a hearing aid.

When her racing pulse began to resume a normal pace and her breathing slowed, she reentered the house. Mustering all the courage she could, she closed the front door and stood in the middle of the entryway.

"I don't know what you want, but I'd appreciate it if we could wait until I'm asleep to discuss it. I really need to get some work done and you're kinda freaking me out."

Sarah picked up the CD player, put it on the end table, and plugged it back in. With trembling fingers, she pushed the play button, relieved when the velvety sound of Benny Goodman's band wafted through the air.

Cautiously, she returned to the dining room and gathered her work tools. A subtle breath blew against her ear, the word *sorry* dissolving against her skin. For some reason, her body relaxed and her mind cleared as if the faraway voice was somehow familiar to her. Shaking off the remaining trepidation, Sarah went to the kitchen to begin inventorying its contents.

MORE THAN AN HOUR LATER, Sarah searched for something to eat in the well-stocked fridge and pantry. Obviously, Dusty's mother had made sure they'd have everything they needed while staying here. Nothing else otherworldly had occurred since the morning music fiasco for which Sarah was grateful. Amazed by her fortitude, she was proud of her ability to tolerate the ghostly encounters more readily than she had in her youth.

Fixing a ham and cheese sandwich, Sarah grabbed a bottle of water, and sat at the kitchen table. She glanced over her notations from the morning's inventory, pleased with her progress. This estate wasn't nearly as complex or as extensive as the Monroe estate, making things move at a faster pace. Granted, she had half as much time, but the efforts would be well worth it. She hadn't met Dusty or his mother but from everything Danni had told her, they were genuinely nice people. Danni was positive her client was innocent, although her friendship with Brady may have influenced her opinion. The sparks between Danni and Brady were subtle, but they hadn't gone unnoticed.

Sarah smiled. The idea of Danni finding someone after all these years warmed her heart. As if channeling her best friend, the Batman theme bellowed from her pocket.

"Hey Danni, what's up?"

"Just checking in. Have you gotten much accomplished?"

"Actually, yes."

"You hesitated. Has something happened?" Danni asked.

Sarah blew out a breath. Danni knew her better than anyone in the world so there was no sense trying to hide the morning scare fest.

"Had a minor incident this morning but everything is alright now."

"What happened? And why didn't you call me?"

"I didn't want to interrupt you with one of my ghostly episodes. I'm fine."

"Sarah, you can always call and leave a message. I'll call back as soon as I can."

"You need to focus on clearing Dusty's name. I can handle the ghosts."

"Suit yourself but I want details when I get back to the house this evening."

"Deal," Sarah replied, thankful to have such a supportive friend. Not many people would have stuck around after learning their best friend was haunted by dead people seeking to find peace from their untimely demise.

5

The day passed with the swiftness of a hurricane when Sarah heard Danni's car tires crunching across the gravel drive.

Moments later, Danni's voice called out, "Sarah?"

"In the back room," she replied, wiping her hands on her shorts as she treaded to the entryway.

Danni had already kicked off her heels and was heading for the bar in the parlor. Pouring a drink, she looked at Sarah. "Want one?"

Sarah nodded and took the crystal highball class from Danni. She plopped onto the wing chair and took a sip, letting the bourbon burn down her throat. Danni downed her scotch in one gulp before pouring another.

"Rough day?" Sarah asked.

"You could say that," Danni said, slumping onto the settee. "So far, I've interviewed half a dozen people, all of whom knew Dusty and Tara well. They all report the couple was very much in love."

"That sounds like a good thing."

"Except two of them heard Dusty and Tara arguing the

evening she was killed. Another person said they were having financial difficulties."

"Most couples fight and have problems with money, doesn't mean they kill each other. Besides, with your persuasive skills, you'll be able to convince a jury he's innocent."

Danni swirled the amber liquid in her glass before downing it.

"What's the matter?" Sarah asked.

"I'm not certain I can convince anyone he's *not* guilty. Even Brady made a comment about Dusty and Tara fighting a lot lately."

Sarah sat up straight. "Oh my gosh, you don't believe he's innocent."

"My responsibility is to represent him to the best of my ability which I intend to do."

"You didn't answer me," Sarah said, arching her brows.

"Tell me about your encounter of the ghostly kind," Danni said, walking to the bar to refill her drink.

Typical Danni. Change the subject when things got too intense.

Sarah sat back in the chair and shared the crazy encounter with the CD player not playing, then blaring, then not playing.

"The strangest part was hearing the ghost apologize after I confronted it about scaring me. Have you read anything in the *Dreamist* book about that?"

"Nope. Haven't come across a chapter about remorseful specters," Danni chortled.

Although Sarah was an intelligent woman, her inability to decipher riddles had plagued her throughout life. Since the *Dreamist* book was written in this manner, she'd enlisted Danni's help for interpretation. They'd made decent progress over the course of the year but still had a long way to go before mastering all of the idiosyncrasies of her dreamist skills.

"I guess we'll see what happens in my dreams tonight," Sarah sighed.

Danni stood. "I'm going to change. Brady is coming over to take us out for dinner."

"Sure you don't want to be alone with him?"

Danni smirked. "If I wanted to be alone with him, we wouldn't be going to a public place."

"Where are we going?"

"Corner Pocket. Apparently, there aren't many options in town."

"The burger I had was amazing. I can handle eating there again."

Sarah's heart palpitated at the idea that Garrett might be there too. *Stop it*, she thought, scolding herself for behaving like a teenager with a crush. Why on earth was she thinking like this? It didn't matter that he made her palms sweat and her heart race. She was only here for a couple of weeks and then she'd never see him again.

Following Danni to their room, Sarah searched through her clothes for something cute to wear. She chose a coral V-neck that made her skin glow and a pair of black leggings that accentuated the curves of her legs. She dabbed on concealer, pulled her hair into a messy bun, slipped on a pair of flip-flops, and scurried downstairs while Danni finished changing. Just because she couldn't have a relationship with this guy didn't mean she couldn't have a little fun flirting with him.

DANNI AND SARAH walked into Corner Pocket where Brady stood at the bar talking with Garrett. Sarah's heart skipped like a stone across water at the sight of him. He was definitely a looker. Dallas sat at his owner's feet until he saw Sarah. Bolting across the floor, he propped his front legs on her knee, his soulful brown eyes staring up at her as his tail wagged.

Leaning over, she scratched behind his ears. When she stood up, she noticed Garrett staring at her from the bar, his green eyes glimmering. She and Danni walked over to the guys with Dallas leading the way.

"I see you've been greeted by the welcoming committee," Garrett said, with a broad smile, making Sarah's insides flop.

"He seems to like me," she responded with a sheepish grin.

"How was your day?" Brady asked Danni. "Get any good leads?"

"Nothing substantial, but it's only been two days," she replied.

"What'll you have to drink?" Brady asked.

"Beer," Danni said.

"Cabernet," Sarah added.

Brady ordered the drinks and then motioned to a table, his hand resting in the small of Danni's back.

They bid goodbye to Garrett and took their seats at a nearby booth. Moments later, the waitress delivered their drinks along with menus.

As Sarah sipped her wine and looked over the food selections, Brady and Danni prattled on about legal endeavors when a shadowy figure eclipsed her. Gulping down her fear, Sarah glanced up slowly, gasping when she saw the same corpselike entity from the other night hovering beside her.

"Are you OK?" Danni asked, staring at her friend.

"Just swallowed too fast," Sarah replied, hoping to squelch any further queries as the decaying figure dissipated.

Sarah's nerves bristled as she struggled to focus on the conversation, all the while trying to determine why she'd seen the same specter in the restaurant twice in a matter of days. Her appetite waning, she ordered onion rings, hoping it would be an early night. Something was off, she could feel it creeping across her skin.

Fortunately, Danni and Brady decided to make it a quick

meal since Danni had so much to do. Brady covered the check and they all headed for the door when Garrett waved them over to the bar.

"What's up?" Brady asked.

"I was wondering if I could buy you guys a drink?" he offered, his eyes fixed on Sarah.

"I've got work to do. My paralegal quit so I'm having to do everything myself." Brady shrugged, obviously annoyed by the situation.

"I have an early appointment in the morning," Danni said. "But Sarah can stay, if you don't mind giving her a ride back to the manor."

Sarah shot a warning glance at Danni whose smile mimicked that of the Cheshire cat.

"I wouldn't want to put you out," Sarah stuttered.

"You're not putting me out," he said, his emerald eyes locking onto hers. "You're welcome to join me, if you're not otherwise engaged."

"Go on, have some fun," Danni prodded, nudging Sarah's shoulder.

Sarah's gut knotted at the idea of being alone with him. Hanging out with gorgeous guys was outside of her comfort zone. She had little to no experience in this realm. Not wanting to seem rude, she acquiesced.

"If you're sure it's no trouble," she said.

Garrett patted the stool beside him. "It's no trouble at all."

Danni gave a sly grin and pinched Sarah's upper arm. Sarah's lips formed a straight line as she gave Danni a menacing glance.

"I'll leave the door unlocked and the porch light on," Danni chuckled. Brady clutched Danni's hand and led her out of the restaurant.

Sarah slid onto the stool, her pulse racing. She felt like a high school kid on prom night, or what she thought it would feel like. Sarah hadn't attended prom or any other coed events in high school. With her haunted issues, dating was out of the question. Except for Danni, Sarah had been the proverbial loner.

"Another Cabernet?" the woman behind the counter asked.

"Anything stronger?" Sarah queried.

"Wine and beer only."

"Cabernet is fine," she replied.

The server hurried off to pour the wine as Garrett looked at Sarah.

"What else do you drink?" he asked.

"Woodford Reserve."

"Good stuff. I drink it on occasion," he said, his bearded face aglow in the shady bar lights.

Moments later, the woman placed a glass of red wine in front a Sarah and a beer for Garrett.

Garrett lifted his bottle and smiled. "Cheers," he said, clinking Sarah's glass.

They each took a sip.

"Tell me about your role in helping with Dusty's case."

Sarah pursed her lips. "I see word gets around."

"Small town life," he replied, scrunching his shoulders.

Sarah hesitated, contemplating how much to reveal. Being a small town, chances were, Garrett already knew the facts and was trying to make conversation.

"Melinda hired me to host an estate sale. She needs to raise funds for Dusty's defense."

"Is this what you do for a living, or is it a side job?"

"I have an antiques and estate business in Beaufort." Sarah said, taking another sip. "What do you do?"

"Construction mostly. In my spare time I hunt ghosts."

Sarah nearly choked at his declaration.

"You hunt ghosts?" she asked, wiping a droplet of wine from her lip.

"That doesn't freak you out, does it?" he asked, his cheeks coloring.

"Not at all. Actually, I live in an 18th century house with its own ghosts."

"Really?" his body seemed to relax as he rested his chin in his hand.

"I don't talk about it much but since you already broached the subject of hauntings, I figured it wouldn't send you running."

"It takes more than the undead to send me running," he said with a smile.

"Oh really? You seem a bit overconfident. Perhaps you haven't encountered any truly frightening ghosts," Sarah taunted. This guy had no idea what scary was until he'd experienced the nightmares that had plagued her throughout her life. Nevertheless, Sarah appreciated Garrett's cheerful demeanor. He smiled a lot and was easy to be around. *If only he lived closer.*

Garrett leaned in, the scent of his aftershave tickling Sarah's nose.

"I can assure you; I've seen some pretty scary things that would send you racing for the door."

Sarah chuckled. "Doubtful."

"I can prove it to you," he challenged, taking a swig of his beer.

"Then by all means, do so," she replied playfully. Despite her conscience telling her not to get involved, she couldn't help enjoying a little flirtation.

Before Garrett could answer, two men entered the restaurant and headed toward them.

"Hey guys," Garrett called out. "Your timing is perfect. I was getting ready to tell Sarah about our haunted expeditions."

The man with brown eyes and dark hair pulled into a ponytail, smiled, and offered his hand. "I'm Harry, and this is Ralph. We're part of the ghost hunting crew."

Sarah returned their handshakes. "I'm Sarah Holden. I'm helping Dusty James' mother with an estate sale."

Their expressions shifted from jovial to morose.

"That's a sad situation," Ralph said, shaking his head. His sandy blond hair fell haphazardly about his round face and his deep blue eyes had a kind countenance. "Dusty's a good guy. Wouldn't hurt anyone, especially Tara."

"Have you talked with Danni Cook about this?"

"Who's he?"

Sarah chuckled. "*She's* representing Dusty."

"Got it," Ralph said, a flush reddening his cheeks.

"Why don't we get a table?" Harry suggested. "It'll be more comfortable, unless you two want to be alone."

"Not at all," Sarah and Garrett chimed in unison.

Sarah's heart skipped a beat. She had her reasons for not getting close to Garrett but what was his reason for avoiding her? Part of her was relieved for the interruption while deep down she was disappointed to have to share Garrett. Then again, there was no way she could get involved with a man who lived three hours away. Conflict bubbled in her gut. This guy could be the perfect match. He believed in ghosts and actually hunted them, yet Sarah was hesitant to make a move. Even if she'd wanted to, with her lack of romantic experience she wouldn't know what to do.

They settled at a table by the front window. The waitress took Harry and Ralph's orders as Dallas curled at Sarah's feet.

"I spoke with Mrs. George about the filming at the plantation house Thursday night. She's good with it," Harry said.

"Glad to hear it," Garrett replied.

"Is this one of your ghost hunting jobs?" Sarah asked.

"Yup. We've been trying to get into this place for months. The George Plantation is said to be the second most haunted place in town."

"What's the first?" Sarah asked, cocking her head.

"Edgefield Manor," Ralph replied.

"Sounds intriguing," Sarah gulped, trying to hide her shock. She'd never met anyone firsthand who not only believed in ghosts but actually sought them out.

"You look a bit pale," Harry said, with a snicker. "Don't let this ghost stuff bother you."

Sarah took in a deep breath and bit her lower lip. This guy actually thought she was afraid of a few ghosts? Ha, what a joke! If he knew about her nightmares and otherworldly encounters, he wouldn't be so quick to insinuate she was intimidated by the spiritual world. Dallas let out a yap, making them all jump.

"Hush, Dallas, or you'll get us kicked out of here," Garrett said to his canine companion.

Thankful for a change in the conversational direction, Sarah smiled. "I'm surprised you're allowed to have a dog in a restaurant."

"The owner is a friend of mine and doesn't mind so long as Dallas stays with me and keeps quiet."

"And if anyone asks, we tell them it's his therapy dog," Ralph laughed.

"He's a therapy dog?" Sarah said, raising her eyebrows.

"He's not a therapy dog, more of a ghost radar. He does a great job sniffing out spirits."

"Forgot about his ability to see spirits," Sarah said, with one eyebrow raised, skepticism dripping from her words.

"Don't know if he sees them but every time he focuses on an area and growls, we've been able to capture images on video."

Sarah shook her head and took a sip of her Cabernet. "Tell me more about your haunted escapades."

The waitress placed the drinks on the table as Ralph started explaining what they did. Occasionally, Harry added some dialog about various old houses and a former mental asylum where they'd captured misty figures and glowing orbs on film.

Intrigued by their stories, Sarah flinched when Dallas leapt into her lap and stared off, a low rumble resonating through his body.

"What has you so upset little fella?" she asked, rubbing his chest.

The hair on the back of the dog's neck ruffled and his lips curled into a snarl. All three men looked in the direction where Dallas was staring while Sarah sucked in her lower lip to prevent a scream from materializing. Across the room, the decaying figure with sunken eyes and part of his head missing, stared in her direction. He floated over the floor, his blood-spattered hand stretching out. Before he reached her, Dallas jumped from her lap with a growl. When his paws hit the floor, the image evaporated. Obviously satisfied with himself, Dallas stopped, shook his head, and returned to Sarah's lap.

Harry and Ralph looked at each other and burst into laughter while Garrett rubbed his forehead.

"What was that all about?" Sarah asked, perplexed by the entire scene. Her skin still crawled from the experience and the fact she'd now witnessed the same spirit twice in one night.

"Looks like Dallas saw a ghost," Harry chuckled.

Sarah glanced at Garrett whose broad smile sent a flush skittering across her cheeks. Taking another sip, Sarah looked at the men as they watched her.

"Is there a ghost behind me?" she asked, puzzled as to why they were staring.

"Nope, just wondering if you believe yet?" Ralph added.

"In ghosts? Sure, I can buy into the idea of spirits walking about," she responded.

"Maybe you'd like to accompany us on one of our filming excursions," Harry suggested, downing the rest of his beer.

"I'd like that," she said, wanting to go along with their conversation yet secretly hoping they didn't take her up on it. The last thing she needed to do was go searching for ghosts.

Garrett grinned. "We've got the shoot at the George Plantation Thursday night if you want to come along."

"Let me check with Danni and make sure it doesn't interfere
with anything she has planned. I still have a lot of work to do at
the manor."

Ralph and Harry gave each other a knowing glance making
Sarah straighten up.

"What was that look about?" she asked, her chin tilted up.

"Me thinks ye be a wee bit scared," Harry said in an Irish
accent.

"I'm *not* afraid," she blurted out. "I'll go with you guys."

As soon as the words left her lips, Sarah regretted them.
How had she let herself be goaded into going on a ghost hunt?
Dallas raised his head and licked her cheek as if trying to
comfort her. Apparently, the dog could sense her discomfort.
Maybe it wouldn't be too bad. After all, most of these ghost
hunters were frauds anyway. At least that's what Sarah wanted
to believe. However, the earlier encounter with the half-headed
specter and the incident with Dallas made her realize she
might have set herself up for disaster.

"Let me take you home," Garrett offered, breaking Sarah's
ruminations.

"Sounds good. I've got an early morning."

Dallas jumped to the floor as Sarah stood with the others.
They stepped into the balmy summer night beneath a splat-
tering of stars and a glowing half-moon.

"It was nice meeting you guys," Sarah said with a smile.

"Same," they replied.

"Meet at your place tomorrow?" Harry asked Garrett.

"Yup."

With a wave, the two men walked down the street as Garrett
led Sarah to a gleaming dark blue king cab pick-up. When he
opened the door, Dallas shot onto the front seat and stared at

them with his tongue hanging out as if to say, "where are you riding?"

"Cab," Garrett commanded. The little dog hopped to the roomy back seat and laid down with a sigh.

Garrett helped Sarah onto the front seat and closed the door before walking around to the driver's side. She blew a breath across her lips. As if all his other qualities weren't enticing enough, he was a gentleman too. Keeping herself emotionally disconnected from him was getting harder by the minute.

She rested her head against the soft tan leather of the headrest as Garrett turned the key in the ignition. The engine purred to life as he shifted into reverse. Sarah reached over to pet Dallas who had his front paws planted on the center console when she noticed camera equipment in the back seat. *Must be what they use for the ghost hunts.*

"I thought you worked construction," Sarah said.

"I do."

"How do you keep your truck so clean?" she asked, trying to make polite conversation.

He chuckled. "This is my personal truck. I have an old beater I use for work."

"Oh," she muttered, trying not to stare at him. She felt like the high school geek getting a ride home from the captain of the football team. She was an adult for goodness' sake, so why was her stomach twisting in knots?

"What do you drive?" Garrett asked.

"An old pick-up truck," she giggled, "affectionately known as the Beast."

His deep baritone laugh sent shivers across her arms.

"I call mine Bertha."

"Why Bertha?"

"I had a high school teacher, Bertha Reynolds, who was ornery and accepted no excuses. She rode my butt all through history, wouldn't let me do anything less than my best." His cheeks crinkled as he smiled at the memory. "She taught me how to work hard and love history."

"Did you go on to study history?"

"Nope. Graduated from the University of Paris Island instead."

"You're a Marine?"

"Yes ma'am. Did four years and then called it quits."

"You didn't like it?"

"Loved it, but when my grandmother fell ill, I was the only one to care for her. My enlistment was up with the Marine Corps, so I got a job doing construction here in Edgefield."

"Does she still live here?"

His joyful countenance dissolved. "She passed away a few years ago."

"I'm sorry," Sarah said as they made their way down the main drag, the city lights fading into shadows as they turned down a back street. A suffocating silence enveloped the truck as Sarah struggled for a segue to the conversation. "Where did you get the name Dallas?"

His smile returned as he gave her a quick glance. "Since he's a Jack Russell, I considered calling him JR but it was too common. I was a fan of the show Dallas when I was a kid, especially the season where they tried to figure out who shot JR so I decided to call him Dallas."

"I remember that show," Sarah said with a chuckle. "It was one of the first prime-time soap opera style series."

"Pretty mild stuff compared to the reality shows on TV today."

"Ain't that the truth?" she huffed.

Garrett turned the truck down the drive and pulled up to the front porch. He put it in park, leapt out, and hurried to open Sarah's door. Helping her to the ground, he stared down at her, the front porch light casting shadows across his handsome features.

"Thanks for the ride," Sarah said, her insides quivering.

"Anytime," he smiled. "You don't have to come Thursday night if you don't want to. Not everyone is comfortable with the haunted stuff."

"I'm up for it," she replied, her mind turning to mush beneath his gaze.

"If I don't see you before then, I'll pick you up around 7:30 Thursday night."

"Looking forward to it," she replied with a slight smile.

"Yap!" echoed from the truck as Dallas settled on the front seat, his nubby tail wagging.

"Goodnight, Dallas," Sarah said, rubbing the top of his furry head.

She scurried up the porch stairs as Garrett got into the truck and disappeared down the drive.

"Hey Danni!" Sarah hollered, closing the door. She made her way into the dining room where Danni was typing furiously on her laptop amidst stacks of papers.

"Hey," she replied, not looking up from her computer. "Did you have fun?"

Sarah slipped onto the chair next to her friend and rested her chin in her hand.

"Met two of Garrett's ghost hunting friends. They invited me along for one of their haunted hunts on Thursday night."

"Um-hmm," she grunted, typing away.

"I agreed to go along."

"You what?" Danni declared, her head jolting upright as her brows furrowed. "Have you lost your mind?"

"Apparently, so," she replied, her eyes dancing with mischief.

Now that she had Danni's full attention, Sarah continued.

"It's not like I'll be sleeping. The worst thing I have to deal with is seeing a few creepy shadows and maybe some ghostly images."

"Aren't we brave all of a sudden?"

"I won't be alone, and Dallas is a pretty good warning system."

"A dog who sees ghosts and chases them away? I still have a hard time believing it."

"And communicating with dead people in my dreams is normal?" Sarah snorted.

"You've got a point. Nevertheless, this is pretty far out there."

"Wouldn't have believed it if I hadn't seen it myself," Sarah replied, leaning back. "I kinda like it. It's nice to have an alarm system announcing incoming ghouls."

"His owner isn't hard on the eyes either," Danni said with a mischievous grin.

"There's nothing between us, nor will there ever be."

"Are you nuts? You've found a good-looking man who hunts ghosts. You couldn't find a better match."

Sarah shrugged and glanced down at the table.

"What's going on?" Danni asked. "There's no viable excuse for avoiding him."

"These guys are only out to capture pictures of the afterlife. It's a hobby for them. My ghostly encounters are woven into my DNA."

"And your point?"

"They may be open to the existence of ghosts but that's a far cry from accepting someone who can communicate with the dead in her dreams."

"Just because people in your past couldn't accept your gift doesn't mean these guys will be the same. You need to give them a chance."

"I'll stick with my uncomplicated single life," Sarah said with a sigh. However, her mind whizzed with the idea that she may have found a man who could accept her haunted proclivities.

"You're not right, you know that don't you?"

"But you love me anyway," Sarah giggled. "Speaking of love, did you spend any time with Brady after you left the restaurant?"

Danni exhaled. "Told you there's nothing between us, he's just an old friend."

"If you say so," Sarah said, heading toward the staircase. "I'm going to bed."

"Goodnight," Danni called over her shoulder.

Sarah padded up the stairs to the sound of Danni's fingers tapping away at the keyboard. Despite the ghostly images that had plagued her first night in the house, and some of the macabre images about town, Sarah felt oddly relaxed. Something about this town was welcoming and she was beginning to enjoy her time here. Even better, she'd met a man who wasn't repulsed by the supernatural, giving her hope she might not have to spend her life alone.

6

S arah's dreams rattled down the tracks of her subconscious like a train with no destination. One minute she was sitting at the booth at Corner Pocket and the next she was in her historic mansion in the heart of Beaufort. Then she was back in the dark corridor with worn wood floors and the door with its icy brass knob that stung her skin. Swallowing hard, she looked around the space imploring herself to run away, but her feet kept plodding toward the door. *Stop*, she screamed in her head. Now more than ever she wished she had Dallas with her. Maybe his barking could break the spell and she could leap from this dream to the safety of wakefulness.

With guidance from the *Dreamist* book, Danni had taught her how to be present in the dreams but they'd yet to figure out how to consistently interact with the specters or to escape. Then again, if she left the scene, the ghosts wouldn't be able to get their message across and gain the help they needed to move on to eternal rest.

Might as well get this over with. With trembling fingers, she reached for the brass knob. The door screeched open and an eyeless shadow glided toward her, its lips a thin line as the words *don't trust him* echoed through Sarah's skull, making her head ache. She stumbled backwards, her heart pounding with the force of a bongo drum. As she turned to run, she saw a shadowy form of an older lady with white hair and a gentle smile who waved her forward. Looking back over her shoulder, Sarah saw the gruesome creature with the bashed in skull still moving her direction.

Abandoning all logic, she ran towards the older woman who vanished when she reached her. A hand clutched Sarah's upper arm, sending electric jolts pulsing through her limbs, its foul breath brushing the side of her face as the entity shrieked, *he's hiding it!* Sarah clutched her head to block out the ear-shattering sound as she crumpled to her knees screaming for it to stop.

Breathless, Sarah sat up, her nightshirt clinging to her sweat-soaked back. Danni snored softly in the next bed.

This dream was different than the others. There'd been another ghost, a reassuring one who seemed like she was trying to lead Sarah away from the malevolent entity. Folding her knees to her chest, Sarah rocked back and forth, trying to ease the trepidation gripping her muscles until she felt the fear diffuse. She'd discuss this with Danni in the morning and see if they could figure out what was happening.

DAWN PEEKED THROUGH THE WINDOWS, splashing shades of amber across the walls to the lilting serenade of birdsong. Sarah washed up, dressed, and headed to the kitchen, hoping to catch Danni before she left. Sadly, all she found was a note and a half empty pot of coffee. She'd have to discuss the latest dream development when she saw Danni later in the evening.

Sarah ate half a bagel and then resumed her work in the kitchen. There were only a few things left to catalog before moving to the library and then the upstairs rooms. Hopefully, the bedrooms wouldn't take too much time since they appeared to house nothing more than memorabilia, old toys, and vintage junk. Still disconcerted by the bizarre CD player experience from the previous day, she decided to try again since music helped her stay focused. Loading a Billie Holiday CD, she pressed play, sending Billie's sultry voice floating through the room. *Perhaps the ghost wasn't a fan of Benny Goodman and would prefer Billie Holiday*, she thought with a grin.

Sarah grabbed her pen and ledger and headed for the pie safe when she accidentally knocked one of Danni's folders off the kitchen table. Bending over, she scooped up the contents, her chest tightening and her fingertips numbing as she gazed at a front-page newspaper article about the murder.

She stared at the picture of a slender woman with a broad smile, piercing eyes, and shoulder length hair, the same eyeless woman from her dreams. Sarah tossed the paper to the ground and backed away from it. Tears crested in her eyes as she processed what she'd seen. Tara James, the woman who was murdered, was haunting her dreams. But why?

Then it struck her. Tara's mother-in-law owned this house! Surely, Tara had been here dozens of times. Sarah must have touched something she'd handled and now she was dreaming about this woman.

Regaining her wits, Sarah pulled the cell phone from her pocket and dialed Danni's number. Voice mail.

"Ugh," Sarah muttered. At the beep she left a message. "Danni, call me as soon as you get this. It's urgent."

Frustrated, Sarah hung up, took in a deep breath, held it for a count of five, and repeated. When her heartrate steadied and her limbs stopped quivering, she set about doing her work. Thankfully, after a year of learning to accept her dreamist abilities, she was braver about her ghostly encounters. Granted, it had been a while since she'd dealt with anything this formidable; however, she was determined to see it through.

Sighing, she grabbed her work tools and rummaged through the vintage cooking items lovingly displayed in the old pie safe. It seemed her job here would encompass more than just clearing out inventory. Now she'd be unraveling a haunted mystery as well.

Sarah had made good progress when the Batman theme clamored from her cell phone.

"Hey Danni," she answered, relieved her friend had finally returned her call.

"What's going on? You sounded distressed in your message."

"I'm not sure how to tell you this but I think your murder victim is haunting my dreams."

Danni gasped. "Are you serious? How do you know?"

"I've had a few dreams and then today I accidentally knocked one of your folders off the table and saw a picture of the dead woman."

"You've been having dreams?" Danni asked, her voice elevated. "Why didn't you tell me?"

"I didn't realize they were of significance until I saw the newspaper article."

"Have you had lunch yet?"

"No."

"Meet me at Edgefield Deli. I want to know *everything*," Danni said, excitement accenting her words.

Sarah hung up, changed into her running shoes, and headed for town. By the time she reached the restaurant on the corner of the main drag, Danni was already there with two sweet teas waiting. Sarah slid onto the ladder-back chair and slumped back.

"I'm so sorry Sarah," Danni said. "I completely forgot you didn't have a car. You should've said something. I'd have picked you up."

"You know I prefer to walk. Besides, I needed the exercise. I'm a little freaked out right now."

"What'll you ladies have today?" the waitress asked, her dark hair pulled into a high ponytail.

"I haven't had a chance to look at the menu yet. Can you give us a minute?" Sarah said, wiping the sweat from her forehead. Her shirt clung to her body as if she'd been in a wet t-shirt contest.

"Be back in a few," the waitress replied, her smile revealing perfectly white teeth and dimples.

Sarah opened the menu and scanned the selections. Hunger rumbled her gut even though her stomach was in knots.

"Tell me about the dreams," Danni said, resting her elbows on the tabletop.

Sarah inhaled, leaned forward, and spoke in a hushed tone. "The first one was the night before we left."

"You had a dream before we left and didn't tell me about it?" Danni exclaimed.

"I didn't think much of it at the time. I figured it was a random vision since we were watching that horror flick."

"Good gracious, you can't even enjoy a scary movie without your dreamist skills taking over."

They stopped talking as the waitress walked towards their table with a smile.

"Ready to order?"

"I'll have the BLT with the homemade chips," Danni said.

"And I'll have the cobb salad."

The waitress walked away as a couple came in and sat at a nearby table. Sarah leaned forward and resumed their conversation in a whisper. She knew all too well that small town gossip usually started by overhearing something at a neighboring table in a restaurant.

"Anyway, in the dream I was in this strange place I didn't recognize. There was a woman with no eyes and her mouth was a thin slit, like she was trying to tell me something but couldn't form the words. It was pretty creepy."

"When is dealing with dead people in your dreams not creepy?" Danni asked, rolling her eyes.

Sarah chuckled, releasing some of the tension gripping her frame. "I've dreamed about her a couple of times since we got here. I didn't know who she was until I saw the newspaper article this morning."

Danni's eyes grew to the size of quarters as a grin curled her lips like the Grinch.

"What?" Sarah asked, afraid of the scheme brewing in Danni's brain.

"If you can communicate with Tara in your dreams, then you can find out who murdered her."

"What if Tara says it's Dusty?"

Danni's shoulders slumped as she paused. "She won't. He's innocent, I'm sure of it."

Before Sarah could respond, the waitress approached and placed their food on the table. They thanked her and started eating.

"How much has she revealed so far?" Danni asked, taking a bite of her sandwich.

"Not much. The only thing I've been able to discern are the words "Don't trust him" and "He's hiding it.""

Danni scrunched her face. "That doesn't tell us anything."

"Sorry, that's all I've got."

"We need to expedite this. Refresh my memory, how did you figure out what happened to Nora?"

A year prior, with Danni's support, Sarah had been able to interpret her haunted dreams to expose a century old missing person case that had actually been a murder. For more than a hundred years, the town believed Nora Monroe Hamilton had run off with her lover when in fact she'd been murdered by her husband in a jealous rage. Nora had sent Sarah on a wild goose chase with photos and other memorabilia to reveal the long-buried secret. The people involved had been dead for decades thus there was no rush to expose the truth.

This time was different. She didn't have the luxury of waiting for the facts to be revealed. There was a deadline for discovering the truth which complicated things, not to mention a man's life was at stake.

"It just kind of happened. Don't you remember? I had clues around the house that correlated with the visions which finally led us to the truth."

Danni leaned forward, her eyes locking onto Sarah's.

"I need answers fast. The evidence is piling up against this guy."

Sarah hesitated before speaking. "Maybe he's guilty."

"I refuse to accept that," Danni replied. "My client is innocent."

"Is he innocent or is that what you want to believe because Brady asked you to represent him?"

Danni's expression froze as if she'd been slapped in the face, and for a moment Sarah worried she'd upset her.

"Brady has nothing to do with this. I believe in my client's innocence."

Sarah scrutinized Danni's response. She knew her well enough to know when she was struggling with a case. It was apparent she and Brady were close, although how close remained to be seen. Obviously, Sarah would have to approach this with the utmost delicacy.

"Then I believe in his innocence too. If we work together, we should be able to decode my dreams and find the evidence we need to clear Dusty. By the way, there was another ghost in the dream who guided me away from Tara."

"Do you know who it was?

"No, but she was very comforting. Tara's image was disturbing and a bit frightening. This lady was more like a favorite kindergarten teacher. She was an older woman with a kind countenance and a gentleness about her. I felt drawn to her."

"Interesting," Danni said, tapping her finger on the table as she stared off in thought. "I'll have to look through the *Dreamist* book again. Maybe I can decipher what this means."

"Did you bring it with you?"

Danni frowned. "I left it at home. I was so focused on getting here I didn't even think about grabbing it."

"Not a problem. If we work together, I think we know enough to interpret these dreamscapes and hopefully get the evidence you need to acquit your client."

Danni offered to give Sarah a ride back to the house, but she declined, instead choosing to enjoy the walk through town. Fragrant blooms perfumed the air and colored the landscape. Downtown Edgefield was lovely with a vast array of architectural styles and friendly greetings from residents.

Despite a childhood filled with ghosts and haunted dreams, Sarah loved the salty marsh breezes of her hometown, the comradery of the citizens, and the mystic beauty of the moss draped oak trees. Beaufort was like a family member, always welcoming and comfortable, regardless of the turmoil swirling through her life. If she weren't so content at Monroe Manse, she'd consider living here. Even though her time at the manse had been turbulent, she'd grown to love the old house with its creaks and groans and a library stocked with rare antique books.

By the time she reached Edgefield Manor, her skin glistened and salty droplets trickled down her back. The walk left her feeling rejuvenated and ready to work. Stepping into the house, she headed for the kitchen when a strange sound emanated from the parlor.

Sarah's back tensed, her eyes scanning the room. In the far corner, the CD player clicked and the curtains shimmied in an invisible breeze. Cold chills erupted across her skin. She looked around, trying to catch a glimpse of anything ethereal but nothing appeared. *You're being paranoid*, she thought. Her breath caught as she walked over to the CD player and pushed the off button. Apparently, she'd been in such a rush earlier to meet Danni, she had forgotten to turn it off. Satisfied with her rationale, Sarah trudged to the kitchen to retrieve her tools and start inventorying the library.

AFTERNOON SHIFTED TO EVENING, sending colorful shadows dancing across the library walls as Louis Armstrong belted out a duet with Ella Fitzgerald. Sarah was in a steady work rhythm, the music keeping her focused on the job at hand. Even better, she'd managed to work all day without any ghostly encounters. Sadly, most of the books were Readers Digest condensed stories, run of the mill best sellers, and paperbacks. Nothing of great value was found. At best, she'd be able to sell them for a buck a piece.

Scanning her ledger, she analyzed what she had so far. The camel back velvet settee with matching chairs in the parlor were mid-19th century and in excellent condition. Unfortunately, these type of parlor sets brought very little money in the current market. The Aubusson rug was large and its deep hues of red, blue, and green were still vibrant. With the right buyer, it could bring a couple thousand. The paintings were typical for the period, primarily European pastoral scenes housed in ornately carved frames. None of them boasted famous signatures.

The Duncan Fyfe table and Chippendale chairs in the dining room were beautiful but not in style. Stained wood furniture just wasn't selling. The current trend was painted pieces which made Sarah cringe. The idea of painting perfectly good antique furnishings was distasteful. Still, she should be able to squeeze a few hundred out of the set. The kitchen items were unremarkable and outdated. Country pine and oak pieces hadn't moved well in years. Nevertheless, the amalgamation of items would add to the bottom line.

If she continued at this pace, she'd be able to finish the first floor and start on the second tomorrow. Her cell phone blared, breaking her concentration.

"Hey, Danni."

"I'm neck deep in this stuff and may not make it back for a while. You OK doing dinner on your own?" Danni asked.

"Want me to pick up something and bring it to you?"

"No, thanks. Brady's going to take me out after I finish."

"I see," Sarah purred.

"He's thankful I'm helping him out so he's trying to take care of me. Like I keep saying, we're only friends."

Sarah could almost hear Danni's eyes roll.

"Have fun. And be home by a decent hour, young lady!"

"Yes mother," Danni chuckled.

Sarah shoved the cell phone back in her pocket and headed for the kitchen. She had a bad habit of skipping meals when engrossed in her work. However, she was hungry and now seemed like a good stopping point. She started the kettle and rummaged through the fridge. Nothing appealed to her, so she grabbed a package of peanut butter crackers from the cabinet, fixed a cup of tea, and plunked down at the kitchen table with her ledger. Sipping her tea, Sarah made a few notes as the sun

made its final descent in a vibrant parade of peachy-gold
shadows across the far wall.

Her cell phone rang out, making her jump. Oddly, this
wasn't a familiar ring, especially since the only people who ever
called were Danni or her parents. Since her parents were
always trotting around the globe and only called when
changing locations, she doubted it was them. Looking at the
screen, she saw the words 'unknown number.' Just what she
needed, telemarketers bothering her. Then again, maybe
Danni's phone had died, and she was calling from the courthouse. She clicked the green button and held the phone to
her ear.

"Hello."

Static crackled.

"Hello? Is anyone there?" she asked, annoyance tinting her
words.

A voice muttered something amidst the clatter.

"Could you repeat that? I couldn't understand what you
said," she declared, trying to discern what the person on the
other end was saying.

Frustrated, she started to disconnect when a voice broke
through the discord and said, *don't trust him.*

Sarah dropped the phone and stood abruptly, knocking the
chair backwards to the floor with a crash. Her chest tightened
as she reached down and picked up the phone, simultaneously
hitting the red button. She plopped it on the table, waiting to
see if it rang again when a banging at the door startled her. Was
the ghost knocking on doors now?

Cautiously, she made her way to the front door, nearly catapulting to the floor when her shoe caught the edge of the rug in
the entryway. Regaining her balance, Sarah flung the door
open to find Brady standing there with a pizza box and a goofy
grin.

"Danni sent me. She said you'd be dining on granola bars

or peanut butter crackers for dinner and wanted to make sure you had something substantial to eat."

"She has you doing her bidding now?" Sarah asked, stepping back so he could enter. Something about his surprise visit was strange. Why didn't Danni call to let her know he was coming over?

"Always glad to help," he replied.

Brady walked past, the smell of pepperoni and cheese making Sarah's stomach grumble and her mouth water. She was hungrier than she'd thought. Dismissing her unease, she followed him to the kitchen like a rodent behind the Pied Piper.

"Thanks for bringing dinner, but you really didn't have to," Sarah said. "I don't want to keep you from Danni or your work."

Brady placed the pizza box on the table and smiled. "I needed a break from everything, and this was a welcome interruption. Besides, I have to keep a certain distance while she's working so nothing appears unethical."

"Hadn't thought about that," Sarah said, noticing the shadows beneath his eyes. "I know it has to be hard watching your cousin go through all this."

"He's more like a brother than a cousin. We grew up together," he muttered, clearing his throat. "When my real brother disappeared, we became even closer."

"Have you been able to visit Dusty?"

"Every day. I want him to know we're fighting for him and we won't let him be railroaded on circumstantial evidence. Danni is the best attorney I know and I trust her to get an acquittal."

"Danni is a special person," Sarah said, watching Brady's reaction for any signs of interest. She'd love to see her friend hook up with a great guy.

"That she is," he replied with a glint in his eyes.

Sarah smiled. "You like her, don't you?"

His cheeks colored as he glanced at the floor.

"I'm sorry. I didn't mean to pry. I'd like to see Danni happy."

"She's unhappy?" he asked, concern wrinkling his forehead.

"Not unhappy, but I think she gets lonely sometimes. Especially when I travel for auctions." Sarah said. "Would you like a drink?"

"Better not," he replied.

Sarah sat at the table and motioned toward the chair beside her. Brady sat down, his confident demeanor unusually deflated.

"Has she dated anyone seriously since her divorce from Scott?" he asked.

"Danni is something of a work-a-holic so there's no time for romance."

"She was a free spirit in law school. Shocked me how she could spend so much time socializing and still pass," he said, a sea of memories washing over his expression.

"That always drove me crazy in college. I'd study for days, and all Danni had to do was show up to class, skim her notes, take the test, and get an 'A,'" Sarah chortled. "If you don't mind my asking, why didn't you ask Danni out in law school?"

"Because we were friends and it never seemed like the right moment, you know? Guess I was afraid she'd turn me down and the friendship would be shattered. Then she met Scott and that was the end of that," he shrugged. "After law school I met Sofia. Stole my heart the first time I met her. But after four years of marriage, I discovered I'd never really given her my whole heart."

"Sorry it didn't work out between you two."

"It was entirely my fault. I was at the office all the time. I think she felt neglected."

"Maybe this is a second chance with Danni."

Brady fidgeted with his hands in his lap. "You think so?"

"Won't know unless you try," Sarah replied, smiling as she

rested her hand on Brady's. "I hate to do this to you, but I really need to get back to work."

Brady's cheeks flushed. "Of course, I'm so sorry. I need to get some things done too. I made reservations for Danni and me at Brookstones Grill tonight. I think she'll like it."

"Sounds like you've already taken the first step."

Sarah escorted Brady to the front door where he stopped and stared down at her. *He really does have the most mesmerizing blue eyes*, she thought. Much to Sarah's surprise, Brady wrapped her in a hug.

"Thanks for being such a great friend to Danni and for the encouragement to try again."

"Anytime," Sarah replied, stepping back. "Have fun tonight."

"Plan on it," he said with a twinkle in his eye as he stepped onto the porch and jaunted down the stairs toward his car.

Between the strange phone call and Brady's unexpected visit, Sarah's mind was racing. All the same, she was glad she'd had a chance to talk with Brady about Danni. He really was a nice guy and would make a great match for her closest friend. With everything going on between the estate sale, the trial, her haunted dreams, and Garrett, Sarah's muscles were twisted like a wet rag.

Although she was hungry, going for a run would do more to help her relax. She decided to wait on the pizza and put the box in the fridge. Hurrying upstairs, Sarah changed into her running clothes and stretched, ready to burn off some nervous energy. The warm summer evening slapped her with its humid hand as she stepped into the darkness. She didn't normally run this late, but the main road was well lit, making it the perfect avenue for a nighttime jog.

With each footfall, her breathing fell into a steady rhythm and beads of sweat trickled down her neck and back. An occasional car drove past but otherwise she was surrounded by chirping crickets and crooning cicadas. The moon wasn't quite full but large enough to cast a glow across lawns and illuminate sidewalks. The number of streetlights increased as she neared the town square.

Jogging past several old buildings, she smiled at the smell of old wood and mildew seeping onto the street through antique glass doors. Rental signs perched in many of the empty display windows. The only evidence of life seemed to be at the eateries about town, except for the bakery and the deli which sported *closed* signs.

As she rounded the corner, a figure materialized in the alley between the courthouse and Corner Pocket. Danni assured her the town was safe, but criminals existed everywhere. Undoubtedly this place was no different. She picked up her pace, rushing past the alley. Once past it, she peeked over her shoulder to see if the figure was gone. Relieved when nothing appeared, she looked forward and spotted a putrefying corpse with part of his head missing, the same one she'd seen at Corner Pocket. With a scream, she leapt sideways onto the roadway, causing a car to slam on its breaks accompanied by a blast of its horn.

Hopping back to the sidewalk, she leaned over trying to catch her breath when a hand gripped her upper arm. She screamed again, fear buckling her knees as Garrett steadied her.

"Are you OK?" he asked, worry furrowing his brow.

"Yeah, I wasn't paying attention," she replied, not meeting his gaze. Her heart thrummed within her chest as the image of the man with the shattered skull flashed through her mind.

Harry and Ralph joined them. "What happened?" Ralph asked.

"I'm so embarrassed. I decided to cross the street and didn't look both ways. My mind was elsewhere," she said, her eyes darting around to see if the ghastly vision lurked nearby.

Garrett released her quavering arm. "Why don't you join us for a drink. I'll give you a ride home afterwards."

Too rattled to brave the shadowy streets and encounter another entity, Sarah agreed. Even though she'd seen the same ghost in the restaurant, the patrons and lights made it less frightening.

She followed them inside and slid onto the bench seat of the booth where Dallas leapt into her lap and nuzzled her chin.

"What'll be?" Harry asked. "This round's on me."

"Cabernet," Sarah replied, taking comfort in Dallas' affection as she rubbed his ears.

Harry walked to the bar, placed the drink order, and returned. Moments later, the waitress placed frosty mugs of beer in front of the guys and a rounded glass of wine in front of Sarah.

"Gave you an extra pour, sweetie. After your near miss out there, I figured you could use it."

A blush spread up Sarah's neck and across her cheeks. How embarrassing. The entire restaurant crowd had probably witnessed her stupidity. Too bad they didn't see the bloody cadaver that sent her jumping into the road.

"You sure you're, OK?" Garrett asked, concern veiling his expression.

"I'm fine, thanks."

Sarah took a long sip of the wine, letting its slow burn dissolve the cords of tension wrapped around her lungs.

"How are things going at the mansion?" Ralph queried, tipping the beer mug to his lips.

"Got a lot accomplished today. Hopefully, I can finish the first floor in the morning and start on the upstairs. What about you guys? Get any more bookings for ghost hunts?"

Harry's eyes sparkled at her question. It was obvious he loved their haunted adventures.

"Actually, we've been invited to film an old abandoned

industrial building in North Augusta. Place is bound to be crawling with ghosts."

"Why's that?" Sarah asked.

"It has something of a frightful history," Ralph added. "Legend has it one of the workers was a serial killer. Came across as the quiet, well-mannered type. He was polite, worked hard, and got along with everybody. Apparently, he would follow select female employees to their homes, murder them, chop up the bodies, and bury them beneath the basement floor of the factory."

"How very Tell-Tale Heartish," Sarah said with a grimace.

"He probably would have gotten away with it until he decided to dispose of some smaller body parts down the toilet. Backed up the system. Talk about a nightmarish discovery. It's said there was blood leaking all over the bathroom floor."

"That's pretty disgusting," Sarah replied, taking another sip of her drink.

"It's what led to his conviction and execution. Someone saw him running from the bathroom right before the unfortunate crimson flood," Ralph said.

"Sounds like a creepy place."

"And very haunted. Anyway, in two weeks we'll be setting up cameras and spending the night there." Harry's eyes twinkled like a five-year-old with an upcoming trip to the candy store.

"You're welcome to join us for that one too," Garrett offered.

The grisly figure from the street streamed through Sarah's head making her stomach churn. "No, thanks. I'll pass on that one. A bit too gory for me."

Garrett ordered another round for everybody as they talked about more pleasant things. At this point, Dallas was sitting in Sarah's lap with his head resting on the table as the conversation drifted back to ghosts. The wine settled in her empty stomach, fogging her head.

"You don't have to let him stay in your lap. I can put him on the floor," Garrett offered.

"I don't mind. We're becoming good friends," Sarah said, scratching behind Dallas' ears.

When they'd finished their drinks, they stepped into the muggy summer night. Standing on the sidewalk, Harry and Ralph chatted about the upcoming Thursday night ghost filming at the George Plantation. Sarah's eyes darted about making sure nothing otherworldly appeared from the shadows.

"Are you alright?" Harry asked, looking around.

"Yeah, just studying the area."

Harry's lips curled into a grin. "You saw something earlier, didn't you?"

Shocked at his question, Sarah stiffened. "What do you mean?"

Garrett smiled. "This place is known to have a few specters of its own."

"You mean Corner Pocket?"

"The whole town!" Ralph declared. "You can't toss a stone in this place without hitting a ghost, or um, going through one."

"What makes you think I saw something?" Sarah asked, swallowing hard.

"You have the same frightened look most people get when they've seen something they can't explain. Besides, I doubt you're the type to jump in front of moving cars."

Hesitating, Sarah weighed her response. "I may have seen something move in the shadows."

"Old Man Howard," Harry chuckled.

"You know who the ghost is?" she queried, her brows arching.

"You're not the only one to see him," Garrett said.

"What does he look like?"

"Decrepit man, mean expression, half his head is gone," Harry said.

Sarah gasped. That's exactly what she'd witnessed, except her version was in advanced stages of decay. Goosebumps prickled her skin even though she was sweating in the oppressive night air.

Ralph patted Harry on the back. "You called that one right."

Sarah looked at Garrett to determine his take on this so-called sighting, but he just smiled at her, his eyes glimmering in the glow of the street lamp.

"He's serious?" she asked.

Dallas barked as Garrett nodded. "Afraid so. Old Man Howard has been scaring folks for more than a century.

"And how did he end up with half his head missing?" Sarah asked, fearful of the answer.

"He and Bertram Sparks got into an argument over a woman. Bertram challenged Howard to a duel in the square except Howard never showed. Bertram was so disgusted; he posted a sign on the courthouse wall calling Howard a coward."

"Howard the coward? How droll," Sarah snickered.

All the guys chuckled, and Dallas let out a high-pitched yap as Harry resumed the story.

"Howard's cousin, Franklin, saw the sign and confronted Bertram, saying he wasn't a gentleman. Back then, that was a serious insult. Bertram pulled out his pistol and shot Franklin in the chest, killing him instantly. What Bertram didn't know was that Howard was lingering in the shadows. When he saw his cousin shot dead, he marched to the square and confronted Bertram. Weapons were fired, blowing off part of Howard's head."

"What happened to Bertram?" Sarah asked, flabbergasted by the tale.

"The court found him to be within his rights since he was defending his good name."

"Unbelievable," Sarah replied, shaking her head.

"That's nothing," Harry snorted. "You should hear the other

tales. They call us bloody Edgefield for good reason."

"I'd like to hear some of those stories," Sarah said, "But it's late and I need to get home."

"I'll give you a ride," Garrett offered.

"I can walk."

"Not a chance. You've had a couple of drinks and I'd feel better knowing you got home safely."

"Might as well do as he says. Otherwise, he'll follow you home like some sort of maniacal stalker," Ralph said in an ominous tone.

"Looks like you're driving me to the house," Sarah responded, shrugging her shoulders.

"See you guys tomorrow evening," Garrett said with a wave.

"Goodnight, Dunk," Harry called as he and Ralph started down the street.

"Dunk?"

"Their nickname for me. Short for Duncan, my last name."

"Dunk and Dallas, I could have some fun with this," Sarah grinned slyly as he helped her into the truck.

As they rode down the main street, Garrett glanced Sarah's direction.

"Did you really see something earlier when you were running?"

"I saw something move in the shadows and it startled me. I doubt it was half-headed Howard the coward," she replied with a huff. Although she suspected it had been him, she wasn't ready to reveal it yet.

"Maybe you should run during the day instead of night-time. It's safer."

"It's too hot during the day."

"Not in the morning. Dallas and I go for a run before work. You're welcome to join us."

Sarah contemplated his offer. "I'll think about it, but I really need to get things ready for the estate sale."

Garrett pulled down the drive and put the truck in park. Jumping from the cab, he scooted around to the passenger side, and helped Sarah from her seat. Dallas barked his goodnight from the open window as Garrett walked Sarah to the door.

"If you change your mind about running with us, give me a call and we'll swing by to get you."

"Sure." Sarah pulled out her phone and programed Garrett's number while he did the same. Something about the exchange of phone numbers sent a spark of excitement through her heart. She'd never done this before.

He bid her goodnight and got into his truck. Sarah watched him back down the drive, Dallas' head hanging out the passenger side window. Darkness ensued as the headlights of the truck turned onto the road. A shudder rattled Sarah's body. Not wanting to see anything of the spiritual sort, she hurried inside.

Danni was typing away at the dining room table. Sarah had been so focused on Garrett she hadn't noticed her friend's Mercedes parked outside. Danni was already in her preferred attire of a t-shirt and leggings with her sandy brown hair secured with a scrunchy.

"Where have you been," she asked without looking up.

"Went for a run and then ran into Garrett and his ghost hunting gang."

Danni stopped typing. "Oh really?" she said with a sly grin, wriggling her eyebrows.

Sarah rolled her eyes. "No drama, Danni. He was at Corner Pocket when I ran by. He invited me to join him and his friends."

Pursing her lips, Danni straightened in her chair. "And he just happened to be standing outside Corner Pocket on the offhanded chance you were going for a nightly jog?"

"Not exactly," Sarah waffled, catching her friend's attention.

"What happened?" Danni's voice took on a serious tone.

"Kinda had an encounter with someone."

"Or something?" Danni declared. "You don't have encounters with *someones*, you have encounters with ghosts! Spill it."

Sarah sat next to Danni and exhaled. "I decided to go for a run..."

"Why?" Danni interrupted, scrutinizing her friend. "You usually run in the mornings, not after dark."

"I got a phone call, from a...something that said *don't trust* him. Then Brady showed up with a pizza. He said you'd sent him over to make sure I ate something other than peanut butter crackers." Sarah sighed.

"Sorry about that. I figured you hadn't eaten anything substantial. Brady has been so uptight about Dusty's situation; I figured it was a good distraction for him. What happened after he came by?"

"Once Brady left, I was still unnerved by the mysterious phone call and decided to go for a run. When I got to the square, a creepy figure with half his head missing appeared. I screamed and bolted in front of a car. Garrett, Harry, and Ralph ran out to see what had happened and invited me to join them for a drink, which I was more than ready for."

"You actually saw a ghost with part of his head missing?"

"Yup, brains and all," Sarah shuddered. "Then the guys described him and I knew he was the one I'd seen."

"You admitted you saw the ghost?" Danni exclaimed, nearly jumping from the chair. "When did you decide to go public with this?"

"I didn't tell them I'd seen it. They figured it out. Apparently, I'm not the first to see a spirit in that area."

"This place gets stranger by the day," Danni said, shaking her head. "So, tell me about this ghost."

Sarah filled Danni in on the sordid story before walking to the next room for a drink.

"Do you think the ghost on the phone is connected to what

you saw?"

"Probably not," Sarah replied, returning to her seat. "From what the guys said, the entire town is crawling with specters."

"You should feel right at home," Danni snickered.

"By the way, how was Brookstones?" Sarah asked. It was her turn to egg on Danni about her gentleman friend, especially since she didn't feel like discussing the half-headed ghost any further.

"I was too engrossed in rereading one of the interviews to go out, so Brady picked up enchiladas from a little restaurant off the highway. He moved the reservations to tomorrow night."

"Did you find anything that might help Dusty?"

"Not sure," Danni sighed. "There's something about this case that doesn't ring true. I feel like I'm missing something right in front of me."

"I know it's frustrating. Sorry I can't help."

Danni downed the rest of her Scotch and went for a refill. Sliding back onto her chair, she took a sip of her drink. "Maybe we'll get lucky and Tara's ghost will reveal the murderer in your dreams tonight."

"Doubtful," Sarah replied, her shoulders slumping.

"We're learning more about your skills. You already know how to prompt a dreamscape by touching something personal that belonged to the ghost. If we can get a better grasp on your interactions during the dreams, we'll probably be able to solve this mystery in no time."

"What we need is a way for me to ask the entities what they're trying to tell me and save me weeks of sleepless nights." Sarah yawned. "Speaking of which, I'm beat and going to bed."

"Have you eaten anything?"

"Nope. Drank my supper."

"You could heat up the pizza."

"Thanks, but I'm too tired to eat. I'll have some in the morning. Nothing like cold pizza for breakfast."

"Ahh...the breakfast of college students after pulling an all-nighter," Danni smiled, shifting in the chair. "Add warm beer and you have the breakfast of college students on spring break."

"G'night," Sarah replied with a grin. No matter how old Danni was, she'd never let go of the good old college days.

"Sweet dreams," she called out as Sarah walked past. "Or should I say, haunted dreams?"

"Not funny," Sarah hollered back as she made her way up the stairs.

Sarah plopped down on the bed, her muscles protesting the earlier run. She'd not been on a regular running schedule for the past few weeks due to some out-of-town trips to antiques markets. Now she was feeling it.

After a quick shower, she changed into her nightclothes and stretched. Wrenching the window open, she smiled as the symphony of crickets wafted in on summer's warm breath. Weary, she slid between the cottony sheets and rested her head on the pillow. Too nervous to close her eyes for fear the half-headed man would flood her thoughts, she went over the day's events trying to make sense of the cryptic phone call and the recurring message from the beyond. Her heart thudded a bit harder when her mind wandered back to Garrett. How she wished she could pursue a relationship with him. But it wasn't feasible. Eventually, her eyelids began to lower and she drifted off to a land of walking corpses and unsolved murders.

THE STALE SCENT of old building mixed with walls of antiquated books assaulted Sarah's nose, drawing a sneeze. The space was void of any living soul, making it feel dank and foreboding. She trudged toward the end of the corridor and stood before the wooden door. Reaching out, she turned the brass knob and stepped into the darkened area. Once her eyes adjusted to the blackness, Sarah descended the stairs, her body taut with expectation. This was normally when the woman with empty eye sockets and the bashed in skull appeared. An icy cold draft crept through the inky darkness as Sarah continued down the creaking staircase, the air growing colder with each step.

When her foot made contact with the cement floor, she moved forward as soft music began to play. She scanned the space trying to figure out what was in this part of the basement. Floor to ceiling shelves housed voluminous notebooks and leather-bound journals. She slid one from the shelf but couldn't make out the words in the dark. Her hair bristled as foul breath tickled her ear whispering, *it's not here, he took it.*

Spinning around, Sarah's gaze rested on Tara's pallid face, her eyeless stare boring a hole through Sarah's fortitude. She started to bolt up the stairs but took a deep breath and willed her legs not to move. With a quaking voice, Sarah collected all of her courage and confronted the wavering form in front of her.

"What do you want to tell me, Tara?"

Shocked she was able to form the words, Sarah watched as the ghost's cadaverous lips wriggled but didn't move. When her bony hand reached out, Sarah lost her nerve and dashed up the stairs two at a time. Halfway up, a hand grasped her shoulder and started tugging her back. Sarah wrenched free and managed to get up two more steps when another hand grabbed her arm while another twined in her hair and still another gripped the back of her neck. Several others scraped at her ankles. Her heart was pounding with the force of a jackhammer.

Gripping the handrail, Sarah pulled herself forward when bony fingers, some with skin, others with bits of flesh, clawed at her clothes, dragging her back. The words, *don't trust him,* began to grow like a chant until it was blaring in her ears and echoing through her mind. Her knees began to buckle when a wrinkled hand reached through the door, its plump fingers wrapping around her wrist. All of a sudden, the noise faded, and the hands fell away as this gentle creature led Sarah up the stairs and into the corridor. With a few deep breaths she was able to steady her breathing and heartrate.

Something about this particular entity was comforting, not frightening. She followed the ethereal figure with its rounded form and glistening white hair to the front of the building. The woman turned with a smile, melting away the apprehension pulsing through Sarah's veins. Before she could ask this grandmotherly spirit who she was, a hand grabbed hold of Sarah's arm and shook it.

With a scream, Sarah bolted upright, sending Danni stumbling backwards with a howl.

Breathless, Sarah looked at her friend who was leaning against the other twin bed clutching her chest.

"What the heck, Sarah?" Danni gasped, her voice shaking.

"You scared me half out of my mind!" Sarah declared.

"You were mumbling in your sleep."

"And you thought waking me up was a good idea?" Sarah queried, her eyebrows arched.

"Not now," Danni smirked.

Sarah rubbed her eyes. "What did you hear?"

"It was unintelligible, but I thought I heard you say Tara's name. I figured if I woke you, maybe you'd be able to tell me what she said."

Sarah could tell by the look on Danni's face she was worried.

"This dream was bizarre. At first it was only Tara. Then others joined in."

"Others?"

"I didn't see their faces, but they were pulling at my arms and my hair chanting *don't trust him*. Tara said something about *he took it* and *it isn't here*."

"Took what?"

"Don't know. I started to panic and tried to pull free from them when another hand reached for me and led me away."

"Who was it?"

Sarah's shoulders instantly relaxed at the thought of the old woman with the gentle touch and the warm smile.

"It's an older woman, the same one from my dream last night."

Sarah pondered the presence of this kindly ghost and her role in whatever secret Tara was trying to reveal.

"And she's not frightening?"

"Not at all. She's like the epitome of the grandmother image. Sweet but her spirit is strong, almost as if she can block out the scary apparitions."

"Maybe it's Edie's mother, your biological grandmother."

"Could be," Sarah replied, brushing a strand of hair from her forehead. "She was probably a dreamist too."

Danni slumped onto her bed with a yawn. "Doesn't sound like you garnered anything useful. I'm turning in."

"Thanks, I'm wide awake now," Sarah grumbled as Danni burrowed under the covers.

"Sorry," Danni croaked. Within minutes her soft snores kept time with the twittering cicadas outside.

Sarah stared at the ceiling, ruminating over the dreamscape and the meaning behind Tara's words. What was missing and what connection did it have to her murder? Obviously, she was trying to communicate something of significance. What Sarah couldn't comprehend was how someone she never knew, who'd never lived in this house, was visiting her dreams. Granted, Tara's in-laws owned the homestead, so she'd probably spent time here over the years. Regardless, why had Sarah dreamed about her the night before she and Danni came to Edgefield?

Sarah sighed. It was a mystery in need of solving if they wanted to prove Dusty's innocence.

After tossing and turning most of the night, Sarah rose to the caress of summer breezes drifting through the sheer curtains. The air was laced with the fragrance of roses and lantana. Sarah loved summer with its colorful blooms and flitting butterflies. Although not as humid, the temperatures in Edgefield were just as stifling as the Lowcountry. At least at home there were marsh breezes to help move the steamy air and make it feel less oppressive. She swung her feet from beneath the covers and stood.

Walking across the room, Sarah glanced at the curtains that were now flapping wildly in the morning breeze. As she stared at them, they began to wave and flutter until they took the form of a slender body, its face contorted as the air whistled through the sheer fabric, *he has it.*

Sarah's breath caught; her legs immobile like cemetery statues. A moment later, the air went still, and the curtains settled against the wall. Sucking in a breath, Sarah stepped backwards until she reached the door, her eyes fixed on the window should the image reconfigure in the gauzy curtains. Once in the hallway, she barreled down the stairs and into the kitchen where Danni was sipping her morning java.

"Mornin'," Danni said, taking a bite of her bagel. "What's got you in such a state? You look like you've seen a..." Her words trailed off as she set the bagel on the plate and straightened in her chair. "What happened?"

"The ghost took form in the curtains and said, *he has it.*"

"What does that mean?" Danni asked, her face scrunching.

Sarah plopped onto the chair next to her. "I have no idea. None of this makes sense."

"Was it the same ghost from your dreams?"

Nodding, Sarah fought back the urge to run from the house and never return. "It was definitely Tara. I still don't understand how she's able to communicate with me or who she's trying to implicate. It's not like I know anybody in this town."

"Actually, you do. You know Garrett and his ghost hunting friends."

"And Brady," Sarah added.

"Brady doesn't live here, not to mention he was at his house in Columbia the night of Tara's murder," Danni said.

Sarah contemplated Danni's words and all of the warnings the ghost had spoken.

"Up to this point, she's said not to trust him, that he has *it,* whatever *it* is, and that it's not here. I just don't get it."

Danni leaned forward, propping her elbows on the table. "That's because you're looking at it in segments. Try viewing it in the context of Tara's situation."

"She doesn't have a situation, she's dead."

"Exactly. Maybe she's trying to lead you to whomever committed the murder."

Sarah could see the hope brewing in Danni's eyes. Obviously, she was struggling with this case and willing to try any avenue to prove her client's innocence, even a supernatural one.

"I don't see how any of this could possibly lead us to the

guilty party. Tara feels more like a menacing presence than a welcoming one. And then the old woman shows up and everything seems OK."

Danni slumped back in the kitchen chair. "I still think you need to check into Edie's family line. Maybe the older spirit is a distant relative. Since dreamist abilities only pass through females, it's logical the benevolent ghost is somehow related to you."

Sarah considered the possibility. "I suppose it makes sense. But how am I to know if I have a long-lost relative from Edgefield?"

Danni gave a sly smile. "The genealogical library is downtown. Why don't you start there?"

"This town has a genealogical library?"

"Don't underestimate this place. It might seem like a sleepy little southern town, but it's got a lot to offer."

"Do they have computers?"

"Probably, but you hate those things," Danni said.

"I may not like them, but I also don't have access to my usual resources. I need to research some of the items in the house. Maybe I could investigate my lineage and the inventory at the same time."

"Sounds like a good idea."

Now that she had a plan, Sarah felt a slight sense of relief. If she identified the older woman from her dreams, perhaps she could communicate with her and figure out what Tara was trying to disclose.

"I've got to get going. I'm doing a couple of follow-up interviews with some of Dusty and Tara's friends." Danni swigged down the last gulp of coffee and rose from the chair. "See you later."

"Thanks for your help with the spirit stuff."

"Glad to be your ghost hunting sidekick," Danni chuckled.

"I'm not hunting ghosts! They're hunting me!" Sarah hollered.

"Regardless, I need answers. I'm worried about Brady. I've never seen him this distraught. Dusty's arrest is hitting him hard."

"I'll do my best," Sarah said, hugging her friend.

"Don't forget, I'm having dinner with Brady," Danni said. "Will you be OK on your own this evening or do you want me to send over lover boy?"

"No need. I'm a big girl, I can handle a few spirits," Sarah replied.

With a nod and a sly grin, Danni left the room.

Sarah jaunted up the stairs and scoured her suitcase for something comfortable and cute to wear. She grabbed a butternut yellow t-shirt and a pair of khaki shorts and went to the bathroom to shower. As she turned the shower knob, she mulled over Danni's comment about sending Garrett to the house to stay with her. It was a nice idea.

Stepping beneath the steaming spray, Sarah exhaled. Why was she so hung up on this man? In a few weeks she'd never see him again. She'd resolved herself to a life of celibacy, leaving no reason to pine over a guy she'd only be around for a short period of time. She needed to let it go, regardless of his deep green eyes, strong stature, and his cute little dog.

After a hot shower, Sarah headed toward town with a notepad and pen stashed in a small leather backpack style purse. The sun was beginning to shroud the day in an oppressive heat as droplets of sweat glistened against Sarah's forehead and neck. Her stomach rumbled, reminding her she'd not eaten since lunch the day before, prompting her to head to the bakery first.

She rounded the corner and stopped abruptly when an old man with a crooked smile and missing teeth, glowered at her. She started to move past him when he lifted his right hand, aiming a pistol her direction. Immobilized by fright, she gasped as his finger contracted and a puff of smoke materialized from the barrel of the gun. Instead of hitting her, the bullet whizzed past, striking a man behind her. She watched as he clutched his chest and crumpled to the ground in agony before vanishing. When she turned back around, the man with the gun had also disappeared. Hoping to avoid any more spectral savagery, Sarah hurried into the bakery as quickly as her trembling legs would allow.

The aroma of cinnamon and fresh brewed coffee temporarily distracted her from the frightful occurrence she'd just endured. Ordering a cinnamon roll and a large hot tea, Sarah settled at a table near the back of the bakery. Occasionally, her gaze meandered toward the massive front window, catching glimpses of people strolling past. Much to her relief, none of the passersby seemed to be of the spectral sort, instead they seemed quite real.

Still rattled by the ghostly encounter outside of the bakery, Sarah leaned back in the chair, wishing Danni was here. After living a lonely life of haunted dreams and spirit filled visions, Sarah found solace in the support of her best friend. In her loyal fashion, Danni had stood by Sarah's side, helping her understand the *Dreamist* book as well as accepting her strange abilities to communicate with the dead through her dreams.

After finishing every morsel of the cinnamon bun, including the crumbs of icing on the plate, Sarah started across the square to the Tomlinson Genealogical Library. The tan brick building had a simple façade with American and South Carolina flags flapping on either side of the front door. Despite the warm temperatures, a chill trickled down Sarah's spine as she opened the door and stepped inside.

She stopped in her tracks as the door swooshed shut behind her. Her eyes darted about the large room with its floor to ceiling shelves housing dozens of leather-bound volumes. A host of pottery and architectural artifacts lined the tops of bookcases. Her lungs constricted and her breakfast roiled in her stomach as she took in her surroundings.

This was the building from her dreams.

"Hey, Sarah," a male voice called. "What brings you here?" Harry strutted toward her with a broad smile.

"You work here?" Sarah queried, her insides quaking while she tried to reconcile her disbelief.

"This is the job that pays the bills so I can indulge in the business of hunting ghosts."

Sarah forced a smile as she recalled something about Tara dying in a library.

"This isn't the place where Tara...?"

Harry's chipper demeanor faded. "She died over there," he said pointing across the room toward a long hallway.

Sarah's mouth went dry. The corridor was the same one from her dreams with a door at the far end. The same door with the icy brass knob that burned her palm when she grasped it. This was the location of Tara's eyeless spirit and the old woman with the comforting countenance she'd been dreaming about.

"I'm sorry," Sarah muttered, spots of light flashing before her eyes.

"Everyone loved Tara. I still can't believe she's gone."

"It's hard to lose someone, especially like that."

"Crushing is more like it," he said, exhaling. "Sorry, we don't need to discuss this right now. Tell me, what can I do for you today?"

Relieved to change the subject, Sarah grinned. "I need some help with a genealogical search as well as an appraisal guide for antiques."

Harry's smile broadened. "Follow me."

He led Sarah to a large room in an adjoining space. Apparently, two separate buildings had been remodeled into one. A couple of computers sat in the back corner near a short hallway with a sign pointing to the restrooms. Harry pulled out the chair for Sarah who sat and stared at the blank screen in front of her.

"Um, Harry," she said hesitantly, "I'm not very good with computers."

"What are you looking for?"

"First, I need to find some websites for china, crystal, and silver."

He leaned over and tapped out a few words on the keyboard and hit enter. The screen lit up with a host of different sites covering everything from vintage china patterns to identifying crystal manufactures to silver holloware and stemware.

"That's great. Thanks."

"Anything else?"

"Not right now. I would like to do some genealogical research in a little bit."

"Let me know when you're ready and I'll show you where to start."

"Thanks, Harry, I really appreciate it."

Harry walked away as a middle-aged woman stepped through the front door. Sarah started making notations about silver patterns and their values. Shortly after showing the woman a series of antique ledgers in the other room, Harry returned.

"What are you doing?" he asked.

"Taking notes."

"There's no need for that. Just hit print. It'll save you a ton of time."

He showed her how to send what she needed to the printer and returned to the woman in the next room. Sarah followed his instructions, printing all the information she needed for the appraisal process.

This is so much faster, she thought, momentarily considering purchasing a computer for her business. When the last sheet of paper inched from the printer, she grabbed it and stacked it with the others. Turning back to the computer screen, she startled when it glowed a bright white with the words *don't trust him* scrolling across the monitor faster and faster. Sarah gasped and stumbled into the computer chair, sending it rolling backwards. Instantaneously, Harry was by her side.

"Everything OK?" he asked, his expression veiled with concern.

"The screen..." she pointed to the monitor which was now black.

"Sorry about that, this machine tends to crash easily." He scooted in front of her, pushed a button, and the screen glowed back to life.

"Crashed?"

He furrowed his brow. "You really don't know about computers, do you?"

Sarah scrunched up her face. "Afraid not. My cell phone is the most technological piece of equipment I own, and I can barely maneuver that."

"These computers are pretty outdated. They get overloaded easily and stop working, or crash. If it happens again just reboot it."

"Reboot?" Sarah asked, her eyebrows arched.

"Wow, you are a novice. Push the power button, wait a few seconds and then press the button again."

"Thanks," she said, gathering the print outs. "I think I've got what I needed."

"Want a folder for those?"

"That'd be great."

Sarah followed him back to his desk in the main section of the building. Just beyond his work area was an old vault with a white exterior door shielding a black interior door with scrolled gold lettering.

"What do you keep in the vault?" she queried as Harry pulled a manila folder from his side desk drawer.

"This building was a bank at the turn of the last century. We house supplies in there now. Of course, we don't close the door or lock it since nobody knows the combination," he chuckled.

Sarah took the folder from Harry and stuffed the papers inside. "Can you help me with my genealogical research now?"

"Glad to," he said with a smile.

He showed her to a section of books organized by South Carolina counties and dates.

"Who are you looking for specifically?" he queried.

And then it hit her. Why was she looking into her family line? Edie was an only child as was her mother before her. She'd seen photos of them and now that she thought about it, neither of them resembled the old woman from her dreams. Whatever the identity of the grandmotherly entity, she obviously wasn't related to Sarah. As she pondered what to do next, an idea popped into her head. Maybe the older woman from her dreams was somehow attached to Dusty. After all, she kept leading Sarah away from Tara's gruesome corpse.

"I don't mean to sound morbid, but I need to research Dusty's lineage."

"Why?" The pained look on his face tugged at Sarah's heartstrings.

"I'm trying to help Danni out. She likes to know the family dynamics of her clientele in cases like this." Guilt filled Sarah's chest for lying about the circumstances. She couldn't tell someone she barely knew she was trying to identify a ghostly woman from her dreams, even if he did believe in spirits. If Harry learned how far the spiritual realm stretched, he'd never believe it.

"If it proves Dusty's innocence, I'll gladly help. What do you need to know?"

"I need to know about Dusty's grandparents, aunts, and cousins."

With a puzzled expression, Harry removed a few books and walked over to a round tiger oak table with four matching chairs. Sarah pulled out her notepad and pen and listened as Harry explained how to utilize the reference books.

"These provide the basics of the family line, who's still alive, and which county they reside in. When you finish with these, I'll help with the next step."

Sarah gave a nod and paged through the voluminous tomes, jotting down names and dates. If she could identify the old woman, perhaps she could figure out her purpose, communicate with her, and use the information to help Danni with her case.

An hour later, Sarah was nowhere near ascertaining the name of the mysterious entity from her dreamscapes. Both of Dusty's grandmothers were still living, although his aunt, Brady's mother, was deceased. For a moment, Sarah considered the possibility that the lady from her dreams might be kin to Tara but quickly dismissed it. Why would Tara's ancestors lead Sarah away from her, especially if she was trying to relay information that may or may not acquit her husband? Unless he really was guilty.

8

S arah walked back to the mansion beneath blue skies with storm clouds moving in from the south. She only hoped she could make it back before the rain burst forth. She didn't need the paperwork in her backpack getting soaked.

Taking the front steps two at a time, she managed to scoot onto the porch as droplets of water began to pepper the ground and ting against the metal roof. A roll of thunder skittered across the atmosphere, making Sarah jump as she jiggled the key in the lock. A strong wind pushed her through the door into the shadowy space.

Torrents of water poured from the roof, splashing against the porch floors. Drawn to the window, Sarah watched in awe as Mother Nature's summer storm pelted the flowers and trees with life-giving nourishment, accompanied by an occasional tremor of thunder. The tension in her body melted to the rhythmic beat of the storm.

Sarah started toward the kitchen when Glenn Miller's, *In the Mood* blasted from the CD player. She stopped in her tracks, fixating on the machine. Swallowing hard, she crept toward it, staring in disbelief at the Glenn Miller CD lying beside it. How could it be playing Glenn Miller without the disc? Although the machine had been doing some pretty crazy things the past couple of days, this was by far the strangest. Another roar of thunder echoed, blowing the front door open, the scent of honeysuckle wafting through the room.

Sarah ran to the door and forced it shut against the fierce wind pushing across the threshold. Once closed, she locked the deadbolt. A loud click came from the CD player, punctuating the last notes of the song and enveloping the room in an eerie quietude.

Looking around, she placed her hands on her hips.

"I appreciate that we have similar taste in music but doing scary things isn't helping me figure out what you're trying to tell me."

She braced herself for some sort of ghostly comment about not trusting someone or that something wasn't where it should be. When silence ensued, she swallowed the unease clogging her throat and went to the kitchen to fix a cup of tea. As the water heated, Sarah ruminated on how well she'd adapted to the ghostly encounters. She was much more comfortable than she'd been before learning about her dreamist abilities. If only she could hone them quicker, maybe she could figure out what Tara was trying to tell her. A twinge of sorrow gripped her heart. Had she known her biological mother, perhaps she could have helped her with this haunted gift. When the kettle squealed, she filled the cup and bobbed a teabag in the steaming water.

Opening her backpack, Sarah retrieved the folder filled with the price guides and pertinent information for appraising the items she'd unearthed over the past few days. She scripted notations in the margins of her ledger. Some of this stuff was worth more than she'd anticipated. But estate sales were fickle events. You either had shoppers wanting something for nothing or serious collectors looking for a deal. An auction would generate higher prices. Sadly, the time constraints on this job didn't give her the option of organizing and hosting an auction. Melinda needed as much money as possible, and fast.

AN HOUR LATER, the sun had chased the storm clouds away, leaving behind clear blue skies and a symphony of songbirds. Sarah had organized all of the items for Melinda to look over so she could decide what would stay and what would be sold. Sarah went to the kitchen for another cup of tea. Lost in her thoughts, she startled when she heard the front door slam shut.

"Sarah, are you here?" Danni hollered.

"In the kitchen," she replied.

Danni plunked a stack of files on the kitchen table, kicked off her heels, and walked to the fridge. Glancing at Sarah's teacup, she shook her head.

"You're not right," she said, grabbing a soda and twisting off the cap.

"How so?"

"Always drinking hot tea, especially when it's sweltering and sticky outside. That storm left a tidal wave of humidity in its wake."

"Tea cools you when it's hot," Sarah responded, joining Danni at the kitchen table. "Any new leads to help Dusty?"

"Nada. It's really aggravating. Everyone believes he's innocent, yet no one can provide proof."

"Didn't you say the evidence is mostly circumstantial?"

"Pretty much. He and Tara had an argument, he went home, drank until he passed out, and woke up the next morning. Before he realized she was missing, the police showed up and arrested him."

"How'd they know to arrest him? There has to be more to this than just an argument," Sarah said, taking a sip of tea.

"Since Tara was murdered with a fireplace poker Dusty made that was found in their shed, it kinda cinched the allegation."

"That's what doesn't make sense. Why would someone use something so obvious, hide the weapon in a place where the police were sure to look, and then pass out at home without concocting some sort of alibi? With this line of thinking the man would have to be the world's dumbest criminal."

"You're right, it doesn't make sense," Danni said, rubbing her eyes with her palms. "What about you? Get anywhere with identifying the old woman in your dreams?"

"Not really. But I was able to identify the location."

"Where is it?"

"The genealogical library."

Danni sat straighter in her chair. "The same place Tara was murdered?"

"Yup."

Danni rubbed her arms. "You're creeping me out."

"Imagine how I felt when I walked in there this morning," Sarah responded. "Anyway, it didn't occur to me until I was there that Edie was an only child and so was her mother, which means the old woman probably isn't related to me."

"How do you know it's not your grandmother? You never met her."

"I've seen a photo of her. She was slender with dark gray hair. This woman was plump with white hair."

"Maybe it's someone on the Devereaux side," Danni said, shrugging one shoulder.

Sarah shuddered at the thought. It was hard enough learning she'd been adopted as a baby and the parents she'd known and adored her entire life were not biologically related to her. Discovering that William Devereaux, the town philanderer who'd been hitting on her since high school, was actually her half-brother had nearly sent her over the edge. Thankfully, her biological father wasn't in any hurry to claim her since her conception was one of disrepute. And Sarah was more than happy to keep that part of her past a secret. The Devereauxs were the last group of people she wished to claim as family.

"Doubtful it's one of the Devereauxs. Remember, only women can be dreamists."

"Your bio dad has a mother, doesn't he?"

"Ugh, hadn't considered that." Sarah slumped in her chair. "No, this woman can't be related to them. She's got a calming presence."

"You know there may have been at least one decent person in their family line."

"Not likely," Sarah said with an eye roll. "Anyway, I researched Dusty's family hoping to find a connection, but nothing turned up. Tomorrow I'm going to look into Tara's family."

Danni arched her eyebrows. "Hadn't thought about that."

Sarah sipped her tea as Danni chugged the soda.

"Do you have plans for dinner?" Sarah asked.

"Nope. Brady had to make an unexpected trip to his office in Columbia for a case he's working on. He'll be back in a couple of days. It's beginning to look like we'll never get to Brookstones Grill."

"Sorry about that," Sarah said, taking her empty cup to the sink. "Why don't we go to Corner Pocket?"

"Hoping Mr. Dreamy will be there?" Danni teased.

Sarah turned with one hand planted on her hip. "Why are you so intent on making us an item? I happen to like the food there."

"Of course, it's all about the food. The scenery isn't bad

either," she added as she scooted from the room before Sarah could retort.

DANNI PARKED her Mercedes in front of Corner Pocket and gave Sarah a sly smile.

"What?" Sarah quipped.

"Nothing. You just seem a bit anxious," she replied, arching her eyebrows.

"I have no idea what you're talking about."

Danni's expression softened from prankster to best friend. "I see the way he looks at you, and it's more than a friendly gaze."

"You're being ridiculous," Sarah said, sliding out of the car.

Despite her adamant denial of any interest in Garrett, Sarah's heart sank when they entered the restaurant and he wasn't there. Scolding herself for getting hung up on his absence, she followed Danni to a table on the other side of the room.

The waitress took their orders as Sarah scanned the place. She wasn't sure what she was looking for, the guys or the grisly visage of Old Man Howard.

"Earth to Sarah, where are you?"

"Sorry, I was just making sure that half-faced man wasn't lurking about."

"Yeah, that would be creepy," Danni said as the waitress placed a pitcher of beer and two frosted mugs on the table.

Danni poured the beers and clinked her mug against Sarah's. "Here's to freeing an innocent man."

"To Dusty's innocence."

They each took a long draw.

"Speaking of which, I'm surprised you agreed to dinner instead of burying yourself in paperwork," Sarah said.

"I needed a break to clear my head. This case is pushing me to the limits," Danni replied, taking another swig.

"Why's that?"

"Not sure. The evidence may be circumstantial but it's also irrefutable. Yet somehow, I know he's truly innocent. I just have to figure out how to convince a jury of it."

"I don't envy you," Sarah replied.

"Wanna trade jobs?" Danni asked.

"Wanna trade dreams?" Sarah responded.

Danni straightened in her chair. "Absolutely not!"

"Then stop all your whining and prove Dusty's innocence," Sarah scolded as the waitress placed their food on the table.

After chowing down on onion rings and burgers, they paid the check, bid goodbye to the bartender, and a few of the regulars at the bar, and walked into the sultry night air. Despite the oven-like atmosphere, Sarah suddenly felt chilled. A draft filtered down the back of her shirt, kicking up her heartbeat a notch. Turning slowly, she gasped when a spectral woman with a sinister smile, shadowed eye sockets, and scraps of skin clinging to her skeletal form, lunged toward her before dissolving into the night.

"You, OK?" Danni asked, the Mercedes lights blinking to the key fob signal.

"Fine, caught a chill," she mumbled, rubbing her arms, as her gaze darted about the area.

With eyebrows arched, Danni leaned against the open car door. "Just a chill when it's a hundred degrees out here?"

"Let's go back to the house."

Sarah slid into the car, not wanting to discuss anything otherworldly. She was tired of all the spectral activity. Her inability to fine tune her skills was weighing heavily on her. Why couldn't that blasted *Dreamist* book say what needed to be said without all the riddles and mumbo-jumbo?

"Do you want to talk about it?" Danni asked as they drove

through town, the streetlamps glowing from behind a fog of moths and fireflies.

"Not really," Sarah replied, staring out the window.

Much to Sarah's relief, they made it back to the manor without any spectral visions or gruesome images. Despite the momentary respite, Sarah suspected there'd be more haunting before the night was over.

9

S arah climbed the stairs, her shoulders hunched and her legs as heavy as lead weights. Thankfully, Danni hadn't questioned her sudden change in mood because she didn't feel like discussing it anymore. What she wouldn't give for one day of a ghost-free existence.

Grabbing her nightclothes, she showered, and climbed into bed. Danni was propped up against several pillows, her dollar store readers perched on the bridge of her nose as she scanned another file. Sarah nestled beneath the coverlet. Night breezes caressed her skin, helping to release the pent-up tension gripping her muscles.

"Any luck?" Sarah asked.

"Not an ounce," Danni replied, pulling the glasses from her face and setting them with the files on the nightstand. "This case is wearing me out. I can hardly hold my eyes open."

"Let's call it a night," Sarah said, switching off the lamp.

As darkness enveloped the room, Sarah could hear Danni shifting in the bed.

"Goodnight, Danni."

"G'night."

Moments later, Danni's rhythmic breathing drifted through the room while Sarah stared at the ceiling. What was she missing about the dreamscapes? If she could solve this mystery, maybe she could get a few nights of restful sleep. Obviously, Tara was trying to tell her something important. So, why was the old woman interfering? It didn't make sense. If Dusty was as innocent as everyone proclaimed, then the message Tara was trying to convey should be easy to decipher. Yet, the vague phrases were cryptic in nature and did nothing to reveal the identity of the murderer.

Yawning, she ruminated over the facts of the murder and Tara's repeated phrase, *don't trust him.* Sarah sat up. What if Tara was trying to say Dusty was guilty? Although the phrase *don't trust him* could be interpreted as Dusty lying about his innocence, the other phrases, *he has it* and *it's not here,* didn't make sense.

The wind kicked up, sending the curtains billowing across the night table nearly knocking the lamp to the floor. Sarah caught the teetering light, jumped up, and closed the window. Danni continued to snore. *If only I could sleep that soundly,* Sarah thought as she slipped back under the covers. Finally, exhaustion fingered Sarah's arms and legs, sending her off to dreamland where answers were just out of reach.

SARAH STARED down the long corridor of the genealogical library, except this time all the books were sprawled across the floor. Some were face down while others had pages scattered about. Sarah stepped carefully around the tumbled tomes, curious to see who showed up in this particular dream. Reaching for the ornate brass knob, Sarah jumped when the door flew open and Tara's image materialized, her decaying breath brushing against Sarah's cheek with the words, *don't trust him.*

Nausea swirled in Sarah's stomach as the eyeless creature floated past, revealing a gash in her temple with blood flowing down her neck and shoulder. Although repulsed by the vision, Sarah was determined to see this through. She followed Tara's lifeless figure as it glided across the pathway of fallen books. Making her way toward the front of the building, the ghost's quivering skeletal hand pointed to a desk. Sarah stepped closer, the strong scent of rot intermingling with the musty smell of old books. A frigid aura swirled about Tara like a cyclone when the old woman appeared in the far corner. Before she could make her way to the old woman, a thud startled Sarah from the dream.

GASPING, Sarah sat up, her eyes darting about the darkened space as she tried to get her bearings. She glanced across the room expecting to see Danni sprawled on the floor, but she was snoozing peacefully.

Blasted, Sarah thought, *why hadn't they brought the Dreamist book with them*? They needed something to guide them. Sarah swung her legs to the side of the bed and stood. Whatever had made the noise that woke her had to be somewhere in the house. The wood floors were cool beneath her feet as she ambled into the darkened hallway.

Silence enveloped the area, sending a shiver down Sarah's back. Something was amiss, she could sense it. Descending the stairs, she flipped on the overhead light and peered into the front parlor. Sarah scanned the room, looking for the source of the sound. Everything was where it should be. The dining room and kitchen yielded the same results. Satisfied that nothing ghostly had knocked anything around, Sarah started up the stairs when the hairs at the base of her neck bristled.

Despite her prickling nerves, Sarah made her way down the hall and opened the first bedroom door. Shadows danced across the floor, but nothing was misplaced. She tried the next room and found a box laying on its side with the contents fanning around it. Stepping closer, she lifted the cardboard container and placed a photo album and two leather bound journals back inside. *Nothing ghostly here*, she thought, placing the box back on top of the stack. Content the sound had been nothing more than the box toppling to the floor, she started back across the hall. Unbeknownst to her, decomposing finger-tips caught strands of her hair, sending a shiver down her back as she hurried into her room and shut the door.

10

Sarah walked along the fragrant streets to the square for another day of research into Dusty and Tara's family line. So far, she'd been able to ascertain that Tara's ghost was trying to warn her about someone, likely the killer, and an amiable elderly woman intervened when the fear was overwhelming.

As the town square came into view, Sarah saw two old men with scraggly white beards, one in a plaid shirt with khaki pants tucked into knee high leather boots, the other wearing a stained cotton shirt with dark trousers. Each sat behind a cannon aimed at the other from across the center of town. At first, she believed it to be some sort of civil war reenactment, except this was early morning on a weekday and there were no spectators. The plaid shirted man yelled something at the other gent about being a yellow-bellied fool. The man in dark trousers returned the insult and lit a match which he held to the back end of the cannon. Sarah's eyes widened as the other gent did the same. Cars drove past as if this were a common occurrence. Rushing through the front door of the library,

Sarah called out for Harry who materialized from the back room.

"G'morning, Sarah," he greeted.

"Harry, call the police! There are two men in the square..." she gasped as she turned back toward the door. The two old men and their explosive weaponry was nowhere in sight. Sarah's skin prickled. There's no way they could have moved the cannons and disappeared so quickly.

Harry walked up beside her and looked out the door, a broad smile parting his lips. "You've got a good eye for this stuff," he remarked.

Baffled by the scene and its instantaneous disappearance, she looked at Harry. "What are you talking about?"

"You keep seeing our resident ghosts. Old Man Howard the other night and now the dueling cannoneers."

"You saw them too?" Sarah asked, her voice cracking.

"A lot of people see them. It's not unusual."

Without warning, a riderless horse raced past in a flash of brown fur.

"Oh my gosh! Was that a ghost horse?" Sarah exclaimed.

"No," Harry laughed. "That was Mr. Brown's mare, Silky. She's quite real. You'd think Mr. Brown would've learned by now not to try to ride her until later in the day since she doesn't care for early morning outings."

"Will she be, OK?" Sarah queried, concerned for the horse's safety.

Harry grunted. "Yeah. She goes down to the park at the end of main street and grazes until Mr. Brown catches her."

"And this is a regular occurrence?"

"More of an occasional incident."

Exasperated, Sarah tilted her head. "Is there anything normal in this town?"

"Only the unexpected," he replied with a sheepish grin. "What can I help you with this morning?"

"I'd like to look into Tara's family line."

A veil of sorrow clouded his dark eyes. "Funny you should say that. She was actually researching her heritage when she..." he paused, obviously distressed about his colleague's demise. Taking in a deep breath, he continued. "What exactly do you want to know?"

Sarah froze like a burglar caught with a bag full of stolen jewels. How on earth was she going to explain the reason for investigating the women in Tara's family? She couldn't tell him she was searching for the identity of a genial older woman who was making appearances in her haunted dreams.

"It's part of the research to help Danni since her paralegal is back in Beaufort."

"If you think it will help. Follow me," he said, walking back to the area where Sarah had been the day before. As Harry pulled leather bound volumes from the shelf, Sarah glanced at the front door, half expecting to see a kangaroo hop by or a ghostly Revolutionary war unit march past. Instead, her gaze settled on the desk nearest the door. Tara's ghost had pointed at that desk in her dream.

Harry plunked two massive books down on the table.

"These will give you the basics. The more detailed volumes are with her research in the vault. Haven't had the heart to reshelve them yet."

"Thanks Harry. Sorry for asking you to do this, but it may help Dusty." It wasn't really untrue. If Sarah could figure out what was going on in her dreams, she may be able to help Danni find the person responsible for Tara's death.

Harry flashed a half-hearted smile and started toward his desk. His sullen demeanor tugged at Sarah's heart. He really did seem to care about Tara.

"Harry," she said.

"Yeah."

"Whose desk is that?" Sarah asked, pointing at the large oak desk covered in files, books, and a pottery jug filled with pens.

"That was Tara's desk," he sighed. "One of these days I'll clear it off, but not yet. Makes me feel like she's going to come back to work."

A shiver raced up Sarah's spine, making the back of her neck tingle. Was Tara trying to tell Sarah there was something in her desk that could help her husband? More importantly, how was she supposed to search it without raising suspicion with Harry? When the time was right, she'd find a way to snoop through the drawers, although she had no idea what to look for.

Then Sarah remembered that touching something belonging to the deceased could connect them in her dreams. Once Harry was helping a patron, she'd take an item from Tara's desk. Until that time, Sarah perused the books hoping to find a grandparent or elderly aunt of Tara's who could be appearing in her nightly visions.

Much to Sarah's dismay, none of Tara's grandparents or aunts were deceased. She thought about going further back to great-grandparents but decided against it. The chances of discovering the ghostly woman's identity were slim. For now, she'd concentrate on finding out what Tara was trying to tell her, starting with her desk.

The morning had been painfully slow in the way of foot traffic, setting Sarah's nerves on edge as she waited for Harry to be distracted so she could swipe something from Tara's desk. After two hours she got her break when Ralph sidled through the front door.

"Hey Harry," he called. "Got something to show you in my truck. You won't believe what I found at the flea market! If I can adapt it, we can use it Thursday night."

Harry rose from his chair and looked at Sarah.

"Sarah, would you mind watching the place for a minute while I check this out?"

Ralph looked her direction and smiled. "Hey Sarah! Didn't see you sitting there."

"Hello Ralph," she replied. "Take your time Harry, I can handle things until you come back."

As soon as Harry stepped out the door, Sarah raced to Tara's desk and sat in the leather chair. She opened the top drawer and found a stapler, paper clips, assorted highlighters, and a box of envelopes. The next drawer housed a phone book, a receipt pad, and a package of lined paper. Glancing toward the door, Sarah could see Harry and Ralph hunched over the back of a pick-up truck. She slid the second drawer shut and opened the bottom drawer. Several manila folders filled the space along with a three-hole punch and a package of mints. Sarah started to close the drawer when the folders shifted, revealing the edge of a book. Her breath caught when she pulled the small brown volume from the drawer and stared at the simple title, *Dreamist*. Stunned by her discovery, Sarah shoved the book under her shirt and hurried back to the table as Harry walked inside.

Conjuring an innocent expression, Sarah smiled. "Was it something good?"

Harry blew out a long breath. "Heck yeah! If he's able to convert this thing, it could amplify our electronic connection to the transistor and possibly give us a clearer signal to the ghosts."

"That's great," Sarah replied, her nerves on edge. She wanted to leave as soon as possible and read through the *Dreamist* book to determine if it was the same as hers. Checking her watch, she closed the research books, and stood, careful not to let the *Dreamist* book slip out from beneath her shirt.

"Thanks for all your help, Harry. I'm going back to the house to do some more inventory." Sarah turned her back to him, slipping the small book into her backpack along with her pad of paper.

"Did you find what you were searching for?"

"I found more than I anticipated."

"We'll be at Corner Pocket tonight if you want to join us."

"Depends on how much I get done this afternoon. Thanks for the invite," she replied, scurrying out the door.

Sarah practically ran the several blocks to Edgefield Manor despite the sweltering summer temperatures. Once inside the house, she slumped onto the settee and pulled the *Dreamist* book from her backpack. A twinge of guilt ruffled her chest at the idea of taking something from a dead woman's desk. However, she quickly dismissed the thought. If she was going to help Danni clear Dusty's name by interpreting Tara's haunted messages, she needed this book for guidance.

With shaking hands, Sarah opened the book and scanned the weathered pages. It appeared to be the same as the one she'd found at Monroe Manse after Edie's death. The question now was how Tara had obtained this copy.

11

S arah read through a couple chapters of the *Dreamist* book with little success. Like her copy, everything was written in riddles. Since Sarah had never been very good at deciphering this sort of thing, she'd have to wait until Danni came home. Hopefully, the book would help them interpret Tara's messages and identify the old woman who kept intervening when Sarah felt overwhelmed.

Placing the book on the coffee table, Sarah went to the kitchen to fix a cup of tea and gather her work tools. She'd spent more time at the library than she'd planned and now she needed to play catch-up with the inventory. Danni always gave her a hard time for being distracted from the job at hand and the last thing her friend needed was more stress.

The days seemed to be flying by since they'd arrived in Edgefield. Tomorrow night, she'd be going with the guys to the George Plantation for a ghost hunt. Part of her dreaded what she might see while another part of her was intrigued. She'd never been with people who not only believed in ghosts but sought them out. It was one of the things that made Garrett even more appealing. Not that his sculpted cheeks, deep green eyes, and seductive smile weren't attractive. *Stop it*, she thought, *you'll be going home soon and will never see him again.* Yet she couldn't get him out of her head. He could be the perfect match. After all, how many men had she met who hunted ghosts?

Per her usual manner, Sarah buried herself in work in an effort to escape the turmoil swirling within her soul. Between trying to finish the inventory, interpret the dreams, and stave off her burgeoning attraction to Garrett, her life felt like a dinghy racing toward a waterfall. Somehow, she'd see this through with the help of her best friend, and a shot or two of bourbon.

SARAH MANAGED to breeze through the inventory on the second floor. Although the furnishings were in good shape and had some value, the current decorating trend of mix and match made complete bedroom sets hard to move. In addition to the furniture, there was a plethora of boxes filled with sentimental items like photo albums, scrapbooks, and miscellaneous mementos from sporting events and graduations. Sarah had yet to explore the attic and the basement but had little hope they'd possess anything other than family memorabilia.

The crunch of tires over gravel alerted Sarah of Danni's return. She ran down the stairs and poured a hefty shot of scotch for Danni and a bourbon for herself. Danni was going to freak out when she showed her the *Dreamist* book.

"Sarah," Danni hollered followed by the front door closing. "You here?"

"In the parlor," she replied.

Danni dropped her brief case on the floor, slipped off her shoes, and headed toward the bar.

"Already got it poured," Sarah said, holding up the glass.

Taking the drink, Danni gave a weary smile. "There's a reason we're friends," she remarked. "It's like we share a brain.

Maybe your dreamist abilities are making you a bit psychic. How'd you know I had a horrible day?"

"I'm definitely not psychic, although I do know how your mind works. I have news to share," she said, sitting on the settee.

Danni plopped onto the wing chair across from her, taking a long sip. "Unless you took a nap and Tara revealed the murderer in your dreams, I doubt it will lift my spirits."

"What happened?" Sarah asked.

Danni ran her hand across her face. For the first time in days, Sarah noticed the deep recesses around her friend's eyes as if she hadn't slept in weeks.

"The prosecutor is pushing for the trial to move forward as quickly as possible. Apparently, he has his eye on a congressional seat and wants to make a big impression on the voters, especially with a case as publicized as this one."

"Wouldn't he look better if truth and justice was served instead of a conviction?"

"Pfft. The only thing voters care about is results, regardless of how they're achieved. The way he's spinning this thing, Dusty looks like a drunken, disgruntled husband who murdered his wife in cold blood. While most of the locals know better, the people in the surrounding areas believe what the media is blasting."

"What do you believe?" Sarah asked gently.

"He didn't do this. But the longer it takes to prove it, the more likely public opinion is to sway against him. Meanwhile, the investigators are so focused on Dusty that the real killer could be long gone or walking among us."

"Let's examine the facts for a minute. From all accounts everyone loved her. If Dusty didn't kill Tara, then who did?"

"Not a clue."

"Who would have motive to murder her?" Sarah asked. "It

obviously wasn't a random act since a fire poker made by her husband was used to kill her."

"She wasn't robbed and nothing was taken from the library so a burglary isn't likely."

"What about an affair?"

Danni mulled over Sarah's words before shaking her head. "She doesn't sound like the type of person who would do that sort of thing. By all accounts, she and Dusty were very much in love and dedicated to their marriage."

"Betrayal and money are usually at the root of all crimes, at least that's what a very wise lawyer once told me." Sarah lifted her eyebrows.

"Ha! Throwing my words back at me. With pressure from the prosecutor to rush things, I'm running out of time with this case. Nevertheless, I'm filing paperwork to stop the expedited trial date but have my doubts about it being approved." She rubbed her eyes and took another sip of her drink. "Tell me about your news."

"Sarah held up the *Dreamist* book. "Found this hidden in Tara's desk at the library."

"Why didn't you start with that?" Danni declared, leaning forward with eyes blazing.

"Because you were upset, and I was trying to be a good friend."

"A good friend would've told me to shut my trap and then shared *her* news."

The right side of Sarah's mouth curled up. Danni didn't mince words; you always knew her opinion whether you wanted it or not.

"In my dream last night, Tara's ghost pointed to a desk in the library. I didn't think much of it until I went back there this morning. Harry informed me it was Tara's desk. The poor guy seemed devastated by her death. He hasn't even cleaned out her stuff yet. Anyway, I figured when he wasn't looking, I'd snatch something personal so I could try to make a better connection with her in my dreams."

Danni's phone blared, making her jump. "Hold on," she said, glancing at the screen. "I need to take this."

"Hey Brady," she said, walking to the bar to refill her drink. "What's going on?"

Sarah leaned back against the settee, rested her head against the curved back, and closed her eyes. Exhaustion enveloped her like a warm blanket as she started to drift when Danni's voice called out.

"Don't you dare go to sleep without telling me the rest of this story," she said, curling her stockinged feet under her as she settled onto the chair.

"What did Brady want?"

"To tell me he's coming back earlier than planned." Danni waved her hand in the air. "Continue."

"I waited most of the morning for someone to come in so Harry would be distracted but the place was dead."

"Quite literally," Danni said.

Sarah rolled her eyes and continued. "Luckily, Ralph came by which gave me ample time to go through the desk drawers. Didn't find anything out of the ordinary until the last drawer. That's when I discovered this tucked beneath a bunch of office supplies."

"Do you think she found it in the library?"

"Not sure. I've never seen another copy until today."

Danni gasped. "Oh my gosh, do you think she was a dreamist too?"

"I suppose it's possible. From what I understand it's not like Highlander where there can be only one," Sarah quipped.

"We need to figure this out. If she *was* a dreamist then maybe we can find a way for you two to communicate through direct clues instead of random messages."

"Maybe this is why she's been in my dreams. Not because she's been to the house but because she and I share a gift."

"Whatever the reason, we need to work on this. It may be Dusty's only chance."

AFTER AN HOUR of studying the riddles in the Dreamist book, Danni's eyes were practically crossed.

"This is insane. What the heck does this mean?" Danni moaned.

"Read it to me again," Sarah said, her head beginning to ache.

Danni exhaled and squinted as she read from the small tome.

Look deep inside,
Where thoughts do hide,
You'll know what to choose,
If you follow the clues.

LISTEN TO THE VOICES,
That guide you to choices,
Revealing the proof,
That leads to the truth.

INDIVIDUALITY IS the key to life,
Listen carefully to avoid strife,
Otherwise, you may stray,
And miss the path that guides the way.

LOOK to those with the same ability,
And forego your own fragility,

From dreamist to dreamist facts do transfer,
Giving clarity to the most difficult of answers.

"Do you think it's referring to *how* you communicate with another dreamist while you're dreaming?" Danni asked.

Sarah shook her head. "I'm at a loss. I thought for sure you could make sense of this."

"It's like a whole bunch of hocus pocus and mumbo jumbo. I can't figure it out," Danni replied, rubbing her forehead.

With the pressure of the trial, Danni's usual riddle solving capabilities seemed stymied. Sarah could tell her friend needed substance.

"Let's take a break and order a pizza," Sarah offered.

"Sounds like a plan," Danni said, walking to the fridge for a beer.

They ordered a pizza and continued trying to decipher the strange chapters.

However, the only thing they were able to garner was that dreamists could communicate with one another. How to do so intelligibly remained a mystery.

When the pizza arrived, Sarah and Danni took a break and devoured the deep-dish pepperoni pie with cheese stuffed crust. Returning to their quest to learn more about the dreamist connection, they skimmed through the book once again.

"This is starting to aggravate me," Danni sighed. "I'm too tired to make sense of this stuff. Why didn't they just write everything in a straightforward manner?"

Sarah reached across the table and grabbed Danni's hand. "Don't get worked up over this. You're exhausted and your brain has been stretched to its limits trying to put together a defense for Dusty. Maybe we should get some sleep and try again tomorrow."

Danni let out a slow breath. "You're probably right. But the sooner we figure this out, the sooner you can get some answers from Tara."

"Maybe. Who's to say she knows the identity of her murderer? It could've been a stranger."

"Not likely since he used something so personal to kill her."

"Good point. What I don't understand is why this other woman keeps pulling me away from Tara. It doesn't make sense."

Sitting straighter, Danni wrinkled her lips. "Why don't you ask her?"

"Huh?"

"The older woman. When you see her again in your dreams ask her what she's trying to tell you. For that matter, ask Tara the same thing."

"I don't know that I can," Sarah replied.

"Have you ever tried?"

"Not really. The only thing I've ever done is attempt to escape."

Danni shrugged her shoulders. "Give it a try. What can it hurt?"

Hopefully nothing, Sarah thought.

AFTER WASHING UP, Sarah changed into her night shirt and plodded across the floor. Danni was already sound asleep. Sitting on the edge of the bed, Sarah ran through everything she'd learned so far as a dreamist. The ability was passed through the females in the family line. Dreamists could communicate with each other, although Sarah had yet to learn the intricacies of that aspect. And handling something that had been touched by the deceased could open a direct line into their memories. Sarah sighed. Was that really all she and Danni had garnered from the *Dreamist* book after a year of studying it? They'd also read something about controlling what happened in the dreams; however, they'd only been able to interpret part of the instructions so far.

Now Tara was showing up in Sarah's dreamscapes as well as whispering cryptic phrases in her ear. What did it all mean? More importantly, how could she communicate with Tara while maintaining her safety? She remembered being strangled during one of the dreams about Nora when she was clearing the Monroe Manse estate.

Too tired to think about it anymore, Sarah took in a deep breath and rested her head against the pillow. A summer breeze billowed through the curtains as she closed her eyes and prepared herself for a night of vivid visions, hopefully with information that could help Danni with her case.

12

S hadows skirted across the wood floors of the library corridor as Sarah traipsed toward the door at the back. She stared at the brass knob, aware it would sting the palm of her hand and that Tara's grisly appearance waited on the other side. Inhaling deeply, Sarah reached for the knob when icy fingers dug into her shoulder. She turned slowly to see Tara's eyeless face inches from her own, blood seeping from the wound in her head onto the shoulder of her dress.

Sarah's eyes grew wider and her mouth dropped to release a scream but nothing came out. She wanted to run from there, far from Tara's gruesome image, and never return. Out of nowhere, the older woman appeared next to Tara. Resting her wrinkled hand on Tara's shoulder, she smiled, sending a wave of comfort through Sarah's body. While Tara's lips didn't move, the words, *read the book*, resonated inside Sarah's head.

"Which one?" Sarah managed to mumble.

Tara's bashed-in head tilted as if questioning what Sarah was saying.

"I'm in a library. Which book should I read?" Sarah sucked in a breath. How had she managed to speak?

Without warning, the scene shifted. Tara was sitting at the same table where Sarah sat when researching. Tara paged through a heavy volume, making notes on a yellow legal pad. The lights in the library were off except for the section where she sat. Getting up, she walked to the shelves when a searing pain radiated through her skull and then all went black.

Sarah shot upright in bed, holding her head and rocking until the pain faded. In all her life, she'd never had a headache like the one hammering her skull now. As the aching subsided, she thought back on the images, trying to decipher what she'd seen and how it all tied together. Tara had been killed by blunt force trauma to the side of the head with a fire poker. Obviously, Sarah had just witnessed the murder, so why not show her who did it?

Massaging the stiffness from her neck, Sarah decided she'd share all of this with Danni in the morning. Maybe they could figure it out together. Now that she'd found a copy of the *Dreamist* book in Tara's desk drawer, they'd have a reference to guide them. And for future trips, Sarah made a mental note to always pack her copy. Apparently, she'd have to carry it with her when she traveled since ghosts were everywhere.

Surprisingly, Sarah was able to drift off to sleep and slumber through the rest of the night without any grisly visions or skull shattering experiences.

Sunlight tickled Sarah's eyelids, nudging her from a fitful sleep. Slipping from bed, she dressed for the day, and hurried downstairs hoping to catch Danni before she left.

"Mornin'," Danni mumbled as Sarah entered.

"Not had your first cup of java yet?" Sarah asked, starting the kettle for tea.

Danni grunted as she leaned against the counter, staring at the coffee maker as it sputtered and spit.

"You know, it doesn't go any faster no matter how hard you try to coax it with a menacing glare."

Danni shot her a look of disdain before returning her gaze to the bubbling brew. Mornings were something in which she and Danni differed greatly. While Sarah loved the early part of the day with its fresh scents, birdsong, and flamboyant sunrises, Danni didn't function until late morning or her third cup of coffee, whichever came first. When the coffee maker sounds went from sputtering to a hiss, Danni filled her cup. She slouched into a chair, her uncombed hair and drooping eyelids making her appear like a college student the morning after spring break ended. Sarah fixed her tea and joined Danni at the kitchen table.

With a few sips of coffee, Danni's eyes seemed to lighten as she sat a bit straighter. "Any good dreams last night?"

"Hard to say." Sarah said. "These dreams are much different than the ones at Monroe Manse. Nora was able to show me visions of what happened whereas Tara keeps showing me the same thing in the same place. Her eyes are black holes, and her lips don't move, yet I can hear her voice. I can't make any sense of it. And the old woman keeps showing up. As soon as she does, all my fear subsides, and Tara doesn't seem so frightening."

"We need to find a way to get more information from her, and fast."

"The only difference in last night's dream was that she told me to read a book," Sarah offered.

"Don't suppose she said which one?"

"No, which makes it more of a mystery. There are hundreds of books in that place. The least she could do is point to it like she did when she led me to her desk." Sarah slumped back in the chair and ran her fingers through her hair.

"Do you think she was referring to the *Dreamist* book?" Danni asked.

"I suppose it's possible," Sarah shrugged. "I asked her to show me which book but before she could, the scene changed. Tara was researching something and then walked to the shelves. Next thing I knew, my head felt like it was about to explode."

Danni's brows furrowed as she took another sip of coffee. "Tara doesn't speak but you can hear her voice, an unidentified woman shows up to quell your fears, and now you're getting headaches."

"Last night was the first time I experienced any pain. It was agonizing, like someone was bashing in my head."

"What happened right before the pain?" Danni asked, sitting up straighter.

"Nothing. She was researching something, got up, everything went black, and then my head started pounding. When I woke up, it was a dull ache that slowly dwindled away."

"This is amazing! I think you dreamed Tara's murder!" Danni declared, her eyes dancing.

"Except I didn't see the killer."

"The forensics report showed she was most likely approached from behind and struck on the side of the head. There's a chance she didn't see who did it."

Sarah thought for a moment, trying to remember anything she may have overlooked in the dream, but nothing came to mind. "Are you saying there's a possibility Tara didn't know who murdered her?"

"Based on the coroner's report and the fact everything went black before you felt the pain, I'd say it's feasible. Up until now we assumed she was hit in the head after turning around, thus reinforcing the belief that Dusty had done it. Logic dictates she wouldn't have turned her back on someone she didn't know or didn't trust," Danni said, getting up to pour her second cup.

"Still doesn't explain why she can't speak or the presence of the other woman."

"Sounds like we need to do some more reading in the *Dreamist* book. If we can figure this out maybe we can clear Dusty and go home," Danni replied.

Out of the corner of her eye, Sarah noticed movement near the window. Not wanting to break the connection, she turned her head slightly, her heart pounding against her chest like a sledgehammer. A flurry of white hair and a rotund figure flashed before her and then disappeared. For a brief moment, a sense of calm washed over her.

"You, OK?" Danni asked, sitting down.

"Yeah, just caught a glimpse of something," she replied, rubbing the goosebumps from her skin.

Danni's eyes widened as she scanned the room. "Was it Tara?"

"I think it was the old woman, but I can't be sure."

"What makes you think it was her?"

"She had white hair, and I got that same sense of peace I get when she appears in my dreams."

"Wonder what she wanted?" Danni said, sipping her coffee.

"Hard to say," Sarah replied, shrugging her shoulders. "If I could identify her, perhaps I could figure out what she's trying to tell me."

"Sounds like we have a day of research ahead of us," Danni declared.

"Don't you have work to do?" Sarah asked, surprised Danni would want to spend the day interpreting ghostly visions.

"I'm supposed to meet with Dusty this morning. I still have several interviews; however, if we can figure out what Tara is trying to tell you I might not have to keep chasing dead-ends."

Sarah shook her head. "I think you're putting too much emphasis on this dreamist stuff. Even if Tara did reveal something, you'd still have to prove it in court. I don't think the judge is likely to take the testimony of a ghost who visits my dreams."

Danni snapped her fingers. "Come with me to visit Dusty.

Perhaps he can shed some light on what Tara is trying to tell you."

"I'm not sure that's such a good idea. How do we explain my seeing his dead wife in my sleep? He's likely to fire you for insanity and then report you to the ethics board."

"We aren't going to charge in there proclaiming ghostly intervention. But if we ask the right questions, we may be able to garner the information necessary to make sense of your nocturnal visitations."

Sarah wrinkled her nose "Guess it couldn't hurt."

Danni hopped up from her chair, poured her third cup of coffee, and headed for the doorway. She stopped and gave a mischievous smile which Sarah knew meant she was ready for battle. "Let me get a shower and change and then we'll head over to the jail. I have a feeling we're about to crack this case wide open."

Danni hurried from the room, leaving Sarah to contemplate everything that was happening. Something seemed off, although what that was remained to be seen.

THE JAIL'S brick exterior had classic turn-of-the-century elements with a large archway over the double doors, lantern style lights on either side of the entrance, and dental moldings around the roofline. However, the interior boasted worn linoleum floor tiles, a sterile atmosphere, and the unfriendly glares of guards, making Sarah feel as if she were about to be ambushed. Danni walked up to one of the uniformed men, showed her ID, and nodded toward Sarah. The tall, burly man with thinning hair shot Sarah a suspicious look before escorting them to a small room. The space was barren except for a metal table with two chairs on one side and a single chair on the other. Once they sat down, Danni opened her briefcase and took out a legal pad and pen.

"I'm surprised they let me in without taking all of my information," Sarah said.

Danni gave a sly smile. "Brady is friends with most of these guys. They grew up together. He told them to give me anything I needed which includes bringing along people who can help with Dusty's defense."

Sarah chuckled. Small town life was the same no matter where you went. Knowing the right people could get you farther than any degree or title. You just needed to work the system and you could achieve almost anything.

Moments later, Dusty shuffled through the door escorted by a stern looking guard with a shaved head and a tattoo of a skull and anchor on his left forearm. Dusty sported the proverbial orange jumpsuit bejeweled by metal cuffs and chains. Although Sarah had never met Dusty before, his sunken eyes and sallow complexion spoke of a man in turmoil.

"Hey Dusty," Danni said as the guard anchored his charge to the chair. "I brought a friend along with me. This is Sarah Holden. She's handling the estate sale for your mother."

"Thanks for helping out. I really appreciate it," he said, a slight smile shifting his somber expression. "Have you had any luck finding out who killed my wife?"

"Actually, we need your help," Danni continued.

"I'll help any way I can, but I've already told you everything I know."

"It's not about what you've disclosed, it's about something Sarah found in Tara's desk drawer."

Sarah's eyes grew to the size of marbles as she gave Danni a 'what the heck' glare.

Obviously picking up on Sarah's angst, Danni rolled her eyes and whispered. "Now is not the time for playing games. We don't have the luxury of waiting for the truth to fall into our laps."

Sarah's chest tightened. She was still adjusting to her

dreamist skills and wasn't ready to go public with it, especially with someone she didn't know.

"What did you find?" Dusty asked, his eyes shadowed and his expression grim.

Sarah drew in a deep breath as Danni explained.

"Sarah found a book titled *Dreamist* in the bottom desk drawer of Tara's desk at the genealogical library. Do you know why she had it? Was it part of her genealogical research?"

In all the years they'd been friends, Sarah had never seen Danni so direct in her approach to garnering information. The case must be truly flimsy for her to be this aggressive in her questioning.

At the mention of the book title, Dusty's expression altered. He sat straighter and started shifting in his seat. "Why are you asking about *that*? It has nothing to do with my case."

His response sent chills bumping across Sarah's skin. Apparently, he knew something about the contents of the book. It was shocking enough to discover another copy but to find another person with knowledge of it was uncanny.

"Dusty, tell me what you know. It's important," Danni said, her words tinged with frustration.

Looking back and forth between Sarah and Danni, Dusty blew out a breath. "I don't think the book has any value so there's no need to appraise it for the estate sale."

"That's not what I asked," Danni retorted, leaning towards him. "I need to know why Tara had that book."

"And I'm telling you it has nothing to do with her murder," his words were practically a growl.

Danni sat back, her lips pursed, and her arms folded across her chest. This was not a good sign. Sarah knew from years of experience her friend's patience was running thin.

"Fine," Dusty blustered in defeat. "The book was Tara's, but it wasn't part of her genealogical research, per se."

"Where'd she find it?" Danni queried, still stalwart in her stance.

"She inherited it," he said flatly.

Sarah shuddered. There was only one reason Tara would have inherited that book. She was a dreamist!

Danni and Sarah exchanged knowing glances before Sarah spoke.

"Do you know the significance of it and why Tara would keep it in her desk?"

"I suppose it's not a secret now that she's gone," he muttered, his voice cracking. "Tara had a gift of sorts, something she inherited from her mother. You're going to find this hard to believe, but she could communicate with ghosts in her dreams." His shoulders sagged as if he'd unloaded a lifetime of secrets in one sentence.

"Tell us more about it," Danni said, a sly grin curling her lips.

Shock wrinkled his forehead. "You want to know about my wife seeing dead people in her dreams? You're not trying to build an insanity defense for me, are you?"

Danni chuckled. "Not at all. Let's just say Sarah and I are believers."

Dusty rolled his shoulders and proceeded to explain how Tara had learned about her ability at an early age. Her mother and grandmother had the gift and watched for early signs of it developing in Tara. They intervened after she had her first nightmare.

Sarah's heartrate accelerated. She loved her adopted parents. Nevertheless, it would have been nice to have had someone who understood what she was going through and to guide her through it. Instead of getting help for the terrifying nightmares, she was sent to a shrink under the pretense she was emotionally disturbed.

"So how does this help my case?" Dusty asked.

"We're trying to understand Tara's life. It will help me build a better defense. After all, not many men would accept the idea of their wife being able to commune with the dead."

"I'd rather you not mention this in court. Most people wouldn't understand this kind of thing, more or less believe it. This could tarnish Tara's credibility as a genealogist and I won't let that happen," he declared, his eyes glistening.

"At this point, I don't need to use it but if it comes down to an acquittal--."

"Absolutely not! Tara was a beloved member of this community. I won't have her memory marred by judgmental hypocrites because she possessed a gift many would deem unsavory," he retorted. Dusty leaned forward and met Danni's gaze with an icy stare. "I've done enough to hurt my wife while she was living, I'll not let anything harm her memory."

"What do you mean by you hurt her while she was living? If you're holding something back, I need you to tell me right now. Keeping secrets only makes you appear guilty."

"There's nothing I can say except I will carry the weight of her death for the rest of my days." Standing up, he shuffled over to the door, banged his shackled fist against it, and hollered, "Take me back to my cell."

"That was bizarre," Sarah whispered as she and Danni were buzzed out of the interview room and walked to the parking lot.

"Now you understand why I'm having such a hard time coming up with a defense for him. One minute he proclaims undying love for Tara and the next he makes off-handed comments about feeling guilty regarding her death."

"All he said was that he'd carry the weight of it all his life. That sounds more like grief than guilt."

"He's made other statements when I've interviewed him. Once he said he felt responsible for her death. Couple that with the circumstantial evidence, the lack of an alibi, not searching for her when she didn't come home, and statements from friends who heard them arguing a lot lately, and you've got a case that's going down like a boat taking on water."

"Nevertheless, he continues to profess his love for her."

"Let's hope it's enough to sway the jury to reasonable doubt."

Sarah ruminated on the interview. Dusty's adoration of Tara and the acceptance of her bizarre dreamist skills accented every word he spoke. If he was guilty, he deserved an academy award for his performance as the adoring husband.

13

———————

Sarah and Danni drove back to the mansion to the hum of the Mercedes' engine. Neither had spoken a word since they'd left the jail. Discovering another dreamist with whom Sarah had no familial connection was overwhelming. How many others were out there? After a lifetime of feeling demented and alone, Sarah realized she was part of a faction of individuals who could decipher messages from the deceased. Yet she was still hesitant about sharing her gift.

It's not as if the *Dreamist* book was on the best seller list or you could check out a copy from the library. There was good reason being a dreamist wasn't common knowledge. Most people would have a person locked up if they proclaimed an ability to communicate with the dead via their dreams. Even her parents believed she was mentally ill after the incident at Nancy's slumber party in middle school.

Sarah's chest constricted at the thought. What if Dusty figured out she was a dreamist and told others? Would they accept or shun her? And what would Garrett think? Would he deem her crazy or accept her peculiar talents?

"Get a grip," Sarah muttered under her breath. Garrett's

opinion meant nothing. In a week or two, she'd be back in Beaufort. Her heart fluttered at the idea of never again seeing his expressive gaze and burnished locks, not to mention her growing affection for his dog, Dallas.

"What'd you say?" Danni asked, parking the car in front of the house.

"Nothing, just thinking out loud."

"In other words, speaking?" Danni chuckled. Thankfully, she didn't pursue the topic further. The last thing Sarah needed was Danni teasing her about having a crush. And she definitely had a crush!

They walked inside and headed straight for the kitchen. Danni grabbed a soda while Sarah started the kettle for tea. When the kettle let out a high-pitched squeal, Sarah poured the steaming water over an Earl Gray teabag and joined Danni at the table.

"Now what?" Sarah asked, swirling the teabag in the cup.

"Not sure. We need to study the *Dreamist* book and find a way for you to ask Tara's ghost for details about her murder. Otherwise, I'm not sure Dusty has much of a chance."

"It can't be all that bad."

"I haven't made any leeway getting an extension on the newly imposed court dates. I need something substantial and fast." Danni chugged a few swallows of her Mountain Dew.

"I've made pretty good progress with the inventory. I can spare some time to look through the book, but I think it's a risky use of time. Anything we uncover is questionable. It's not like you can call Tara's ghost to the stand."

"No, but if you can get her to reveal provable facts, I can follow up with those leads instead of wasting time chasing information that may or may not be relevant to the case."

"May as well get to work," Sarah said. "I'll get the book."

Sarah jaunted up the stairs to their room and grabbed the

small leather tome from the night table when a chill caressed her cheek and the words *don't trust him*, tickled her ear.

Sarah scanned the room. "Tara?" she muttered. "I know you're a dreamist like me. Please tell me how to communicate with you so I can help Dusty."

The book flew from her hand and landed face down on Danni's bed. Frozen, Sarah shifted her gaze around the room searching for signs of a ghostly image. When nothing appeared, and she felt comfortable nothing else would go flying, she crept to the bed and lifted the book. Oddly, it had landed open on Chapter Ten. Since none of the chapters had titles, perhaps this was Tara's way of guiding her to the answer.

All of a sudden, the scent of jasmine wafted through the room, massaging the tension from Sarah's shoulders. She loved the smell of jasmine, yet this wasn't the time of year for the fragrant vine. Glancing out the window, she noticed roses and hydrangeas in full bloom, their soft petals and vibrant hues coloring the yard, but no jasmine. Sarah hurried from the room to the kitchen where Danni was setting up her computer.

Sarah slid onto the chair and handed Danni the book.

"Read chapter ten," she said.

"But we've only made it through chapter eight. I think we need to go in order since the skills seem to build on each other."

"Well, the ghost implied we need to read chapter ten."

Danni's stature straightened as her eyebrows arched. "You spoke with Tara?"

"I spoke, she tossed the book onto your bed. When I picked it up, it was lying face down on chapter ten. I figure this is her way of letting us know what to do next."

Recoiling from the book on the table, Danni scrunched her face. "Why the heck did she toss it on *my* bed? She's not trying to say something about me, is she?"

Sarah shook her head with a sly smile and a chuckle.

"You're defending her husband; I doubt she's going to hold a pillow over your face while you sleep."

"I've adjusted to your haunted escapades and helping with this dreamist stuff, but I draw the line at being smothered by a specter!" Danni exclaimed, her complexion paling.

"You and I both know they can't kill us, at least I don't think they can," Sarah replied, furrowing her brow and cocking her head. She knew it was mean to torment her dearest friend like this, but she was having fun.

"Sarah Holden, I'm serious! Death by ghost is not how I want to go out."

"And how do you plan on going out?"

Danni's demeanor relaxed a bit as she smiled mischievously. "On the beach with a drink in my hand. That way high tide can drag my worn-out corpse into the ocean. I think burial at sea would be a dignified ending."

"More like shriveled up old lady with pickled organs being hauled to the depths as shark bait."

"Way to ruin my plans. You make it sound so disgusting," Danni said, her shoulders drooping.

"Since we're not near a beach and you're not close to being an old drunk on the verge of death, let's deal with the current situation and figure out what Tara is trying to tell me."

Danni skimmed the pages of chapter ten again. Rubbing her eyes, she let out a slow breath. "I'm usually pretty good with these things, but I can't get my mind to work. Too bad they don't offer courses on this."

"Maybe they do and we haven't discovered them yet."

"Ha! You should start a dreamist society and offer workshops. If you garner enough interest, you could hold annual conventions at your house. Then you could write Monroe Manse off as a business expense."

"Very funny. Let's figure this out and save the marketing for another day," Sarah said, rolling her eyes.

. . .

TWO HOURS LATER, Sarah and Danni sat at the kitchen table as confused as ever. They'd read the verse several times with little progress as to the meaning behind it. Sarah re-read one of the riddles out loud as Danni typed the verse into the computer.

Steady your heart to squelch the fear,
That blocks understanding and silences voices.
Listen to the one who is near,
For in her words lie all of your choices.
Calmness is the key,
To helping you see.

Due to the complexity of the book, Danni was keeping a log of dreamist interpretations on her computer for reference. As a team, they'd been able to decipher and strengthen Sarah's skills over the past year. However, once Sarah moved into Monroe Manse where she first learned that her lifelong nightmares were actually an inherited skill, she'd not had many haunted dreams. Now that they were at Edgefield Manor, the hauntings had resurfaced.

"Let's go over this once more," Danni said in her closing argument voice. "I think this is saying when a deceased dreamist tries to communicate with a living dreamist, the living one has to be open to the conversation. This may explain why you haven't been able to communicate with Tara. You were too frightened which impeded the process."

"Tara is a gruesome sight. Her eyes are hollow, her mouth is pinched shut, and she's got a gash on the side of her head."

"That's it!" Danni declared, nearly jumping out of the chair. "Your fear has silenced her. That's why the older woman keeps showing up, to take the fear out of the scenario."

"But I still don't know what Tara is trying to communicate."

"Then we're missing something," Danni said, scrunching the right side of her mouth.

"Although she's made several comments, she routinely says *don't trust him* and *he took something*," Sarah said, slumping back in the kitchen chair. "This is so frustrating."

"When Nora spoke with you in the dreams, how did she do it?"

"Nora didn't speak to me directly, she showed me visions of what happened. Her words either came through the recorder or as whispers in my ear. I didn't make the connections at the time because I was so scared. It wasn't until afterwards it all made sense."

"That's the key. You have to relax when you see Tara and concentrate on what she's trying to say."

"I've never been very good at controlling what I dream. I'm sure there's something about it in that blasted book. Why not just say how to do this stuff instead of putting everything in riddles," Sarah grumbled.

"Probably because this information is some sort of secret code. Think about it, when was the last time you heard people talking about dreamists in a coffee shop or saw a documentary about it? I'm sure many of these women were deemed crazy or possessed. Maybe the book was written in code to protect those who had the ability."

"Makes sense. Still, it would be a lot easier if they said everything plainly."

"I realize Nora didn't frighten you visually, but Edie did, and you were never able to communicate with her."

"Good point," Sarah replied. "But it was terrifying when I saw Nora in skeletal form, and she'd say *he's guilty*. As for Edie, I only saw her once in my shop. At first, I didn't know she was a ghost. Of course, her empty eye sockets quickly gave that away."

"Tell me more about the cryptic messages Nora left on your tape recorder."

"There wasn't anything specific that stands out. It was bad enough having her haunt my dreams and whisper things in my ear but hearing her voice on tape mumbling from the great beyond was horrifying!" Sarah replied with a shiver.

"Which is why it took so long for you to figure out what she was trying to communicate. It was the visions in your dreams that eventually led you to the truth, more so once you were able to remain calm."

"So, you're saying I have to keep my wits about me *and* remember to ask questions while I'm sleeping," Sarah said, arching her eyebrows.

Shrugging one shoulder, Danni grimaced. "Pretty much."

"Is there a chapter on that, because I don't know how to do this while I'm asleep."

"What did you say before Tara tossed the book?"

Sarah thought for a moment. "I asked her how I was supposed to communicate with her."

"Ask her for more specifics about how to achieve that."

"Guess it couldn't hurt," Sarah said.

Danni hopped up from the kitchen chair. "I'm going to run to the bathroom so you two can have some privacy."

"You want me to ask her now?" Sarah cried out.

"No sense waiting," Danni declared, darting from the room.

"Coward!" Sarah hollered as her friend disappeared. Taking in a deep breath, Sarah closed her eyes and rolled her shoulders. "Tara, help me understand how to figure out what you're trying to tell me."

The temperature began to climb, sending beads of sweat across Sarah's forehead as she concentrated on every sound in the room. The hum of the fridge intermingled with the ticking of the clock on the wall behind her. Sarah's mind began to wander. Images of Tara's morbid expression and the decaying hands grabbing at her in the basement of the genealogical library filled her head. She swallowed hard when fingers clutched her shoulder, squeezing a scream from her lips.

Jumping from the chair, Sarah spun around to find Danni standing there wide-eyed.

"Doggonit Danni! You can't sneak up on me like that," Sarah gasped, holding her chest.

"Calm down," Danni said. "Just wanted you to know I was back in case you were communicating telepathically. Get any answers?"

"Seriously? You just scared me half to death! Any connection with the dead has been severed."

"Interesting way to put it," Danni smirked.

Sarah inhaled. "I asked Tara to clarify how to communicate with her more clearly, but nothing happened. This will probably take longer than the average bathroom visit," Sarah responded, her limbs quivering from the rush of adrenaline.

"She's a ghost. How long could it take?" Danni shrugged. "Maybe there's a limit on how many interventions a ghost can do each day."

"That's probably chapter eleven," Sarah quipped.

"Don't know about you, but I'm hungry. Let's get some lunch."

Sarah shook her head and rested her hand on Danni's shoulder. "Always about the food with you."

"And the booze," Danni said, grabbing her keys. "Let's go somewhere outside of town. I've had my fill of burgers from Corner Pocket."

"Any ideas?"

"Brady mentioned a great Mexican place near the highway."

"Sounds good to me."

They both jumped when Danni's phone rang.

"Hey Brady," Danni said, a broad smile forming. "Uh huh... OK... great. See you then."

"What's up?"

"Brady's on his way back and claims we're actually going to Brookstone Grill tonight."

"Care to place a bet on that?" Sarah giggled as they walked to the car.

AFTER LUNCH and an afternoon of inventorying and pricing items for the estate sale, Sarah took a quick shower and prepared for ghost hunting with Garrett. Brady had already picked up Danni for their dinner at Brookstone Grill. Danni had pulled up the website on her phone and shared it with Sarah.

The restaurant was housed in a stunning old Queen Anne Victorian. Two shades of brick created an elegant façade with a wraparound porch welcoming all who meandered up the boxwood lined walkway. There was no doubt in Sarah's mind the place probably housed a few ghosts of its own, making her leery of wanting to dine there. Nevertheless, if there was any mention of spiritual encounters, Danni was sure to tell her about it.

Hovering over her suitcase, Sarah contemplated what to wear. What was the appropriate attire to hunt ghosts? Even though there was no chance of a relationship, she wanted to look nice for Garrett. She decided on jeans, a buttery yellow scoop neck shirt, and sneakers. No point being any more uncomfortable than she already was.

Why had she agreed to this? Her life was haunted enough without hunting for specters. With a sigh, she rubbed her forehead. She knew why she was going and it wasn't to spy on spirits. Her interest was solely in spending time with Garrett. No matter how hard she tried to deny it, she liked him.

Adding a man to her life would definitely complicate things. Even a man with the most soulful eyes, gentle demeanor, and an adorable dog. The fact he believed in ghosts made him nearly perfect. After tonight, she'd have to limit her time with him. She needed to focus on the estate sale so she could finish up and resume a normal existence, whatever that was. For Sarah, life with ghosts infiltrating her dreams or randomly appearing in her wakeful hours was routine.

A knock at the door, accompanied by an enthusiastic bark, caught her attention. Hurrying to the entrance, she opened it to find Dallas with his tongue hanging out and his tail wagging. Garrett stood there in a dark blue polo shirt, jeans, and sneakers. His eyes twinkled in the dim porch light as a smile spread across his face.

"Ready to go?" he asked, excitement glimmering in his gaze.

"Ready as I'll ever be," she replied, stepping onto the porch. Her heart thrummed with the speed of hummingbird wings at the sight of his dazzling smile and the way his sculpted shoulders filled out his shirt.

"If you're not comfortable with this, you don't have to come. I'll understand."

Sarah waved a hand in the air. "What's to be afraid of? They're only ghosts, not serial killers."

"Maybe not in death, but who's to say what they did when they were alive,"

Garrett replied, leading Sarah to the truck with Dallas toddling at her heels.

UNBEKNOWNST TO HER, the curtains in the upstairs window fluttered as a shadowy figure hovered by her bed, watching her climb into the truck and disappear down the drive.

Twenty minutes later, they turned down a gravel lane encased by scraggly trees and knee-high underbrush. What had once been a showplace was now a neglected shell of its former glory, its only claim to fame the reputed hauntings.

As the truck lurched back and forth over potholes and

uneven gravel, the hairs on Sarah's neck bristled. Shadows skirted between trees in a creepy waltz and the air was as still as death. In the dimness of a partial moon, a Greek Revival manor with massive columns peered through the darkness.

Harry and Ralph were already there standing by a truck with several pieces of equipment. Garrett hopped from his truck, rushed to open Sarah's door, and helped her down. Dallas scurried about, happily greeting the guys and getting scratches behind his ears from his fellow ghost hunters. Garrett hefted a large camera and tripod on his shoulder while grabbing a duffle bag with his other hand. The energy was electric as if dozens of spirits were floating about.

"What can I do?" Sarah asked.

"Grab the box off the tailgate of my truck," Ralph said. "Garrett was here earlier scoping out where to set up the cameras."

Sarah lifted the box while Harry and Ralph gathered the remaining items. Stepping through the double doors of the run-down mansion, Sarah took in a deep breath. The stale scent of old house was sprinkled with a hint of mildew and dust. A grand entry with winding staircase alluded to a once opulent home now brimming with faded furnishings and cobweb-laced corners. A spacious parlor was situated on one side of the hall and a dining room on the other, each with massive pocket doors. A crystal chandelier hovered overhead, many of the prisms sprinkled in shards on the floor below. The place definitely had a high creep factor.

"Which rooms are we filming in?" Ralph asked, holding a camera bag and audio equipment.

"I think it's best if we set up in the front parlor and also the first bedroom on the left upstairs. We can monitor from the kitchen at the back of the house," Garrett said.

Harry placed several bags on the parlor floor and started setting up a tripod with a fancy-looking camera as Ralph climbed the stairs to ready things in the bedroom. Garrett waved Sarah to follow him.

They walked down the narrow hall to an outdated kitchen replete with peeling linoleum floors, painted cabinets, one of which was dangling from the wall, and gold-colored appliances. Sarah set the box on a rickety enamel-topped table that wobbled beneath the weight.

"What can I do to help?"

"Unpack that box and I'll show you how to connect this stuff."

Sarah started removing all sorts of electronic devices as Dallas sniffed around the perimeter of the room. Garrett connected wires and plugs. Moments later, Ralph rolled in a small generator.

"Got everything set up in the bedroom and thought I'd help out in here," he said.

They spent the next half hour getting the monitoring equipment up and running

when Harry joined them.

"Got three cameras ready to roll in the front parlor since that's where the bulk of the sightings have been reported."

"How long has the house been empty?" Sarah asked.

"Twenty years, at least," Harry replied. "When Mr. George died, his kids didn't want to live here but couldn't agree on what to do with the place. Some wanted to rent it out while others wanted to sell. Sadly, it was a stalemate, resulting in the old place being abandoned and falling into disrepair. Now the only people who come here are teens on a dare. Everyone has reportedly seen a lady in blue. The Georges didn't like the idea of ghosts and for years avoided our requests to film. Finally, they changed their minds. I think they're hoping we can prove the place isn't haunted so people will stop trespassing."

Sarah rolled her shoulders. It wasn't likely they'd prove that. She could feel the suffocating presence of several spirits.

"You alright?" Harry asked.

"Yeah, just a little stiff from all the things I moved around earlier while I was doing inventory."

"We'll all be stiff tomorrow. Hauling this stuff always does me in," Ralph added.

Thankful her excuse was readily accepted, Sarah walked over to where Garrett was adjusting equipment. Once everything was set up, checked, and double-checked, Ralph sat down at the monitors.

"Harry and I are going to keep an eye on the cameras while Ralph stays here to watch the screens," Garrett said. "Who do you want to stay with?"

Before Sarah could answer Dallas let out an ear shattering bark that resonated through the room. His brown eyes were fixed on Sarah and his tail wagged furiously.

"Looks like Dallas wants you to join his team," Harry chuckled. "Of course, that includes Garrett. We try to work in pairs when we can."

"Who do you usually partner with?" Sarah asked Harry.

A shadow crossed his eyes as he glanced at the floor. "Tara used to partner with me."

"Tara was part of this group?"

"She helped when she could. Tara enjoyed the specter stuff. Used it in her *Deadly and Deceased* cemetery tours."

"Did Dusty come along too?" Sarah asked, curious about this new information.

"He didn't seem to like her coming with us," Harry replied.

Even though she wanted to know more, this wasn't a good time to dig deeper, so she changed the subject. "I'm happy to join whoever wants to take on the novice for the evening."

"You can work with us," Garrett offered followed by a yap from Dallas. It was as if the dog understood every word spoken and offered his opinion as he saw fit. Garrett turned to Harry. "You OK flying solo tonight?"

Harry nodded.

"Everyone put your cell phones on mute," Garrett instructed as he handed each of the guys a walkie-talkie. Sarah switched her phone to vibrate and stuck it in her back pocket.

With her heart thumping at the idea of being alone with him, not to mention the possibility of seeing spirits, Sarah followed Garrett and Dallas up the stairs to the second-floor landing. Wallpaper sagged in several places and the ceiling was stained with coppery splotches where the roof had leaked. They entered the bedroom with its tattered curtains and grimy bed linens.

"We'll watch from over here for any signs of movement. Dallas is pretty sensitive to spectral activity and will alert us if anything enters the room." As if on cue, the dog plunked his tail end onto Sarah's foot and stared at the far wall.

"He's really taken to you," Garrett said with a chuckle.

"I like him too," she said, patting his fuzzy head.

"Let's get to work." Garrett settled behind the camera while Sarah leaned against the wall and focused on the area Dallas was watching. She'd heard that animals had a strong sense for the spiritual world and this little pup seemed to have a keen awareness for the supernatural. Perhaps he'd act as a warning system so Sarah wouldn't be surprised by any ethereal activity. The last thing she wanted was to disrupt the guys with her ghostly intuition.

As the evening wore on, the wind picked up, rattling shutters and swirling through broken windowpanes. The blustery conditions stirred up the dust and debris littering the worn wooden floors. Pings and thuds reverberated within the mildew ridden walls, making Sarah's heart palpitate. Every so often, Garrett checked his watch suggesting he was bored. Absolutely nothing had materialized, and a sense of relief was beginning to take hold.

"Seems like a lot of waiting," Sarah whispered. While glad

nothing ghostly had manifested, she felt a strong sense of unease regarding the situation with Garrett. She'd not had much experience with guys, especially one this good-looking.

His smile fluttered across her skin. "It takes a lot of patience to do this and sadly, it usually ends with nothing more than empty footage. However, when we do capture something on tape, it's an adrenaline rush."

"Have you always been into the ghost thing?" she asked.

"Most of my life."

"How did you get interested in it? Scary movie or a ghost story?"

Garrett fidgeted with the camera's tripod. "Can't really say what prompted it, I've always had a penchant for it. Something in trying to prove the unproveable, I suppose."

Sarah nodded.

"What about you? Did you grow up with ghost stories at slumber parties and haunted houses at Halloween?"

Sarah's breath caught. The only slumber party she'd attended as a kid had ended in disaster when she shared a haunted dream with the group. "Never attended any haunted houses but we have an annual ghost walk every October bene-fitting a local shelter."

"Is it scary?" he asked.

"Wouldn't know," she shrugged. "I never went."

"Why not?"

Sarah gulped. How had she backed herself into this corner? She'd been so caught up in trying to make casual conversation she hadn't paid attention to where the topic was heading.

"I'm not much of a people person so large groups are uncomfortable for me." *Great*, she thought. *Now he thinks you're an anti-social recluse.*

"I wouldn't have thought that. You seem pretty outgoing to me," he replied.

No matter how hard she tried to divert her feelings from his easy-going demeanor and mesmerizing green eyes, her heart turned to mush beneath his gaze. She'd spent much of her life trying to avoid human interaction, especially with the opposite gender. Now she found herself with the most captivating, not to mention good-looking, man she'd ever met. Desperate to change the topic, Sarah steered the conversation in another direction. She needed to get off the road of the past before his questions entered dangerous territory.

Sarah startled when her phone buzzed in her back pocket. Sliding her cell from her jeans, she glanced at the number.

Ugh. Of all the times for her parents to call they chose this very moment. Garrett gave her a concerned glance.

"Sorry, but I have to take this," she mumbled, scurrying from the room to answer the phone.

"Hey Mom," Sarah whispered.

"Sweetheart, I can't hear you. You need to speak up," her mother said. "We're in Egypt and don't always get a strong signal."

"Give me a minute," she replied, looking for a place where she could speak louder without disturbing the spirits. She tiptoed across the dusty floor as her mother clamored for her to speak up. Much to her surprise she discovered a door at the end of the hall leading to an upstairs porch. Once outside, Sarah spoke in a normal tone.

"Sorry Mom, I had to step outside to talk."

"Where are you?" she asked, her voice steeped in concern.

Without thinking, Sarah blurted out the answer, regret tightening her chest as the words fell from her lips.

"I'm at an old, abandoned mansion with some friends."

"Abandoned mansion? Whatever for?" her mother's intonation rising. "And who are these friends? Is Danni there?"

"Danni's working. I'm in Edgefield, remember? I'm helping with an estate."

"It's in an uninhabited house?"

Sarah chuckled at her mother's concern. She still worried about everything she did, despite the fact she was a grown woman now.

"I'm at a different house with a ghost hunting group. They're hoping to catch some spiritual activity on film."

Silence resounded from the other end.

"Mom? You still there?"

"Sarah Holden, please tell me you're not getting tangled up in that haunted nonsense again. Don't you remember how disastrous it was the last time you claimed to see ghosts?"

Sarah's shoulders tensed. How could she ever forget? After sharing her haunted dream at a slumber party, the ghost having been the deceased grandmother of the hostess, she was ousted from the small group of girls. To make matters worse, her parents had to pick her up in the middle of the night. The following day she was sitting across from a psychologist because her parents believed her introverted nature was leading her to seek out negative attention.

"Mom, this is just for fun. I'm not conjuring up the dead or sacrificing children."

"Your father wants to speak to you."

Sarah could tell by the tone of her mother's voice she was distraught about the situation and was hoping her father could talk some sense into her.

"Hey pumpkin." Her father's pet name for her, melted Sarah's resolve. She'd always been a daddy's girl.

"Hey Dad. Are you guys having a good time in Africa?"

"Absolutely, although the look on your mother's face tells me that might be changing soon."

"She's overreacting. There's no need for concern, I'm with some new friends I met in Edgefield. They like to film ghost sightings and invited me to join them."

"Is Danni with you?"

"Why does everyone think I need Danni with me at all times? I'm perfectly capable of taking care of myself, Dad."

"Didn't answer my question."

"She's working. These guys are perfectly safe," Sarah huffed.

"Guys?"

Sarah's head slumped. Now her father's tone was taking on the same skepticism as her mother's. It's not like Sarah had boyfriends growing up to give him practice at playing the over-protective father.

"These are really nice guys with good jobs. They aren't brainwashing me into a cult, and as far as I know they aren't murderers."

"Sarah, you're not helping," her father responded in a hushed tone, letting Sarah know her mother was within hearing range of the conversation.

"Dad, I promise I'm fine."

She heard the whoosh as he released a breath. "Alright. We'll call tomorrow. Be safe."

"Always," Sarah replied. "Love you, Dad."

"Love you too."

Sarah stuffed the phone back in her pocket and returned to the room. Garrett glanced at her, his eyebrows raised.

"My parents," she whispered. "They're in Africa."

With a nod, Garrett gave a half smile, causing Sarah's insides to flutter.

"How much longer will you guys wait?" Sarah asked.

He let out a long sigh. "Not much longer. Don't think we'll capture anything tonight. Sadly, this is the gamble we take. I'm hoping the family will let us try again."

At that moment, Garrett's radio crackled. A low growl emanated from Dallas' throat as the fur at the nape of his neck bristled. Garrett's eyes widened as he lowered his left eye to the camera. Dallas' growl increased in volume as he crept closer to the corner. Sarah glanced at the floor in an effort to avoid witnessing anything ghoulish. It's probably just a mouse, she told herself.

A shallow light glimmered from the far corner, increasing in brightness as it flowed across the dust covered floors. Garrett stood firm, adjusting the camera angle as he focused on the shimmering orb.

Ralph's voice whispered over the walkie talkie. "Are you seeing this?"

"Got it," Garrett replied. The entity began to take form and in a quick flash dissipated saying, *don't believe him* before the room went dark.

Dallas stood down, his growl subsiding as his fur relaxed against his back.

"What just happened?" Sarah asked, her insides quivering like a Jell-O mold.

"Don't know yet. Hopefully, we just caught an apparition on tape."

Garrett made a few adjustments to the video camera and spoke into the radio. "Did you get that, Ralph?"

"Yup," echoed over the speaker.

Garrett motioned for Sarah to follow, and she was more than happy to comply. No way was she going to linger by herself in the spooky room of a purportedly haunted house.

The wide plank floorboards creaked and groaned with each footfall as she followed Garrett and Dallas downstairs. All of a sudden, a prickling sensation skittered across Sarah's scalp. Turning, she noticed a shadowy figure at the top of the stairs, its eyes hollowed and its lips seared into a thin line. She recognized the image immediately. It was Tara. But why was she here? Sarah closed her eyes and took in a deep breath.

This wasn't the time to reveal her secret abilities. Before she could dismiss her unease, Garrett looked at her, his expression steeped in concern.

"You, OK?" he asked.

"Yeah, just a little lightheaded. Should've eaten more protein at dinner."

Thankfully, he seemed to accept her response and continued down the stairs to the kitchen where the guys huddled around the monitor.

"Get anything significant?" Garret asked.

"We got something," Harry said, moving over so Garrett and Sarah could see the screen too.

Stillness mixed with the grainy picture until a flash of light illuminated in the far corner of the upstairs bedroom, accompanied by the yip from Dallas. The split-second image was unmistakable to Sarah. In that quick glimpse, Tara's eyeless visage appeared on the screen, but her words didn't record. Was Sarah the only one who'd heard her say *don't believe him*?

"Did you see that?" Harry exclaimed.

"I did," Garrett mumbled.

Ralph hit the replay button as they watched the video again.

"Definitely something in the corner," Ralph replied.

"Good work guys. Now we just need to figure out who the ghost is."

Shock permeated Sarah's body. To her the image on the screen was clearly Tara, yet Garrett and his crew didn't seem to recognize her. And these guys called themselves ghost hunters? If they considered a flash of light in the corner of a room significant, they were the lamest ghost hunters to ever film. She'd expected high tech images with all of the equipment they'd hauled in. And the light could have been lots of things other than a spirit. It seemed the only true ghost hunter in the group was Dallas who'd proven himself to Sarah on multiple occasions.

"We'll take this back to my garage and run it through some filters to get a clearer image. I'll send a copy to my brother,

Walter, and see what he can do with it. Until then, we should do some more research on the house. Maybe that will help reveal the identity of the ghost," Ralph suggested.

Sarah swallowed hard. How could they not see the image on the screen was clearly Tara? Then again, maybe her own imagination was imposing Tara's features on the ghost. She'd dreamed about her for more than a week. Surely, Garrett and his friends weren't frauds. No doubt, they're ghostly encounters had garnered them a great deal of attention in town. With Garrett's good looks, much of that attention was probably female.

Glancing at the image on the screen once more, Sarah's stomach churned. This wasn't her imagination. The ghost in the upstairs room was Tara, of that she was certain. Waves of nausea rolled across her stomach. Was Tara telling her not to trust Garrett?

14

Garrett dropped Sarah off at 1:00 a.m. Weary from the day's work and emotionally drained from the ghostly encounters, Sarah trudged up the stairs. Much to her surprise, Danni was already asleep with the *Dreamist* book laying open, face-down on her chest. The scene warmed Sarah's heart. Danni had supported her in every aspect of her life, even ones beyond belief involving specters and frightening entities. Hopefully, Danni would have some time in the morning to go over what she'd read.

For now, Sarah just wanted to wash up, get some sleep, and wipe away any prospects of finding a man who actually understood and saw ghosts. The disappointment over Garrett's lack of ghost detecting skills weighted her shoulders, not to mention Tara's warning. Consciously she'd known there was no hope of a relationship with him; however, her subconscious had permitted a small seed of hope to flourish. Her shoulders slumped. The ghost thing had been the tipping point for any expectations of a relationship, but they'd dissolved as quickly as sugar in a teacup.

Not wanting to disturb Danni, Sarah padded down the hall to use the en suite bathroom off the master bedroom.

Stepping into the bedroom, she flipped on the overhead light and shook her head at the boxes filled with memorabilia and other items only of value to family members. Outdated décor blighted the room with mauve painted walls and rose bedecked borders edging the ceiling. A matching comforter set covered the bed with ruffled cotton swags framing the windows. Piles of winter coats and old dresses camouflaged a good portion of the bed.

Sarah stepped into the bathroom and washed her face before slipping into a nightshirt. A yawn filled her lungs as the stale scent of paperboard and old magazines stung her nose. As she turned off the bathroom light, a shiver traced her spine, catching her breath and freezing her to the spot where she stood. She watched the boxes against the far wall of the master bedroom begin to shudder and totter. Without warning they toppled over in a cloud of dust.

Racing over to the avalanche of old photo albums, newspaper clippings, and other ephemera, Sarah started cleaning up. She focused intently on the contents of the boxes, fearful something ethereal would appear if she happened to look around. Her fingertips tingled when she lifted an old scrapbook. Carefully, she flipped through its yellowed pages.

Nostalgia oozed from the photos, bringing a smile to Sarah's face. She perused a profusion of family snapshots depicting kids playing near a pond, picnic tables full of food, and older folks seated in rockers on the front porch of what appeared to be an old farmhouse. The words, *he took it*, echoed through her head at the same time a hand grabbed her shoulder. With an ear shattering scream, Sarah jumped up, dropped the album, sending the pictures scattering across the floor.

Danni groaned, rubbing her forehead. "Why are you so jumpy?"

"Maybe because you snuck up on me *again!*" Sarah exclaimed, clutching her chest while trying to catch her breath.

"I didn't sneak up on you," she replied, her voice still groggy with sleep. "I said your name and walked over to you."

"Didn't hear you," Sarah mumbled, kneeling on the floor to gather the photos. "Why are you up?"

"I heard a crash and came to see what happened."

Sarah stared at her friend. Danni usually slept like the dead. The boxes had made a thump but nothing that would wake someone who could snooze through an earthquake.

"What time is it, anyway?" Danni muttered.

"About 1:30."

Danni's eyes widened. "You're just now getting home?" she asked with a sly grin. "Sounds like it was a great first date." She waggled her eyebrows like a goofy teen whose best friend got caught sneaking in after curfew.

"It wasn't a date," Sarah quipped. "I was with three guys."

"That sounds wrong in so many ways. You may want to stick to a late night with a hot guy who chases ghosts."

Sarah sighed. "You know I was with Garrett and the guys *hunting* ghosts, not chasing them. This isn't Scooby Doo."

"Hunting, chasing, dating, it's all the same."

"Nevertheless, we filmed some scenes in one heck of a creepy house, watched a flash of light appear on the tape, and then packed up. If these guys hope to make a living hunting ghosts, they're going to starve."

"Yikes. I've heard of guys disappointing in the area of romance but never the specter category."

"Regardless, Garrett dropped me off like the platonic gentleman friend he is. The only goodnight kiss I got was from Dallas," Sarah said, pursing her lips and squaring her shoulders.

"Pretty bad when the best action you get is from a dog," Danni replied with a smirk.

"At least Dallas is legit. Every time he senses something, a ghost actually appears."

Danni shook her head. "Can I help you with any of this?"

"Sure," Sarah replied as Danni knelt down and helped her gather loose photos.

Danni glanced through a few and grinned. "These kids look like they're having fun. I always wondered what it would be like to live in the same place your entire life instead of traveling the globe to a dozen different Marine bases."

"Funny, I used to think it would be great to get a fresh start by being a Marine brat and moving every three years, especially with my middle school history. It would've been nice not to have to hide my unusual talents."

"At least you don't have to hide things now," Danni said with a reassuring grin.

"Not from you," Sarah mumbled.

"OK, what's up? I know that look, something happened tonight. Did you see a ghost at the mansion?"

"Not just any ghost, I saw Tara."

"What?" Danni exclaimed. "I'm going to need refreshments for this story. Let's go downstairs."

"We need to clean this up," Sarah said.

"It can wait until tomorrow. I wanna know what happened!"

They flipped off the light and headed to the parlor where Danni poured herself a scotch and a bourbon for Sarah. Danni sat in the wing chair across from the settee where Sarah perched, sipping her drink.

"Tell me what happened."

"I was upstairs with Garrett when something appeared on the other side of the room. The camera caught the apparition but for some reason when the guys played it back, they couldn't decipher who it was. It was definitely clear to me." Sarah took a long draw from her glass.

"And?" Danni said impatiently.

"It was Tara. She looked the same as she has in all of my dreams with the empty eyes and unmoving lips. I heard her say, *don't trust him.*"

"What did the guys think it meant?"

"They didn't hear it. Apparently, her words didn't record on tape. Like I said, they couldn't make out any details on video. Ralph said something about running it through filters to get a clearer image."

Danni leaned forward, enthusiasm brightening her expression. "If they see Tara maybe they can figure out what she's trying to tell us, like evidence to clear Dusty."

"We can't ask for testimony from a ghost. Aside from the fact a jury would never buy into it, no judge would allow it. Not to mention, I am not sharing my secret skills with these guys. They may be self-proclaimed ghost hunters, but they don't have a clue about the spiritual world. With their lack of abilities, I doubt they'd buy into the 'communicating with the dead in my dreams' scenario."

Danni snorted. "You do care what *he* thinks."

"Not at all. I'd prefer not to be viewed as some sort of sideshow freak. I've had enough of that in my life." Sarah exhaled as she slumped back.

"These guys wouldn't view you as a freak, they'd likely ask you to come on board as part of their team. You could be the key to their success. A real ghost conduit. Think about it, Sarah. You may have found the man of your dreams, even the haunted ones."

"Great, just what I need, a guy who wants to film me while I dream about ghosts."

"Gives a whole new meaning to kinky," Danni said with a sly grin.

Sarah shook her head and finished the last swallow of her bourbon. "It's late and I need to get some sleep. Let's talk about this in the morning."

They set their glasses on the bar and started up the stairs.

"Who do you think Tara is referring to when she says *don't trust him*?" Danni asked.

"Not sure. It's not the first time she's said it."

"Has she ever said it when Garrett was around?"

Sarah thought for a moment. "Maybe, once or twice. Do you think she's trying to warn me about him and his lack of spiritual capabilities?"

"Hard to say. Depends on how well she knew him."

"According to Garrett, she helped with some of their ghost hunting pursuits."

Danni halted abruptly at the top of the stairs. "You don't think Garrett did anything inappropriate, do you?"

"Like what?"

"I don't know, maybe she realized he didn't have any real connections to the dead and threatened to expose him. After all, Tara was a dreamist and would recognize a fraud."

"Doubtful. I can't imagine he'd murder someone to protect his reputation as a ghost hunter. And I don't believe Harry would hang out with him if he'd done something to Tara. Harry was definitely fond of her."

"Maybe we need to ask Dusty about his wife's relationship with Garrett."

"If they were involved, I doubt he knew about it," Sarah said, crawling beneath the sheets.

Disappointment coursed through Sarah's body. What if something had happened between them? Dusty wouldn't be the first husband to kill his wife in a jealous rage. Was that why he felt so much guilt about her death? Then again, if Tara was in a relationship with Garrett maybe he was the one who'd murdered her. Men were known to kill when their reputation was in jeopardy. With Garrett's military training, he'd know how to kill a person with minimal effort.

The entire scenario was too much to absorb. Sarah rested

her head against the pillow, her chest tight and her mind racing with possibilities.

"Goodnight, Sarah."

"Goodnight, Danni."

"Stop worrying. I'm sure Garrett didn't do anything awful," Danni said, rolling over to face the wall.

In the darkness, Sarah smiled. She loved how Danni knew her well enough to sense what was bothering her without her uttering a word. Closing her eyes, Sarah pondered what Tara was trying to communicate. As she contemplated the different scenarios, her muscles relaxed and she drifted off to a land of ghostly visions and haunted houses.

SARAH AMBLED down the hallway of the genealogical library to the door at the end. Gulping down her apprehension, she reached for the knob expecting the icy chill that usually burned the palm of her hand. Before she grabbed it, a weathered hand gently grasped her wrist, washing her in a peaceful sensation. She turned to see the old woman, her blue eyes sparkling and a slight smile plumping her wrinkled cheeks.

Sarah started to ask why she was there when the door swung open, and Tara's image appeared. The words, *don't trust him*, resonated in Sarah's head. She managed to form the word, *why* when a bright light engulfed the room.

When the glare subsided, Sarah found herself in the farmhouse from the photos. The scent of freshly baked bread lingered in the air as a soft breeze billowed through lacey curtains. Looking around, she noticed children playing in the yard outside, the same children from the photo album. They ran around the yard, laughing and chasing each other in a game of tag. Although young, Sarah recognized some of the faces, including one little girl who resembled Tara. Three of the boys also bore strong resemblances to Garrett, Harry, and Brady.

She remembered something about them growing up together, although Garrett was only here in the summer months when he stayed with his grandmother. The squeals of delight and triumphant declarations of victory emanating from the yard beyond the paned windows suggested a happy and carefree existence. That's when Sarah noticed another little boy slumped against the trunk of an old oak tree, his face scrunched in a pout. He had the same dark eyes and wavy hair as Dusty. The other kids charged past him as little Tara turned and mouthed to Sarah, *don't trust him.*

SITTING UPRIGHT IN BED, Sarah glanced around the darkened room in an effort to get her bearings. Outside, an owl hooted in harmony with twittering crickets. The night was stagnant without so much as a whisper of a breeze. The dreamscape had been bizarre, hopping from recent events to the past. Still, Tara's warning made no sense. Whomever she was trying to reveal as being treacherous remained a mystery. Sarah desperately hoped it wasn't Garrett. Then again, Tara could've been referring to any of the others. Disappointment clutched her chest. She'd grown fond of the guys in such a short time. Regardless of who Tara was trying to identify as untrustworthy, the outcome would break Sarah's heart and possibly destroy Danni's case.

15

Sarah poured steaming water into a mug and plopped in a teabag as she sat at the table. Danni was dressed in a coral cotton blouse, form fitting fawn-colored skirt, and matching pumps. She sipped her coffee and stared at Sarah with a blank expression.

"Explain the dream again," Danni finally said, setting her cup on the table.

"I started out in the library. When I went to open the door, the old woman grasped my wrist and then Tara appeared. Next thing I know, I'm at the same farmhouse from the photos upstairs watching all the kids run around the yard. One little boy appeared to be sulking beneath a tree while the others played. That's when the little girl, who I'm certain was a young Tara, turned and said, *don't trust him.*"

"Don't trust who?"

"I'm not sure. The only ones who've been around when she's said this before are Garrett, Dusty, or Harry."

"Harry? How does he play into this?" Danni asked.

"They worked together. Based on his emotional state when he speaks of her, I gather they were rather close."

Danni set her jaw and furrowed her brow. Sarah recognized the look. Danni had an idea and was working through the different scenarios.

"We should focus on who had access to the library the night Tara was killed, as well as who knew she'd be there alone," Danni offered.

"Dusty and Harry would be the most likely choices, although Garrett could have known too," Sarah shrugged.

"We definitely need to discuss this with Dusty," Danni said.

"You want me to tell him about my dreams?" Sarah exclaimed.

"No, we need to take the photo albums with us and get some information about his childhood. Apparently, Tara is trying to reveal something using the pictures and the dreams, just like Nora did."

Danni was right. Nora had led Sarah to information using artifacts and old photos. All Sarah had to do was connect the dream sequences with the clues and a story unfolded leading to the mystery behind Nora's disappearance.

"What about the *Dreamist* book? Did you garner any information from it?" Sarah asked.

"Not much. By the time I got back here, I was so tired I couldn't make sense of the stuff. I'll try again later," Danni said, putting the coffee mug in the sink.

"What time did you get back?"

Danni's cheeks colored as she picked some lint from her skirt. "Late."

"Your reservation was at 7:00. It couldn't have been that late when you finished," Sarah taunted, enjoying giving Danni a little ribbing after all her teasing about Garrett.

"After midnight," Danni said hurriedly.

"What on earth did you do after dinner that kept you out until that hour... Ohhh," Sarah said, her jaw dropping. "Oh my gosh, why didn't you tell me?"

A sheepish smile crinkled Danni's eyes. "I'm not one to kiss and tell."

"Sounds like it was more than a kiss."

"Perhaps," Danni purred. "By the way, the house where the restaurant is located was spectacular. You'd love it. Heart pine floors, original mantels, and antique chandeliers. The bar room looks like an English pub."

"Not interested in the house," Sarah grinned. "I want to hear more about the evening."

"We'll talk about it later. For now, we need to focus on interpreting the *Dreamist* book. How about we go to the bakery for breakfast?"

With a chuckle, Sarah rose from her chair. "Glad to see all the ghost stuff and upcoming trial drama hasn't affected your appetite."

"Nothing affects my appetite," she snorted. "Let's take some of the photo albums to Dusty after we eat. Maybe he can divulge some information explaining Tara's messages to you."

With a nod, Sarah carried her tea upstairs where she changed into a shell pink tank top and khaki shorts. After pulling her hair into a ponytail, she walked across the hall, and grabbed the scrapbook along with the photos that had come loose. A chill rattled her body as she rubbed a tickle from the back of her neck, unaware of the translucent hand grasping at her ponytail.

SARAH AND DANNI waited in the dingy visiting room as the guard brought Dusty in. His demeanor was more subdued than their last meeting and his skin was beginning to take on a grayish pallor. He plunked down on the hard metal chair and forced a slight smile.

"Anything new on my case?" he asked.

"Not yet, but we may be getting close. We found this album

at your mother's house and were wondering if you could identify some of the people in the photos."

"Sure, but how is this going to help me?" he asked as Sarah
slid the scrapbook across the table. The guard watched carefully as Dusty opened the red leather cover and paged through
the faded photos, his eyes misting as his lips spread into a
broad grin.

"It may seem inconsequential, but I need to understand
your relationships both past and present," Danni said.

Not questioning her further, he stopped at the page with
the photo of the kids gamboling around the two-story
farmhouse.

"This is my aunt's home. We spent our summers playing in
the creek and eating watermelons and fresh tomatoes."

"Who are these people?" Danni queried.

"This is me sitting at the base of the tree and that's Brady,
Harry, and Garrett. Garrett used to spend the summers here
with his grandmother, Ola. Everyone loved her. She made the
best oatmeal cookies in the world. She's the reason Garrett left
the military. He wanted to take care of her."

"Who's the little girl?"

Dusty swallowed hard. "That's Tara," he whispered, his
voice cracking. "Her mother owned a nursery and worked long
hours in the summer. When Tara wasn't helping her, she'd
hang out with all of us. She may have been a girl, but she could
outrun and outclimb any boy. I remember the time I caught
Harry trying to steal a kiss from Tara behind that very tree," he
said with a chuckle.

"Harry liked her?" Danni asked.

"He had a serious crush on her," he replied, swiping a tear
from his eye.

"Did she feel the same about him?"

A laugh boomed from Dusty's lips. It was the first time
Danni or Sarah had seen him so carefree.

"She gave him a black eye. As far as I know he never tried again."

Sarah muffled a laugh at the idea of Tara's strong-willed personality. She would've liked to have known her.

Danni continued her questioning. "Harry never mentioned any feelings for her after that?"

"Not that I'm aware of," he shrugged, his sullen demeanor returning.

"How old were you guys in this photo?"

"About ten," he said. "I still don't understand why you want to know about all this."

Ignoring his statement, Danni went on.

"When did you start dating Tara?"

"High school. We were in the history club. She and I partnered up to research the gravesites in Brookfield Cemetery for a presentation the club was doing as part of the town's annual history symposium."

"Interesting topic for a couple of high school students," Sarah said, intrigued by the story.

"Harry was part of the group too. The three of us spent weeks documenting and photographing the gravesites and researching the background of each one. I guess that's when Harry took an interest in hunting ghosts."

"How did Garrett get involved with the ghost hunting?" Sarah asked.

Danni gave her a sideways glare, making Sarah shrink back in her chair.

"I was only trying to figure out how the ghost hunting group came together," Sarah said meekly.

"That's a funny story," Dusty said as the guard cleared his throat with a smug look.

"Nevertheless, we need to focus on the case, not the haunted escapades of a group of friends," Danni said. "According to what you've told me, the only time Harry showed a romantic interest toward Tara was the summer when he was ten. How about as an adult?"

"You can't possibly think Harry had anything to do with Tara's murder. He adored her," Dusty declared. "Like I said, Harry had a crush when we were kids, nothing more, and Tara never reciprocated."

Danni pursed her lips and arched her eyebrows. "Are you sure?"

"Absolutely. Harry wouldn't hurt Tara, for any reason."

"Not even jealously?" Danni asked.

Dusty leaned forward, his gaze locking onto Danni's. "He wasn't jealous. He had a crush on her one summer and never showed any interest after that," Dusty said sternly.

"Was there anyone else who may have been interested in her?"

"No," he grumbled.

"I'm not trying to upset you, but I need to explore all the angles. If we can't prove your innocence, we have to create reasonable doubt. Money and love are two of the biggest motivators for violent crimes. I need you to think with your head, not your heart."

"And I'm telling you, no one ever made a move on her. Once we started dating, the other guys stopped pursuing her."

"But there were other guys?" Danni asked.

"I don't know, maybe," he replied, his voice edged in frustration.

"Who was it?" Danni's tone was taking on an authoritative vibe.

"I caught Garrett holding her once in the old cemetery."

"When you were kids?"

Dusty's jaw clenched. "When we were in high school."

"Who did she spend time with over the past few months?" Danni queried.

"The same people she always hung around with. Mostly

people at the library since she was always doing genealogical research. When she started spending as much time there as the employees, they gave her a desk. Tara was a volunteer. Sometimes she'd help Harry and the guys with one of their ghost hunts. Otherwise, she was at home with me or at her parent's house." Dusty buried his face in his hands. "This is all my fault."

"What did you say?" Danni asked, leaning in closer.

Rubbing his eyes, he took in a deep breath and met Danni's stare. "Nothing. Do you have any other questions?"

"Did she have any girlfriends?"

"Not really. Like I said, she was pretty immersed in her work. The rest of the time she spent with family."

"If you think of anyone who might have held a grudge against Tara, even as far back as high school, I need to know about it."

Dusty shook his head. "If I think of anyone, I'll let you know. Everyone loved Tara," he mumbled, his eyes watering.

"Thanks Dusty. We'll talk again soon," Danni said, gathering her briefcase as the guard grabbed Dusty's elbow and led him through the barred metal door.

"That was interesting," Danni muttered.

Sarah swallowed the bile burning her throat. In addition to Dusty, there seemed to be several new suspects, one of which was Garrett.

CRUISING DOWN THE MAIN DRAG, Danni and Sarah rehashed all of the information gleaned from their visit with Dusty.

"Do you really think one of their childhood friends killed Tara?" Sarah asked, hoping Danni wouldn't bring Garrett into the list of possible murderers.

"Not sure. Regardless, I've got to investigate all of them."

Sarah stared out the window of the car, her chest tight. *Why was she so concerned about Garrett being involved?* She'd only known him a week and had no intentions of pursuing him past the trial. And now he could be a suspect. Add the long-distance relationship issues, his pitiful attempt at being a ghost hunter, and fear of rejection due to her dreamist abilities, and the scenario to avoid him was cinched.

"Who are you going to question first?" Sarah asked.

"Harry. He seems to have a pretty strong attachment to her."

"Anyone else?"

Danni gave a sideways glance at her friend. "I'll have to speak with Garrett as well."

Sarah shifted in the seat.

"Of course, you could always do a little investigating for me," Danni added.

"How?" Sarah asked, suspicious of Danni's suggestion.

"Ask Garrett about Brookfield Cemetery. Maybe you can get some of the dirt on the place and why high school students found it so interesting."

"I'll call him when he gets off work."

A goofy smile spread across Danni's face, making Sarah pause. Even though she knew she shouldn't, she asked the question anyway.

"Why are you grinning?"

"I know what a difficult task this is for you, and I appreciate your willingness to take on the burden of calling Garrett," she replied dramatically.

"You don't have any room to talk after your post-dinner exploits last night," Sarah declared.

"At least I got my engine tuned-up instead of letting it rust away," Danni said with a snort.

Sarah punched Danni's upper arm, wrenching a yelp from her.

"What was that for?" Danni squalled.

"The sarcasm," Sarah said, looking away so her friend didn't see the smile creeping across her face. No matter how hard Sarah tried to hide it, her attraction to Garrett wouldn't squeak past the one person who knew her better than anyone else in the world. Of course, Danni's chosen profession as a top-notch barrister made it nearly impossible to sneak anything past her. Worst of all, was having to face the fact her heart was growing fonder of Garrett with every passing day, despite all the reasons why she shouldn't give him a second thought.

Regardless of her romantic dilemmas, Sarah was thrilled her friend had found someone that made her happy. At the same time, she worried what would happen when the trial was over and everyone returned to their respective homes. Even worse, what if Dusty was convicted? Danni took her job seriously and losing a case that meant so much to her lover would make it even more devastating. Forcing the thought from her mind, Sarah convinced herself that Dusty would be acquitted and somehow everything would work out between Danni and Brady.

AFTER DANNI DROPPED HER OFF, Sarah left a voice mail for Garrett asking him to call when he got home from work. The thought of him left her palms sticky and her heart racing as she gathered her work tools and headed upstairs to finish the last room. Work had always been a good distraction from her troubles, and she hoped it would take her mind off the man tugging at her heart.

Outside of the furniture, nothing much of value had been discovered in the other bedrooms and she suspected this one would be the same. Once she finished this room, she'd start the appraisal process, discuss the estate sale with Melinda, and tag the items. The urgency to raise funds was increasing, especially with the lack of progress finding evidence to prove Dusty's innocence. His constant mutterings about feeling guilty over his wife's death didn't help matters.

After searching through several boxes of outdated magazines, old report cards, and numerous journals, Sarah was no closer to finding anything of worth. She'd even perused some of the old scrapbooks hoping to find an alternative suspect for Tara's murder, but nothing surfaced.

Deep in thought, Sarah sat on the floor and slumped against the bed when her phone rang, making her jump.

"Hello," she said, trying to steady her breathing.

"Catch you at a bad time?" Garrett asked, his baritone voice purring through the phone.

"Not at all, I was working and lost track of the time," she responded, her heart drumming at the sound of his voice. Then again, it may have been the phone startling her from her stupor.

Silence charged the atmosphere.

"Sarah? You still there?" he asked.

"Yes," she replied.

"You asked me to call you."

Feeling foolish, Sarah shook her head.

"Sorry, I think all the dust in this place has infiltrated my brain," she chuckled nervously, trying to gather her wits and speak like a partially intelligent woman instead of an awkward adolescent. "Were Ralph and Harry able to clean-up the video of the ghost from the George Plantation?"

"Not yet. It's really strange. There's some sort of interference on the tape. They're trying to work through it."

"Has that ever happened before?" Sarah asked, certain he'd come up with some sort of hype about their paranormal abilities. If they were legit, they'd be able to filter the image and see it was Tara.

"Only once," he said.

Sarah waited for him to elaborate. When he didn't, she

considered asking him about it but changed the subject instead.

"Since we're talking about ghosts," Sarah said, "I was wondering what you know about Brookfield Cemetery."

"It's a pretty cool place. I'd love to take you there some time. Since you didn't seem fazed the other night, I'm thinking you'd probably be OK with a cemetery tour."

"There's a tour?"

"Actually, Tara used to take groups through there on a regular basis. She knew every tombstone and piece of ironwork in that place. I don't have the dramatic flair she did, but I know all the stories if you want to go."

At first, Sarah was shocked people would want to traipse through an old graveyard at night until she thought about the ghost tours in her own hometown. People flocked there every year to hear spine-tingling tales of the dead floating about the streets and old mansions. Once she'd tried to walk through the old graveyard behind the Episcopal church after dark. She made it three steps into the walled cemetery when she felt a strong pressure encompass her. It was like having a pillowcase over her head in the heat of summer. Overwhelmed, she ran back out and never set foot in a graveyard after dark again.

"Sounds like a plan," she said, hoping the spirits wouldn't be too active. At least she'd have Garrett and Dallas with her. Maybe it wouldn't be so frightening with them. After all, she'd done well during the ghost hunt, even with Tara's ghostly image appearing.

"Pick you up about nine o'clock?" he asked.

"See you then."

Danni had gone with Brady leaving Sarah alone to prepare for the cemetery walk. She dressed in a pair of jeans, a black t-shirt, and neon orange sneakers. Her hair was swooped into a ponytail and she'd dabbed on some concealer with a bit of lip color. Even though she couldn't start a relationship, she wanted to look her best. Grabbing her cell phone, Sarah hurried down the stairs when she heard truck tires crunching across the gravel drive.

Opening the door, she watched Garrett amble up the walkway. Dallas perched on the edge of the open window of the truck. The small dog let out a welcoming yap when Sarah stepped onto the porch and locked the door behind her.

A slight tingle rustled Sarah's insides. Despite the darkness, Garrett's green eyes sparkled beneath his chestnut hair. He was definitely a good-looking man.

"Looks like you're ready to roll," Garrett said with a smile.

"Yup," she replied. Nervous about the spiritual aspect of the cemetery, she knew she'd have to garner all her courage and self-control to deal with any entities they might encounter.

He opened the truck door and helped her inside as Dallas hopped to the backseat. They drove several blocks to an old brick church with a garden of gravesites to the side. Garrett parked the truck, turned off his headlights, and looked toward the shadowy monuments and tombstones.

"Welcome to Brookfield Cemetery."

Sarah's stomach flopped. Now that she was here, her resolve was beginning to falter. This was a terrible idea. Why hadn't she just asked what he knew about the place instead of agreeing to come here?

As if sensing her discomfort, Dallas' wet nose nuzzled Sarah's cheek. She reached over and scratched behind his silky ears, her blood pressure dropping a bit. Something about the little dog was reassuring, allaying some of her consternation.

"Looks a bit run down," she said, staring into the eerie expanse.

"Tara and several of the historical society members have been trying to raise funds to refurbish some of the gravesites.

Tara was well-schooled in the symbolism of the headstones and knew every detail of the family burial plots. We referred to her as a cemeterian."

"Is there a record of all her research?"

"Absolutely. It's all at the genealogical library. Harry used to give the tours when Tara wasn't available. Now he's training Darlene so she can take over. She has a natural storytelling ability and loves history, making her the logical choice."

"Darlene?"

"One of Dusty and Tara's friends."

"I'm glad there are people to carry on her work," Sarah responded with a smile.

"Ready?"

"Let's go," Sarah replied, taking a deep breath.

Garrett grabbed a couple of flashlights and handed one to Sarah as he helped her from the truck. Dallas leapt from inside and waited with tail wagging. They started down the brick pathway, uneven from tree roots and years of neglect, through the burial plots of Brookfield. Without a care, Dallas toddled ahead, disappearing into the darkness.

"Keep your flashlight trained on the ground. Many of the bricks are loose and I don't want you to fall."

"Thanks for the warning," Sarah replied, focusing on the walkway. "Where'd Dallas go?"

"He's scouting for varmints or ghosts, whichever he finds first."

"Is that safe?" she asked, concerned Dallas might encounter a raccoon or something larger.

Garrett shook his head. "He's pretty smart. Doesn't take on anything he can't handle and will scare the life outta anything that threatens him."

"Even the ghostly type?" Sarah hoped the answer was yes.

"He has a keen ability for chasing them off," he chuckled.

Distracted by the conversation, Sarah stumbled on a tree

root. Garrett grabbed her arm, catching her before she fell. Her skin tingled at his touch, sending a thousand butterflies flitting about her stomach. His eyes met hers as she steadied herself, wondering how someone so handsome and charismatic could be a suspect in something as sinister as a murder. Sarah inhaled as she searched for a safe question to ask.

"Tell me about Tara's research on this place. Is there a reason this particular graveyard caught her attention?"

"Aside from the fact there are several South Carolina statesmen buried here and the unique features of the graves, I think she was intrigued by the stories."

"You mean of the people buried here?"

"That and the odd manner surrounding some of their deaths and burials."

"Odd?"

Dallas let out a series of warning barks from the far corner of the graveyard, making Sarah jump.

"He found something," Garrett said, shining his flashlight in that direction.

Dallas was barking like mad, his tail wagging with the force of a jack hammer.

Garrett whistled and the little dog came bounding over to them. Dallas lowered his haunches at Garrett's feet with his tongue hanging low as he panted.

"Let's start over here," Garrett said, leading Sarah off the brick path toward a cluster of marble headstones. "These are the Gretsky sisters. They had a penchant for cooking with herbs, specifically hemlock."

Sarah's hand flew to her mouth. "Did they kill anyone?"

"They never used enough to cause death; however, they did make several people sick, mostly corrupt business owners and politicians. Word spread pretty quickly and people avoided eating anything they prepared. One day, they accidently mixed the wrong jar of herbs in a batch of tea."

"They inadvertently committed suicide?"

"Yup."

Sarah followed him past a beautiful wrought iron fence surrounding an obelisk monument. Pausing, she ran the flashlight beam across the smooth surface. "This looks like someone important."

"Former governor," Garrett replied as he continued to a fallen tombstone with what appeared to be moss creeping across the right side.

Sarah stepped up beside him and shone her flashlight on the crumbling marker.

"Who is this?" she asked.

"This is Edward Pooler, eccentric extraordinaire."

Sarah raised an eyebrow and cocked her head.

"This guy left explicit instructions in his will that he should be buried wearing his velvet smoking jacket, sitting in his favorite chair behind a plate of glass."

"You're not serious," Sarah replied incredulously.

"Very. His family honored his request since the will stated no one would inherit unless his demands were followed. Needless to say, with a million-dollar estate at stake, the family obeyed his wishes."

Sarah glanced around but only saw the decrepit tombstone. "Where was he buried?"

"Here." Garrett directed the flashlight to a square metal cover at the base of the tombstone. "If you lifted this trap door, you could climb down the ladder and view his dead body sitting in a chair."

With a gulp, Sarah looked at the metal cover and then back at Garrett. "Seriously? We could climb down there and see a corpse in a coat?"

"Not now. After years of kids sneaking down there on a dare, the family had it filled with gravel."

Shaking her head, Sarah blew out a breath. "That's the strangest thing I've ever heard."

"Not yet," he said with a chuckle.

Dallas trotted alongside them as they meandered through the graveyard. Garrett told stories of a woman so smitten with her first husband, she insisted on being buried in the same coffin.

"They exhumed him to add her?" Sarah queried.

"Yup. Placed her face down on top of him."

"That's pretty creepy. I can't believe anyone would actually dig up a decaying body to add a fresher one."

"This is Edgefield. People here respect the requests of its citizens no matter how bizarre."

Enthralled with the stories, Sarah was surprised at how relaxed she felt walking through the cemetery. They'd been there for half an hour when the serenity of the evening was interrupted. A biting chill trickled down Sarah's spine, making her body shudder. At that moment, Dallas stopped and stared off, a low growl emanating from his throat as the hair on his back bristled.

Sarah tried to calm her racing pulse by taking a deep breath, holding it for a count of five, and releasing slowly while Garrett scanned the area with his flashlight. Dallas' growl increased in volume and his muscular stature tensed.

Then Sarah saw it. A misty figure swirling in the dark. Closing her eyes, she willed away the terror squeezing her lungs. When she opened her eyes, the misty figure had dissipated. Garrett walked a few steps forward, apparently trying to determine what had alarmed his dog. Sarah turned the other direction, a scream erupting from her lips as she stared into the eyeless visage of Tara who was only inches from where she stood. Stumbling backwards, Sarah lost her balance and started to fall as Dallas rushed over barking frantically. Tara's deadpan stare prickled Sarah's skin as she sailed toward the ground when Garrett's hands caught her.

"Are you alright?" he asked breathlessly, lifting her to her feet.

"I'm fine," she muttered. "I must've caught my heel on a tree root or something."

Glancing up, she noticed the frightening image had disappeared. Her insides quivered like jelly as she scanned the area for any signs of Tara.

Nothing.

"I think we've had enough fun for one evening. How about we get a drink?"

"I could use one," she replied with a nod.

They walked back to the truck with Dallas leading the way, his stubby tail bouncing back and forth in rhythm with his stride.

They drove a couple of blocks but instead of parking in front of Corner Pocket, Garrett drove down a back street and parked in front of a charming cottage with a screened porch spanning the front of the house. A single light shimmered from within, welcoming them to come inside.

"This is your house?" Sarah declared, her gaze riveted on the home that was all too familiar to her.

"Yup," Garrett replied with a sheepish grin.

"When were you going to tell me you lived next door to Edgefield Manor?"

His grin broadened into a mischievous smile. "I wanted to see how long it took you to notice."

Sarah glanced at the wall of trees and underbrush that lined the far side of his yard dividing the properties. She'd noticed the cottage when walking to town but never suspected Garrett resided there, especially since the copse of trees blocked visibility between the two houses. The fact that Edgefield Manor was at the end of a rather long drive whereas

Garrett's cottage was situated toward the front of his property also prevented a clear view from one house to the other.

Garrett slid from the truck and walked toward the passenger side. Dallas leapt to the ground and jaunted up the walkway. Unsure what to do, Sarah stared straight ahead when he opened her door.

"I'm sorry, I wasn't trying to be elusive. Where I lived never came up in conversation and I didn't want to seem..." his words trailed off as he looked toward the house.

"Devious?" Sarah replied, arching her eyebrows.

"Now that I think of it, I should have asked if you were OK coming to my place."

Sarah's insides twisted at his brazenness. He'd had plenty of opportunities to say "Oh, by the way, my house is next to the one where you're staying." How could he have been so deceptive about where he lived?

Her mind veered to another thought, making her stomach twist. Tara's ghost had uttered *don't trust him* when Garrett was around. What if he was the killer? Surely, he wouldn't be daring enough to murder her when Danni was right next door. *Stop it*, she thought. Despite the turmoil swirling in her gut, something in her head urged her to trust him. She only hoped it wouldn't lead to her demise. Then again, Sarah's instincts were usually pretty reliable. The guy was nothing more than a ghost-hunting pretender and probably a player, albeit a good looking one, but that didn't make him dangerous.

"No worries," she replied, hopping out of the truck.

Dallas stopped halfway up the path, turned, and let out a bark as if telling them to hurry up. He continued to the porch door and waited, his tail wagging so hard it blurred in the glow of the porch light.

Garrett opened the door to the screened porch fronting his cottage, its hinges squealing in protest. He motioned for Sarah to follow. Dallas trotted past her and waited at the front door while Garrett fiddled with the key in the lock.

"Old houses," he snickered. "The lock on this door always swells with the humidity in summer."

"I understand that," she replied. Her palms were sweaty and she could feel the moisture gathering down the small of her back. Whether it was nerves or the steamy atmosphere remained to be seen. She desperately wanted to get into the air conditioning before she looked like she'd just stepped out of a sauna.

When the lock clicked, Garrett turned the knob and used his shoulder to nudge the door open. Dallas scurried inside, his toenails clicking against the wide plank floors. Sarah followed Garrett down a broad hallway spanning the length of the house. Turning on lights along the way, he led her to the last room on the left. As he flipped the switch, an overhead light flickered to life illuminating a quaint, old-fashioned kitchen. The scent of pine oil filled the space. White painted cabinets lined the far wall and a small oak table anchored by a braided rug was situated in the center of the room. Above a farmhouse sink with a drying rack on one side, was a window framed in blue checked curtains. The room looked like something from a 1950s movie.

"The only thing I've got in the house is beer," he said apologetically.

"That'll be fine," she replied.

Garrett pulled two beers from the vintage fridge and handed one to her before grabbing a piece of ham for Dallas who perched on his haunches awaiting his treat. Tossing the chunk to his dog, Garrett sat across the table from Sarah and popped the top of his beer with a swoosh.

"Were you able to get much accomplished today?" Garrett asked, taking a swig of his beer.

"I did. Granted, most of what I found was family memorabilia. There are several photo albums with pictures of Dusty when he was young. Looked like he had a wonderful childhood."

Garrett stared at his beer and smiled. "Spent a lot of time with Dusty, Harry, and Brady growing up. We were like the Little Rascals, except Tara was part of the group. No she-haters amongst friends." He lifted the can to his lips and took several gulps.

"You guys were pretty close, huh?"

"Best friends I've ever had. Even though I was only here during the summer months, these guys were like brothers, and a sister, to me. I know this sounds kinda sappy, but I loved them all. Even their parents. We'd spend the days playing at Brady's family farm and the evenings at different houses. Used to be an ice cream parlor where the bakery is now. Couple times a week we'd go there for hot fudge sundaes or root beer floats."

"Sounds like a great way to grow up."

"It was an amazing childhood," he said, nostalgia veiling his expression. "What about you and Danni? How long have you known each other?"

"We met in high school when her father was stationed at the air base. Up until then, I was pretty much a loner. Spent most of my time reading."

"Interesting. You don't strike me as the introverted type."

"I was until Danni came along. She's the kind of person who throws you out of the nest, even if your wings are clipped."

"Fly or die?" he asked, his eyebrows arched as a smile parted his lips.

"That's a great way to put it," Sarah giggled, her shoulders releasing some of the tension. Something about Garrett's laid-back demeanor made her feel at ease. "Of course, some of Danni's antics landed her in trouble with her parents, especially the summer she got arrested for protesting."

"Danni was arrested?" Garrett's eyes widened.

"Yup. Danni was all about preservation and fighting for the underdog. The judge released her without *legal* consequence, although her father wasn't as lenient."

"Wow, I wouldn't have thought her to be so brazen. Then again, I don't really know her."

"What about you guys? Any misconduct during your summer visits?"

"Just the typical childhood pranks and adventures. Mostly, we played in the woods or searched for hidden treasure. One summer, Harry got it in his head that a group of pirates had come through town in the 1700s in an effort to escape capture. He and Brady concluded there must be treasure somewhere in Edgefield, most likely on Brady's homestead since it was far from town and therefore less likely to be discovered."

"I assume you never found the buried treasure."

"Actually, we did. I'm independently wealthy but joined the Marines to have something to do and then went into construction for fun," he said with a wink. "What about you? Any buried treasure hunts in your past?"

"Funny you should ask. I inadvertently stumbled upon my fortune."

"Seriously?" Garrett leaned back in the chair.

"Last year, I was clearing out a multi-million-dollar estate and discovered I was the heir. Turns out my parents adopted me from what was believed to be the last living descendant of the Monroe fortune. When my biological mother died, everything in the family homestead came to me."

"That's incredible," Garrett said with a whistle. "And you're still working?"

"I love what I do. The best part is now I have the freedom to take on the estates that pique my interest instead of every offer that walks through the door."

"You sound like Tara," he said wistfully. "She left the job at the title office to do genealogical searches for people full time.

It was hard on them financially, but Tara was a natural at research, not to mention her knowledge of the town's history was extensive. People loved her and shared their stories openly. She remembered all of it." Garrett got up and grabbed two more beers, handing one to Sarah.

"You two were close?" she asked.

"We were all close with Tara," he sighed.

"Was Dusty always in love with her?"

Garrett snorted. "At some point during our lives, we each had a crush on her. Dusty's stuck and grew into something much deeper."

"You had a crush on Tara?"

"During middle school," he responded, a slight blush coloring his tan cheeks. "By that time, she already had eyes for Dusty, and we all knew it."

"You must've been disappointed."

"Angry was more like it. It was a hard summer for me. My mother was dating a guy I didn't like, and my real father had just died. The only thing that kept my mind off of reality were my feelings for Tara. Her rejection was like a slap in the face. Made me question whether true love existed."

"I can't imagine you being so bitter," Sarah said with a slight grin.

"Between my mother's romantic entanglements and a broken adolescent heart, my view of relationships was tainted for years. I suppose that's why I never married. I was so busy guarding my feelings I closed off my heart. Believe it or not, I resented Dusty a bit when they married. It wasn't anger as much as jealousy." Garrett shook his head. "I don't know why I'm telling you all of this."

"It's the natural progression of the conversation. I'm glad you feel comfortable enough sharing these things with someone you hardly know."

"You have a way of making people feel at ease. I've noticed it with Harry and Ralph."

Sarah pondered his statement. She'd never considered herself to be the kind of person who put others at ease, at least the living sort.

"Of course, Dallas adores you."

At the mention of his name, Dallas raised his head and gave a soft 'woof' before nuzzling his nose between his front paws.

"I like him too," Sarah said, glancing down at the dog curled at her feet. Sarah felt relaxed with the situation and Garrett's willingness to share his feelings with her. Maybe she should share her secret. After all, she and Danni would be gone when the trial was over. Since Garrett believed in ghosts and there was no future with him, it didn't seem like such a big deal. Sarah took a long swallow of beer, hoping it would give her the courage she needed to divulge her dreamist abilities. Garrett shifted in his chair and yawned.

"It's getting late and I have an early morning," he announced, swigging the rest of his beer. "I don't mean to end this so abruptly, but I need to be up at five tomorrow morning. The job is in North Augusta."

Sarah's heart sank. As always, her timing was off. It was probably better she hadn't said anything, especially since she didn't know much about him outside of her fledgling crush and a few childhood stories.

"I'll walk you home," he said as Dallas jumped to his feet and led the way.

They walked across his yard in silence to the side garden of Edgefield Manor. Sarah felt uncomfortable with Garrett's sudden decision to end the evening. Maybe he regretted revealing his adolescent feelings for Tara. Did he think Sarah would make inferences about his past and Tara's murder? And if he was the killer, would he try to harm her?

Her ruminations dissipated like steam when Sarah noticed Brady's red Mercedes parked under the huge oak.

Garrett looked at Sarah with a sly grin. "Is it OK for you to go inside?"

A giggle shook Sarah's shoulders. "Are you inferring Danni and Brady might be otherwise engaged?"

"That's what I'm inferring."

Not wanting to give away the burgeoning romance between Danni and Brady, Sarah played it safe. "Knowing Danni, she's completely immersed in her work."

"Even with Brady there?"

"Absolutely," Sarah said.

"She's not interested in guys?"

"She's interested but was married once and I don't think she's looking to repeat it anytime soon."

"I'm not saying they're planning a wedding," he replied, waggling his eyebrows.

Sarah smacked his arm. "Get your mind outta the gutter. Danni wouldn't put me in that situation. Brady probably brought over something to eat and stayed to answer any questions Danni had about the case. I assure you, it's safe for me to go inside."

Sarah's stomach twisted. Despite her protestations, she wondered if in fact Danni and Brady might actually be 'busy.'

Garrett nodded as they meandered up the brick walkway. At the front door, he turned to face Sarah as they stood in the glow of the outside light. Moths fluttered about, smacking against the glass panels of the lanterns.

For an instant, the world seemed to stand still. Garrett looked down at Sarah, his eyes glimmering in the dimness of the lights, a slight grin lifting the corners of his mouth. Sarah's heartrate increased as he leaned towards her when the front door flew open. Sarah jumped back a step as Garrett straightened up.

"Great timing. Brady was heading out," Danni declared. Sarah noticed Brady's shirt was untucked and Danni's hair was tousled.

"Wow, that *is* great timing," Sarah said, her insides quivering like a worm at the end of a hook. Turning to Garrett, she smiled. "Thanks for the tour, and the drinks."

"Anytime," he replied with a nod. "See you guys later."

Dallas barked a goodnight as he and Garrett strode down the brick path.

Brady stepped onto the porch and gave a bow. "I shall take my leave, ladies. Good evening."

Danni gave Brady a shove. "Get out of here with all that chivalry nonsense. I know you better than that."

A laugh rolled from his mouth as he walked to his car. With a wave he slipped behind the wheel and drove off.

"How was the graveyard walk?" Danni asked as Sarah edged past her.

"Interesting," she replied, going straight to the bar. Hopefully, another drink would settle her quaking limbs before Danni started asking personal questions.

With arms crossed, Danni pursed her lips. "What's up?"

Sarah sighed. Sometimes she hated how well Danni could read her.

"Nothing's up. He showed me around Brookfield, shared a few crazy stories about its residents, and then we went to his place for a couple of beers," Sarah said, sitting down.

"You went to his house?" Danni exclaimed with a gasp. Plunking down beside her on the settee, Danni bumped her shoulder against Sarah's. "He's a good-looking guy. Don't be shy about liking him."

"It's not that," Sarah said sullenly. "Did you know he lives next door?"

"What?" Danni exclaimed. "Why didn't he tell us?"

"Didn't give a reason," Sarah replied with a wave of her hand and a roll of her eyes.

"This is great. You don't have to go far to *visit* him."

"Cut it out. We're only here for a short period of time. Besides, I'm not sure he's interested."

"Why do you say that?"

"We talked about his summers here when he was a kid. He mentioned having a crush on Tara when he was younger."

"So?" Danni said, shrugging her shoulders.

"The way he spoke about her made me believe he still has feelings for her. He denied it, of course."

"First, the woman's dead so no competition there. Second, she was married to Dusty." Danni said matter-of-factly.

Regardless, It's not a good time for a relationship. And in case you've forgotten, I can't exactly date with my *special abilities*." Sarah emphasized the last two words by making quotation marks in the air.

Danni shook her head, astonishment sweeping over her expression. "Seriously? You're questioning a relationship with this guy because of your dreamist skills? He hunts ghosts! This is the perfect match!"

"Just because you're starry eyed doesn't mean I'm going to follow suit," Sarah huffed.

"Come on, give the guy a chance. I can tell you like him."

Sarah shook her head. "My dreamist abilities would only complicate things."

"You've got to stop seeing your gift as a hindrance and view it more as something that makes you special. It gives you a sense for the feelings of others that most people can't grasp."

"Hmph. Garrett made a similar statement earlier about my putting others at ease. I just don't see it."

"What else did dream-boy say?" Danni asked with a sly look.

"It doesn't matter. He lives in Edgefield and I live in Beaufort. Don't forget, I witnessed his so-called ghost hunting abilities and trust me, they're as illusory as the ghosts he proclaims to hunt," Sarah replied. "It wouldn't work out."

Sarah knew most men's egos couldn't handle their girlfriend outshining them in a favored hobby. While Garrett claimed to believe in spirits, he might not accept a woman who could communicate with them in her dreams, especially when his abilities were so superficial. Even Danni had issues with Sarah's spectral skills when she first learned about them. Sarah exhaled. She was glad she hadn't told him about her ghostly proclivities. There was no need to complicate her life with dating drama. The hauntings were dramatic enough.

"Suit yourself, but I think you're missing out on a *dreamy* opportunity," Danni said with a wink. "Tell me more about what you learned this evening."

Sarah gave a slight smile. Just like Danni to needle her about her love life and then get back to finding clues to exonerate her client.

16

Sarah recounted the bizarre stories of the cemetery, Dallas' barking fit, and the gruesome sight of Tara's face. Then she elaborated on Garrett's confession about his feelings for Tara when they were younger.

"I know it was an adolescent crush, but the sadness still radiated in his eyes," Sarah said.

Danni stared off as she pursed her lips.

"What's the matter?" Sarah asked, taking a swig of her drink.

"How upset was Garrett about Dusty and Tara getting together?"

"He liked her when he was a teen. I can't imagine he'd hold a grudge that long. Although, he did admit to some bitterness about their marriage."

"Do you think his resentment festered enough that he killed her and set up her husband for it?"

A lump formed in Sarah's throat at Danni's line of questioning. She didn't like the turn it had taken, probably because she'd wondered the same thing.

"I don't want to believe Garrett would hurt anyone," Sarah

declared, trying to resolve the conflict in her heart.

"This isn't *anyone*. This is a woman he's professed to have feelings for who supposedly broke his heart and later married one of his childhood buddies. A marriage he confessed to being cynical about. Men have killed for a lot less," Danni said. "Think about it. The man is gorgeous and doesn't have a girlfriend."

Sarah's gut churned. What if Garrett really was the killer? Would he actually go to such extremes over a decades old crush? A broken heart coupled with resentment could eat away at a person's soul. Even though she'd never have a future with him, she couldn't accept the idea he'd murder someone he proclaimed to care about.

"Earth to Sarah! Hello!" Danni exclaimed, waving her hand in front of Sarah's face.

"Sorry, my mind was wandering," she replied with a yawn. "I'm really tired."

"I know you like the guy, and don't try to deny it," Danni said, holding up her hand. "But if he did this, he needs to be brought to justice."

"That's an awfully big if. He had a crush on her when he was a teen, got rejected, and went on with his life. I got the feeling his jealousy was more about the desire for a relationship than wanting Tara specifically. For goodness sakes, he served in the Marine Corps and is well respected in this area."

"Those are the same things people say after a serial killer is arrested," Danni said.

Sarah rolled her eyes.

"I'm not saying he did it."

"Sounds that way to me," Sarah retorted.

"All I need is reasonable doubt. If the detectives want to follow up with an investigation that's their business. Mine is to clear my client of the charges."

Desperate to change the subject, Sarah leaned her head

back against the curve of the settee when her mind shifted.

"Speaking of romantic endeavors, tell me more about your evening with Brady. He looked pretty pleased when he left earlier."

"It was wonderful. We drove to Aiken for dinner at this fabulous old inn," Danni replied, her eyes twinkling. "You would have loved the place. Antiques, original mantels, exposed beams, and probably a ghost or two.

"So, dinner was wonderful. And then?"

"He brought me back here and we had a drink. He's pretty stressed about a case and wanted my opinion on some things. Without his paralegal, he's having to do all the work himself which is why he went home for a few days."

"And?"

"And I was able to relieve his stress," Danni said with a grin as she walked to the bar and poured a scotch. "Want something?"

Sarah shook her head no.

"Why did Brady have to go all the way back to Columbia to work?"

"Apparently, there were some things he could only accomplish at his office. I feel badly for him. It's a bear not having someone to help out. I couldn't function without Anita."

"Ha! We should all be so lucky to have an Anita to research everything, keep the office running smoothly, and know what you need before you ask."

"She's pretty amazing and I'm thankful she puts up with me. Nevertheless, this thing with Brady was totally unexpected. We've been such good friends, I'm almost afraid of ruining that connection."

"He never gave any indication he was interested before now?" Sarah asked. After her conversation with Brady when he brought the pizza over, Sarah knew the answer but wanted to find out if Danni was aware.

"Not really. He was always so immersed in his studies, except for the occasional party or prank," Danni snorted.

"Maybe Brady did it," Sarah chortled.

"Did what?"

"Killed Tara."

"Not possible. He wasn't in town at the time. Not to mention, Brady would never hurt a woman," Danni said matter-of-factly.

"How do you know?"

"I remember watching him defend a female classmate when her boyfriend got aggressive. When we talked about it later, he said the one thing his mother always told him was to respect women and never lay a hand on them, no matter what."

Sarah looked at her friend. "What about men?"

"Huh?"

"You said Brady would never hurt a woman. What about a man?"

Danni paused, her cheeks coloring. "Men are a different matter. Brady has a bit of a temper when he's been drinking. Once, I saw him smash a guy's nose because he spilled Brady's beer."

"And you don't think a man with a bad temper when he drinks could be a suspect?" Sarah asked, leaning forward.

"Like I said, he wasn't in town, and he doesn't hurt women."

"Would he be able to make that determination if he was drunk?"

"Absolutely! Listen, I get you're not happy about Mr. Handsome being a suspect, but there's no need to turn this on Brady. I've known him for more than a decade. He's not the type to do something like this. A barroom brawl maybe, but not murder."

Sarah sighed. "You're not going to say anything to him about Garrett, are you? I mean, we're talking about an adolescent infatuation."

"I'm not going to say anything yet. I want to do a bit more

digging first. No need to ruin Brady's opinion of a lifelong friend, especially when we're relying on a few ghostly utterances and a confession of a decades-old broken heart."

Sarah stood in a stretch. "I can't hold my eyes open any longer. I'm going to bed."

"I'll be up in a little bit. I want to do some more research before I turn in."

With a nod, Sarah headed for the stairs. Research for Danni meant mining for anything unsavory in Garrett's past. Regardless of where her friendship with Garrett progressed, Sarah hoped she hadn't inadvertently implicated him by sharing information with Danni that could wreck his life.

Flipping on the overhead light, Sarah traipsed across the room, grabbed her nightshirt, and stepped into the bathroom. The three-bulbed light shrouded the mirror in a shadowy glow, making Sarah's eyes appear sunken and her cheeks hollow. She reached for the soap, turned on the faucet, and washed her face.

Blotting her face dry, she picked up the moisturizer bottle as the room took on an icy feel. With a shiver, she let out a blood-curdling scream when she looked back in the mirror and saw Tara's face instead of her own, the words *don't trust him*, resonating in the small space.

Sarah rushed into the bedroom as Danni's footfalls pounded up the stairs.

"What happened?" Danni asked breathlessly.

"I was washing up and saw Tara's reflection instead of my own," Sarah responded, resting her hand on her thumping chest. "She said *don't trust him*, again."

"Was it really her ghost or was it your imagination? Face it, it's kinda hard *not* to think about her."

"Maybe," Sarah responded. "The light in the bathroom is terrible and I did look a bit peaked when I glanced in the mirror. However, I definitely heard the words, *don't trust him.* I'm certain of that."

Bam!

A crash echoed down the hall, making both women jump.

"Guess it wasn't my imagination," Sarah whispered as a tingling sensation slithered up her spine and across her scalp.

"Could've been a critter in the attic. Maybe a raccoon or something," Danni offered, arching her brows.

"Might as well check it out," Sarah said, filling her lungs with air and releasing slowly.

She plodded across the hall with Danni close behind. They peered into the first room, but everything appeared to be in its place. The next room was the same. Splinters of light from a nearly full moon pierced through the sheer curtains of the back room.

Sarah switched on the light, casting a warm glow across the space. On the far wall, a stack of boxes had tumbled over, their contents spilling like a waterfall. They walked over and started gathering up the piles of papers, old journals, and manilla envelopes filled with old photos. Instinctively, Sarah started sorting through some of the items when Danni jumped up and gasped.

"What's wrong?" Sarah asked, her body freezing as her eyes scanned the area for something mystical hovering nearby.

"Spider," she muttered, pointing at the eight-legged creature scurrying across the rug.

"It's running away from you," Sarah responded, exasperation tinting her words.

"You don't have to be so mean about it. You know I can't stand the scurvy little things." Danni replied with a shudder.

"Get it together and help me with this stuff," Sarah said, shaking her head.

Slowly, Danni lowered herself to her knees and started

stacking some of the folders when she stopped to look at one file in particular.

"What is it?" Sarah queried, craning her neck to see what Danni found.

"Looks like birth certificates for several of Dusty's family members."

"I'm surprised they aren't in a lock box."

Danni studied a sheet of paper behind the birth certificates. "This looks like a rough sketch of a family tree."

"Maybe someone started investigating the family line before turning it over to Tara."

"Or perhaps these things were part of Tara's research."

Without warning, the window flew open, flapping the curtains like laundry on a windy day. A strong gust filtered through the space blowing everything about, except the folder Danni had been looking through, which stayed eerily still. Sarah ran to the window and managed to push the paned glass shut as the words, *he took it*, reverberated in her ear.

"Took what?" Sarah shouted, stomping her foot.

"What are you talking about?" Danni asked from the doorway where she'd scampered, her complexion as colorless as a corpse.

Closing her eyes, Sarah's head dropped as she tried to process all that was happening. Now more than ever, she needed to keep her mind clear.

"I don't understand this," she muttered before lifting her head and meeting Danni's troubled gaze. "She whispered 'he took it' in my ear. What is she trying to tell me?"

"I really need to read through that *Dreamist* book," Danni said, apologetically. "I haven't spent as much time on it as I should have."

Sarah walked acros the room and hugged her friend. "It's not your fault. We need to do this together." Stepping back, she gave Danni a reassuring grin. "Right now, you need to focus on defending Dusty, not worrying about some crazy haunting that may or may not have anything to do with the trial."

"How can you question it? Isn't this what the *Dreamist* book taught us last year? Ghosts haunt your dreams when there's something unsolved in their manner of death."

"Good point."

"It makes sense that Tara is trying to share clues with you. We just need to figure out how to interpret them."

"It seemed easier with Nora."

"Probably because you were related," Danni said. "Unless Tara is a long-lost cousin, we'll have to determine how to interpret her messages."

"Looks like we have a bit more work to do before turning in for the night."

"Let's take a look at the *Dreamist* book and leave this mess until tomorrow. If we can figure out what Tara's trying to say, then we can decide if this stuff is relevant."

AFTER AN HOUR of listening to Danni read and reread a few chapters, Sarah's brain felt like scrambled eggs. Danni was sitting on the bed, her legs stretched out as she leaned against the wall. "This isn't making any sense to me right now. I'm too tired. Why don't we get some sleep and try again in the morning?"

"Sounds good to me," Sarah responded. "Maybe Tara will visit my dreams and tell me how to interpret that blasted book."

"Do me a favor, if she does, please wait until morning to share. I need some shut-eye. It's been a busy day."

"And night," Sarah chuckled.

Danni scrunched up her face and hurled a pillow across the room, smacking Sarah in the face.

Sarah lobbed it back before sliding beneath the covers.

Tossing the pillow on the floor, Danni placed the small

leather tome on the night table, hunkered beneath the sheets, and rested her head on the pillow. "G'night."

"Goodnight," Sarah replied, lying down.

In a few moments, Danni's cadenced breathing filled the room.

Mentally, Sarah scolded herself for putting off learning about her unusual abilities over the past year. Once she was settled at Monroe Manse it hadn't been a priority, not to mention, the disturbing dreams had ceased. Had she known the need for her skills would resurface like this, she'd have taken it more seriously.

Sarah's mind wandered from Tara's frightening appearance in the bathroom mirror to her scratchy voice muttering, *he took it*. Took what? And to whom was she referring? Although Sarah hoped Dusty would be cleared of all charges, she didn't want Garrett to be the reason.

Unable to sleep, she slipped from bed and returned to the back room. Kneeling beside the avalanche of papers, she started sorting through them. Perhaps Tara would speak with her again if she kept looking for clues.

An hour later, Sarah had constructed a make-shift family tree with birth certificates, a plethora of old photos, and a few dozen hand-written letters between what appeared to be Dusty's and Brady's grandmothers. From what she could garner from the correspondence, their grandmothers had been raised more like sisters than cousins. With nothing extraordinary jumping out at her, Sarah was beginning to believe she'd wasted her time. She had a bad habit of getting side-tracked by old memorabilia when cleaning out estates and Danni was always too happy to remind her of it.

Standing, she brushed the dust from her knees, turned off the light, and went back to her room. Danni was still sound asleep as Sarah snuggled beneath the coverlet and promptly drifted off to dreamland.

17

"We shouldn't be here," Garrett said as he and Tara meandered past the overgrown lantana in the cemetery.

"Where else are we going to meet? I can't exactly stroll to your house without notice. At least no one comes around here after dark. The last thing I need is for word to get back to Dusty that we we're together."

"Have you decided how to handle the situation?" Garrett asked, beaming the flashlight along the uneven ground as they rambled amongst the graves.

"Not yet. I think Dusty has had all he can take. If he knew we were discussing this, he'd have a fit. I can't afford to push him much harder or he'll snap. You're the only one I can trust."

Tara stumbled but regained her balance as Garrett reached out to steady her. She looked at him with a slight smile. "You know I've always adored you," she said.

"Not enough to go out with me," he responded.

Tara inhaled and walked ahead of Garrett without responding. Approaching one of the tombstones, she reached down to set a fallen flower vase upright when the dream shifted.

Now Sarah was in the scene and it was her hand straightening the vase when bony fingers poked through the weed ridden gravesite, curling around her wrist. An ear shattering shriek crossed Sarah's lips as the skeletal hand started pulling her down into the dirt.

With heart pounding, Sarah jolted upright and looked around the dimly lit room. Danni's bed was made. Sunrays splashed across the far wall in shimmering shades of apricot and gold. This dream had been more disturbing than the others. Garrett and Tara were adults and their conversation inferred there was a secret between them, one Tara didn't want Dusty to know about. Rubbing her temples, Sarah tried to make sense of the dream when Danni appeared in the doorway wrapped in a towel with her hair dripping across her bare shoulders.

"What's the matter?" Sarah asked, her voice scratchy.

"Stupid water heater must've died! Thank goodness I managed to rinse the soap from my hair before ice cold water started pouring across my body." She shivered. "Won't need any caffeine to get me going now."

"I'll call Garrett," Sarah said.

"Ooo..." Danni replied like a ten-year-old taunting a classmate. "You've got a handyman on call, how nice."

Sarah stuck out her tongue. "He's a contractor, and the only one we know in town, Goofus. It was a logical deduction!"

"Keep telling yourself that," Danni giggled as she returned to the bathroom to dress.

Apparently, Danni had dismissed Garrett as a possible suspect or she wouldn't be so liberal with her teasing. Sarah dialed Garrett's number.

"Hey." He answered on the first ring, his voice skittering across her skin. Dallas barked in the background. "Dallas says good morning."

Sarah smiled. She loved that little dog. "Sorry to bother you so early but it seems the hot water heater has gone out. Do you know anyone we can call?"

"Got a guy I can send out this morning. I do all the work for Melinda so it shouldn't be a problem," he replied.

"Thank you."

"If you need to take a shower, you can go to my place," he offered. "I'm getting ready to head out. There's a key under the mat."

"Isn't that a bit obvious?"

"What do you mean?"

"It's the first place a burglar would look," Sarah replied.

"Ha! No one's going to break in. Mrs. McDaniel, the older woman who lives across the street, doesn't miss a thing."

"Good to know you have someone to call the law."

"Call the law? She's packing. Anyone who tried to break in would likely leave with a butt full of buckshot, if that's where she aimed."

"Will she shoot me if I go over?" Sarah asked, her voice raising an octave.

"I'll call her and let her know you'll be coming."

"Thanks Garrett, I really appreciate this."

"Not a problem."

He hung up and Sarah fell back on the bed, closing her eyes. Her chest tightened every time she heard his voice and she couldn't get his tanned face out of her mind. The secretive nature of his meeting with Tara in her dream only complicated things. The idea of him being a killer weighed on her mind. She really didn't need this kind of drama in her life right now.

"What's up?" Danni asked as she walked across the room buttoning her creamy silk blouse.

Sarah sat up, her shoulders slouching. "Garrett is sending someone out to repair the water heater."

"Sounds like *friendship* has its perks," she said with a sly smile as she plunked onto the bed and pulled on her heels.

"He does all the maintenance on Melinda's properties, Smarty Pants," Sarah retorted. She got up from bed with a stretch, gathered her clothes, and sauntered into the bathroom.

"You gonna take a cold shower after talking to him?" Danni asked.

"Nope. I'm going to brush my teeth, go to Garrett's to take a *hot* shower, and then go to the bakery for a cinnamon bun," she called out from the bathroom.

"Oh yeah, nothing going on between you two," Danni snickered.

Sarah popped her head out of the bathroom with the toothbrush protruding from her mouth. "I hurd dat," she said as white foam dribbled from her lips.

"See you later, *if* you're not otherwise engaged," Danni winked before stepping into the hallway.

Sarah spit the toothpaste into the sink and rinsed. On the surface, she knew Danni was only toying with her; however, Sarah was growing fonder of Garrett with each passing day. If Danni wasn't arguing with her about going to Garrett's place, then she must have changed her mind about his potential involvement in Tara's death. Sarah dashed down the stairs where her friend stood by the front door.

"Have you dismissed Garrett as a suspect?" she asked.

"Not at all," Danni replied resolutely. "As a contractor, he's probably already at work which means you'll be safe. I'll ask Brady about him when he comes to the courthouse after visiting Dusty."

"Please don't say anything about what I told you last night," Sarah pleaded.

"I'll keep you out of this but if the evidence points to Garrett, you know I won't let up until he's arrested."

"I know," Sarah groaned. "I wouldn't expect anything less."

"Cheer up. There's a good chance he's not involved."

"A very good chance," Sarah replied, despite the tiny hint of doubt in her heart. If only she could figure out what the previous night's dream meant, perhaps she could dismiss her suspicions too.

Danni grabbed her briefcase and headed out the door.

Sarah went back upstairs, dressed in a t-shirt and running shorts, and packed a fresh set of clothes. Trudging downstairs, she grabbed the backpack with her research tools and headed toward Garrett's house.

By the time she walked to his cottage, she was dripping with sweat. She'd never believed any other place could be hotter or stickier than the Lowcountry. Apparently, she was mistaken. This place was like a pizza oven.

Shafts of light streamed between tree branches, casting a glowing aura across the neatly cut grass and heirloom hydrangeas with bubblegum pink puffs the size of Sarah's hand. She stepped onto the screened porch, scooped the key from under the mat, and unlocked the front door. The scent of old house tickled her nose when she entered.

Closing the door behind her, she glanced around the space. She hadn't appreciated the architectural details the night before, or the fine antiques filling the rooms. Garrett had good taste. Part of Sarah wanted to explore while the other part felt strange being in a man's house she barely knew. Nevertheless, with her skin sticky and her ponytail clinging to the back of her neck, she needed a shower.

The bathroom was the second room on the left and still sported bright white subway tile on the walls with an octagonal black and white mosaic on the floor. The shower curtain was a bright yellow that matched the curtains on a tiny window to the side of the toilet. The room had something of a feminine, albeit outdated touch.

After showering and dressing, Sarah shoved her running clothes into the backpack and started for the front door when temptation prompted her to take a quick look around. She glanced into the large space to her right. Obviously, a front parlor-turned-living room, she was impressed with the mixture of early twentieth century tiger oak pieces mixed with several Mission style furnishings. The brick fireplace was painted white with a simple mantel and surround. A deep brown leather sofa sat across from a massive 1920s armoire. Stepping into the room, Sarah took in the masculine yet warm feel of the décor. The armoire door was cracked open, calling her to take a peek.

Inside she found a TV, VCR, and a small stereo with a turntable and CD player. *Typical,* she thought. Spotting a CD cover, she picked it up and smiled as she read the title. Benny Goodman was one of her favorites. Sarah knelt down and perused an antique wooden box filled with other favorites; Glenn Miller, Duke Ellington, Louis Armstrong, and more. Her heart fluttered. This guy was getting harder and harder to dismiss. They had the same taste in music, were into the spirit thing, and seemed to share a love of antiques and old houses. Too bad his idea of ghost hunting bordered on parlor tricks and slumber party antics.

She could overlook the mild theatrics surrounding his attempts at filming ghosts if only she could be certain he wasn't involved in Tara's demise. He was such a great guy; how could he possibly be a killer? Sarah exhaled, her shoulders wilting like a fern in direct sunlight. It seemed the most gruesome murderers were always described by neighbors and colleagues as modest, amiable people until bodies were discovered in the backyard garden or a basement freezer.

Sarah walked across the hall, hesitating at the partially closed door before her. Deciding it wouldn't do any harm to take a peek, she peered around the door and gasped at the sight. Built-in shelves filled with books covered three walls. Her heart palpitated. One more thing to connect them. Books were her weakness and had been her closest companion as a child, until she met Danni.

The walls were painted a deep green with striped silk curtains framing the front window. Although not as large or elaborate as the library at Monroe Manse, the collection of books was impressive. Without thinking, Sarah stepped into the room to take a closer look at the titles.

A chill prickled her skin as she turned to the wall behind her. Instead of books, this wall sported a red brick fireplace encased by a dark oak mantel bordered by two Eastlake parlor chairs. Sarah froze as she gazed at a large portrait above the mantel. Soft blue eyes stared from beneath a neatly styled coif of snowy white hair. The older woman's features were creased with wisdom, but her expression suggested a soft and genteel countenance. Sarah swallowed hard as tears trickled down her cheeks. This was the comforting woman from her dreams who appeared when Tara's gruesome visage terrified her. Sarah's heart sank and her stomach knotted.

How could the woman from her dreams be staring at her from a portrait in Garrett's home? Her mind raced with possibilities about this bizarre coincidence. Perhaps, the old woman was a well-known local whose portrait Garrett had purchased at an estate sale. Or maybe this woman had known Tara and was teaming with her in the afterlife to expose Garrett as the murderer. Any suppressed hopes Sarah held about his innocence began to fade.

At that moment, Billie Holiday's sultry voice belted out *It's a Sin to Tell a Lie*. Sarah's muscles stiffened. Surely, Garrett hadn't come home. Dallas would have zeroed in on her whereabouts if he had. Traipsing from the room, she followed the sound to the front parlor, the music growing louder as she approached the armoire. Reluctantly, she pulled open the door and stared at the phonograph spinning out the tune. The temperature dropped, encompassing her in a glacial embrace when a hand rested on her shoulder. She spun around, catching a glimpse of a dissipating mist. As mysteriously as the music had started, it stopped and the room warmed.

She'd had enough.

Grabbing her backpack and the key, Sarah hurried from the house, locking the door and replacing the key under the mat. Tears blurred her vision as she power-walked toward town. Her heart had been tossed about like a ship on stormy seas, drowning her appetite. Once in the square, she sat on one of the park benches to compose herself. If she went to the library in this state, Harry would ask questions and Sarah wasn't adept at lying.

Summer's hot breath ruffled her damp hair as she watched three gentlemen dressed in old-fashioned attire strolling down the street. Her pulse raced at the idea she was witnessing another supernatural event. Normally, she would shy away from the scene; however, it was broad daylight and curiosity won out. Daytime specters weren't as frightening, so the risk seemed minimal as she started down the sidewalk.

Keeping her distance, she watched as the men conversed along the way. They seemed incredibly real, then again, many of her sightings often did. At that moment, she looked around and sucked in a breath. Despite the time of day, there wasn't another living soul in sight.

They passed a row of empty brick storefronts each hosting a sign advertising affordable rent and the number to call for a lease. On the next corner was a 1950s style gas station-turned-convenience-mart and across from that was a white house with a sprawling wraparound porch and a sign that read Edgefield Museum. The three men climbed the stairs and stood by the front door.

Sarah slowed her pace, watching to see if they vanished through a wall or performed some otherworldly task. The tallest man looked her direction and gave a nod. Blowing out a breath, Sarah mentally scolded herself for her foolishness. They were real.

Perhaps they were dressed for some sort of event at the museum. Sarah loved museums and decided to check it out. With everything going on, she hadn't paid much attention to the businesses outside of the square. Maybe the museum could provide more information about Tara and Dusty's family history, as well as the identity of the older woman from her dreams whose image was now showing up in her waking hours.

"Mornin', young lady," the tall gent said with a smile that peeked from a full mustache and beard. "Just getting ready to open up if you're interested in a tour."

"You visiting our fine city?" the shorter man asked. Dressed in cotton trousers and a plaid shirt, his crystal blue eyes shone through a pair of thick glasses.

"Actually, I'm here to handle an estate sale," she responded.

"Ahh, you're the one helping Melinda with the funding for Dusty's defense," the third man said, rubbing the scruff prickling from his chin. He wore a wide-brimmed leather hat and despite his age, still exuded a robust deportment.

"You know about that?" Sarah asked, puzzled these strangers knew why she was in town.

"Small town, Miss. Know everything that's going on. And if we aren't aware then we'll hear it from somebody else," the first man chuckled.

"Sounds a bit like my hometown."

"Where you from?" the second man asked.

"Beaufort."

"Nice place," the third man added. "Had a brief stay on Paris Island many moons ago."

"Don't know where my manners disappeared to," the first one said. "I'm Eli and this is Robbie and Isaac."

The two men gave a nod and a smile.

"I'm Sarah Holden. I'm here with my friend, Danni Cook. She's representing -- "

"Dusty," they said in unison, making Sarah chuckle.

"Would you like to see the museum?" Eli asked.

"I don't want to interrupt you guys."

"We were just making some last-minute plans for the shootout this evening," Isaac said.

Sarah gasped. "You're planning a shootout?"

"It's a reenactment from the prohibition period. This town has a history of shootouts. Every summer we reenact one of them."

"And these things actually happened?"

Eli grinned. "A lot of interesting things have happened in this town. Come into the museum and I'll share a few."

Robbie and Isaac bid goodbye with a promise to meet before the evening's events to go over any last-minute changes. Sarah stepped through the museum door that Eli held open. The scent of old house and antiques wafted through the air as she took in her surroundings. What had once been an elegant home was now beautifully adapted into a museum space.

Glass fronted cases displayed a myriad of architectural pieces, pottery shards, Native-American relics, and other pertinent memorabilia for the town. A bodice sporting a silk mourning gown stood in the far corner and several Civil War regiment flags graced the opposite wall. The front room hosted a complete Eastlake parlor set with several oil portraits of former notable Edgefield residents covering the walls. Once the estate sale was over, she'd have to come back and spend some time studying all of the exhibits.

"Tell me more about these shootouts," Sarah said, trying to absorb the history encompassing her.

Eli grinned. "One of the most talked about incidents was the Booth-Toney shootout. It occurred on August 12th of 1878. However, the trouble started brewing in 1869, when there was a squabble between the families, resulting in Benjamin Booth killing Luther Toney. For obvious reasons, the families were at odds with each other after that."

"I can understand why," Sarah said.

"Then in 1878, the Booths and the Toneys ended up in a bar during a political celebration. Didn't take long before a confrontation broke out and spilled into the street with more than fifty men. Shots were fired in all directions. When the gunfire stopped, one Toney and two Booths were dead in the street and several residents were wounded."

Sarah gulped as Eli continued the tale.

"When all was said and done, nine men were indicted and later found not guilty."

"How?" Sarah asked, flabbergasted something so violent could occur in broad daylight without the guilty parties being convicted.

"No one came forward," Eli snorted. "Juries in Edgefield have always understood the peculiarities of gentlemen. This incident was about defending family honor which sadly, ended in violence."

Sarah shook her head while Eli discussed one of the displays. "If you thought the shootouts were scandalous, wait till you hear about Becky Cotton."

"Who's she?"

"One of the most notorious killers in Edgefield history. She murdered her first husband with an ax to the head while he was sleeping."

Sarah cringed. "How very Lizzie Borden."

"There's more. While on trial for his murder, for which she was acquitted, she managed to catch the eye of a male juror. She was said to be a very beautiful woman. Supposedly, she went on to murder two more husbands, one with a needle through the heart and another by poisoning."

"And she was never convicted?"

"Nope. She did meet a violent end when her own brother caught her flirting with yet another man near the courthouse. He picked up a large stone and knocked her in the head, killing her on the spot."

"I've heard about Edgefield's colorful history," Sarah said, shaking her head, "but this is unbelievable."

"Our past contains more than just bizarre occurrences. We've made our mark on the state in many ways."

Eli shared other remarkable historical facts about the town such as Dr. Landrum founding a prosperous pottery industry, William Gregg developing the most successful textile factory in the south, and Edgefield's claim to fame for producing ten South Carolina governors and several statesmen.

"This has been incredible," Sarah said as they finished. "Thanks for the tour."

"You should attend the shootout this evening. Most of the town will be there. Aside from the entertainment, there's food and a band."

"Depends on how much work I get accomplished today."

"Then you best get to it," Eli replied. "You haven't experienced a good time till you've been to an Edgefield reenactment."

"I'll do my best."

Sarah started for the front door with Eli on her heels. He slipped past her and opened the door with a bow.

"Until we meet again, Miss."

Sarah blushed at his chivalry. Instead of going to the library, she decided to go back to the house. If she could get enough done, she'd attend the reenactment.

AFTER A FAIRLY UNEVENTFUL day of tagging items for the sale, Sarah decided she'd go to the shootout. Danni was working late and Brady was occupied in his hotel room with his own cases, leaving her no reason to hang out alone at the house. For all she knew, Danni might join Brady and not come home tonight. Dressing comfortably in running shoes, jeans, and a Gamecocks t-shirt, she gathered her hair in a clip and headed for the square.

The aroma of hamburgers and hotdogs wafted through the air as she neared the center square. The road was cordoned off and a crowd of people filled the grassy areas and sidewalks to watch the event. Apparently, the entire show would take place in the street. She recognized Eli, Robbie, and Isaac standing in front of the genealogical library. They looked her direction and waved.

"You made it!" Eli declared, walking towards her. His 1920s suit was perfectly fitted along with a fedora hat. Robbie and Isaac were dressed in working-class style clothing with period correct caps. Each sported a holster with a gun.

"Since I got so much done, I thought it would be a fun way to spend the evening," Sarah smiled.

"Glad you could make it," Robbie said with a broad grin.

"Your friend didn't come with you?" Isaac asked.

"She had to work."

"Follow me, I'll get you a spot right up front," Eli added when a man came running up to him, his face flushed.

"What's the matter?" Eli asked.

"Sheila can't make it. She has food poisoning. What are we going to do?"

Eli removed his hat and wiped the sweat from his brow. "This is a problem. We need her."

"Hey guys," Harry called out. He marched toward them wearing a black suit and red shirt, with a bowler hat perched on his head. "Something wrong?"

"Sheila's sick and can't make it. We need her to assist the reverend with the destruction of the liquor," he sighed. "Where are we going to find someone to replace her on such short notice? This thing starts in half an hour."

A mischievous grin spread across Harry's face as he gazed at Sarah.

Picking up on what was likely to follow, Sarah shook her head and held up both hands. "No way. I don't know anything about shootouts or acting."

"It's simple," Robbie said. "You'll be portraying a Temperance woman. All you have to do is bust up the pottery when the reverend announces his intention to end the sin of alcohol consumption in the city."

Sarah glanced down at her attire. "I'm not dressed for it."

"No problem. Sheila's dress is at the library. You look to be the same size," Harry said.

"Do you think she'd mind if I wore her clothes?" Sarah's heart raced as she tried to find any excuse to get out of this.

"Actually, they were Tara's. Sheila was one of the few people with a similar build and agreed to play the role." Harry's voice cracked when he said Tara's name.

Gulping down her anxiety, Sarah realized she was stuck. Four sets of eyes stared at her imploringly. They'd all been so kind and welcoming to her. How could she turn them down?

"Alright, show me where to change," she said, her shoulders sagging as smiles spread across the faces of the men in front of her.

Harry led her through the library past rows of books to a large room at the back filled with metal file cabinets and piles of manila folders. A shiver rankled her body and her scalp prickled. There was a strong sense of something in this room, although what it was remained to be seen. Grabbing a garment bag, Harry handed it to Sarah.

She unzipped the bag and gazed at a short, fringed dress.

"I thought I was portraying a Temperance woman?"

"You are," he replied.

"But this is a flapper dress. Temperance women dressed modestly."

"It's all we have for this time period."

"I'm sure it will be fine," Sarah replied.

"You can change in the restroom at the end of the hall."

Closing the bathroom door, Sarah slipped into the fringed dress and cloche hat. The wide heeled shoes were a bit snug, but she wouldn't have to wear them for long. Once she was dressed, she checked her reflection in the mirror when her stomach wrenched, and she regretted coming. She wasn't a stage person. Being on her own with a good book was her comfort zone. Thank goodness Danni wasn't here to see this. She'd never let her live it down.

With a deep breath, Sarah stepped from the bathroom. She looked for Harry but didn't see him. *He must have joined the others*, she thought. As she made her way through the stacks, the air seemed to still as the temperature plummeted. Sarah's breath fogged before her, making her realize she'd made a terrible mistake.

She was wearing Tara's clothing in the very building where she'd been murdered. This couldn't be good. Not wanting to witness any apparitions, Sarah inhaled and sprinted for the front door. Stepping into the muggy evening, she released the breath she'd been holding as the door closed behind her. Ralph had joined the group who was now staring at Sarah like zombies. Robbie's mouth dropped and Isaac let out a whistle.

"You look fabulous," Eli said, breaking the tension.

The others nodded enthusiastically.

"Anyone ever tell you that you look great in a past era?" Harry asked.

"I've never dressed in a past era, so no," Sarah chuckled, her body beginning to relax at their compliments.

Harry offered his arm which Sarah gladly took. Everyone

started talking about how authentic she looked and how she was going to have a great time. And they were correct.

The event was more fun than she could have imagined. Not knowing anyone seemed to alleviate some of her timidity. It didn't matter if she made a fool of herself, she'd never see these people again after she finished this job. And so, she gave the performance of a lifetime. The gent portraying the reverend preached about the sin of alcohol and its negative impact on the townsfolk. When he called for the jugs of whisky to be destroyed, Sarah stepped forward. Several cracked pottery jugs from the local potter sat upon a table next to the reverend. At his command, she dropped the first one with a crash and proceeded to the next as the reverend continued his message of abstinence.

When the last jug was shattered across the pavement, Eli stepped forward and pointed a gun at the reverend, shouting something about the destruction of whiskey being alcohol abuse. A puff of smoke accompanied a pop from the fake pistol as Eli squeezed the trigger. Robbie, Isaac, Harry, and Ralph joined the fray. A series of whoops and gasps emanated from the crowd as the scene progressed into a makeshift wild west show. Men took positions in various business doorways while others flagrantly shot back and forth in the street. Several Model A's, on loan from the local car club, were parked in strategic places, adding shelter for the gun-wielding actors. It was like watching a movie, except you could smell the smoke and your ears rang from the gunfire.

When the dust settled and the smoke dissipated, a dozen men lay in the street as Eli announced the end of the program and the start of the cookout. Applause erupted and the crowd made their way toward smoking grills and tables of homemade potato salad, coleslaw, macaroni and cheese, and various types of cookies.

"You were great!" Eli declared, approaching Sarah.

"It was fun," she responded, surprised at having enjoyed it as much as she had.

"Miss Holden, I had no idea you had a hidden talent for acting," a familiar voice sounded behind her.

Whirling around, Sarah stared at Garrett. Her stomach flopped and a flush colored her cheeks. How embarrassing. Unable to speak, she stared at his dazzling smile and strong jawline. He wore jeans and a pale blue button-down shirt with the sleeves rolled to his elbows, showing off his sculpted forearms. Harry stepped up beside her and placed his arm around her shoulders.

"She did a great job, didn't she?" Harry said.

"Thanks," Sarah mumbled.

"Indeed," Garrett replied, flashing a smile.

"I'm going to get a burger. You guys comin'?" Harry asked.

"Not just yet," Garrett responded.

"Guess I'll have to eat yours, slowpoke," Harry said before jaunting across the grassy area to the crowded food tables.

"Where's Dallas?" Sarah asked, finding her voice.

"Gunfire makes him a bit nervous so I leave him at home for these events."

"Makes sense," she replied, looking around.

"Are you hungry?"

"Actually, I could use a bite."

Garrett and Sarah strode across the square, the fringe of her dress swaying with each step. Children squealed and gamboled about while their parents chatted on the benches nearby. The smell of burgers made Sarah's stomach growl. She and Garrett fixed their plates and sat at one of the fold-out tables where they talked about their day.

"Want to come back to the house for a drink?" Garrett asked after they'd thrown away their paper goods. "I picked up a bottle of bourbon today on my way home."

Sarah desperately wanted to go, but the memory of the

portrait and the mysterious Billie Holiday music at his house rankled her nerves. He seemed like such a great guy and yet an internal battle between attraction and suspicion raged within her. What were his intentions buying a bottle of bourbon and inviting her to his house? And how did he know he'd even run into her tonight? Was he attracted to her or was he trying to get close in order to sway her opinion should he be viewed as a suspect? He had to know she and Danni were close. After all, everyone else in town seemed to know about them.

Although Sarah had always been levelheaded in everything she did, relationships were unchartered territory for her. And this one was leading her down a reckless path. A lifetime of haunted dreams had precluded any serious dating. Now she was faced with an attractive man who believed in ghosts and was possibly a suspect in a murder. *Ugh*, she thought, *how had her life become so complicated in only a few days?*

It would be rude to turn him down after he'd gone to the trouble of buying her favorite libation. As for the strange occurrences and discoveries at his house that morning, she reminded herself Garrett would be there, leaving little chance for anything supernatural to cause a ruckus. Sarah had been cautious her entire life. Just once she wanted to have some fun. *What the heck*, she thought, suppressing the skirmish raging in her mind. It was only a drink and she could handle that. Maybe while she was there, she could learn more about the identity of the woman in the portrait over the library mantel.

"Sarah?" he said, breaking her concentration. "It's a drink, not a marriage proposal."

"Sorry, my mind wondered for a moment," she replied, feeling her cheeks warm. "A drink sounds good."

Eli, Robbie, Ralph, and Isaac walked over.

"Hey guys," Sarah called out.

"We were just getting ready to head back to the house for a drink," Garrett said. "Care to join us? I stopped at the liquor

store after work today. Figured you guys would want to come by
after the event."

Sarah's heart sank and her shoulders sagged. She was an
idiot! He was only being friendly, nothing more. Now she was
stuck with no way to extricate herself from the situation. At
least she could feign exhaustion and go home early.

"I'm going to change clothes," she announced.

"We'll wait here for you," Robbie said.

Sarah sprinted across the road and into the library. The
setting sun cast wavering shadows across shelves of books,
lending an eerie feel to the place. Add the fact it was the scene
of a murder, and the creep factor ratcheted up several notches.
Determined to get in and out of there without any ghostly
sightings, Sarah rushed to the back room, grabbed her clothes,
and changed as fast as she could, careful not to look around.
She replaced the dress on the hanger and returned to the bathroom, doing a quick check of her hair and overall appearance.

Hurrying down a wall of bookshelves, she turned the
corner and nearly knocked Harry over.

"I'm so sorry," she gasped. "I wasn't paying attention."

Harry furrowed his brow. "You, OK? You look like you've
seen a ghost."

"Don't be silly," she said with a wave of her hand. "I didn't
want to keep you guys waiting."

"I've got to lock up everything before I head to Garrett's."

"See you there," she replied.

She stepped into the warm night air to the buzz of streetlamps and the crooning of crickets and cicadas. The moon was
making its first appearance in the darkening sky as she joined
the others.

They started down the slope of the side road that led to
Garrett's house. Dallas was waiting in the front window,
wagging his tail, and barking as they approached. As soon as
Garrett opened the door, Dallas darted out and ran straight for

Sarah. Propping his front paws on her leg, he let out a spirited *yap.*

"Hey Dallas," she said, reaching down to pet his head.

Obviously content with the greeting, he turned and ran back into the house. Everyone gathered in the front parlor where a small table-turned-bar was decked out with glasses of varying shapes along with bottles of bourbon, vodka, and rum. A small cooler sat beside it filled with ice and beer. Garrett immediately slid into bartender mode, fixing drinks for all of his guests. He handed Sarah her bourbon and grabbed a beer for himself. Picking up a small remote, he pointed it at the open armoire, and started the music. Les Brown's *Paper Moon* hailed from the stereo as everyone stood around talking about the reenactment.

"Danni would've enjoyed this evening," Sarah said, sipping her drink. "I'm sorry she missed it."

"It wouldn't hurt for her to take a little break from the case and have some fun," Garrett said, shrugging one shoulder.

The hair on the back of Sarah's neck bristled. Why would he want Danni to take time away from the case? Everyone knew Dusty's life was on the line. Surely, someone who proclaimed to be his friend would want his attorney to work day and night to free him.

"What did you think of the shootout?" Robbie asked, pulling Sarah from her thoughts.

"It was fun. I loved seeing all the costumes, and the old cars were fabulous."

"We do this twice a year. If you ever want to join us again, we'd love to have you," Eli offered.

"Thanks, maybe I will."

Garrett's eyebrows arched as he took a swig of his beer. "Sounds like Edgefield is growing on you," he said with a half-smile.

"I'm developing a fondness for it. I don't think I've ever known a town with so much character."

"You got that right," Isaac said with a snort. "And that's saying a lot coming from me. I traveled the world as a Marine and never ran across a place with as much scandal and intrigue as this town, not to mention the best people."

"That's the truth!" Robbie added.

The conversation drifted from the evening's events to recollections of past shootouts to what could be done to make the next one better. Two hours later, the guys announced it was time to head out.

After Garrett said goodnight to his friends, he returned to the front parlor.

"I should probably head back to the house," Sarah said, even though she secretly wanted to stay. With the guys around, she hadn't had a chance to ask about the portrait in the library and she desperately wanted to know more about the mysterious woman from her dreams.

"Stay for one more drink?" he asked, his glimmering eyes and the curl of his lips tugging at her heart.

King Porter's *Stomp* floated through the air from the same turntable where Billie Holiday had played earlier that morning. Despite her trepidation, Sarah was determined to discover the old woman's identity before she left.

"Another drink would be nice," she replied, humming along with the recording.

"You seem to like this music," he said.

"Listen to it all the time. I love classic jazz and big band music."

His smile grew as he put the drinks on the coffee table and held out his hand. Sarah tensed. He couldn't possibly be asking her to dance!

"I, um…" she stuttered.

"Don't dance?" he said, raising his eyebrows.

"Not really, no."

"Then let me show you."

Sarah accepted his hand as he gently pulled her to the center of the room and showed her a few steps. She'd always heard a good lead could make a dancer out of anyone, and Garrett proved it. Sarah quickly fell into step.

When the song ended, Sarah smiled.

"Where did you learn to dance like that?" she asked.

"My grandmother taught me. Every summer I was forced to listen to big band music and jazz. Eventually, I fell in love with it. Now I go to Fitzgerald's when I want a good dose of the era."

"What's that?"

"A jazz club. Everyone wears period attire from the 20s to the 40s."

"I can't believe you're into this stuff," Sarah said, shaking her head.

"Why?"

"I don't know, maybe because you're a Marine and hunt ghosts."

"Ghost hunters and Marines tend to love history," he replied as *Moonlight Serenade* started playing.

His gaze locked onto Sarah's, making her knees weaken. Without a word, he pulled her into his arms and led her around the room in a silky step-by-step dance that flowed with the sultry sound of the horn. Her heart pounded so hard within her chest she felt certain he could feel it.

The music stopped, enveloping the room in an uncomfortable silence. They stood staring at each other when Dallas let out an ear shattering bark, breaking the spell.

Sarah stepped back, chewing her lower lip as she glanced at the floor while Garrett rubbed the back of his neck. Dallas trotted from the room, seemingly pleased he'd managed to get their attention. He stopped in the hallway and barked again.

"What's wrong with him?" Sarah asked.

"Not sure," Garrett said, furrowing his brow. "Dallas, come here."

The little dog lifted his nose and scurried into the library at the same time something invisible squeezed Sarah's shoulder, sending a shudder through her body. Thankfully, Garrett had already started toward the hall and didn't notice her unease as she rubbed the chill from her arms.

Sarah followed him into the library where the blue-eyed gaze of the woman in the painting cut through her. She turned to see Garrett petting Dallas's stomach as the dog lay on his back with his paws curled in the air.

"Who's the woman in the portrait?"

Garrett rose to his full six-foot stature.

"That's my grandmother, Ola."

Swallowing the golf ball size lump in her throat, she considered his words. The woman in her dreams was Garrett's grandmother. The same dreams where Tara's horrific visage kept saying, *don't trust him*. Tears stung the back of Sarah's eyes as she fought to dam them up. In that instant, she wanted to flee and never look back. Everything about Garrett was ideal from his captivating smile, piercing green eyes, gentle demeanor, and his love of the same things she held dear.

"How long has she been gone?" Sarah asked, wanting to know about Ola's death.

His expression melted as his gaze shifted to the portrait.

"Three years ago. Heart attack. She was stubborn about certain things, specifically her diet. She loved to cook and didn't skimp on the stuff that makes food delicious."

"How old was she?"

"Eighty-nine," he replied softly, staring at the painting.

"Not bad for someone who supposedly ate *too* well," Sarah said.

"Still too short for me," he replied, turning back to Sarah. "But I suppose that's true of anyone we love. We can never have them long enough." Dallas nuzzled Garrett's leg with his nose as if he understood his person's sorrow.

The situation was growing more uncomfortable by the moment. The conflict swirling through Sarah's mind was beginning to make her head ache. Now that she'd identified the woman and garnered some information about her death, she knew she needed to go, yet deep down she wanted to stay. Nevertheless, she'd stayed longer than she'd planned.

"It's getting late and I have an early morning," she said, feeling a twinge of guilt. She didn't have to be up at any specific time but needed an excuse to leave.

"Of course," he said, running his fingers through his hair. "Sorry I didn't ask when you needed to go home."

Sarah followed Garrett from the room. He held the door as Sarah walked out, Dallas toddling beside her.

They walked down the shadowy street to Edgefield Manor chatting about mundane things like the recent heat wave and the upcoming peach festival.

When they reached the front door, Garrett scuffed the porch floor with the toe of his shoe.

"Go with me to Fitzgerald's?" he asked, flashing a sheepish glance at Sarah.

"When?"

"Tomorrow night. They're featuring a new band and I'd love to have a dance partner."

Sarah contemplated his offer, trying to find an excuse to turn him down gently. Things were getting stranger by the moment. One minute she felt certain he was an upstanding guy and the next she was wondering if he'd killed a woman. Add to that the three-hour distance between their residences and his pitiful approach to hunting ghosts, and Sarah was stuck. Her heart said one thing while her mind screamed another.

Apparently, he picked up on her hesitation.

"It's not a date, just a bit of fun for two big band afficionados."

His smile lassoed her heart and squeezed out an acceptance.

"Sounds like fun," she responded. "How should I dress?"

"Call Melinda. She has a closet full of period clothing spanning a hundred years. Pick out anything between the twenties and forties."

"I'll get in touch with her in the morning."

"Pick you up around 8:00 tomorrow night?"

"See you then."

With a nod, he strode down the brick walk with Dallas tottering at his side. Sarah stepped inside and peered through the sidelight window, watching Garrett's silhouette disappear into the night, indecision needling her nerves.

18

S arah climbed the stairs, her legs heavy and her feet aching. It had been a long but enjoyable evening, although her mind was spinning like a cyclone. Danni wasn't home, letting Sarah know she was probably with Brady. Too tired to wait up, she changed into her nightshirt, crawled into bed, and plopped her head against the pillow, leaving the lamp on so Danni wouldn't stumble around in the dark. Her friend was dangerous enough with good footing in the daylight.

Ruminating over the evening's events, Sarah tried to make sense of everything she'd learned. Garrett's grandmother was haunting her dreams but in a calming way, while Tara's gruesome image kept warning her *not to trust him*. Dusty was in prison for murdering his wife whom he claimed to adore. Everyone in town believed him to be innocent except for the DA. All of the evidence pointed to Dusty even though a dullard would've found less obvious ways to dispose of a murder weapon.

Sarah closed her eyes and took a few deep breaths, hoping it would help her relax. If only she could make some connections between the dreams and what she'd learned about Tara,

Garrett, and Harry over the past few days. Her breathing slowed as her muscles loosened and consciousness gave way to slumber.

A GROUP of children frolicked in a sprawling field of daisies bordered by rows of corn and staked tomato plants. Summer heat baked their heads and shoulders as they gamboled about chasing each other. Squeals of delight, and an occasional taunt about someone being too slow, floated across the soft breeze. Sarah recognized the group from the photos she'd perused earlier. Watching the bucolic scene, she smiled when Tara dashed past with Garrett on her heels.

They rounded the end of the corn row when Garrett doubled back and blocked Tara's path. Mischief percolated in his gaze as his lips curled into a smile. Tara planted her hands on her hips and squinted, perspiration beading her brow.

"Don't even think you can beat me, Garrett Duncan! I can outrun you any day of the week!" she challenged before whirling around and racing back toward the towering oak the kids had designated as base. Garrett ran as quickly as his gangly legs would go but his target was much faster. Tara tagged the tree and turned with a triumphant glare.

"Told you! You'll never be fast enough to catch me!" she declared.

Panting, Garrett slumped forward with his hands on his knees. "Go ahead and gloat but one day you'll see what I'm really capable of."

Dusty, Harry, and Brady sidled up to them, their faces flushed with a sparkling sheen of sweat.

"Who's *it*?" Harry asked.

"Garrett, *again*," Tara blurted.

"Slowpoke," Brady said.

"Who you callin' slow," Garrett asked, puffing out his scrawny chest.

"You, sloooow poooke," Brady taunted.

"Care to make a bet?"

"With the slowest kid in school? Sure. What's the wager?" Brady asked, folding his arms across his chest.

"Loser has to walk through Brookfield Cemetery after dark, *alone.*"

A series of 'Oohs' drifted from the lips of the onlookers. Everyone knew Brookfield was haunted and no one dared go in there after dark, especially alone.

"You're on," Brady said, offering his hand which Garrett shook.

"Race you from here to the end of the cornfield and back. First to tag the tree wins," Garrett announced.

Harry stood in front of the two boys who took a runner's stance.

"On the count of three," he exclaimed with his hands in the air. "One, two, three!" Harry yelled, lowering his hands, sending the runners sprinting forward.

Clods of dirt bounced up as the two boys sped to the end of the corn rows before turning back. They were side by side as they headed toward the tree, Brady's face beet red from exertion while Garrett's chest puffed out as he tried to push his body ahead of his opponent.

Sarah felt her lungs tighten and her breath catch as she watched them draw closer to the tree trunk. At the last moment, Brady shot forward, tagging the trunk a split second before his friend. Brady fell to the ground, his chest heaving while Garrett leaned his head against the tree, panting in defeat.

"Looks like you've got a date with the dead," Brady said between gasps.

Garrett looked at his friends as they stared at him incredulously. Squaring his shoulders, he raised his chin. "No problem. I'm not afraid of that place." His words were steady, unlike his wobbling knees.

"We'll see. I say we all wait in the church yard and see how fast Garrett can run when ghosts are chasing him," Brady laughed.

"Care to make this a bit more interesting?" Garrett asked, furrowing his brow.

"How?"

"I'll walk through the cemetery alone and then you do the same. The one who stays the longest, wins."

"What does the loser have to do?" Brady responded, narrowing his eyes.

"Spend the night there."

Brady's expression melted like butter on a hot biscuit. Everyone knew he was skittish when it came to anything supernatural. Harry and Tara exchanged glances before Brady shrugged one shoulder.

"You're on," he said smugly. "I'm faster than you, and definitely braver."

"We'll see about that," Garrett replied with a menacing grin.

The scene shifted to nightfall with an incandescent full moon, its beams shimmering across the walkway leading into Brookfield Cemetery. The five friends stood at the edge of the road, staring at the eerie shadows wavering against the headstones as if the spirits of those buried beneath were watching them.

"Since you're the loser, you have to go first," Brady announced.

"I might not run as fast as you, but I'll stay in there longer than you will," Garrett grinned. "Harry, you got the stopwatch?"

"Yup. I'll start it as soon as you cross the threshold."

Young Garrett stood tall, his head held high, and marched into the darkness.

The air seemed to thicken as Sarah watched intently, her eyes trained on the walkway and any sign of Garrett's return. As she observed, a finger traced the back of her neck as the words *don't trust him* tickled her ear.

Sarah bolted upright in bed, her nightshirt clinging to her back. Her stomach turned. The message she'd heard for days was finally clear. Tara was trying to warn her that Garrett couldn't be trusted.

The clock on the night table read three in the morning. Sarah had only been asleep for a couple of hours. Apparently, Danni had made it home. She was on her side, snoring like a buzz saw. Desperate to share the dreams with her friend, she considered waking her but decided against it. Danni needed to get her sleep if she was going to function at her best.

Garrett's charming smile and dazzling eyes flashed through Sarah's head. She'd been a fool to get hung up on a guy with whom she had no future, not to mention he could be a killer. Aggravated, she rolled over and let sleep lead her away from the turmoil simmering in her heart.

SUNLIGHT DAPPLED the heart pine floors in the main parlor of the farmhouse as breezes drifted through the windows. Dressed in shorts and knit shirts with sneakers and dirty socks, Brady, Tara, Harry, Dusty, and Garrett sat around a Monopoly board, the scent of baking cookies permeating the air. Their eyes grew wider when a high-pitched *ping* echoed from the kitchen, followed by the sound of the oven door opening and closing.

Cookies!

The kids knew better than to race in there before being invited. Brady's mother, Mrs. Anderson, was kind but strict, not allowing anybody in her kitchen unless they belonged there.

"Those cookies sure smell good. Hope your mom doesn't wait too long," Harry said, licking his lips.

"I'm with you Harry," Tara added.

The mantel clock chimed as Mrs. Anderson walked in with a tray of cookies and five sweaty glasses of milk. Brady's mother was a lanky woman with seal brown hair curled at the ends, deep blue eyes, and a smile that revealed perfectly white teeth. She placed the tray on the coffee table and handed out milk glasses.

"Enjoy," Mrs. Anderson said, walking from the room.

Small hands grabbed at the warm, gooey, chocolate chip cookies. The boys shoved them in their mouths, leaving spots of chocolate dotting their hands and cheeks. Instead of partaking in the confectionary feast, young Tara turned toward the mantel clock with its gingerbread trim and spider web design on the lower glass panel.

Suddenly, Tara's image began to shift. Her hair lengthened as her body grew taller, taking on an hourglass shape. All the while, the others continued eating cookies. The clock started chiming relentlessly, growing louder and louder with each dong as an army of spiders scurried from beneath it.

Pointing at the timepiece, Tara muttered the words, *it's time.* When she turned around, dark shadows eclipsed her empty eye sockets, and her skin was a pallid shade of gray. Blood trickled down the side of her head as she pointed toward Sarah. *You're not listening.*

19

S arah stirred, her shoulders stiff and her nightshirt drenched with sweat. Rolling over, she leaned up on one elbow and glanced around the room. Morning peered through the curtains, casting a golden glow across the floor and walls. Danni's bed was already made. Sarah rose in a stretch, longing for a run until the idea of encountering Garrett squashed her enthusiasm. She needed to clear her head, not inundate it with unrequited romantic feelings.

With the previous night's dream lingering in her mind, she changed and made her way downstairs. Danni sat at the kitchen table sipping coffee, dressed in her typical business suit and the stiletto heels that added another three inches to her stature.

"Good morning," Sarah said with a yawn. "Noticed you got home after me last night. Did you have fun?"

"Indeed," she replied with a sly smile, apparently not willing to discuss the subject further. "How'd you sleep? You moaned a few times so I figured you were being haunted."

Sarah sighed. "You could say that."

"What did you dream?" Danni's eyes gleamed as if Sarah

were about to reveal the suspenseful conclusion to a mini-series.

Fixing a cup of tea, she joined her friend at the table.

"I dreamed about Tara, Garrett, Harry, Dusty, and Brady when they were kids. They were playing at a farmhouse."

"Like the one in the photos we found?"

"Exactly," Sarah replied, slouching. "Which means this was probably connected to seeing the photos and not a message from Tara, except..."

"Except what?" Danni practically yelled.

"Right before I woke up, the dream got creepy and bizarre."

"When are your dreams not creepy and bizarre?"

"Good point," Sarah said. "Anyway, all the kids were at the farmhouse and Brady's mother brought them cookies and milk. It seemed like a harmless scene until the clock on the mantel started chiming loudly and Tara transformed into her corpselike self."

Danni grimaced.

"Then she said, *it's time* and *you're not listening*. How could she say such a thing? I'm listening. Maybe if she communicated plainly instead of using cryptic messages, I could figure out what she's trying to disclose." Sarah rubbed her eyes, contemplating everything from the dreams. "Then again, I could be dreaming about the photos we found in the master bedroom."

"Doubtful. Chances are Tara is trying to tell you something. Is it possible you touched an item she may have handled before you went to sleep?" Danni asked.

Sarah straightened up. "I completely forgot to fill you in on everything from last night."

With a sheepish grin, Danni propped her elbows on the kitchen table. "Do tell."

"Nothing like that," Sarah said, rolling her eyes. "I met some guys at the museum yesterday. They invited me to participate in a shootout."

"What?" Danni exclaimed.

"Not a real shootout, a reenactment of one. It was set during prohibition, and I have to admit, it was a lot of fun," Sarah said, wrinkling her nose. "Anyway, I wore clothes that belonged to Tara."

"That's got to be it," Danni declared. "Maybe wearing her clothes changed your perspective and her messages. Now she's able to address you more directly."

"So, last night's dream might have been Tara changing tactics?"

"Sounds like it. What else did you see in the dream?" Danni queried, getting up to refill her mug.

Sarah didn't want to disclose the part about Garrett and his apparent rivalry with Brady. Danni was already suspicious of him, and she didn't want to implicate him further. No doubt, Danni would take Brady's side.

"Sarah, what aren't you telling me?"

It was times like these she hated Danni's uncanny ability to read her thoughts.

"There was another dream where Garrett and Brady were bantering about who was faster. It seems Garrett wasn't a speedy runner and he lost a race against Brady. The loser had to spend time alone in Brookfield Cemetery. Then Garrett issued a second challenge to see who could stay in the cemetery longest."

"After dark?" Danni asked, furrowing her brow.

"Yup. Harry, Dusty, and Tara waited with Brady while Garrett walked around the graveyard by himself without a flashlight. Harry was timing him."

"What happened?"

"Don't know. Something tapped my shoulder and whispered, *don't trust him* and then I woke up."

"Don't trust Harry?"

Sarah shrugged her shoulders. "Hadn't thought about that. Or she could have been referring to Garrett or Brady."

"Can't be Brady if she's trying to lead us to her killer. Remember, he wasn't in town which leaves Harry or Garrett."

"That reminds me, after the shootout, Garrett invited several of us back to his house and you won't believe what I saw!"

"Tara's ghost?"

"No, the old woman."

Danni's eyes grew to the size of half dollars. "You saw her ghost in his house?"

"Not exactly, more like her portrait."

"Garrett has a portrait of the old woman who's been haunting your dreams in his house? Did he say who she was?"

"His grandmother."

Danni gasped, shaking her head. "This is getting stranger by the minute."

"Tell me about it. I can't understand why she'd be in my dreams. I never knew her and she has no connection to Tara that I'm aware of."

Danni checked her watch, swigged the last of her coffee and rinsed the mug.

"I really want to hear more about this but I have to play lawyer today so I won't be available until later. We'll sit down this evening, analyze the dream further, go through the *Dreamist* book again, and figure out why Garrett's grandmother is haunting you," Danni said, squeezing Sarah's shoulder as she walked past.

"Thanks, Danni!" Sarah called after her.

Frustrated with the situation, and the looming deadline to get everything ready for the estate sale, Sarah slumped back in the chair and sipped her tea. This happened every time she handled an estate. She'd get sidetracked and then have to rush to get caught up. Except this time a man's life was on the line.

Then again, it wasn't like Danni was demanding payment for her services up front.

Pulling out her cell phone, Sarah dialed Melinda's number.

"Hello?"

"Hey Melinda, it's Sarah Holden. Could you come by sometime today and let me know if there's anything you don't want included in the sale?"

"I have some time this morning. How about ten o'clock?"

"See you then."

Sarah clicked off the phone and finished her tea. Devoid of any appetite, she decided to peruse the stuff in the master bedroom so she could clean it up before Melinda arrived. Trudging toward the stairs, Sarah stopped when she caught sight of something from the corner of her eye. She stepped back, and gazed at the floor-to-ceiling gilded pier mirror with the marble topped shelf near the base. The mirror was clouded in places but still provided a sparkling reflection of the space.

Moving closer, she studied the silvery glass and pondered all the people who had gazed into this same mirror over the years. A timeless Lowcountry legend told how people's souls could be trapped in a looking glass. This was why some cultures covered mirrors during the mourning period. They believed the soul of the deceased was stuck in the mirror and could call the living to join them in the afterlife. Sarah chuckled at the idea. Whether true or not, it made for great storytelling.

At that moment, the glass began to shift and contort as a misshapen face formed, its pallid lips mouthing the words *he took it with him, he can't be trusted.*

Sarah stumbled backwards, away from the unearthly form, her heart beating against her chest with the force of a battering ram. When she looked back at the mirror, it had returned to a gleaming flat surface. Adrenaline coursed through her veins. She'd had enough of trying to maneuver her dreamist idiosyncrasies. She was going to figure out how to communicate with Tara and get this haunting over with.

Marching up the stairs, Sarah entered her room, snatched the Dreamist book from the night table, and plunked onto the bed. She paged to chapter ten, the one Tara's ghost had indicated, and started reading.

After reading and rereading the riddles several times, Sarah's eyes brimmed with tears of frustration. She wasn't a stupid person, yet she couldn't understand the words on the page.

Calm your heart to squelch the fear,
That hinders the mind and silences voices,
Focus your thoughts on the one who is near,
For in her words lie all of your choices.

Sarah plopped back on the bed and squeezed her eyes shut, helplessness streaming down her cheeks. After a lifetime of dealing with haunted dreams and unexplainable visions, she felt defeated. When she and Danni discovered her odd abilities were actually a hereditary skill, she had a glimmer of hope. But daily activities had distracted her from developing her abilities further. Now she was faced with a haunting that could save a man's life and she couldn't make sense of it. The stress of it all weighted her chest like a fifty-pound sack of potatoes.

She decided to try some relaxation techniques before Melinda arrived. Taking in a deep breath, she held it for a count of five, and released. Sarah repeated the ritual several more times until the tension dissolved from her muscles. Without meaning to, she drifted off into a sea of dreams.

AUTUMN FOLIAGE STAINED in hues of gold, mango, and crimson fluttered as a cool breeze whispered through tree branches. Harry and Tara walked through Brookfield cemetery across a carpet of fallen leaves crunching beneath their steps.

"We fight all the time," she said, Harry by her side with his arm draped around her. "I wish it could be like it was when we were kids."

"We all do," Harry said, giving her shoulder a squeeze. "Everyone has their ups and downs."

"If only we could get past all this financial stuff so we could work on our relationship. As it is, we're in danger of losing the forge and the business. Of course, Dusty isn't aware I know about it. How he's managed to keep the secret for so long is a mystery."

Harry stopped and faced her. "Give it time. No man wants to admit defeat when it comes to providing for his family. Dusty loves you and I know you love him."

Tara scraped the ground with the toe of her shoe. "I do love him but I don't know how much more animosity I can tolerate."

Harry took Tara's hand in his. "Regardless of what happens, I'm always here for you."

Tears crested in Tara's eyes as she pulled Harry into an embrace. Oddly, Sarah could feel the despair racing through Tara's conscience and the uncomfortable feeling that someone was watching the scene. The breeze picked up, sending leaves skittering across gravesites when the sound of a door slamming echoed amongst the tombstones.

Gasping, Sarah sat up, sweat trickling down the small of her back as she tried to get her bearings. The clock read 10:00. She must've dozed off.

"Sarah, are you here?" a voice called from downstairs.

Leaping from the bed, she ran to the bathroom to check her appearance before hurrying down the steps where a petite, fair-haired woman stood in the entryway. Obviously, this was Melinda. Her solemn expression and puffy, red-rimmed eyes showed the emotional turmoil of coping with her son's arrest.

"You must be Melinda," Sarah said, offering her hand. "It's nice to finally meet you in person."

"Nice to meet you too," she replied, shaking Sarah's hand. "Are you alright? I didn't catch you at a bad time, did I? You seem out of breath."

"Not at all," Sarah replied, her cheeks warming. She rarely took naps, especially when she was expecting a client. "I, um, got caught up in something and lost track of the time."

"Thank you for doing this."

"I'm happy to help," she replied, motioning for Melinda to follow. "I've tagged everything on the first and second floors. If there's anything you don't want in the estate sale, just remove the tag. There wasn't much in the bedrooms except furniture and memorabilia. I haven't had a chance to go through the attic or the basement yet."

Melinda waved a manicured hand in the air. "Don't bother. There's nothing but rusted bicycles, old tools, and probably a few rats. Anything of value would be in the living areas of the house."

"That'll help move things along," Sarah said, relieved her work load was reduced.

Melinda took in a deep breath as her eyes scanned the room. "I have so many fond memories in this house. Everything seems to have a story."

"I'm sure it's not easy having to part with so many sentimental things."

"It's worth it if it saves my son," she sniffled.

"Dusty is in good hands, I can assure you," Sarah said, patting Melinda's shoulder.

"Danni seems quite driven," she replied.

"She's an excellent attorney."

"I'm thankful my nephew was able to get her."

"They've been friends for a long time. She was happy to help Brady out."

"Indeed," Melinda replied, arching her eyebrows. "Maybe something will spark between them. Brady's been burying himself in work since his wife left. And now with Tara gone and Dusty being accused of her murder, well, he's had a few rough years. He deserves some happiness."

"Hopefully, Dusty will be acquitted, and everyone can move on with their lives," Sarah responded, secretly relishing the idea that Brady and Danni seemed to be building a relationship. "If you have any questions, I'll be in the kitchen working."

With a nod, Melinda started looking through the items, her expression grim. It couldn't be easy getting rid of family heirlooms, especially under the circumstances.

While Melinda perused items, Sarah sat at the kitchen table updating her ledger. An hour later, Melinda stepped into the kitchen where Sarah sipped a cup of tea.

"I see you're a tea drinker," she said with a smile. "My grandmother drank tea her entire life, never touched a cup of coffee."

"Sounds like someone I would enjoy meeting," Sarah replied.

"You would've liked her. My brother, Brady's father, was the opposite. Had to have strong black coffee. He and Brady's mother, Janey, would fix a pot of coffee in the afternoon and drink the entire thing," she sighed, sorrow shadowing her features.

"They're both gone?" Sarah queried.

"Yes. Parker died of pneumonia after a botched surgery and Janey from a heart attack. To make things worse, Brady's brother, Thomas, disappeared when he was a teenager and has never been found. As I said, poor Brady has been through so much. He and Dusty are more like brothers than cousins. He needs Dusty to be acquitted. Brady is helping with the attorney fees, thank goodness, but it still won't cover all of the court expenses."

"I feel confident we'll make enough from the estate sale to take care of the rest."

"That would be a true blessing. I know this sounds crazy, but sometimes I wonder if our family is cursed. I've lost my brother, sister-in-law, nephew, mother, father, and now my daughter-in-law. I will *not* lose my son too," she said, wiping a tear from her flushed cheek.

"Sorry there's nothing more we can do to help."

"You've done so much already. Go ahead with the estate sale and use all of the items you've tagged. There's nothing here more important than my son's freedom," she said, squaring her jaw and lifting her chin.

"I'll make arrangements for two weeks from Saturday. That should give locals and people from the surrounding areas time to make plans to attend."

"Let me know what I can do to help," Melinda offered, flashing a quick smile.

"I've got everything under control, but thanks."

Melinda stepped through the door, leaving Sarah to ponder her current situation. How was she supposed to solve this mystery *and* run the estate sale? Regardless, Sarah was determined to make the most money possible to help Dusty. From everything she'd heard from those who called him friend, Dusty was a kind and gracious man who adored his wife. Somehow, time constraints or not, she was going to help prove it.

SARAH MADE arrangements for ads to run in the local papers, radio, and one spot on the morning news broadcast. Hopefully, word would get out and bring in a horde of customers.

The Batman theme blared from Sarah's pocket. "Hey Danni, what's up?"

"Wanna get lunch? I've got some news."

"Sure. Where do you want to go?"

"Somewhere outside of town," Danni replied.

"You'll have to pick me up."

"Be there in thirty minutes."

Sarah slipped the phone back in her pocket and resumed her work. Danni was obviously upset about something; she could hear it in her voice. Furthermore, she didn't have any spare time to be going out of town for lunch. Sarah's gut stirred. Maybe Danni found evidence against Garrett and wanted to break the news in person.

Tears stung her eyes. What if he was guilty? Sarah chased the idea from her mind. There was no use getting upset. It's not like they were engaged. Heck, they'd only had a few dances in his living room, a ghost hunting rendezvous with two other guys, and a few drinks at his place. He'd never made a move, although there were a couple of moments when she thought he might.

Why was her life always so complicated? Never had a boyfriend, never went to prom, never even had sleepovers when she was younger, until Danni.

Even though Sarah was content with her life and her career, sometimes she just wanted a normal existence, free of specters, haunted dreams, and loneliness. She had her best friend but since meeting Garrett, she wanted more. Sarah sighed. Figures she'd find an almost perfect match and he'd turn out to be a homicidal maniac.

The sound of Danni's Mercedes barreling down the drive caught Sarah's attention. She swiped the tears from her eyes, rinsed her cup in the sink, and hurried outside, locking the door behind her. She hopped in the car and they sped off to the sound of gravel flinging from the car tires.

"What's going on?" Sarah asked.

"Found some pretty detrimental stuff this morning," Danni replied, staring straight ahead, her jaw set.

"Like what?"

"Insurance policies."

Sarah closed her eyes and took in a deep breath, relief massaging the tension from her shoulders. Surely, this didn't involve Garrett.

"I'm assuming the insurance was for Dusty and Tara?"

Danni nodded. "Dusty took out policies for both of them three months ago."

"Sounds like a normal thing. It's not like he only took out a policy on her, he got one for himself too."

"Except his wife was murdered and he's on the hook for it," Danni groaned.

"Why would he take out an insurance policy on himself if he was planning to kill his wife?" Sarah asked.

"Maybe he thought it would take away the appearance of guilt."

"I suppose," she said. Sarah shifted in the seat when her latest dream popped into her head. Harry and Tara had been discussing Dusty's financial difficulties and the strain it was putting on the marriage. Was this what Tara was trying to tell her? Dusty killed her for the insurance money and inadvertently got caught?

"What is it? You've got that weird look you get when you've had one of your dreams."

Sarah exhaled. "I fell asleep earlier while waiting for Melinda to come over and had a dream. Harry and Tara were talking about Dusty's financial problems. Tara said it was causing trouble in their relationship."

Danni blew out a breath. "This isn't good."

"I know how it looks, but there's still a possibility he didn't do it," she said, her heart sinking as the words left her lips. She hated adding to her friend's stress levels.

Danni pulled into the parking lot of a Mexican restaurant, switched off the ignition, and looked at Sarah. "I've got a host of possible suspects, the ghost of the murder victim haunting my best friend's dreams, a mountain of evidence suggesting my client's guilt, and a judge who keeps moving the court dates forward. Regardless of who actually killed her, I'm running out of time to prove Dusty's innocence."

"Somehow we'll figure it out," Sarah said with as much confidence as she could muster, even though she had no clue how they would accomplish it.

AFTER LUNCH, Danni dropped Sarah off at the house and went back to her make-shift office at the courthouse. Glancing around the entryway, Sarah pondered how things had gone off track so quickly. She felt like a derailed train as her heart battled with her head. So far, the evidence pointed to Dusty who continued to make comments blaming himself for Tara's death, which wasn't helping his case. Harry's 'I can't live without her so no one else can have her' scenario was also a possibility, albeit weakly based.

Then there was Garrett with his charismatic personality and adorable dog. Despite his affable demeanor and handsome face, he'd been trained to kill people and could have gained access to the library the night Tara was killed. Sarah's heart sank. How could she be attracted to a man whose own grand-mother, or the ghost of her, was siding with a murder victim in her dreams? Sarah could come up with dozens of reasons why Garrett wasn't involved, except for Ola's consistent presence in her nightly visions. That alone suggested Garrett as a suspect. Thankfully, his motive was sketchy at best.

This was supposed to be a simple job. Clear out a house, have an estate sale, then go home. Now, Sarah was trying to help clear a man's name by searching for evidence that could implicate a guy she liked. And if Garrett was guilty, what would happen to Dallas if he went to prison? Would he let her take his dog after she'd helped gather evidence against him? Would he even know she'd been involved?

Sarah felt a sudden urge to get out of the house, despite all of the work to be done. She grabbed her backpack and rushed through the door. Maybe she could find out more about Garrett's grandmother at the genealogical library and put this mystery to rest.

20

A rush of cool air greeted Sarah as she walked through the glass doors of the library. Her skin was sticky with sweat and her breathing labored. She'd walked hard and fast to town, driven by the turmoil raging within her mind. Never would she have believed her dreamist skills would lead her to this conundrum.

Oddly, the library was empty except for Harry who had his back to Sarah while he spoke on the phone. Approaching his desk, Sarah was shocked to hear the anger edging his words.

"I don't care! We can't let anyone know about this!" he hissed. "This could influence the outcome of the trial! It stays buried; do you understand? I'm not taking the fall for this!"

Feeling awkward, Sarah cleared her throat. Harry spun around, a smile dissolving the shock from his face as his tone of voice softened.

"I'll get back to you about those books tomorrow. Thanks for your help."

He hung up the phone and stepped from behind the desk.

"What can I do for you, Sarah?"

Taking in a deep breath to steady her nerves, Sarah forced a smile. "I've done everything I can at the house for now and thought I'd come back to do a little more research on the family. Buyers like to know the provenance of the pieces they purchase. Sometimes it helps bring a bit more money."

"Of course," he said, wiping the beads of sweat forming on his brow. "Do you need my help?"

"Not yet," Sarah replied, noticing Harry's uncharacteristically rigid stature. He'd always been laid back, but now his left eye twitched and he jiggled his leg. Whatever he'd been discussing on the phone was obviously quite serious for this sudden change in demeanor.

Sarah stepped into the adjacent room and sat at the computer. Taking out her notepad, she jotted down everything she'd heard Harry say. It was probably nothing more than a misunderstanding on her part. She didn't want to believe Harry could possibly be involved in anything untoward. Sarah's fingers clicked across the computer keys when a thought popped into her head. On several occasions, Tara's ghost had said *don't trust him* during the childhood scenes.

Sitting straighter, she ruminated on what Harry had said. *It would influence the outcome of the trial; I'm not taking the fall for this.* What was he trying to hide? Could he actually be involved with Tara's death? The murder had happened in the library and he knew the building well.

Sarah's lunch swirled in her stomach. She liked Harry and couldn't conceive he'd do anything nefarious. Then again, if Harry and Dusty were guilty why was Garrett's grandmother showing up in her dreams? A wave of relief splashed over her. Perhaps Ola was trying to let Sarah know Garrett *wasn't* involved. Burying her face in her hands, Sarah exhaled. The idea of Garrett's innocence was the most positive thing to happen in the last twenty-four hours.

Nevertheless, she needed to figure it out as quickly as possible. If only she knew what Ola was trying to impart, maybe she could make sense of what Tara was trying to say. Her thoughts bounced around like a ping-pong ball. At that moment, she remembered Garrett would be picking her up at 8:00 to go to Fitzgerald's.

Pulling out her cell phone, she dialed Melinda's number. Voice mail. It was almost three o'clock and she needed to find something to wear when she remembered the flapper outfit from the shootout. She walked to Harry's desk where he sat typing away on his desktop.

"Harry, would it be possible for me to borrow the flapper outfit again?"

"Sure, I don't think anyone will need it anytime soon."

"Thanks. I really appreciate it."

"Where are you going to wear it?" he asked.

"Fitzgerald's."

A sly grin creased his eyes. "Garrett is taking you dancing?"

"Um, yeah. I love big band music and he offered to take me." Sarah could feel the heat rising up her neck and coloring her cheeks.

"You'll have a good time. Garrett's a regular there," he said with a wink.

Anxious to get away from the awkward exchange, Sarah gave a quick smile and hurried to the back room to get the costume. She walked past the row of metal file cabinets and grabbed the dress and hat when a chill rankled her body. Sarah gulped down the fear bobbing in her throat when a voice whispered in her ear, *don't trust him.* Turning slowly, Sarah's eyes rested on Tara's bloodied head, her finger pointing at the back wall before she dissipated into nothingness.

Sarah started to run from the space when she noticed several framed sepia photos in the area Tara had indicated. Gathering her courage, she padded over to get a closer look. Although in sepia, many of the pictures depicted scenes from recent reenactments. There was one of Tara in a black crepe mourning gown from the 1860s with Dusty at her side in his civil war uniform. They appeared to be standing in Brookfield Cemetery. The one beside it showed Dusty, Harry, Eli, Robbie, and Isaac dressed in 19th century attire in front of a horse drawn carriage in the square. The next photo showed a lanky woman standing by a debonair gentleman in front of the library. Another man with a broad smile and thinning hair held a plaque. A group of kids stood by her, many of whom Sarah recognized as Harry, Dusty, Brady, and Tara. The caption read, "Mayor awards Mrs. Parker Anderson the illustrious Edgefield Preservation Award for her efforts in preserving the town's history and helping to fund the genealogical library."

She studied the photo for a few moments, a smile curling her lips. Garrett wasn't in it. But Harry and Dusty were. Obviously, Tara was implicating one of them. The question was, which one?

BY THE TIME Sarah made it back to the house, she was soaked with sweat. Her heart was lighter at the idea Garrett wasn't involved, although the reason for his grandmother's appearance in her dreams remained a mystery. Nonetheless, she'd have to think about that later. She hopped into the shower and washed away the grime and perspiration from walking all over town in the heat of summer. Relieved Garrett might not be involved in the murder, she was suddenly looking forward to the evening.

Sarah plodded down the stairs, fixed a cup of tea, and worked on the inventory for the estate sale. As eventide grew near, she closed her ledger and decided to eat something. She'd need energy for dancing. Slathering peanut butter on a bagel, Sarah sat at the table and went over her list of things to do for the sale. After eating, she headed upstairs to change.

Slipping on the fringed dress, she flipped the end of her

ponytail under and secured it with a ribbon so her hair looked like a bob. Sarah remembered an old jewelry box with costume pieces in the master bedroom closet and decided to look for accessories to jazz up her outfit.

While hunting through the closet, Sarah noticed a shoebox on the top shelf she'd overlooked when doing the inventory days earlier. Sliding the box from the ledge, she opened the lid, and peered inside. Dozens of letters filled the space, along with a few mementos. She sat on the floor, cradled the box in her lap, and started flipping through the correspondence when the Batman theme jolted her from her mission.

"Hey Danni," Sarah said, placing the box on the floor.

"What are you doing?"

"Looking for some things to embellish my outfit for tonight."

"Uh-huh," she said teasingly. "I know you want to look perfect for Mr. Studly."

"We're only going because we both love big band music."

"Keep telling yourself that," Danni replied.

"He's the one who said it!" Sarah declared, her heart twisting at the fact he made it clear it wasn't a date and they were only going as friends. "Why are you calling?"

"Just wanted to let you know it's going to be a late night for me too. Might have found another lead. Brady is going with me to check it out."

"Sounds cozy," Sarah said.

"This is work, nothing else."

"I thought he had to keep his distance for appearances sake."

"He's not helping in that respect. He's playing chauffeur."

"Got it. Do you really think this is promising?"

"Won't know until I talk to the guy."

"With any luck, it will be enough to get the charges dropped against Dusty," Sarah said.

"Let's hope. Have fun tonight."

"Plan on it," Sarah replied, hanging up the phone.

She put the lid back on the box of letters and replaced it on the shelf. She'd have to look at them later. Right now, she needed to find some vintage jewelry to accessorize her outfit. Sarah located the old jewelry case and scavenged through its contents. She chose a long strand of faux pearls with matching earrings. Draping the pearls around her neck, she clipped on the earrings, and glanced in the full-length mirror. A smile crinkled her eyes. The pearls added the extra pizzaz she was going for. She looked as if she'd stepped straight out of the *Great Gadsby*. In all her days, she'd never felt so...attractive. With a tickle in her stomach, she went back to her room, put on some make-up, and started downstairs when a thud echoed from behind.

Turning, she raced back up the steps, checking each room until she got to the master bedroom. The box of letters had fallen from the shelf, its contents sprawled across the floor. She stared at the box, pondering how it had fallen when the words, *he took it*, tickled her ear.

She gulped down the fear rising in her throat and stuffed the contents back in the box when the sound of truck tires crunching down the drive caught her attention. Hurriedly, Sarah placed the box on the shelf and ran to the end of the hall. Peering out the window, she exhaled, relief washing over her at the sight of Garrett's pickup truck. The letters would have to wait. Her breath caught when she noticed the translucent image of his grandmother sitting in the passenger seat. Ola's eyes locked onto Sarah's, releasing the pent-up air in her lungs. Sarah smiled. Something about the old woman gave her a sense of peace.

Hurrying down the stairs, she flipped on a lamp in the entryway and stepped onto the porch. She locked the door behind her and sauntered down the walkway, her heels clicking with each step as the fringe of her dress swayed with her hips.

Garrett emerged from the truck and walked around to the passenger side to open the door. He was dressed in a tan suit with a waistcoat, bow tie, and fedora hat. Sarah's knees wobbled ever so slightly at the sight of him. He was gorgeous in regular clothes, but period attire brought out the debonair side of him.

"You look amazing," he said, the right side of his mouth curling into a half-grin.

"You look pretty good yourself," she replied with a smile.

Electricity ricocheted up her arm when his hand rested on her elbow as he helped her into the truck and closed the door. The scent of fresh soap and lavender filled the truck as he slid in and turned the key. With his strong profile, the fedora hat cocked ever so slightly on his head, and the way his broad shoulders filled out the suit, it was getting harder and harder for her to suppress her attraction to him.

"You really do look stunning," he said as they drove down the main drag past the genealogical library, the bakery, and the courthouse.

"Thanks," she replied, watching the scenery as they drove through town.

Sarah shivered when they passed Brookfield Cemetery. It felt as if all the souls had gathered to wave as they drove by.

"You OK?" Garrett asked.

"Just caught a chill," Sara replied.

"I can turn the temp up on the air if you want." He reached for the control knob when Sarah stopped him.

"No need, I'm fine now."

With a grin, he gave her a sideways glance. "Brookfield has that effect on people."

If he only knew. Brookfield was nothing compared to the haunted dreams she'd suffered throughout her life.

"I'm sure it does for people who are afraid of ghosts," she responded, still staring out the window.

"And you've shown yourself to be fearless when confronting the undead," he added.

"There's really nothing to fear. Ghosts are entities, not physical forms so their ability to do harm is a moot point." Sarah was well aware of the physical capabilities of the spiritual world after she'd suffered marks on her neck following a dream about strangulation. However, she wanted to seem indifferent about spirits in an effort to thwart any suspicions on Garrett's part. If anyone could detect a person with ghost communicating skills it would probably be him, and she wasn't about to take that risk.

Garrett pulled onto a gravel drive filled with cars and a glowing red neon sign that read, *Fitzgerald's*. The building appeared to be an old gas station from the 50s with large plate glass windows spanning the front covered by a large overhang. To the far side of the building was an old man with his hair slicked back, wearing a dark green button-down shirt, blue pants, and boots. He held a wrench in one hand and waved with the other as they parked.

Sarah returned the wave when his face began to vacillate until he faded from sight. With a gulp, Sarah fiddled with the strand of pearls as Garrett opened the truck door.

"Who were you waving at?" he asked, looking at the front of the building, now devoid of any living souls.

"I was swatting at a mosquito," she said, hoping he'd believe her.

"They're pretty bad around here," he replied, helping her from the truck.

Sarah exhaled; thankful he'd accepted her excuse.

"You should see the ones in Beaufort. They could carry a person off," she chuckled.

"That's why they call them the unofficial state bird of South Carolina."

Sarah looped her hand through Garrett's extended arm as they walked side-by-side into the club. The inside was completely different from the exterior. It looked like one of the juke joints seen in period movies. The lighting was low with a band in the far corner dressed in 1940s fashion. The bar was filled with ladies donning everything from flapper dresses to form-fitted attire with A-line skirts. Several men wore pinstriped suits. A few of the gents had removed their jackets, revealing vests over long-sleeved cotton shirts. Some had fedora style hats while others sported flat caps. The scene was reminiscent of a Clark Gable movie and the atmosphere was saturated with old-fashioned comradery as people smiled and laughed.

Garett led Sarah to a small round table at the back.

"Want something to drink?" he asked.

"Bourbon, neat," she replied. Being this close to him and knowing they'd soon be dancing had her nerves on overdrive.

He strode over to the bar and placed their order. From this angle Sarah noted the strong lines of his physique and confident stature. She'd observed the same thing in the Marines she saw around town with their self-assured demeanor. He walked back and handed her a highball glass, the amber liquid shimmering in the dim light.

"To an evening in the past," he said, holding up his glass.

"To a more genteel era," she replied, clinking her glass against his.

Sarah's eyes fixed on his handsome face as she took a sip. The band started playing Cab Calloway's *Jumpin' Jive*. Several couples made their way onto the dance floor and started swinging and swiveling to the music.

Sarah's chest constricted. What had she gotten herself into? She couldn't dance like these folks. She'd only danced with

Garrett in the privacy of his home but nothing as complicated as this. When she looked up, Garrett was standing in front of her with his hand outstretched. She took in a deep breath. As if reading her mind, Garrett smiled and spoke calmly.

"You'll be fine. Follow my lead, I won't let you down."

She placed her hand in his and followed him to the dance floor amidst the gyrating couples. Her first few steps were clumsy. She focused on Garrett and within minutes she was stepping and tapping her feet as if she'd done this all her life. By the time the song ended, Sarah was panting as perspiration formed below her cloche hat.

"Need a break or do you want to try another?" Garrett asked, his eyes sparkling.

The band started playing one of Sarah's favorites, *Doin' the Jive*.

"Let's do another one," she replied, feeling a bit more confident in Garrett's hands.

They listened as the lead singer belted out the words, guiding everyone through the motions for the dance. Sarah had heard the song all her life but the meaning behind the verses had never registered until now. When the music stopped, she swiped at her forehead.

"Maybe we should take a quick break," Garrett offered.

"Sounds good," she replied, following him across the room.

They sat at the table and sipped their drinks.

"I still don't understand how you got so good at these dances."

"My grandmother taught me when I'd stay with her in the summer. She loved to dance and said every gentleman needed to be a strong lead," he laughed. "She claimed dancing was the key to romance."

Warmth surged across Sarah's chest and up to her cheeks.

"Sounds like a wise woman," she said, hoping to defer any further comments about romance.

Staring off, he took in a deep breath. "She was the best of people."

The band slowed to *Moonlight Serenade* and Sarah's heart melted. She loved this song.

"Care to join me?" Garrett asked, rising from his seat to escort her to the dance floor.

With a nod, she fell into step as he guided her to and fro, his gaze fixed on hers. Her skin buzzed at his touch and she felt her heart dissolving beneath his stare. It was as if this was where she was always meant to be, in the past with a man who didn't grimace at the word ghost or shy away from being polite. If she let her imagination flow, she could almost believe she was back in the 1930s. Because of her haunted visions and newfound dreamist abilities, Sarah had dismissed any ideas of a relationship. But now, swaying back and forth in Garrett's arms, she was beginning to think it possible. Never in her life would she have believed she'd find a guy like this. Good looking, kind, loved big band music, and had the cutest, ghost sensing dog in the world. The entire scenario seemed too good to be true.

Garrett's gaze intensified as the music faded from Sarah's consciousness. He tilted his head, his lips only inches from hers when a high-pitched voice called out, shattering the moment.

"Garrett!"

He stepped back and turned toward a tall, slender woman wearing a bright red dress with a flared skirt cinched at the waist by a wide navy-blue belt. A felt hat perched at an angle on her platinum blond hair and her full lips were accentuated by candy apple red lipstick that matched the nails on her elegantly thin fingers. She was stunning.

"Hey Franny," Garrett declared, scooping her into a hug.

When he released the woman, she looked at Sarah with a sly smile. Her stomach flopped. Deep down she wanted to believe a relationship with Garrett was possible, until this woman's flirtations doused the fire of her hopes. His reaction didn't help, suggesting a mutual affection.

"Don't worry, Honey, he and I are just good friends. Not that I wouldn't want more than that, but you know how he is. Won't commit to nobody." Her carriage and manner of speaking sounded like something out of the time period. She tilted her head at the right time and shifted her shapely legs in an alluring manner as she interacted with him.

"Don't be silly Franny," he replied. Despite the dimly lit room, Sarah could have sworn she noticed his cheeks color. "I'm here for the dancing, not a matchmaking session."

Sarah's heart dropped. When would she get it through her head, he was only being friendly? Then again, she was certain something was about to happen between them before *tootsie* showed up. More confused than ever, Sarah did her best to appear unfazed by the interaction. Life was difficult enough with ghosts occupying her dreams without her heart being kicked around like a soccer ball. Was Garrett interested or not? Did it really matter? Just because he believed in and hunted ghosts didn't mean he'd accept a woman who was haunted by them on a daily basis. She was leaving in a couple of weeks anyway.

"Garrett, one day you're going to meet a woman and never look back. I only hope it'll be me," Franny blew a kiss and sauntered off, her hips swinging seductively.

The lead singer of the band started singing *Bei Mir Bist Du Schön*. The irony of the lyrics cut through Sarah's soul like a serrated knife through butter. The soloist crooned about a lonesome woman who'd met a man and how her heart had lightened and her world was made new. It was bad enough being this close to Garrett, but the song seemed to broadcast the very feelings she was fighting to suppress.

Garrett gave a sheepish grin and offered his arm to Sarah, escorting her back to the table where they sat down. Fidgeting with her fingers, Sarah had a sudden urge to go back to the manor. If this is what heartache felt like, she didn't want any part of it. My goodness, only hours before, she'd suspected he might have killed a woman.

As if sensing her distress, Garrett offered an apology. "Sorry about Franny, she can be a bit brazen at times."

"Sounds like she has a serious crush on you," Sarah replied.

"Franny flirts with everyone. She's harmless, but gets into her role as a 1940s lady and plays it to the limit."

"She's pretty good."

"That she is. Her dancing is remarkable."

Sarah squirmed in her seat. Her confidence was taking a turn down the railway of self-doubt aboard the Chattanooga Choo-Choo.

Finishing their drinks, they danced to a few more tunes before calling it a night. They stepped into the steamy summer air, arm in arm, Sarah's feelings wavering between disappointment and exhilaration from an evening of big band music and swing dancing. Sadly, the almost kiss that didn't happen and Franny's flamboyant appearance weighted Sarah's heart like an anvil.

They rode in silence until the lamplight of Edgefield's town square glimmered against the night sky. Instead of driving straight to the Manor, Garrett turned down his drive.

"Nightcap?" he asked.

"Sure," she replied, wondering why she was agreeing to this. Hadn't she learned anything? Closing her eyes, she admonished herself for being so foolish when another thought nudged its way into her mind. Who cares if he's interested? Enjoy yourself and worry about the fallout later. It was only a drink and gave her an opportunity to garner information that could help Danni with her case, especially if Harry was involved.

As they entered the house, Dallas greeted them at the front

door with several accusatory barks before dashing into the yard. Garrett left the front door open and moments later Dallas returned. He scurried over to Sarah for a little petting and then toddled into the living room where he curled up on his bed.

Sarah followed Garrett into the room and sat on the sofa while he fixed them each a drink. He handed her the glass and she took a long sip, her insides doing somersaults. She was tired, conflicted, and on her third drink for the night. Swallowing hard, she watched Garrett remove his hat and coat and roll up his sleeves before taking a seat in the leather chair across from her. He was one good-looking man. If the dictionary used pictures for definitions, Garrett's photo would be listed under handsome.

Her chest tightened. She felt like a teenager on her first date, or what she thought it would feel like since she'd never dated anyone. *What if he decided to ask about her past?* She'd shared a little with him; however, the haunted dreams and self-isolation in the pre-Danni years was a topic she desperately wanted to avoid. Gathering her courage, she started the conversation in order to thwart any questions from him.

"Tell me more about your summers here in Edgefield when you were a kid."

He smiled, sending a tiny little pulse through her chest.

"Summers here were amazing. I loved spending time with my grandmother. She was the best person I knew." He took another drink. "Of course, growing up with Dusty, Tara, Harry, and Brady led to all sorts of mischief."

"It's nice you were able to reconnect as adults," Sarah said. "Any rivalries that lingered?"

"That's an odd question," he said, raising one eyebrow.

Idiot, she thought to herself. Her query was based on her dreams and she didn't need to reveal things she'd learned while sleeping.

"You guys seem close but I noticed an undercurrent of

competition between you and Harry at times." She took another sip of her drink. Surely, that would pacify him and explain why she'd asked the question.

"I suppose there's always a little competitiveness between guys. Didn't realize it was so obvious to others," he said with a chuckle.

"Guess I've always been a bit sensitive to my surroundings. Sometimes I pick up on things other people don't. It's a good skill to have when haggling for antiques."

"Very perceptive of you. Harry is probably my best friend. He and I often place bets as to who can capture a ghost on film first. Otherwise, there's never been much of a rivalry between me and the guys."

"What about Tara?" Sarah blurted out, mentally scolding herself for her brazenness. The liquor was beginning to loosen her ability to monitor her words.

Garrett seemed unfazed by the question as he swirled the amber liquid in his glass and grinned. "Tara used to beat me at racing, if that's what you're asking, but then again everyone did. I was kind of a slow runner as a kid."

"And now?"

"Boot camp changes you. I worked hard not to be the slowest guy in the platoon. I'm still not going to win any sprints, but I can hold my own in long distance runs. What about you? You run for speed or pleasure?"

"Pleasure. There's something liberating about rising with the sun and running through town as it wakes." Sarah shifted in her seat, pulling her legs under her. "I love the sound of bird-song as breezes filter in from the marshes and the mist that covers the ground before the sun dissolves it."

"You love where you live," he said.

"I do love my home. It's an incredibly special place."

"I feel the same way about Edgefield. Even though I grew up in Walterboro, my closest friends were here. I guess that's

why all this stuff with Dusty is taking its toll on me. I can't stand
the idea he's being charged or could be convicted of killing
Tara." He downed the rest of his drink and walked to the bar to
pour another. Looking at Sarah, he held up the bottle but she
shook her head. She couldn't afford to cloud her mind any
further.

"Tell me more about your grandmother," Sarah said. If she
couldn't gather any meaningful information for Danni, maybe
she could figure out why Garrett's grandmother was haunting
her dreams.

"Grams," he said, his eyes sparkling. "She was my world
growing up. My mom was great but I think I reminded her too
much of my father. She always seemed distant. Don't get me
wrong, she wasn't cruel just...emotionally absent. Everyone
loved Grandma Ola."

Sarah rested her head against the back of the sofa as she
listened to him speak about his grandmother.

"Like I told you before, she's the one who got me interested
in big band and jazz music. And her oatmeal cookies were the
best in the world. Brady used to try to sneak an extra one when
no one was looking."

"What did Ola do for a living?"

"Librarian. Thus, the extensive library in such a small
house."

"I love libraries. I have one in my house as well."

Garrett stood up and placed his drink on the coffee table.
"Come with me, I want to show you something."

Sarah followed him across the hall to the library with
Dallas on her heels. Garrett flipped on the overhead chandelier, its prisms sparkling across the floor in shards of colored
light. Opening a closet door, he rummaged through its
contents while Sarah perused the neatly organized tomes
crowding the shelves when one in particular caught her eye.
Gently, she reached up and pulled the small brown book

from its cocoon and gasped at the simple gold lettering, *Dreamist.*

"What's the matter?" he asked, immediately by her side.

"Nothing," she muttered, feeling lightheaded.

"Are you sure? You don't look well."

Shaking her head, Sarah bit her lower lip. What was he doing with a copy of the *Dreamist* book? Her eyes locked on his.

"Where did you get this?" she finally asked, her voice a mere whisper.

"Grams was always picking up old books at yard sales and flea markets," he said, shrugging one shoulder.

"This is a rare edition not commonly found at flea markets or yard sales," she replied, emphasizing the last few words. For the first time since she'd met him, Garrett seemed flustered. His face colored and he rubbed the back of his neck. Finally, he exhaled and looked at the ceiling.

"You know about the book?"

"Perhaps," Sarah said, pursing her lips.

"What do you know about it?"

"You tell me what you know and maybe I'll reciprocate."

Garrett ran his tongue across his teeth before answering. "It belonged to my grandmother."

A chill bumped across Sarah's skin. "Your grandmother was a dreamist?"

He nodded. "Which means you must be one or you wouldn't know about it."

Sarah closed her eyes. "I am." Without even thinking, she'd just revealed her deepest secret to a man she hardly knew.

Garrett's affable expression washed over her, cleansing away her unease. No shock or aversion. It was as if she'd just told him something mundane like she preferred red wine over white.

"You said your grandmother told you about her dreamist abilities?"

"She did."

His words reverberated through Sarah's chest. "How much did she tell you?"

"Everything. I used to help her with some of the things in the book."

"You understand it?" Sarah asked, the pitch of her voice rising.

"Of course. Grams taught me everything there was to know about it."

Sarah's knees wavered. Garrett understood the book. Finally, there was someone who could help her. Placing the book on the shelf, she sank onto the wing chair by the bookcase.

"Are you sure you're alright?" Garrett said.

"What about Tara?" Sarah asked, remembering she'd also been a dreamist.

His eyes narrowed. "What do you mean?"

Chewing her lower lip, Sarah contemplated how much to reveal. "How *well* did you know her?"

Garrett squared his shoulders and took in a deep breath.

"I found a copy of the book in her desk drawer," Sarah said. "Did you know about her abilities?"

Garrett exhaled. "I was helping her enhance her skills."

"You can do that?" Sarah exclaimed.

"Like I said, Grams taught me a lot about it. Even though males can't inherit the ability, my grandmother wanted to make sure I could help my daughters, if I ever had any, should they receive the gift."

Some gift, she thought. She'd have preferred an aptitude in music or art. Seeing and communicating with the dead didn't seem like an asset to her.

"Danni and I have been struggling with this since I learned about it a year ago."

"Danni knows?" he asked, his eyebrows arched.

"I needed help and she's my best friend. Not to mention, I stink at riddles and that blasted book is nothing but a senseless tangle of words."

"Ha, that's the truth. Fortunately, my grandmother was a whiz with brain teasers." Rubbing his chin, Garrett stood quietly for a few moments. "Has Tara contacted you?"

"Several times but I can't make sense of what she's trying to tell me."

Garrett grabbed Sarah's arm. "This is incredible. Has she said who killed her?"

Hesitating, Sarah tried to reconcile the conflict raging within her. This was the first person she'd ever met who understood her unusual skills. How much should she reveal? While Garrett seemed amenable to the dreamist abilities in his grandmother's life, could he accept another woman who possessed the skills?

Exhaling, Sarah admonished herself. This was not the time to second-guess the situation. Now was the time to share what she knew instead of burying it. "She keeps saying *don't trust him* or *he took it*. Does that mean anything to you?

Shaking his head, Garrett blew out a breath. "Not at all. Obviously, she's trying to lead you to the guilty party. We need to figure out who that is before Dusty gets railroaded for her death."

"Unless Dusty is the conductor of the train."

"No way. I've known them both since I was a kid. Dusty would never hurt Tara."

"If he is innocent then someone else committed this heinous crime. Are you prepared to accept the identity of the guilty person, even if it's someone you know?" Sarah asked.

"Absolutely. Whoever did this deserves to rot."

Sarah rubbed her ankle which was beginning to ache from all the dancing in heels. The mantel clock chimed twelve.

"Looks like you've had enough time on those stilts. I'll drive you home. We can discuss this in more detail tomorrow," he said, grabbing his keys as he headed for the door. Dallas hurried out in front of them.

Relieved, she followed him to his truck and slid onto the leather seat beside him. Dallas hopped into the cab, perching his front paws on the arm rest between them.

"Thanks for not freaking out about my being a dreamist," she muttered.

A smile lifted his sculpted cheeks. "Thanks for telling me. I think we'll make a great team, and with Tara's help possibly clear Dusty of these ridiculous charges."

They drove the short distance to Edgefield Manor where he escorted her to the front porch and smiled. "See you tomorrow."

"See you then," she replied and scooted into the house. One thing was certain, regardless of the hour, she'd have to share all of this with Danni, who was going to freak out when she heard the news.

21

S arah bolted up the stairs and into the bedroom where Danni was sound asleep. The night table lamp glowed in the darkened room as summer breezes ferried the sound of chirping crickets through wispy curtains. Not wanting to scare Danni too badly, Sarah crept over to her friend and gently nudged her shoulder. Danni snorted and rolled over. Sarah tried again with similar results. Blasted, Danni was a heavy sleeper.

This time, she shoved her hard, stirring a mutter but still she slept. Exasperated, Sarah shook her friend.

"Get up Danni!" she exclaimed.

Danni shot upright, mumbling something about getting to court on time. When she looked in Sarah's direction, a scowl scrunched her face.

"Why are you waking me from a perfectly good sleep?" she grumbled, rubbing her eyes.

"Because I have news," Sarah replied with hands resting on her hips.

The declaration smacked Danni out of her stupor, her eyes widening as she swung her feet over the edge of the bed.

"What kind of news? Did Tara reveal the killer?"

"Not yet. This is a complicated story and I think you're going to need a drink."

Danni planted her feet on the floor, stretched, and padded past Sarah for the door.

"Come on," she said. "If I'm going to be awakened in the dead of night with the offer of a drink, I'm not going to waste any time." She exited the room and plodded down the stairs. Sarah followed, shaking her head and smiling. Danni might be a grumpy riser, but the offer of a drink always pacified the beast within.

Sarah walked to the bar, poured Danni a scotch and handed it to her.

"You're not having one?" she asked.

"I've had plenty."

"But you said *we* were going to have a drink."

"No, I said you were going to need one."

Danni plunked onto the settee, the scotch sloshing in the glass, and took a sip.

"What's so important that I need a middle of the night libation?" Danni asked, her voice scratchy.

Sarah took a seat across from her and smiled.

"I found someone who knows all about dreamists," she replied with a sly grin.

Blinking several times, Danni leaned forward, her brows furrowing. "Say that again."

"I found someone who not only understands the dreamist book but can help us with it."

"Who?"

"Garrett," Sarah replied.

"What?" Danni declared, nearly spilling her drink.

"His grandmother, the one in my dreams, was a dreamist. I found the book at his house earlier and confronted him about it."

"You were at his house? I thought you went to some old-timer's club."

"We went to his place afterwards."

Danni raised one eyebrow and straightened in her seat. "Oh really? Do tell."

With a sigh, Sarah lowered her head. "Nothing happened, well except for discovering he knows all about this dreamist stuff."

Slumping back against the settee, Danni took a long sip. "Bummer."

"Will you stop blathering about romance and listen? We have someone to guide us now."

"Wait a minute. I thought dreamists could only be female," Danni said, tilting her head.

"Like I said, his grandmother was the dreamist. Apparently, she was concerned he might have daughters someday and wanted to make sure he knew how to help them in case they inherited the abilities."

"So, he knows about you?"

"Yeah, it kinda slipped out when I found the book."

"This is huge progress for you. You just confided your darkest secret to a gorgeous guy who also happens to believe in ghosts and knows about dreamists. I'd say you just found your perfect match." A Cheshire cat grin spread across Danni's face.

"I'm not looking for a match or anything else. He lives here and I live in Beaufort. I'm not going to do the long-distance relationship thing. Anyway, I really think he sees me as a friend and nothing more."

"Uh-huh," she said, downing the rest of her drink and placing the empty glass on the bar. "I still have to consider him as a suspect until I have evidence otherwise."

"I'm almost certain he's *not* the killer," Sarah said confidently. "If he were, I believe his grandmother would have let me know."

"My head is reeling," Danni said, rubbing her forehead. "While I appreciate you waking me up to share this, I'm too groggy to process all of it. I'm going back to bed. Tomorrow we'll get together with Garrett and see if he can help us interpret what Tara is trying to tell you in your dreams and hopefully clear Dusty."

"Sounds good to me," Sarah yawned.

Exhaustion assaulted her, making her arms and legs feel like sacks of flour. Her back ached and her eyes were dry. If she was going to help Danni solve this case, she needed to be sharp. Following Danni upstairs, Sarah switched off lights as she went.

Once in the room, Danni flopped onto the bed with a groan. "Goodnight," she mumbled, closing her eyes.

"G'night," Sarah replied, going to the bathroom to change.

After washing her face and hanging up the flapper dress, she climbed into bed and turned off the lamp. Her mind danced around the evening's discoveries from the flirtatious woman at the club to learning about Garrett's family connection to a dreamist. Maybe now that she knew about Ola, and had handled her copy of the Dreamist book, her dreams would make more sense. Fortunately, all she had to do was close her eyes and let fatigue lead her to the dance floor of her subconscious where ghostly secrets dwelled.

OLA STOOD in her library with a broad smile.

"So glad to finally get the chance to speak with you," she said, taking Sarah's hands into hers. Wrinkles and deep blue veins made her hands look like a road map. She motioned Sarah toward two chairs on either side of the mantel.

Sarah tried to speak but her lips wouldn't form the words. Why could Ola talk to her but she couldn't respond? Frustrated, Sarah plopped into the chair. When her eyes met Ola's, she felt a sense of calm saturate her frame.

"Still can't speak on command, I see. Not to worry, it will come. There's much you can do with your gift, but you've got to be open to what the book says. Let my grandson help you. He's a good man, you can trust him. Once you're able to understand certain things, the answers will come more readily."

Sarah grinned. How strange to have the blessing of Garrett's deceased grandmother. Now she knew she could trust him and that he wasn't a demented killer. Then the scene altered, and Sarah found herself near the door at the end of the corridor in the genealogical library. The sound of fingernails scraping against the door made her blood pulse. Tara's grayish visage appeared as she mouthed something. Sarah tried to run but her legs wouldn't respond. The clawing increased in volume, blocking out any sound coming from Tara's moving lips.

Tara glided closer at an excruciatingly slow pace, intensifying the terror building in Sarah's chest. She tried to scream or wake herself, but nothing happened. When Tara was close enough for Sarah to detect the putrid rot of her flesh, a voice rang out over the cacophony of scratching and mayhem.

"Give her time, she has much to learn."

Sarah recognized Ola's voice. She looked around for the older woman but only saw Tara slowly retreating until Sarah was alone in the library. Silence saturated her body in an icy embrace when something traced the back of Sarah's neck with a scorching heat, causing her to spin around. This time the scream escaped her lips as a decaying corpse stood behind her, decomposing flesh hanging from its skeletal form.

Sarah gulped down air in an effort to fill her lungs but the only thing it accomplished was a gag reflex at the disgusting taste of decay.

When words wouldn't form, she closed her eyes and focused on Ola's image while silently repeating her name. Suddenly, the corpse dissipated, and Sarah was once again alone in the library. Her limbs relaxed and she was able to walk again. Maybe the answer was on the other side of the door. She'd only been past it once when a legion of hands had grabbed at her.

Somehow knowing she could summon Ola was a comfort. A sense of pride straightened her stature. She'd learned something on her own. The question was, would she remember it in her next dreamscape? Standing in front of the basement door, Sarah felt strongly there were answers on the other side. She grasped the brass knob and turned, the hinges squealing as she pulled the door open. A cold breath exhaled from beyond as she stepped onto the first stair. Her skin prickled and her hair stood on end as she descended to the basement.

"Ola?" she muttered, hoping the older woman would guide her.

Nothing but silent darkness.

A sense of unease skidded across her skin. Turning, Sarah headed back up the stairs when fingernails dug into the flesh of her arm, wrenching a yelp from her dry lips. She yanked her arm free and continued to climb the staircase when another hand grasped her hair, nearly pulling her backwards. She slapped the hand away and bolted up the stairs when a pair of hands wrapped around her ankle, tipping her forward. As she started to fall, she reached for the banister when the door slammed shut, shrouding her in blackness. More and more fingers scratched and clawed at her legs and back as she struggled to escape. Her breath came in labored puffs as she repeated Ola's name again and again, but she didn't appear.

At that moment, the door creaked open, a hand grabbed her wrist, and tugged her into the corridor. The floor shook as the door slammed shut behind her. Releasing the breath she'd been holding, Sarah scanned the space for her rescuer but nobody was there.

He's a monster, echoed through her mind, making her head ache.

"Who?" she managed to utter.

Don't trust him.

"Just tell me who you're talking about!" Sarah yelled into the empty space, shocked she was able to form the words. How had she done that?

Tara's gruesome image appeared before her, shaking her head when another hand gripped Sarah's shoulder.

"Sarah, are you OK?" Danni asked, leaning over her.

"What?" she gasped, glancing around the room at Edgefield Manor.

"You were screaming in your sleep," Danni replied.

Blowing a breath across her lips, Sarah cupped her hands over her eyes.

"I've got to figure this out," she moaned. "The dreams are getting worse, and the ghosts are becoming violent."

Danni turned on the lamp and sat on the edge of Sarah's bed.

"Wasn't Ola there to help?" Danni asked.

"That doesn't seem to stop the others from getting physical."

"Do you think we should call Garrett?"

"Goodness, no!" Sarah exclaimed, sitting up, her body still trembling.

"Do you want to talk about it?"

"Not really. I did learn something though," she said, her voice hoarse.

"What's that?"

"I can summon Ola in my mind. She helped me out a couple of times and then she disappeared. I'm not sure what I did to sever the connection, but I ended up in a situation I don't care to repeat again."

"I know you don't feel like talking about it right now but maybe we should try to figure this out while it's still fresh in your memory."

Burying her face in her hands, Sarah exhaled. "You're right."

"Tell me what happened first," Danni said.

Sarah relayed everything, including Ola's declaration to trust Garrett, right up to Tara's dreadful appearance at the end of the dream.

"The strangest thing was being able to speak towards the end. I don't know how I did it."

Danni stared off for a few moments before speaking.

"I don't know what to tell you except we need Garrett's help. If he's as good with this stuff as he claims to be, then we need him to explain it to us. Having his grandmother's endorsement doesn't hurt."

"I know you're right. Still, it feels strange to share something so...personal with a man I hardly know."

Danni snorted. "Please, you've been eyeing him since we arrived, not to mention all of the 'it wasn't a date' dates you've had. Think of this as an icebreaker."

"Seriously?" Sarah said, shock scrunching her features. "This is a secret I never planned on sharing. I've never even told my parents! And I only shared it with you last year."

"So, you're slow," Danni said, shrugging her shoulders. "You've just had the most amazing and unlikely situation plopped in your lap. Don't tell me you aren't going to take advantage of it."

With a sigh, Sarah leaned back against the white iron headboard. "I suppose it would be nice to understand all of this without having to wait years for us to decipher that wretched book."

"Now you're thinking."

Sarah's phone buzzed, causing them both to jump.

"Who the heck is calling at this hour?" Danni asked.

Sarah glanced at the clock which read 4:07 a.m., sending a

wave of fear racing through her body. Hopefully, her parents were OK.

"Hello?"

"Hey Sarah," Garrett's voice boomed over the phone. "Sorry if I woke you."

"Don't worry about it, we were already up." Sarah looked at Danni and mouthed *Garrett* to which Danni responded with a goofy smile and a waggle of her brows.

Sarah rolled her eyes.

"Is everything alright?" Sarah asked.

"I know this is going to sound crazy, but I couldn't sleep and sometimes I can sense my Grams. I had an overpowering urge to check on you."

Gulping, Sarah tried to process what he was saying. He might not be a dreamist but his connection to his grandmother was obviously strong enough for her to prompt him to call.

"Actually, I had a pretty weird dream. It got a bit physical."

"I'm coming over," he said and hung up the phone.

Sarah clicked the red button and rested the phone on the bed.

"He's on his way over."

"Oh really? Whatever for?"

"Stop it," Sarah said, giving her friend a shove. "He said his grandmother prompted him to call."

"Finally, we're getting some help on this. Obviously, Ola knows you're stubborn and decided to take matters into her own hands." Danni stood up and headed for the door.

"Where are you going?"

"To start some coffee. Get dressed in something that shows off that cute little figure of yours. No need to traipse around in a night shirt, although..."

"Stop right there," Sarah said, holding up her hand. "I'll get changed but there will be NO matchmaking, understood?"

"Ha! Ola's doing a fine job on her own without my help."

Danni scurried out the door before Sarah could retort. Just what she needed, dating help from the dead.

AFTER CHANGING her clothes and pulling her hair into a clip, Sarah padded down the stairs where Danni and Garrett were sipping coffee at the kitchen table. Dallas rushed to Sarah's side as soon as she entered, balancing on his haunches, and pawing the air with his front feet.

Leaning over, she scratched behind his ears and started for the kettle when she noticed a cup of tea steeping on the table.

"Thanks Danni," she said, sitting down and bobbing the tea bag in the steaming water.

"Danni filled me in on your dreams," Garrett said. His voice was gentle and the compassion radiating from his stare melted her heart, making her feel more comfortable about discussing the situation with him.

Sarah noticed he'd brought his grandmother's copy of the *Dreamist* book.

"I have Tara's copy upstairs. Should I get it?" Sarah asked.

"Let's look through this one first," he replied. "Since Grams has been in your dreams and nudging me into this, we need to understand her role. Then we can move on to Tara's."

Danni cocked her head. "Each book is different?"

"Yes. Each family line has an underlying ability with some individual differences."

Danni and Sarah exchanged glances.

"Which chapter explains that?" Sarah asked.

"It's intertwined throughout but Chapter Ten covers it in more depth."

"What?" they declared in unison.

"Have you read that chapter?" he asked.

"We did, but it didn't make any sense," Danni replied.

"Did you read your chapter ten or Tara's?"

"Tara's," Sarah said. "I left my book at home."

"Never travel anywhere without it. It's a guide to help you understand your specific skillset in relation to your dreamist abilities."

"I don't understand," Sarah said, shaking her head.

"Each dreamist shares certain skills but they also have abilities unique to their family line."

"Such as?" Danni asked.

"Grams was a librarian. She used books as a guide to understand what the ghosts were trying to communicate to her. For Tara, it was the genealogical paperwork."

"How can the book predict what your career would be if it was printed a century before?" Sarah asked.

"You're looking at it too literally. Dreamists tend to choose their professions on a subconscious level based upon their specific skillset."

"I'm an estate dealer, how does that relate to haunted dreams?"

"I'd imagine you garner your information from the items you buy and sell," he replied.

Sarah sat back in the chair mulling over what he'd said when Danni spoke up.

"Like when you handle something that belonged to the deceased, you're able to connect with them in your dreams," Danni offered.

"Exactly," Garrett said with a smile.

"So, you're saying my innate dreamist skills led me to work with antiques and estates."

"Sounds like it, if that's what helped you solve previous hauntings."

"I've only solved one, so far," Sarah replied sheepishly.

"Tell me about it."

Garrett leaned forward, resting his elbows on the table as Sarah shared everything that happened with Nora at Monroe

Manse.

"That's it," he said. "Your special abilities are tied to handling old pieces from the past."

"But I've also witnessed ghosts in broad daylight before. How do you explain that?"

"Grams said dreamists are sensitive to all spectral activity. Sometimes the undead appear, usually when your mind isn't occupied."

"That explains the train conductor I saw on the way here," Sarah said with a shiver. It had been an unsettling sight.

Danni grabbed the coffee pot and refilled her mug and Garrett's.

"What do we do now?" Danni asked.

"We figure out what Tara is trying to tell you," Garrett responded, taking a sip of his coffee.

"Especially if she reveals the killer," Danni added.

"Agreed," Garrett replied. "There's no way Dusty did this."

"What if it is Dusty?" Sarah asked.

"I've known him most of my life. He's not capable of something like this, especially with Tara."

"What if it's another friend? Would you be able to accept that?" Sarah queried.

Garrett straightened in his chair. "She's already revealed someone, hasn't she?"

"Actually, there were two of you," Sarah said.

"What do you mean two of *you*?"

"On several occasions, she implicated you, or so I thought."

Garrett plunked the mug on the table, causing coffee to slosh over the sides. "That's outrageous. I had nothing to do with this."

Sarah reached across the table and rested her hand on his. "I know that now, but at the time I was confused. Keep in mind, I'm new at this."

Nodding his head, he blew out a breath. "Explain what

made you believe I was a candidate for this crime, and we'll go from there."

"Tara keeps saying things like, *don't trust him* or *he took it*, generally after I'd been around you or dreamed about you. Tonight, Ola corrected that notion."

"That's good to know. Who's the other suspect?" Garrett asked.

Sarah glanced over at Danni who nodded.

"Harry."

"Absolutely not!" Garrett declared. "He wouldn't lay a hand on her."

"Are you sure, because he keeps showing up in my dreamscapes, not to mention he had a crush on her at one point."

"Having a crush doesn't make a person a murderer. We all had a crush on Tara at one time or another."

"The only people she's revealed in my dreams are you, Dusty, and Harry. Now that I think of it, I overheard a strange conversation Harry was having on the phone when I went to the library yesterday."

"What did he say?" Danni asked.

"Something about the outcome of the trial and not taking the fall for it. He really seemed agitated. When he realized I was there, he hung up and his demeanor changed like a chameleon."

"That doesn't prove anything," Garrett said vehemently.

"I'm sorry to upset you but that's what I heard."

"I'm not upset with you, it's the situation," he said, running his hand through his hair. "I know for a fact none of us would hurt her."

"Then help me prove it," Sarah said.

22

G arrett drew in a long breath and rubbed his forehead. "I need details of what Tara has shown you so far."

"Follow me," she said, heading for the stairs. Danni, Garrett, and Dallas followed as she climbed the steps and walked to the back bedroom where the photo albums were housed. She lifted the red leather one from the box and opened it to the black and white childhood photos of Garrett and his friends at the farmhouse.

"These are some of the scenes in my dreams. Tara's ghost keeps saying *don't trust him* and *he took it.* Do those statements mean anything to you?"

Shaking his head, Garrett stared at the pictures. "Not at all. We were tight, like the Little Rascals, except we didn't have a dog and we welcomed Tara into the group."

"Why do you think she keeps leading me back to the farmhouse and your childhood friends?"

"It's a mystery to me," he replied. "How did your previous haunting transpire?"

"Nora had lived in the house and was murdered there. She

showed me snippets of her life until it formed a picture of what happened. It took a couple of weeks."

A smile creased Garrett's eyes. "The murder took place in the house where you were staying?"

"Uh-huh."

"That's it! You get a better connection with the ghost when you're in the place where the death occurred," Garrett said.

"Are you suggesting I spend the night at the genealogical library?" Sarah asked, shock wrinkling her forehead.

"I'm sure Harry would let you."

"Except Harry might be a suspect," Danni said.

"I know you guys want to believe that, but I'm telling you he would never harm Tara."

Sarah and Danni exchanged glances. Things were getting complicated. If Harry was the culprit, alerting him to their suspicions could place Sarah in danger.

"Is there any way to gain access to the building after closing without informing Harry?" Sarah asked.

Garrett thought for a moment. "We could try jimmying the basement door."

"Still kind of risky," Danni said.

"What if I handled Tara's research instead? Perhaps I'd be able to connect with her on another level without having to be in the same place she died."

"It's worth a try," Garrett replied. "If it doesn't work, then we can consider sneaking you in after hours."

"Where are you going to find her research materials?" Danni asked.

"I know she didn't work from home," Garrett said. "Tara liked to keep her professional life separate from her private life. A lot of the documents she delt with were personal and she felt the families had a right to their privacy."

"Sounds like we need to pay a visit to the library when it opens," Sarah sighed.

"I thought you were trying to avoid the library," Danni said.

"Daytime hasn't been a problem so far. But I'd really like to forego the after-hours visits, if possible.

"Harry should be there by eight," Garrett said.

"I'll go with you," Danni offered.

"Me too," Garrett added.

"No," Sarah said. "If you both come along, it will look suspicious. We can't afford to let Harry know what we're doing. If he's not involved, then there's no harm done and he never has to know about it. But if he is involved, we need to keep him in the dark."

Garrett rubbed the back of his neck. "Makes sense."

"I'll go to the library and look through Tara's research, if it's still there. If I find anything, I'll text you guys."

Danni and Garrett nodded in agreement.

"Thanks for all your help," Sarah said, standing up.

"Talk to you guys later," he replied. "Come on Dallas, let's go home."

Dallas hopped to his feet and toddled over to Sarah. She ruffled the fur on his head before he followed Garrett out the door. Sarah looked at Danni and sighed.

"Looks like I've got some investigating to do."

"So, it would seem," Danni replied.

Sarah went upstairs and showered. Although she'd hardly slept, she felt rejuvenated. Whether her sudden burst of energy was a result of the shower or the fact she finally had someone who could explain the dreamist stuff, remained a mystery. Nevertheless, she was happy to learn more about her so-called gift and hopefully move on to a more normal existence. Of course, having Garrett's help was an added bonus, especially now that he was no longer a suspect.

Sarah took in a deep breath and smiled as she entered the kitchen. Danni was on her second pot of coffee as she sat in front of her laptop.

"Sure you don't want me to come with you?" Danni offered. "It could be dangerous if Harry is the killer."

"What do you think he's going to do? Knock me over the head in front of everybody?" Sarah huffed. "I'll be fine."

"Still think I should go with you."

"No way. He'd be suspicious if you came along. So far, he believes I'm researching Dusty's lineage to provide provenance for the items in the estate sale. If you showed up, he'd know we were investigating something related to Tara's death."

"Promise you'll text if you find anything," Danni said.

"I promise," Sarah replied, grabbing her backpack from the chair.

"Where are you going? It's only seven and the library doesn't open for another hour."

Sarah smiled. "Bakery. Their cinnamon rolls are calling."

"I'm comin' with you!" Danni declared, jumping up.

"Don't you have work to do?"

"Technically, this is related to the case," Danni replied.

"Cinnamon rolls are part of the case?"

"It's fuel so I can be at my best, and it allows me to escort one of my investigators safely to her destination." Danni said, lifting her chin.

"That's stretching it a bit," Sarah muttered.

"Give me five minutes," Danni declared, darting from the room to change.

A few minutes later, Danni hurried down the stairs in a pair of sneakers, denim shorts, and a t-shirt. Her hair was piled on top of her head with a black clip, and her only make-up was some foundation and eyeliner.

Sarah shook her head. "The things you'll do for a pastry."

"It's not just a pastry. It's a divinely created piece of heaven on earth with a mountain of icing on top."

Chuckling, Sarah stepped into the sticky morning haze with Danni close behind. The scent of roses and honeysuckle perfumed the air. Danni walked to her car as Sarah started down the drive.

"Where are you going?" Danni called out.

"To town," she replied with hands on her hips. "What are you doing?"

"Driving. Don't think for a minute I'm going to walk to town in this sauna."

Sarah's head dropped to her chest. There was no arguing with Danni when it came to her resolve to avoid exercise. She hopped in the car, and they drove through the empty streets to the bakery.

A bell jangled as Sarah and Danni stepped through the door into the delicious bouquet of cinnamon and baking bread. A chill rankled Sarah's frame, causing her to turn around. Nothing. She blew out a breath, relieved nothing otherworldly was behind her. Thankfully, Danni was too focused on the baked goods to notice Sarah's discomfort.

After they'd eaten, Danni went back to the house to shower and change into her attorney attire while Sarah made her way across the town square to the library. Harry was hanging the flags on either side of the double glass doors as Sarah approached.

"Good morning, Sarah. How are you this fine day?"

"Very well," she replied. "How are you?"

"Wonderful," he said, holding the door for her.

Sarah took in a deep breath as she walked inside. Glancing around, she half expected to catch a glimpse of Tara, but saw nothing. Somehow, she needed to find Tara's research without raising suspicions in Harry. She decided to investigate Harry's background first and then find a nonchalant way to ask about Tara's research.

Sarah went straight to the computers in the adjoining room and sat down.

"Need help with anything?" Harry asked, suddenly behind her.

"Not yet. I'll let you know if I do." Her skin bristled at his presence, sending a shiver racing down her spine. Now everything Harry did seemed suspect.

"You alright?" he asked.

"Just caught a chill," she responded.

"I can adjust the air if it's too cold in here."

"I'm sure it was coming in from the heat that did it. Thanks anyway."

Harry reshelved a few volumes in the bookcase next to her before returning to the other room. Swallowing the guilt burning in her chest, Sarah started searching the sites Harry had recommended for antique furniture values. Once she was certain he wasn't coming back, she clicked on the search engine and started investigating Harry. Maybe she could find something to dispel her suspicions. She liked Harry and didn't want to believe he was capable of committing a violent crime. Then again, passions of the heart could lead a perfectly calm person to do unspeakable things. Either way, she needed to make sure he didn't catch her looking into his private affairs. There's no way she could explain her actions, or her suspicions, without causing a permanent rift.

AN HOUR LATER, Sarah hadn't found anything of significance. Harry was an ordinary guy who liked to hunt ghosts and go boating in his spare time. Aggravated with the time spent on something yielding no results, Sarah stood in a stretch and logged out of the computer.

She walked to the other side of the building where Harry was immersed behind his computer screen. He jumped when Sarah approached.

"Sorry, didn't mean to startle you," she said.

"I was so engrossed, I didn't hear you walk up," he said, grabbing his chest. "Finished with your research?"

"Actually, I was wondering if you knew where Tara's research was?"

His expression altered and his voice lowered. "Why do you need to see her work?"

"She was doing the genealogical research for the family, right?"

"Yeah."

"Instead of spending all my time hunting for information, I figured it might be easier to look through what she'd already found," Sarah said, pleased with her excuse to peruse Tara's work.

"I guess it'd be alright. I doubt Melinda would mind," he replied. He walked to the old vault and stepped inside. Moments later, he came out with several neatly organized folders and two antique leather-bound journals. "This is everything she left here."

"Would it be OK for me to take these to the house, or do I need to look at them here?"

Harry grimaced as he glanced at the clock on the far wall. "How long do you think it will take?"

"Hard to say. If I'm going to get top dollar for the items at the house, I need as much background information as possible. People will pay substantially more for a piece with provenance." Sarah chewed her lower lip, hoping her explanation appealed to his sensitivity for Dusty's plight. Of course, if Harry was guilty, he might not want her snooping into Tara's research.

"Go ahead and take it. Promise you'll bring it back as soon as possible," he said, his countenance fading to sorrow. "That work meant a lot to her, and I don't want anything to happen to it."

"I understand," Sarah replied with a sympathetic smile.

She hurried out the door and down the street in case Harry

changed his mind. By the time she got to the house, she was winded and dripping with sweat. Plunking onto the kitchen chair, Sarah swiped the perspiration from her forehead. There was a lot of paperwork to peruse so she started the kettle and jaunted upstairs to change into fresh clothes. When she got back downstairs, steam was shooting from the kettle's spout in a high-pitched squeal.

Fixing a cup of tea, she started looking through the documents. Tara's timelines were meticulous. In the first folder was a basic family tree going back three generations, stopping with Melinda's marriage and only child, Dusty. Melinda's brother, Parker Anderson, was already married to Janey and had two sons, Brady and Thomas. Interestingly, there were folders containing the genealogy of Melinda's late husband, Conrad, as well as her sister-in-law, Janey.

Recognizing some of the names and snapshots, Sarah took the files upstairs to the master bedroom to compare with the pictures in the old scrapbooks and photo albums. She pulled several albums from their cardboard tombs and sat on the floor, shuddering when the temperature dropped. Her shoulders tensed and her breath came in short puffs when the floor creaked as if someone was walking toward her.

Icy fingernails clutched her shoulder as the words *he took it with him* tickled her ear. She leapt to her feet and ran for the door. *Stop it*, she thought. Now more than ever she needed to stay calm. Closing her eyes, Sarah inhaled, held for a count of five, and released.

"What did he take?" she whispered, opening her eyes.

A shoebox flew from the closet shelf, the same one she'd looked through days prior, and landed on the floor in front of her. Slowly, Sarah walked over, reached for the box, and opened the lid. Inside were several letters, a dried rose, a faded blue baby's bonnet, and a few black and white photos. A frosty breath tickled her neck. Too nervous to stay up there, Sarah gathered the folders, the box, and several albums, and headed downstairs. As she reached the bottom step, the Batman theme clamored from her pocket, ratcheting her heartrate up to an unnaturally fast pace.

"Hello," she said breathlessly.

"Are you OK?" Danni asked, concern tinting her words.

"I'm fine, only a bit rattled."

"What happened?"

"Not exactly sure. Tara whispered in my ear, *he took it with him*, except this time when I asked what she was referring to, I got an answer."

"You're kidding!" Danni exclaimed. "What did she say?"

"She didn't say anything. Instead, she tossed a shoebox filled with family letters from the closet shelf."

Silence.

"Danni, you still there?"

"Yeah, you just freaked me out," she replied. "Anything notable in the box?"

"Not sure yet. I also have the research Tara was doing for Melinda. I was trying to connect the information to the photo albums when Tara whispered in my ear."

"Sounds interesting. I'm heading your way now. I'll help when I get there, but you have to tell Tara to settle down. I'm still adjusting to this haunted stuff."

Sarah chuckled. "I'll see what I can do."

DANNI AND SARAH rummaged through the contents of the shoebox, organizing the items on the kitchen table in a makeshift timeline. From what they could gather, the letters in the box were between Janey and Parker when they were courting. They found corresponding photos of the young couple with their firstborn, Brady.

"He was a cute baby," Sarah said, gazing at the photo of Mr.

and Mrs. Anderson standing in front of the farmhouse holding a swaddled bundle.

"Too bad he outgrew it," Danni snorted, looking at another picture.

"He's a nice guy, and not bad looking either," Sarah said.

"I didn't say he wasn't handsome, I was speaking of his quirky and troublesome nature," Danni chuckled.

"No doubt you aided in that troublesome nature."

"That's beside the point," Danni said, looking at the photo. "He really was a cute kid."

Nostalgia sailed across Danni's eyes as she flipped through the withering scrapbook pages.

"We should invite him over," Sarah suggested. "He may be able to shed some light on the relevance of this stuff in relation to Tara's research."

"He's back in Columbia. Remember, his paralegal walked so he's having to do her job as well as his."

"I'm sorry he's going through all this. I know he wants to be here to help."

"It's driving him mad not being able to contribute more to Dusty's defense. He loves him like a brother. With his immediate family gone, Dusty and Melinda are all he has left."

"It's a sad situation," Sarah said.

"Heartbreaking is more like it. I've never seen Brady so distraught. He's lost so many people in his life."

"He has you now," Sarah offered.

Danni shrugged her shoulders. "Even so, his mood is sinking with each passing day. In all the years I've known him, he's always been outgoing and jovial. Between Dusty's trial and trying to keep his practice afloat, I fear his health will suffer. He's having problems breathing, and it's not due to the pollen count."

"Hopefully, we'll find some answers, or at least something to provide reasonable doubt."

The sound of truck tires clattering down the drive caught their attention.

"That must be Garrett. He said he'd come by when he got off work," Sarah said, rushing to the front door. Her pulse quickened as she watched him get out of the truck with Dallas at his side.

When Dallas saw Sarah standing in the doorway, he dashed forward, plopped at her feet, and stared at her with his tongue dangling from the side of his mouth. Instinctively, Sarah reached down and tousled his fur.

"Hey buddy," she said to the dog as Garrett walked up.

Shaking his head, Garrett grinned.

"What?" Sarah asked, cocking her head.

"I think Dallas loves you more than he loves me," he replied sheepishly.

"Nonsense. He just likes the extra attention."

"Humph," Garrett grunted.

"Come on in."

Garrett followed Sarah to the kitchen where Danni sat at the table sorting through old photos and papers.

Dallas plunked down at the base of Sarah's chair, his tail wagging. Careful not to step on his paws, Sarah slipped onto the seat while Garrett sat across the table.

"What have you figured out so far?" he asked.

"Not much I'm afraid. It seems the deeper we dig, the farther we get from any definitive answers," Sarah said with a shiver. Her skin prickled as Dallas jumped up and trotted from the room whining.

"What's wrong buddy?" Garrett called out, following his dog.

Sarah and Danni exchanged glances.

"Don't look at me," Danni said. "I'm not the ghost hunter in this group. I'm with the research department."

"Coward."

"Got that right!"

Shaking her head, Sarah rose from her seat and went to the entryway where Dallas continued his whine fest. Kneeling, she stroked his head and spoke in a soft tone.

"What's going on? Did you see something?"

The fur between his shoulder blades rose as his whining transformed into an aggressive bark.

"He doesn't do this unless there's someone here," Garrett replied in a hushed tone.

No one said a word as Sarah watched intently to see what Dallas would do next. Much to their surprise, his barking faded into a whimper. Sarah scanned the area but saw nothing. Whatever was there, it wasn't making itself visible to her. Then a mist formed at the base of the staircase. Gulping down the apprehension forming in her throat, Sarah stared as the mist swirled and wavered until it formed a foggy silhouette of a woman, specifically Tara.

Dallas whimpered once more and cocked his head.

"Do you see something?" Garrett whispered.

Sarah nodded. "It's Tara."

Dallas groaned and laid down on the floor, his head resting on his front paws.

"Is she saying anything?" he asked.

"Not yet."

Sarah started to speak when the area behind Tara wavered, and two silhouettes began to form. Her breath caught as she strained to see what would materialize. Before she could figure it out, a crash emanated from the kitchen.

"What the heck is going on?" Danni hollered, bolting into the room, her eyes wide.

Sarah's shoulders slumped as Tara's hazy figure dissipated along with the others. Apparently, she only showed herself to those with whom she felt comfortable.

Letting out a long sigh, Sarah turned around. "She's gone."

"Who's gone?" Danni asked, her eyes darting around the space.

"Tara was over there. I was getting ready to ask her something when we heard a crash in the kitchen. What happened?"

"I was looking through one of the albums when it flew across the room and slammed into the wall." Danni's hands were trembling.

Glancing at the spot where Tara had been, Sarah felt the hope drain from her body. Was Tara getting ready to reveal something when Danni walked in, or was it just another visitation with a vague statement about not trusting someone? Frustration filtered through Sarah's limbs, making her want to scream.

"Doesn't look like she's coming back," Sarah grumbled. "Might as well get back to it."

"In the kitchen?" Danni exclaimed.

A smile spread across Garrett's face. "Yes, since that's where everything is."

Shaking her head, Danni looked at Sarah. "Don't think so."

"Come on, Danni," Sarah said, gently grasping her friend's elbow. "Dallas will warn you if anything spiritual shows up."

They all returned to the kitchen with Dallas leading the way. Danni and Garrett sat at the table while Sarah walked across the room to gather the album and loose photos. As if sensing her unease, the little dog settled at Danni's feet.

"What do we do now?" Garrett asked.

"Keep searching," Sarah responded, setting the album on the table and taking a seat.

"Eat," Danni added.

Garrett smiled as Dallas let out a few spirited barks. "It is his supper time."

"Any good restaurants that deliver around here?" Danni asked, fidgeting with a loose photo.

"Not this far out. I can pick up something."

"Works for me," she answered.

"Me too," Sarah said. "Any suggestions?"

"Corner Pocket is close and fast."

Danni and Sarah gave him their order and resumed working as Garrett headed out.

"So, another date for you two," Danni chuckled.

"This isn't a date," Sarah retorted, opening another album.

"He's bringing you dinner."

"He's bringing *us* dinner! That doesn't sound like much of a date."

"Aha, then you admit this is a date."

"You're impossible, you know that?" Sarah said, shaking her head.

"But you love me anyway."

With a grin, Sarah rolled her eyes and continued rummaging through the photos and memorabilia.

Danni's phone rang, startling Sarah.

"Hello, Danni Cook. What do you mean? But no one informed me," Danni blurted, her cheeks flushing. "Who made this decision? I don't care...that's not acceptable!" Danni yelled, clicking off the phone and slamming it on the table.

"What's the matter?" Sarah asked.

"They've moved the trial up another week," she responded, massaging her temples.

"Can't you stop it?"

"Apparently not. He said it's the way things are done around here."

"What about taking it to a higher court?"

"Not an option," she moaned. "Brady warned me something like this could happen. I thought he was just poking fun at the small-town judicial system. If I irritate the wrong people, it could hurt the case."

"What are you going to do?"

"Find answers. When Garrett gets back, we need to discuss

how to communicate with Tara and get some applicable information. We're literally running out of time."

BY THE TIME Garrett arrived with the food, Danni was tapping away on her laptop and sipping her second beer after downing her first one. Dallas danced around on his hind legs as Garrett served up burgers and fries. Pulling out a plain burger, Garrett broke it into small pieces, and put it on the floor. With tail wagging, Dallas gobbled it up.

"Everything OK?" Garrett asked, popping open a beer.

"Prosecutor managed to get the trial date moved up, *again*" Danni grumbled.

"You're kidding?" Garrett sat straighter. "Have you called Brady?"

"Got his voice mail. I'm hoping he knows someone who can help."

"Good luck with that. Brady might be a hometown boy, but he chose to practice law elsewhere. Some folks don't look favorably on that."

"This place gets better and better," Danni scoffed.

"Don't give up yet. Brady may still have some connections," Sarah said.

"Let's hope," Danni replied, taking a bite of her burger.

Garrett and Sarah exchanged glances. Now more than ever, she needed his help if they were going to get the answers to clear Dusty's name. Her chest filled with pride. For the first time in her haunted life, she was beginning to embrace her abilities as a gift instead of a curse. If she could help free a man from unfounded accusations, then her skills were worthwhile, no matter how frightening they may seem at times.

Their inability to find anything substantial to clear Dusty shrouded the atmosphere like a wet blanket on a humid day.

When they finished eating, Danni poured a double shot of scotch and slumped into her chair.

"What can I do to help?" Garrett asked.

"Figure out what Tara is trying to tell Sarah," Danni answered, taking a long draw from the glass.

"Have you dreamed anything other than what you've shared?" he asked, his deep green eyes making Sarah's stomach flutter.

"Only Tara saying not to trust him and that he took something," Sarah replied, shrugging her shoulders.

Garrett rubbed his chin when Danni spoke up.

"How did the dreams about Nora differ from the ones with Tara?"

"They were kinda the same, except Nora shared excerpts of her life at the house and the stables."

Danni sat up straight. "This confirms what we were discussing earlier. You have to spend the night at the library building."

"Location plays a major role in your ability to communicate effectively with the spirits. It's one of the aspects Grams was most adamant about," Garrett said.

Sarah shook her head. "How am I supposed to sleep at the library? Especially when Harry might be the killer?"

"Like I said earlier, we may have to be creative with getting you into the building," Garrett replied, his eyes twinkling with mischief.

"You can't possibly be serious about breaking into the place." Sarah responded.

"It can't hurt anything," Danni said with a goofy grin.

"If I'm caught, I could go to jail!" Sarah hollered, shocked at her friend's willingness to sacrifice her freedom to exonerate her client.

"No one will ever know," Garrett responded. "Harry is a creature of habit. He gets there at 7:30 every morning and is generally gone by 5:30 at the latest. If you go in after 8:00 p.m. and leave before 7:00 a.m. he'll never know you were there. Security in that place is nonexistent. I'm sure we can get you in with a screwdriver or a credit card."

Sarah blew a long breath across her lips. "I suppose I could try, but I'm not sure I'll be able to fall asleep."

"What if I come with you?" Danni offered.

"You can't risk getting caught in something illegal. It would hurt Dusty's case."

"Then we won't get caught," Danni replied.

Sarah pursed her lips. "Can't risk it. I'll have to do this on my own."

"I could stay with you," Garrett offered. "Maybe I could help interpret anything you dream."

A sheepish grin crossed Danni's lips, garnering a dirty look from Sarah. As tempting as the offer was, Sarah needed to keep her head clear. Garrett in close proximity would definitely be a distraction.

"I can stay on my own. We can discuss any dreams I have once I get back to the house. I'm not going to implicate anyone else in this scheme."

Danni grasped Sarah's hand. "We'll make sure no one finds out you're there."

"Once we get you settled, I'll park the truck down the block. If you need anything, just text me." Garrett gave her a reassuring smile, melting away some of the dread clutching at her chest.

With a nod, Sarah exhaled. She was about to embark on a radical endeavor to help a man she hardly knew. A wave of adrenaline crashed through her veins. Would she be successful, or would she end up in jail? Regardless, with the help of her best friend and Garrett, she was determined to try.

————

23

S arah dressed in a t-shirt and yoga pants. No sense being any more uncomfortable than she had to be. She ambled down the stairs, where Garrett and Danni waited.

"You ready?" Garrett asked.

"Ready as I'll ever be," she responded.

"Call if you need me," Danni said, embracing her friend.

"I will." Sarah stepped back, grabbed her backpack, and looked at Garrett. "Let's get this over with."

With a nod, he held the door open as Sarah stepped into the sticky atmosphere. The trees were still as death without so much as a quiver of a leaf. Climbing into Garrett's truck, Sarah clicked the seatbelt into place as the engine revved. They drove to town amidst the croaking of bullfrogs and twinkling fireflies. She stared out the window, wondering how she'd gotten herself into this mess.

Garrett shut off the lights as he parked the truck behind the library. He helped Sarah out before rummaging through the back seat for a screwdriver. They walked to the back entrance with Dallas close behind. With a few twists of the screwdriver, Garrett unlocked the door, and held it open for Sarah to enter.

"Isn't there a security system we need to disarm?" Sarah asked, unease scurrying across her skin.

"Nope," he replied.

"Any cameras?"

"Sadly, no. If there had been, Dusty wouldn't be sitting in jail right now."

A flush warmed her cheeks. *Stupid question.*

Dallas bolted past her, wagging his tail with his tongue lolling from his mouth in heavy panting. Even he seemed wired by the idea of ghostly activity. The stale scent of old books welcomed Sarah in a warm embrace. She'd loved the smell of weathered pages and gleaming leather-bound covers since she was a child. Growing up, books were the one thing that helped maintain her sanity when the rest of her world was inundated with spectral visions.

Garrett combed the space with a flashlight as Sarah fell in behind him. Instantly, her chest constricted as she scanned the shadowy basement, remembering the dreamscape where skeletal hands clawed at her. Dallas' little paws clicked across the cement floor and up the stairs where he sniffed the base of the door.

Sarah's nerves were beginning to fray as she followed Dallas and Garrett into the main section of the library. In the dark, the upper floor appeared much like it had in her dreams except Tara's image, with its visionless eyes and sealed lips, wasn't floating towards her. As if sensing her trepidation, Ola's face flashed through her head, instantly soothing her pounding heart.

"Be careful," Garrett said as they maneuvered past tables and chairs. "Sorry about the darkness but we can't risk turning on any lights. I'd have a hard time explaining this to Harry."

"No doubt," Sarah replied with a huff. She really liked

Harry and hoped they'd get the answers needed to eliminate him from the suspect list as well as clear Dusty.

"Where do you want to set up?" Garrett asked.

"This section," she replied, pointing to the table where she'd done some of her research. "I think this is where they found the body."

Garrett swallowed hard, shining the light toward the section just beyond the table. "They found her right over there."

"Then this is probably the best spot. I'll sit at the table and start reading. It won't take long before I fall asleep. I'm beat."

"How are you going to read without light?"

"Good point," she said with a yawn. "Maybe I'll just put my head down on the table and let drowsiness take over. Like I said, I'm pretty tired."

"Do you want Dallas to stay with you?"

Looking down at the little dog, Sarah smiled. "That would be great." Dallas let out a high-spirited yap as if he was excited to be part of the slumber party.

"I'll be in my truck down the back alley. If you need anything, just text me."

The gentleness in his voice swept over her like a silk sheet. His keys rattled as he prepared to leave, making her skin prickle and her fingertips tingle. All of a sudden, the idea of facing Tara's ghost in the place where she'd been murdered seemed daunting. As if sensing her angst, Garrett lingered for a moment, tempting her to invite him to stay.

"Would it be possible...?" she started but stopped herself. She needed to do this on her own. "Never mind."

"What?"

"Nothing. Dallas is all the company I need," she said, stroking the soft fur on the dog's head. Now was not the time for insecurities regarding the undead. The sooner she made the connection with Tara's ghost, the faster she could be rid of this haunting. Having Garrett nearby would only distract her, and she didn't want to delay this any longer. At least Dallas would be able to warn her of any impending spirit activity.

"Text if you need me," Garrett said before disappearing down the corridor.

She listened to the sound of his footfalls on the stairs followed by the thwack of the basement door closing. The sudden tomblike feel of the space was overwhelming. Every little creak and groan of the building seemed amplified in the stillness. Dallas nudged Sarah's leg. With a half-hearted grin she reached down and rumpled his fur.

"Thanks for staying with me buddy," she whispered, plunking onto a chair.

Her skin crawled and the hair on the back of her neck bristled. Dallas curled at her feet and let out a long sigh. She rested her head in her hands, took in a deep breath, and released it slowly. With each inhalation, the tension knotting her muscles began to melt away like ice cream on hot pavement. Exhaustion tickled her eyelids and fingered her limbs. Laying her head on the table, Sarah accepted the call to dreamland where haunted faces and familiar places resided.

AN ICY CHILL gripped her shoulders, making her body quiver. Sarah glanced about and realized she was still in the library; except she wasn't alone. Tara was sitting next to her, seemingly oblivious to her presence. She watched as the ghostly figure made notes from a leather-bound volume cracking from age. The lights were covered by a hazy mist, giving a surreal feel to the atmosphere. Although she was in the dream, she couldn't get her lips to form the questions she needed to ask.

The words *he isn't what he claims* echoed in her ears, yet Tara hadn't moved. Standing, Sarah turned and gasped at a shadowy figure hovering near the basement door. She gulped down the golf ball sized lump lodged in her throat. This had to be the killer. Sarah squinted in an effort to make out his features, but it was too dark. Tara leapt from her chair, her eyeless sockets glaring as the words, *don't trust him* crackled through the air like a megaphone.

Finally, Sarah's lips moved, and she heard herself say, "Don't trust who?"

Sarah flinched as she watched the fire poker swing through the air, slamming against the side of Tara's skull. Blood splattered in all directions covering Sarah's face and chest, releasing a scream from her lips.

Bark, bark, bark!

Sarah bolted upright, sending the chair tumbling from under her. Dallas faced the end of the hall, barking madly.

Nausea crashed across Sarah's body in waves. It felt as if someone had punched her in the stomach after a full meal. She swallowed the bile creeping up her throat and took a few steps toward Dallas who was now snarling. His tail was rigid and the fur on his back stood on end. Something had his attention.

"I can do this," she whispered to herself, forcing her feet to move forward.

The door creaked open, solidifying Sarah in place as Dallas lunged down the stairs growling as he went. For a moment, she considered texting Garrett. *No*, she thought, *I can do this*. Now more than ever, she needed to prove to herself, and to him, that she could handle the situation.

Walking slowly toward the doorway, she focused on each step, careful not to trip in the darkness. Why hadn't she brought a flashlight? She could still hear the faint grumble of Dallas growling downstairs as her foot rested on the first step. Each stair groaned beneath her weight as she descended deeper into the frigid dankness of the ground floor below.

Her fingers gripped the railing as she took each step. As the air grew colder, her courage began to fade. Dallas let out an ear shattering bark that resonated against the walls, making Sarah's heart skip. Instantly, she inhaled, held for a count of five, and released.

When her feet settled on the cement floor, she reached into the blackness searching for the wall. Instead of finding a solid surface, her hand wrapped around what felt like bones, a sticky residue clinging to her fingertips. With a scream, she toppled to the ground, pain stabbing at her hip as she hit the floor.

Scrambling to get to her feet, Sarah felt a set of bony fingers latch onto her wrist, followed by another set gripping her shoulder. The more she struggled to break free, the more hands grabbed and clawed at her. Her lungs constricted, allowing only shallow breaths. She tumbled back again, blind to the creatures pulling at her. Wooziness swirled through her stomach. She tried to scream but panic choked back the sound. Blackness began to veil her vision and her head spun. She was losing consciousness.

Don't pass out, she thought. Dallas barked several times. Suddenly, the twiglike fingers began to withdraw. A velvety tongue lapped her cheek as her breathing began to steady and consciousness took hold. With quavering legs, she managed to push up onto her feet. She needed to call Garrett before the creatures returned. Adrenaline pumped through her veins as she sprinted up the stairs. Stumbling once, she quickly regained her footing and charged into the darkened library. The temperature warmed as she gasped in air and grabbed her cell phone from the tabletop. Dallas was on her heels and sat at her feet while she dialed Garrett's number.

"Everything OK?" he asked on the first ring.

"Not really," Sarah said, her voice raspy.

"On my way."

Moments later she heard his footsteps pounding up the stairs and her heart rate slowed.

"What happened," he asked.

"Had another dream and caught a glimpse of the killer standing in the shadows."

Garrett stepped closer. She could see the anticipation dancing in his eyes. "Who was it?"

"I don't know. All I saw was a figure and then the poker slamming into Tara's head. This time she said *he's not who he claims* and *don't trust him.*" She rubbed the fear bumping along her upper arms. "I asked what she meant but woke up when Dallas started carrying on."

Garrett ran his hand through his hair and furrowed his brow as Sarah continued.

"Dallas was near the basement door barking, so I decided to see what was upsetting him. He scurried down the stairs and I followed. Hands started grabbing at me, causing me to fall." She drew in a long, slow breath. "I started to lose consciousness until Dallas ran to my side and then the creatures vanished."

"Good boy," Garrett said, petting his dog. "Told you he was a good alarm system for ghosts."

"Thank goodness he was here. Another moment and I'd have passed out. Not sure what would have happened, and I really don't want to know."

"Do you want to try again, or would you rather go back to the house?"

The idea of trying again made Sarah's gut twist. But at this point, she didn't care what anyone thought. She wasn't going to face this alone. "Maybe you could stay with me this time?"

"I'll sit at Harry's desk," he smiled, melting away her angst.

"Thanks. Sorry I'm being so silly about all of this."

"It's not silly, it's human nature. Ghosts and other entities are frightening. Even my grandmother got spooked sometimes."

He patted her shoulder as he walked past.

"Garrett."

"Yeah."

"I remember something about the shadowy figure wielding the fire poker."

"What?"

"He was medium height and build."

"That sounds like most people," he replied calmly.

"Now that I think of it, he may have had longish hair, although I can't be sure."

A sliver of light from the streetlamp streamed through the window, highlighting the grimace on Garrett's face. Sarah could feel his disappointment radiating from across the room. She didn't want to believe it was Harry either.

"Let's keep trying," he responded.

"Alright," she replied. Her body felt like a deflated balloon. Fatigue nipped at her arms and legs as she returned to the table and settled onto the seat. Garrett leaned back in Harry's office chair, crossed his arms over his chest, and closed his eyes. Sarah grinned. He was just as handsome reclining as he was dancing. Her heart palpitated for a moment when she felt Dallas curl up on her foot. How had she become so attached to these two in such a short period of time?

Leaning against the table, she rested her head in her arms until sleep swept her away to dreamland.

"Bet you can't beat me at checkers," young Tara declared to Harry. "I've beaten Brady and Garrett. Now it's your turn."

Rain pelted the windowsill of the farmhouse while darkening skies shadowed the parlor in an eerie feel. Gauzy curtains fluttered as the storm's breath blew through the open window, spitting raindrops upon the floor. Brady sat on the sofa, a scowl on his face while Garrett watched his two friends banter over who was better at the game.

"You may have beaten those knuckleheads, but I'm better at

checkers than all of you," Harry declared with his chin jutting out.

"Prove it," Tara retorted, sitting on the floor across from him.

Over the next twenty minutes, they maneuvered their chips across the board.

Thunder shook the wooden floors as flashes of light burst through the front parlor. Nervousness beaded Harry's forehead while Tara sat stalwart with a sly grin curling her lips. The clock on the mantel announced the four o'clock hour, its chimes thumping instead of the melodious bells usually heard. Tara moved her last checker and took the win. Harry's face flushed as he turned his gaze toward her and set his jaw.

"You got lucky. Two out of three to decide who's really the better player?"

Tara sat straighter and lifted her chin. "I can beat you as many times as you'd like."

The scene continued with Tara winning every match. Oddly, the clock thumped out a pitiful clang every hour until the kids disappeared, the storm subsided, and the curtains stilled. The room was as lifeless as the inside of a coffin when the clock began to grow in size. Its thumping chimes increased in volume until the walls reverberated with the noise and started to crumble.

In the far corner, Tara's ghostly image fluctuated like an old television screen getting ready to lose its signal. Her hand quivered as she pointed to the clock, the words, *it's time he was discovered* echoing in Sarah's head. Covering her ears, Sarah startled when the clock exploded, smashing Tara's form against the wall, the right side of her head bloody as she collapsed to the floor.

Sarah gasped as she sat up in the chair, her hands shaking and her back saturated with sweat. Dallas leapt to her lap and started licking her face. Garrett was still in the desk chair, his head slumped forward while he dozed. Embracing Dallas, Sarah buried her face in his soft fur. He nuzzled her cheek until her heart rate slowed and her body ceased its quaking.

Not wanting to wake Garrett, Sarah wrote down everything she could remember from the dream. Too wired to go back to sleep, she tiptoed to the next room and fired up the computer. She'd dreamt of the house several times, yet tonight's vision gave her a stronger sense of its connection to whatever Tara was trying to convey.

After an hour of searching online databases and a few genealogical sites, she'd gleaned a great deal of information. The farmhouse and its 200 acres had been in the Anderson family for generations. A couple years after Brady's parents married, his aunt Melinda married Conrad James. Dusty was their only child. Of course, Brady's parents had him and his younger brother, Thomas, who disappeared when he was eighteen. With Thomas unaccounted for, and the deaths of Parker and Janey Anderson, Brady was the only surviving member of his immediate family.

Edgefield Manor had been occupied by Dusty's family when he was a child until they moved to a cottage on a forty acre parcel several miles from town. Edgefield Manor still belonged to Melinda. Since it was part of the family trust, the property couldn't be sold and thus had become a glorified storage unit, only occupied at Thanksgiving and Christmas for family gatherings.

Sarah sighed. None of this had anything to do with her dream or Tara's comments. The chair in the other room squeaked followed by footsteps.

"How long have you been awake?" Garrett asked from the doorway, his voice scratchy.

"Couple of hours now."

"Why didn't you wake me?"

"You were sleeping so soundly; I didn't want to disturb you. I decided to do some research instead."

Garrett pulled up a chair and looked at the computer screen. Sarah's body tingled when his arm brushed against hers, the woodsy scent of sandalwood and lavender filling her senses.

"Brady's farmhouse? Why are you researching that?" he asked.

"In my dream, all of you were there playing checkers."

Garrett smiled. "I think it was raining. Since we couldn't go outside, we decided to play checkers. Tara beat all of us. Harry was so angry I thought he was going to explode."

Sarah straightened in her chair. "That's an odd choice of words."

"What do you mean?" he asked, cocking his head.

"There was a clock on the mantel that kept chiming, except the sound was muffled, like the striker was hitting against something soft. Anyway, Tara said, 'it was time he was discovered' and then the clock grew in size and exploded. Debris from the clock knocked her to the ground and bloodied the side of her head."

Garrett slumped back in the chair, rubbing his eyes.

"What's the matter?" she asked.

"It's so convoluted. None of it makes sense. Why show us at the farmhouse when we were kids and then allude to the clock killing her. She died here from a blow to the head."

Sarah shrugged her shoulders. "I was hoping you could clarify it."

"The only underlying factor between your dream and her death here at the library is Harry."

"You said he was angry about losing to her?"

"Not enough to kill her twenty years later," he scoffed. "It was a checkers game, not an international conspiracy."

"And there isn't any other connection between the dream and her death?"

"Brady and I were there too, but we didn't do it. Brady lives in Columbia and I definitely didn't kill her."

"I have a hard time believing Harry could have done this," Sarah said. "He seems devastated by her murder."

"I agree. He adored Tara."

He knows, tickled Sarah's ear like a mosquito.

Sarah's gaze dropped to the floor as she took in a sharp breath.

"What?"

"She just whispered in my ear, *he knows*. Knows what? And is she referring to Harry or someone else?"

Garrett shrugged.

"Maybe she is referring to Harry. If he was still in love with her..." Sarah muttered when Garrett interrupted.

"He wasn't *in* love with her. He loved her, like a sister. I know things keep stacking up against him, but I can't believe he'd hurt her or anyone else for that matter."

The computer monitor brightened as the words "you're wrong" scrolled across the screen over and over again.

Sarah scooted the chair away from the computer table as Garrett jumped from his seat. Suddenly, the screen went blank, enveloping the room in darkness.

"What the heck was that?" Garrett muttered.

"Not sure, but Tara seems to have better computer skills than I do. Too bad I can't figure out what she's trying to tell me," Sarah replied, fright seeping into her limbs.

Dallas stood at the threshold of the other room; his muscles tensed as a low grumble emanated from his throat. Garrett rose and started toward the doorway when the dog shot across the room barking wildly. Sarah ran after them. If Tara was here, perhaps Garrett could help her get some clarifying information. By the time she entered the next room, Garrett was staring at something on Tara's desk.

Sarah approached and looked at the paper on top. *You're wrong*, was written multiple times until it ran off the page onto the desktop.

"What is she trying to say?" Sarah asked.

"Not sure, but I don't like what she's inferring."

Sarah touched Garrett's arm. "It may not mean what we think. Do we know where Harry was the night of the murder?"

"At home, asleep."

Sarah's heart sank. It wasn't the response she wanted to hear.

"Should we try again?"

Garrett shook his head. "It's 5:30 in the morning. We need to get out of here before Harry shows up. Let's go back to the manor and discuss this over a pot of coffee. I need a good kick of caffeine."

After logging out of the computer, they grabbed the paper from Tara's desk, locked everything, climbed into the truck, and rode to the house in silence. A translucent mist hovered over the grassy landscape of the square as the sun peered over the horizon, chasing the veil of night from the sky. The lights of the bakery were on, and the thought of cinnamon rolls made Sarah's stomach rumble.

"You hungry?" Garrett asked.

Sarah's cheeks heated as she looked away. "Maybe a little. I was just thinking about the cinnamon rolls at the bakery."

"Let's get some." He turned the truck around and parked in front of the brick building.

"It's closed," Sarah said.

"Not when you're friends with the morning crew. Tiffany will let me in," he said with a wink.

Sarah's chest burned at the mention of another woman's name. Mentally she scolded herself. She was being silly. Tiffany could be a mature woman with snow white hair and ten grand-children. She waited in the truck as Garrett rapped on the glass door. A slender woman in her twenties sauntered over and let Garrett in. Her golden hair was pulled in a high ponytail and her eyes sparkled as she greeted him with a hug.

Cut it out, Sarah thought, chasing the jealousy from her mind. He can flirt with anyone he chooses; after all, they were only friends with limited time left before she returned home. Once the estate was cleared, she'd go back to Monroe Manse, unless, of course, Danni wanted her to stay to the end of the trial. Even though she couldn't have a romantic relationship with Garrett, it felt good knowing he'd be there to help with the dreamist stuff.

With a sigh, she slumped back against the truck seat. If only she could have more. But now wasn't the time to think about these things. She needed to focus on figuring out who Tara was implicating, even if it was painful to consider.

WHEN THEY ARRIVED at the house, Sarah was shocked to find Danni already in the kitchen sipping coffee.

"What has you up so early?" Sarah asked, starting the kettle for tea.

Garrett placed the bag of cinnamon rolls on the table and got plates from the cabinet. Sarah poured him a cup of coffee while Dallas followed her around like a mouse behind the Pied Piper.

"No time for sleep since the judge moved up the deadline," she replied with a yawn. Sniffing the air, she smiled. "Cinnamon rolls?"

"Yup," Garrett said, placing a gooey pastry on a plate and handing it to Danni.

"I didn't think they were open this early," Danni said, closing her eyes as she bit into the iced confection.

"Everything is open when you have the right friends," Garrett responded, with a wink.

Sarah's stomach flopped. Surely, he wasn't involved with that young woman. Danni sighed with delight. "I may need to move here for the baked goods."

Sarah fixed a cup of tea, joined them at the table, and placed a roll on her plate.

"Garner anything from your dreams?" Danni asked.

"Maybe," she replied, glancing at Garrett while sipping her tea.

Danni stopped eating and leaned her elbows on the table.

"Is someone going to enlighten me, or do I have to play fifty questions?"

Sarah shared the dreams, the bizarre occurrences with the computer, and the note on Tara's desk.

"This doesn't sound good," Danni said, furrowing her brow. "How can we find out more about Harry?"

Garrett shook his head. "I know the dreams are leading us in that direction, but I still don't think he did it. I've known him since I was six years old. He's never hurt anything."

"I hate to say this, but what about Dusty?" Sarah asked. "He's been in all of the scenes and the evidence points to him as the killer."

They startled when the grandfather clock in the front entry rang out, except the sound was that of the muffled chimes from the clock in Sarah's dreams. Danni's face paled as she looked at Sarah.

"Please tell me you wound that clock," Danni whispered.

Shaking her head, Sarah looked across the table at Garrett who seemed surprisingly calm. Dallas barked, breaking the tension as the clock went silent.

"Does this have something to do with your dream?" Danni asked.

"Not sure," she replied. "Does any of this make sense to you?"

Garrett blew out a breath. "I remember Grams talking about entities being able to communicate through objects outside of the dreams, but I don't recall all of the circumstances. Sadly, I never wrote any of it down. Always assumed I'd remember everything when the time came."

A loud crash echoed from the entryway, sending them all running in that direction. The three stood in the doorway staring at the grandfather clock, which now lay face down in a puddle of broken glass.

Sarah stepped closer as Garrett scooped Dallas into his arms to prevent him from walking onto the shards scattered across the rug. Picking through the broken fragments, Sarah noticed a piece of paper. She pulled it from the debris, shook it off, and unfolded it.

"It's the provenance of the clock. It must have been hidden inside the case. I didn't see it when I evaluated it."

"Do you think Tara did this?" Danni asked from a safe distance.

"Who else could it be? The question is, why? This doesn't implicate Harry or anyone else. It only says that a Mr. Anderson purchased the clock from a Pennsylvania clock maker in 1843. I assume that's the great-grandfather of Brady and Dusty. It may add to the value for the estate sale but there's nothing incriminating here. Granted, it's not worth much in this state."

Garrett's phone buzzed. "It's one of my crew. I need to get them started on a job."

"I don't want to keep you from your work. We can discuss this later," Sarah offered.

"You have a ghost destroying antique clocks while Dusty's trial date keeps getting moved up. Let's not put this off. We have a murderer to find and a man to exonerate," Danni said, planting her hands on her hips.

"Alright," Sarah said.

"Give me an hour and I'll be back," Garrett said, walking out the door with Dallas under his arm.

Sarah watched them leave, her chest constricting.

"What's going on?" Danni asked, obviously sensing her friend's angst.

"Absolutely nothing," she replied, walking into the kitchen to get a broom and dustpan. The last thing she needed was to admit her attraction to Garrett. Life was complicated enough with a murder trial and a clock-destroying ghost haunting her dreams.

24

"Garrett hasn't been able to help with the dreams?" Danni asked after the mess in the entryway was cleaned up. Pouring another cup of coffee, she pulled a second cinnamon roll from the bag.

"Not really. So far, the dreams seem to suggest Harry as a likely suspect. Neither of us want to believe it," Sarah said with a sigh.

"Why Harry? What's his motive?" Danni asked, slipping into attorney mode.

"That's the issue. There isn't a solid motive. In my dreams, he was upset about losing to Tara at checkers. He had a strong attachment to her at one time but by all reports it subsided when she married Dusty. Aside from the cryptic phone call I overheard at the library about Harry not wanting to take the fall for something that could impact the trial, there isn't anything substantial other than the dreams. In fact, Harry still speaks of her with great affection. It doesn't make sense."

"Tell me again what Tara has said to you."

"She's told me not to trust him, that he's taken something,

and most recently that I'm wrong." Sarah snapped her fingers. "Last night she said, *he knows*."

"What about the clocks? How do they fit in with all of this?"

"Not a clue," Sarah replied, shrugging her shoulders. "The clock stuff started last night too."

"Something tells me the clock is the key to figuring this thing out."

"Well, Tara destroyed the grandfather clock here and it didn't reveal anything."

"What about the clock at the farmhouse?"

"We don't even know if it's still there," Sarah said. "And if it is, what could it possibly tell us?"

"We won't know until we check it out," Danni said, swigging down the last of her coffee. She stood with a stretch, placed her cup in the sink, and walked across the room, stopping in the doorway.

"What are you waiting on? Change your clothes and let's go to the farmhouse."

Sarah rubbed her eyes. "I've barely slept."

Planting her hands on her hips, Danni scowled. "We pulled all-nighters in college. Barely slept means you got some sleep, so I don't want to hear any whining. Let's go!"

"Yes, Colonel," Sarah said, rising from her chair with a groan. Anytime Danni issued demands, Sarah referred to her as Colonel. Being the daughter of a Marine Corps Colonel, Danni was always complaining about his strict manner. It was Sarah's way of letting Danni know she was pushing the limits without entirely disagreeing with her.

SARAH TOOK a shower and changed into running shorts and a t-shirt. Although weary from the night before, she was beginning to awaken. Danni was waiting in the entryway with keys in hand.

"Is Brady back in town?" Sarah asked as they walked to the car.

"Not until tomorrow."

"How are we getting into the farmhouse?"

"I know where he keeps the spare key."

Sarah slid onto the leather seat and closed the car door, her eyebrows raised. "And how did you garner this information if you've never been there?"

"Brady is a creature of habit. He always hid his dorm room key in the same place. I'm sure it's the same with the farmhouse."

As they sped down the road, Sarah noticed the town waking with delivery trucks parked in front of restaurants and shop keepers sweeping walkways. The courthouse loomed over the square like a sentinel keeping watch. Sarah's emotions were a jumbled mess with the estate sale drawing near and Dusty's trial date fast approaching. She'd be returning home soon. The idea of not hanging out with the guys or enjoying Edgefield's welcoming square weighed on her heart. Of course, she knew the core of her despair was not seeing Garrett and Dallas. Forcing the thoughts from her head, Sarah turned to Danni.

"Did you ask Brady if we could do this?"

"We've always had an open-door policy. I used to use his dorm room when I needed a quiet place to study, and he used to hide in my room when he was avoiding the Dean."

"But this is now. How do you know the same open-door policy applies? He might have personal things at the house he doesn't want others to see," Sarah said.

"Given our recent circumstances, I feel certain he'd approve. Besides, he doesn't live there so I doubt there's much in the way of personal things. It's probably filled with child-hood memorabilia, a few girlie magazines, and dust bunnies. Trust me, if we gather any evidence to clear Dusty, Brady will be thrilled."

"He doesn't have an alarm, does he?"

Danni glanced at her friend. "Are you afraid of being arrested?"

"Kinda. This is the second time in twenty-four hours I've entered a building uninvited. Not to mention, it wouldn't look good if Dusty's attorney was booked for breaking and entering."

"Ha! I'm sure there's no alarm and Brady would vouch for us if anything happened, which it won't, so stop worrying."

Danni was right. The farmhouse was miles outside of town with no neighbors close by. All they needed to do was check the place out. Hopefully, the visions from Sarah's dreams would guide her to whatever Tara was trying to communicate.

Sunlight streamed through an avenue of trees as Danni's Mercedes barreled down the dirt drive, kicking up dust along the way. A white clapboard farmhouse loomed before them, its flaking paint and sagging porch giving the place a fore-boding feel. Huge oaks surrounded the structure, blocking the sun and sending shadows scurrying across the façade. The lack of light gave the peeling paint a grayish hue like the pallid skin of a rotting corpse, the windows soulless eyes glaring down upon them. No wonder he didn't have a security system. The house alone would scare off anyone who approached.

Danni parked the car and sat for a moment.

"This place gives me the creeps," she said with a shudder.

"It definitely doesn't look like the inviting family homestead from the photos."

"Might as well get this over with," Danni replied, exiting the car.

Sarah followed her across the crumbling brick walk and up the wilting porch stairs. A faded doormat with only the letters W, L, and M remaining, seemed to wither beneath the forsaken structure. Danni leaned over, ran her hand under the corner of the mat and produced a key.

"Seriously? He hides the key under the mat?" Sarah declared.

"Yup, nothing has changed."

"Garrett does the same. Can't believe people still do that," Sarah huffed.

Danni opened the door, and they stepped inside. Aside from layers of dust and the musty scent, the house appeared as it had in the pictures and Sarah's dreams. The worn floorboards were cloaked in faded rugs and the staircase railing curved at just the right angle for sliding. They stepped into the front parlor which was furnished with an overstuffed sofa, two wing chairs, and a recliner. Paintings were askew on the walls and the once billowing curtains were tattered. The house had a morbid feel as if former residents still lingered there.

"Look," Danni said, pointing to the hearth. "Is that the same clock from your dreams?"

"It is," Sarah mumbled. Walking over to it, Sarah ran her hand along the gingerbread frame. It was a typical Seth Thomas clock with ornate oak trim and a spider web design on the glass front panel. A zap stung Sarah's fingers making her withdraw her hand quickly as the words, *the time has come,* tickled her ear. Sarah sucked in a breath, fearful an army of spiders would follow.

"What's wrong?"

"The clock shocked me," she replied, shaking her hand.

"Is it electric?"

"No, it's key wound. This is definitely what Tara has been leading me to."

"How do you know?" Danni's eyes darted around the room.

"Because Tara just whispered, *the time has come.*"

"She's here?" Danni muttered, leaning in toward Sarah.

Sarah nodded and reached for the latch on the side of the clock. This time there was no shock. Carefully, she opened the front and peered inside. The key rested below the wobbling pendulum.

"Anything unusual?" Danni asked.

"Looks like a regular clock to me."

All of a sudden, the clock began to chime, sending Danni stumbling backwards. Sarah grabbed her chest. Oddly, instead of ding, ding, ding the chimes went thunk, thunk, thunk, just like they had in her dreams.

Closing her eyes, she took a few deep breaths until her heart rate resumed a normal pace. Aside from the clock chiming without being wound, everything about it appeared normal. Sometimes a shaky floor could cause a clock to chime. Granted, this one obviously needed an adjustment since the chimes thunked instead of dinging. Then it struck her. The chimes!

She reached behind the face of the clock, her breath catching when her fingers brushed against something. Swallowing her fear, she grabbed the item and pulled it out, relieved when no spiders appeared.

"This explains why the chimes sounded muffled," Sarah said, holding a folded piece of paper.

"What is it?" Danni asked, peering over her friend's shoulder.

"Looks like a birth certificate with Brady's name on it."

"Let me see that," Danni said, reaching for the frail document. "Nothing out of the ordinary here, except..."

"What?"

"They have the wrong last name. This says Brady Houston. It's Brady Anderson."

"Did his mother remarry?"

"Not that I know of. Maybe this was a distant cousin, or it belonged to the previous owner of the clock," Danni said, shrugging her shoulders.

"Couldn't be the previous owner. I think Brady's family

would've noticed the muffled chimes and found the birth certificate years ago."

"It's the same birthdate so it must be him. All this implies is that Brady's last name changed at some point in his life, which I must admit is strange, especially since he never mentioned it," Danni said, furrowing her brows. "Regardless, why would the ghost lead us to this? It has nothing to do with the murder."

"Tara was doing the genealogy for the family, right?" Sarah asked.

"Yeah, so?"

"What if she discovered something about the family's history and someone killed her to keep it a secret?"

"That would have to be one heck of a secret," Danni replied, her brows furrowing. "We could always ask Brady about it. If Tara's ghost led us here, maybe he can give us the answers we need to find the real killer."

"Why not just give us the answer instead of sending us on a wild hunt?"

"Nora did the same thing. I suppose it has something to do with the dreamist stuff," Danni sighed. "Tara's gotten us this far, let's not ignore the clues, I'm sure they lead somewhere."

"We'll add this to the other documents at the manor."

"I'll text Brady and see if he can come back a day early. In the meantime, we can dig through more of Tara's research. Perhaps something will pop out that didn't make sense before."

Sarah closed the front of the clock and refolded the birth certificate. They headed back to Edgefield Manor beneath blue skies, their hope renewed that the answers to this mystery were forthcoming.

Once at the house, Sarah gathered Tara's research while Danni organized the photo albums and scrapbooks into a crude timeline.

"We can cross-reference the name on the birth certificate

with the names in the genealogy paperwork," Danni said, as Sarah placed Tara's notes on the table. "If we find anything, we can ask Brady. This new piece of evidence suggests someone else may be involved, like a relative with claims to the inheritance."

After skimming through everything, they realized bits of information were missing from Tara's work.

"If she's trying to implicate some long lost relative, it's not listed in any of this," Danni said. "Nothing here explains the name on the birth certificate."

"Obviously, she died before she could complete the work. Unless there's something at the library I missed," Sarah suggested. "I need to go back."

"I'll drop you off, fill up the car, grab something for lunch, and swing back by to get you."

"Good idea," Sarah replied.

They piled into the car and drove across town. Danni stopped in front of the Tomlinson building that housed the library.

"Text me when you're ready for me to pick you up."

"OK."

Sarah's heart hammered in her chest as Danni drove away. She stepped into the building and found Harry at his desk typing.

"Hey, Sarah," he said, standing.

"How's it going, Harry?"

"Pretty good, actually. May have found something on the tape from our excursion."

"I thought you didn't capture anything decipherable that night," Sarah said, walking over to his computer.

"That's what I thought too. I tried some different filtering programs, and something showed up." He pointed to a misty figure on the screen.

"Is that the same room where Garrett and I were?"

"Yup. Unfortunately, I don't think I can get the image any clearer but there's definitely something there."

Sarah's skin prickled. She already knew who was there; she'd seen it with her own two eyes. *He knows*, echoed through her head.

Taking in a deep breath, she forced a grin. "I'm glad the night wasn't a bust. What will you do now?"

"Let the guys know and then set up another filming. With any luck, we'll get better footage and be able to identify the entity."

The excitement in his voice niggled at Sarah's conscience. How could Harry possibly be a killer? Aside from his enthusiasm for the dead, he was a genuinely nice guy. Granted, people always said that after a murderer was exposed. The neighbors would go on about what a friendly person he was and how he never caused any trouble. Whether he was guilty or not, she needed to find out if there was more of Tara's work than what he'd given her.

"Harry, are you sure you gave me all of Tara's research? It seems there are some names missing that might go along with a few of the items at the manor. It will increase the price if I can make the connections."

"Thought I did, but you're welcome to check," he said with a smile. "You know where everything is."

"Thanks."

Walking into the old vault, she dug through the stacks of leather-bound journals, and pulled a folder from the bottom of the pile. Her back stiffened as she opened it and stared at more of Tara's documentation of the family lineage. *Had Harry purposefully withheld this stuff? And if so, why was he giving her access to it now?*

Emerging from the vault, Sarah held up the folder. "Turns out there was more. OK if I take it with me?"

"Are you sure it's Tara's work?"

"Looks like it," Sarah replied, swallowing hard.

She couldn't let him know what she was up to, especially if he was guilty. *Stay calm*, she thought, trying not to reveal the panic clutching her chest.

"Could I see it? We have a few other people who store things in there. I need to be certain I don't give access to someone else's research."

"Sure," she said, handing him the folder.

Sarah froze as his eyes scanned the pages.

"This looks like Brady's side of the family. Do you really need this?" he asked.

"Actually, yes. Turns out there are a few of his family pieces at the house." Guilt fingered Sarah's conscience for lying.

"Humph, wouldn't have thought that."

"Why not?"

"His father had a falling out with Dusty's dad right before he passed. I'm pretty sure all of the things that belonged to Brady's family are at the farmhouse."

Sarah's heart palpitated at how intimately Harry knew the family histories of his friends. Did he know them well enough to murder Tara and make it look like Dusty did it? Maybe this is what Tara meant by, *he knows* and *don't trust him*. Did Harry know Dusty was innocent because he was the one who bludgeoned her to death?

"Hopefully, this information will help," Sarah said, trying to stay nonchalant. Now more than ever, she wanted to get away before he became suspicious and asked more questions.

"Good luck," he said, closing the folder and handing it to her.

Sarah scooted out the door and texted Danni to let her know she'd be waiting at the corner across from the bakery. Sitting on the bench, she ruminated over everything that had happened in the past few hours. Danni pulled up and Sarah hopped in the car. Inhaling the delectable aroma of fried chicken, Sarah smiled.

"Where'd you get lunch?" she asked, peeking in the bag.

"Little place down the road. Fried chicken and potato salad was the special for today," Danni replied. "Any luck at the library?"

"Turns out there was another folder with information about Brady's side of the family. Harry asked why I needed it. I did my best to deflect any suspicions on his part."

When they arrived at the manor and went inside, the sight of the grandfather clock with its missing glass made Sarah's head ache.

Danni grabbed a couple of sodas from the fridge, and they sat down.

"Did you text Brady?" Sarah asked, taking a bite of chicken.

"Yup. Haven't heard back from him yet which is strange. He always responds immediately, unless he's in court."

"Could he be in court?"

"No. He was able to clear his trial schedule for a couple of months so he could be here. Poor guy is still doing all of the prep work. I can't believe he hasn't found another paralegal yet."

Over lunch, they chatted about the trial and the lack of evidence to exonerate Dusty. Clearing the food containers, Sarah yawned. Now that she'd eaten, her sleep deprivation and spectral investigating from the previous night was catching up with her.

"You gonna be OK?" Danni asked.

"I'm exhausted."

"Why don't you lie down for a bit? You need to be sharp if we're going to figure this out."

"Sounds like a plan," Sarah yawned. "First thing I need to do when I get up is find a clock shop so I can have the grandfather clock repaired."

"It was an accident," Danni said. "Surely, Melinda won't hold you accountable."

"It was done by a ghost trying to communicate with me, so I'm indirectly liable. Regardless of the reason, I always take responsibility for any damage when I'm on the job. It's the right thing to do."

"Suit yourself," she shrugged. "I'll be working in the dining room."

"Don't let me sleep more than an hour," Sarah hollered over her shoulder as she trudged up the stairs.

Once in the room, she opened the window and inhaled the rose scented breeze. Plunking down on the bed, she removed her sneakers and rested her head on the pillow. Fatigue wrapped itself around her body like a blanket, lulling her into a sound slumber.

25

T ara sat on the floor of the upstairs bedroom of Edgefield Manor going through boxes of memorabilia. After making several notations from photos, she put together a crude timeline and family tree for her mother-in-law, Melinda. Although she did this every day, there was something particularly satisfying about working on her husband's family lineage.

After two hours of digging through dusty boxes and faded photographs, Tara started to stand when something under the bed caught her eye. She reached down and removed a crumpled shoebox held shut with a rubber band that had long since lost its shape. Sitting on the bed, she plucked the rubber band from the box, lifted the lid, and peered inside at a stack of letters. She was shocked to see they were addressed to Dusty's Aunt Janey.

Curious, she took the first from its envelope and began reading. Heartfelt declarations spilled from the scripted words. She read on, moved by the passion and love exuded on each line. Tara blushed. She felt as if she were intruding on Mr. and

Mrs. Anderson's privacy until she read the name at the end of the page, Edward Houston.

Apparently, Aunt Janey kept some letters from a beau in her high school days, except the date was after graduation. Tara's skin crawled as she continued to read the impassioned phrases. None of it made sense. Brady was born the same year as the dates on the correspondence. Did Mrs. Anderson have an affair while she was married? The next to the last letter in the stack answered her question.

MY DEAREST EDWARD,

HOW COULD you abandon me when I need you now more than ever? We're going to be parents. I'm pained you want nothing to do with our child. Please meet me at the coffee house so we can discuss this further. I know you love me as I love you.

LOVINGLY YOURS,

Janey

THE LETTER HAD BEEN ADDRESSED, but never sent. Tara's mind whirled with the innuendo of the contents. Her husband's aunt, Janey Anderson, was pregnant before coming to Edgefield? Family lore told of a whirlwind romance between Janey and Parker when they met at Newberry College. The couple was married at the town hall and Mrs. Anderson dropped out of college when she became pregnant. Yet this letter inferred a much different scenario.

Stuffing the correspondence into her jeans pocket, Tara placed the box on the shelf in the closet with some of her other research, and headed to town. Surely, she'd find answers at the genealogical library.

A search there revealed nothing of consequence. Tara had already constructed a basic family tree with the documentation from the library and ancestral records. Nothing contradicted the legitimacy of the family history she'd always known. Mr. and Mrs. Parker Anderson had two sons, Brady and Thomas. Two years later, Melinda Anderson married Conrad James, and had one son, Dusty. Both Parker and Conrad had died fairly young, Parker of pneumonia and Conrad of a heart attack, leaving behind their wives and children. But the letters she'd uncovered suggested Janey Anderson had a lover with whom she had a child before her marriage. The question was, where was that child? Did it die or did she put it up for adoption?

The scene skipped to another day. Rain cascaded down the windows of the records office where Tara rummaged through the family wills. Her breath caught when she finally found the one she'd been searching for. Pulling it from the file cabinet, she sat down to read.

LAST WILL and Testament of Parker Anderson

In accordance with the wishes of my father that the Anderson assets remain in the family line, I hereby bequeath all land, property, and financial holdings to my sons, Brady and Thomas. As I have done, they will leave all assets to those of the Anderson bloodline. Adopted children or stepchildren will not be included in the inheritance in order to maintain a true family lineage regarding land and other holdings. In the event that Brady and Thomas are not living and/or produce no heirs, all properties will go to my sister, Melinda Anderson James and her son, Dusty James.

. . .

TARA SLUMPED BACK in the chair, her mind churning with possibilities. She walked down the hall to the room that housed birth certificates. She hadn't given much thought to birth records before now because she knew her husband's immediate family history.

Checking Brady's birth certificate, she found Parker and Janey Anderson listed as the parents. Yet something about the document was different than the others. She made a photocopy of the birth certificate and the will and returned to the house to search the box of letters.

Thunder rumbled as she sorted through the shoebox. The only letter she hadn't read was the last one. Lightning zigzagged across the sky as a chill rambled down her spine. Wrapped in the yellowed parchment of the letter was a birth certificate. This one listed Janey Grant as Brady's mother with Edward Houston as the father. But how could that be? She looked at the copy from the records office which clearly stated Parker Anderson as Brady's father. Then it struck her. The certificate on file was slightly different, as if it were a revised copy.

Tara swallowed hard. If the letter and birth certificate from the shoebox were accurate, Mr. Anderson *wasn't* Brady's biological father, meaning Brady wouldn't inherit his share of the estate. Yet, Mr. Anderson had always claimed Brady as his own.

SARAH JOLTED awake as Danni shook her shoulder.

"Are you alright? You were mumbling in your sleep," Danni said, concern masking her face.

"I'm fine," she muttered, rubbing her eyes. "I was dreaming about Tara."

Danni sat on the side of the bed. "Anything important?"

"Bizarre is more like it."

"Tell me," Danni's face lit up.

Sarah shared what the dream revealed and watched as Danni's expression melted into concern.

"If this is true, then Brady isn't truly an Anderson and wouldn't inherit a thing," Danni said, brushing a strand of hair from her forehead. "He'd be devastated. He loves his family and has always been proud of his birthright. The family name carries a great deal of weight in this area."

"It also makes him a suspect," Sarah added.

"How so?"

"If he knew about the will and his true parentage, he may have killed Tara to keep it from being revealed."

"Except he didn't know about it. Did Tara confront him in your dream?" Danni said in a defensive tone, her back straightening.

"No, but she knew the truth."

"Doesn't mean she shared it with anyone. We only have the birth certificate from the clock. So far, this is all speculation based on a dream."

"This also explains why he never sold the farmhouse. According to the dream, the property can only be bequeathed to someone in the family line."

"Still doesn't prove anything."

Sarah's stomach twisted. In all the years they'd been friends, she'd never faced off with Danni. Apparently, Danni didn't like where she was going with the newfound information. Regardless, Sarah wasn't going to let this little tiff deter her.

"Funny how my dreams are accurate until Brady's integrity is questioned."

"Don't you dare," Danni growled. "I would never look the other way for anyone. For goodness' sake, he wasn't even in town the night Tara was killed."

"Good point," Sarah replied, deciding it was better to take it down a notch. Obviously, Danni wasn't ready to consider any guilt on Brady's part. And she wasn't about to risk their friendship on a haunted dream. "If the information isn't relevant, then why did Tara share it?"

"Maybe it leads to the real killer."

"I suppose it's possible. Let's ask Brady when he gets back in town," Sarah said. "By the way, did he say when he'd be back?"

"He still hasn't responded to any of my texts," she replied. Suddenly, her demeanor shifted. "I've got it! Maybe the killer knew about Brady's parentage and has been blackmailing him. If Tara made this information public, then the blackmailer wouldn't be able to use it against Brady, thus losing his payout. And there's our motive for her murder. The blackmailer killed Tara to avoid losing his leverage against Brady."

"But how did the blackmailer know about all of this?"

"Maybe Tara told a close friend like Harry?" Danni suggested.

"I suppose it's plausible."

"Oh no," Danni declared. "What if the killer went to Columbia and found Brady?"

Sarah's heart palpitated at the idea. It aligned with the dream and everything Tara had revealed so far. *Don't trust him, he has it, it's time.* Somebody in their circle of friends had discovered the truth and may have been blackmailing Brady. And the most likely suspect was Harry. He worked alongside Tara and would have known about her discoveries and research. Add the phone conversation Sarah had overheard at the genealogical library and the evidence mounted. *It's not here, don't trust him.* Harry could have taken information from Tara's research and used it against Brady.

"We need to find Brady," Sarah said.

Danni pulled her phone from her pocket and sent another text to him.

"I told him it was urgent and to call me immediately."

"What if he doesn't respond?" Sarah asked, fear twining through her chest.

"We may need to contact Garrett."

"Good idea," Sarah replied. She texted Garrett and set her phone on the bed. "While we wait for responses, let's search the master bedroom for more clues. That's where Tara found the box of letters."

They started from the room when they heard the front door open and close.

"Danni!" Brady called out.

Danni hurried down the stairs with Sarah close behind. "I'm so glad to see you! I was worried when you didn't answer my texts."

"I hopped in my car and drove straight here when I got your first one. What's going on?" he asked, grasping Danni's hand.

"It's complicated."

Cocking his head, Brady furrowed his brow. "Has something happened with Dusty's defense?"

"Not exactly, although we might have information regarding the motive for Tara's death."

"That's incredible!" he said, embracing Danni and kissing her cheek. "I knew you'd get to the bottom of this."

Sarah and Danni exchanged glances.

"Let's have a drink. The things we've discovered are going to come as a shock."

"OK," Brady replied, concern rippling across his face.

The three of them went to the front parlor where Danni poured drinks for everyone.

Sarah and Danni sat on the settee while Brady stood near the hearth.

"Tell me what has you in such a state," Brady said, taking a sip of his scotch.

"We've uncovered some unexpected information regarding your father."

"Is that all?" Brady smiled. "I know my father wasn't a saint, if that's what you're about to tell me."

"It's more than that. We were at the farmhouse earlier and..."

"Why were you there?" Brady asked, his complexion reddening. "I didn't give you permission to snoop around the property."

"I didn't think I needed permission to gather evidence for this case. You hired me to clear your cousin," she retorted.

Brady licked his lips. "You're absolutely correct. I'm sorry. I guess I'm a bit tense with the court date being moved up."

"How'd you know about that?" Danni said, standing. "I haven't told you yet."

"Heard about it from a friend at the courthouse," he replied, taking another sip of his drink.

"What friend?" Danni asked, firmly.

Sarah watched the interaction, a chill filtering through her body. Witnessing their first lover's spat was awkward. Conflicted, Sarah wanted to give them some privacy while also wanting to stay and support Danni. Another part of her wanted to hear what Brady had to say. Curiosity won out. Getting up from the settee, she moved closer to her friend.

"What difference does it make how I found out?" he said, flippantly. "I have lots of friends in town who keep me apprised of what's going on."

"It would have been nice to tell me about it," Danni said, her cheeks reddening. "The judge is being a complete jerk about everything. If you have so many friends in the court-house, maybe you can explain why Dusty's court date keeps getting moved forward."

Brady's jaw flexed. "I can't interfere, it would be unethical."

"But getting inside information *is* ethical?" she asked, indignation punctuating her words.

Brady took in a deep breath and plastered a smile on his face.

"I don't want to argue with you Danni. Just tell me what has you so concerned. The text you sent earlier was alarming."

"It's difficult to say," she replied, rubbing the back of her neck.

"Then say it. You know I don't like to dance around with bad news. I'd rather you tell me and get it over with."

"We found a birth certificate that doesn't align with what you've been led to believe is your true parentage."

Brady placed his glass on the mantel and took a step closer. "What do you mean?"

"I can't explain the details behind the discovery, but we found a birth certificate for you with a different name than your father's."

His brows furrowed and his stature straightened. Obviously, Danni had captured his attention.

"I'm sorry to drop this on you," Danni said, pity washing over her face as she met Brady's stare. "I've not been able to confirm this yet, but it seems your family inheritance can only go to those who are related to the Andersons by blood. Sounds like something archaic put in place to prevent spouses from inheriting. I don't know what happened between your mother and biological father but apparently some sort of arrangement was made to cover it up. Somehow Tara discovered it. Maybe whoever killed her was trying to prevent the truth from coming out."

Brady looked down at the floor, his shoulders slumping as he nudged the edge of the rug with the toe of his shoe. "Do you have any idea who that might be?"

"We have a theory, although we don't have evidence to prove it yet."

"Who do you think it is?" Brady asked.

"I don't want to say until we know more," Danni replied in a soothing tone as she stepped toward him. "No need making unnecessary accusations."

Brady studied Danni for a moment before he spoke.

"The only thing you've been able to determine is my birth certificate lists another man as my father?"

"That, and the stipulation only blood relatives can inherit."

"Are you saying I'm not the rightful heir to the family property?" Brady ran his hand across his mouth, noticeably shocked by the news.

Danni's eyes misted. Sarah knew Danni was loyal to a fault and clearly delivering this sort of news to someone she cared deeply about was breaking her heart.

"That's what I'm saying. I'm so sorry, Brady." She reached for his hand, but he took a step back.

"Who will inherit?" he whispered.

"Your aunt, and eventually your cousin, Dusty."

"What will people think?" Brady asked, lifting his glass from the mantel and downing the rest of his drink.

"This is all preliminary stuff. I haven't even had a chance to confirm it yet. If it is true, I'll do everything I can to keep it out of the press," Danni said.

"You can't control the media," he replied, meeting her gaze. "You're great at what you do, but there's no way to prevent the gossip train from barreling down the tracks in a small community like this."

"Big deal," Danni said brazenly, throwing her hands in the air. "So, people whisper about you for a while. If this leads us to the real killer, the discomfort of a few local rumormongers won't matter."

"And my inheritance?" he asked with icy words.

"Dusty is a great guy, more of a brother than a cousin, as you've said. I'm sure he and your aunt will split everything with you."

"You assume too much. Money is always thicker than blood,

especially in Edgefield where family lineage is everything. Besides, you just said the will stipulates only blood relatives can inherit," he grumbled. "Who else knows?"

"We haven't said a word to anybody. Like I told you, I haven't confirmed any of this yet. I'll need to do a lot more research."

"Good, that's very good." Raising one eyebrow, Brady nodded as his lips formed a thin line.

"How is that good?" Danni exclaimed. "With the upcoming court date, this leaves us less time to find evidence to clear Dusty."

"It's good because nobody else knows about my unfortunate family line. I don't need this sort of thing spreading through town. After all, I have a reputation to uphold, not to mention properties to inherit." Holding out his hand, a wicked grin crinkled his icy blue eyes. "Now, if you'd be kind enough to hand over my birth certificate."

"I don't have it on me. It's with the other documents in the..." Danni's complexion paled, and she took a step back. "It can't be," she whispered, her hand flying to her mouth.

"I knew you were bright but never imagined you'd discover all of this."

"What's the matter?" Sarah asked, her heartrate quickening.

"Dusty didn't kill Tara," Danni said in a deadpan voice.

"That's the theory," Sarah muttered, her gaze shifting from Danni to Brady. Brady's demeanor was changing course like the ball on a tennis court, making Sarah's gut swirl.

"What did you do Brady?" Danni asked, squaring her shoulders. Despite her attempts to maintain a tenacious presence, adrenaline shook her hands, exposing her distress.

"Why would you ask such a question?" he said playfully.

"What's going on?" Sarah demanded. Her mind was racing with possibilities, although she was having a difficult time settling on a specific one.

"You can't be that ignorant," he sneered. "I'm not my father's son. My mother kept the secret well-hidden until Tara started digging around. Why my stupid mother didn't destroy my original birth certificate is beyond me. The woman was an idiot."

"Sarah, I believe we've found our killer," Danni said matter-of-factly. "How could you do such a thing?"

Sarah's legs wobbled beneath the weight of her friend's declaration and her confrontational demeanor. Why was she being so brazen in the face of a killer? The idea ricocheted through Sarah's brain. Brady really did kill Tara! Although Sarah had alluded to him as a possible suspect earlier, she hadn't believed it was possible until he spoke again.

"I was raised the child of a prominent businessman. The firstborn son of Mr. Parker Anderson. Except I wasn't." Brady's expression turned to stone. "My parents deceived me. Worst of all, my mother kept my birth certificate *and* the letters from my biological father. She had to know someone could discover them and disinherit me."

"You killed Tara to prevent the truth from coming out and then set up Dusty to take the fall. That way everything would eventually come to you," Danni said, disbelief wrinkling her forehead.

"Tara was a fool. She thought I'd be able to accept it. Even assured me she'd speak to Dusty and make sure I had part of the inheritance. Why bother when I could have it all and maintain my good name?" he laughed.

"Except you won't. You'll be in prison," Danni said boldly.

The atmosphere felt like an electric blanket on the hottest day of August. Sarah's chest tightened at the scene unfolding in front of her. Brady was a killer and Danni was inadvertently provoking him with her bulldog attitude. Her mind pinged with possibilities. They were alone with a killer, then again, it was two against one. Worst case scenario, Brady escaped. If nothing else, they'd uncovered enough evidence to get the charges against Dusty dropped.

Sarah hoped Garrett received the text she'd sent earlier asking him to contact her immediately. Since she hadn't heard back from him, he was probably working and couldn't respond. Sarah's ruminations were interrupted by Danni's voice as she hurled another accusation at Brady.

"You're just as foolish as you accuse your mother of being. You didn't destroy the evidence. You hid it like she did!" Danni yelled, slapping his face.

"Tsk, tsk, tsk," Brady taunted, rubbing his cheek where Danni's handprint glowed red. "Letting your emotions get the best of you. Did you not learn anything from Professor Johnson about maintaining decorum in the face of an adversary?

"Adversary? Is that what I am now? After everything that's happened between us? I hold your life in my hands with this evidence," Danni blustered.

Laughter erupted from Brady's lips. "You always were a go-getter. There is no evidence, especially since no one knows about the birth certificate or the letters."

"I do!" Danni hollered. "Do you really believe I'd bury evidence and let an innocent man go to prison because of our relationship?" Danni swatted at a stray tear as her cheeks flushed a deep pink.

"Never believed you would. I know you too well," he winked. "Very well."

"You sleezy jerk. How could you use me like this?" she muttered, the devastation streaming down her face. "You're not going to get away with it."

Danni reached for her phone at the same time Brady pulled a pistol from his waistband.

"Put the phone down," he commanded.

Sarah swallowed the bile searing her throat. Would he actually kill them or was this a scare tactic to make his getaway? She glanced around the room looking for a way to escape or something she could use as a weapon. Like a boa constrictor squeezing its prey, panic suffocated her ability to think as fear slithered through her limbs.

"You won't kill us," Danni said as boldly as she could. "You'd be caught within the hour."

"I killed Tara, and no one was the wiser," he replied.

"If we figured it out, someone else will too." Danni's eyes narrowed as she spoke.

"Not likely. Sadly, there will be a fire destroying this house and all its contents. Investigators will discover the bodies of two women from out of town, here to assist with Dusty's defense." Brady stood taller, a sly smile spreading across his face.

"How will you explain the gunshot wounds?" Danni asked.

"The same way I was able to convince the judge to move the trial dates. I have a friend in the coroner's office who will sign off that you both died of smoke inhalation. The tragedies in our family are widespread."

"You had the judge change the dates? Are you mad?" Danni hollered, her voice shaking.

Sarah grasped Danni's arm. "I think we should be more concerned about the fact he wants to kill us," she whispered, the knots in her stomach tightening.

"I'm going to kill him first," Danni growled, yanking her arm from Sarah's grip and lunging for Brady.

He cocked the pistol and took aim.

"Danni!" Sarah shouted, grabbing her shoulder and pulling her back.

"We've been friends for years. More than friends," she breathed, tears flowing down her cheeks. "How could you do this?"

"Money is a powerful motivator," he replied. "Now if you'll please go upstairs, we can get this done."

"And if we refuse?" Danni said, folding her arms across her chest.

Leave it to Danni, Sarah thought, to take one last stand with a gun pointed at her. Nevertheless, Sarah hoped it would buy them some time. Surely, Garrett had received her text and was on his way. Three people, and a determined Jack Russell, against one demented maniac gave her a sliver of hope.

A chilling glint flashed in Brady's eyes, freezing Sarah to the core.

"I'm an excellent shot. I'll down both of you like a couple of stray deer and drag your corpses upstairs."

Sarah tried to take in a deep breath, but her chest was too tight. Brady actually appeared to be enjoying the moment. How had she and Danni not seen him for the lunatic he was?

"Why upstairs?" Danni asked, apparently trying to delay the inevitable.

"For such an intelligent woman you can be rather dumb at times. If you were on the first floor, you'd be more likely to escape the flames. As it is, you were trapped upstairs and overcome by smoke," he sneered. "Stop stalling Danni. This isn't a court room."

Brady motioned toward the doorway of the parlor with the pistol. Danni glanced at Sarah with a sorrowful expression. They walked to the entryway side by side and started up the stairs with Brady behind them. With each step the air grew colder until Sarah could see her breath puffing before her.

Instinctively, she looked up. Tara's translucent figure hovered over the upstairs landing surrounded by several others. Gulping down a scream, Sarah wondered if this was a sign they were about to die. Was Tara there with other ghosts from the manor to welcome them to the afterlife? They were halfway to the top when she heard Brady gasp.

"What the...?" he yelled.

Sarah turned to see Brady standing as still as a statue, his eyes wide with madness, pointing the gun toward the crowd of specters gathered on the landing.

"What kinda stunt are you trying to pull Danni?" His voice raised an octave as his hand began to shake. "This isn't funny! Turn off the camera or whatever is creating those creatures!"

Danni looked up and then back at Sarah. "What are you talking about Brady? There's nothing there."

Adrenaline pulsed through Sarah's veins prompting her limbs to quake.

"Stop it!" Brady growled through gritted teeth. "Make them go away or I'll make you suffer!"

Before Danni could say another word, Sarah watched Tara and the other ghosts float down the stairs toward Brady. Sarah braced herself. In all of her haunted encounters, she'd always tried to flee if the entities came toward her. It took every bit of fortitude not to do that now. Confusion veiled Danni's face as the shimmering figures drifted past. Tara's decaying fingers reached for Brady as she swept past Sarah who gripped the handrail to steady herself.

Brady's eyes widened as the apparitions drew closer. He leaned backwards; his gaze fixed on the gruesome images before him. His foot searched for the stair behind him but met air instead. Tara lunged forward along with the other entities, causing Brady to lose his balance and tumble down the stairs, the pistol slipping from his hand. He hit the floor with a thud, at the same moment the ghosts dissipated into nothingness. Danni and Sarah stood on the staircase unable to move, staring at Brady's motionless frame as blood oozed from the back of his skull.

A series of barks echoed from outside, accompanied by frantic scratching at the front door, breaking Sarah's trance. The door swung open bringing with it the scent of roses and a flash of fur as Dallas charged in, stopping at Brady's body.

Garrett rushed to Brady's side and took his pulse before realizing Sarah and Danni were standing there.

"What happened?" he asked breathlessly.

"He fell down the stairs," Sarah croaked, her throat as dry as toast.

"Is he...?" Danni mumbled.

Shaking his head, Garrett's expression withered. "He's got a pulse but it's weak." Garrett pulled out his cell and dialed 9-1-1.

For the first time since the ordeal began, Sarah felt like someone had drained all the blood from her body. She crumpled onto the step and leaned against the wall.

"Are you OK?" Garrett asked, hurrying up the stairs.

Danni stood straight, still staring at Brady's body.

"Danni?" Garrett said softly. "Why don't you sit down. You've had a shock."

His voice was consoling, not condescending, making Sarah's heart skip a beat.

Don't be a ghoul, she thought. *This is not the time to be thinking about Garrett. There's a body at the base of the stairs that may not survive.*

Garnering all her strength, Sarah pulled herself up and reached for Danni's hand. "Let's go to the parlor and wait for the police."

Danni nodded; her eyes still glued to the bottom of the staircase. Garrett gripped Sarah's elbow to steady her while she led Danni down the steps and past the body.

"Let me take care of Brady," Garrett said, giving Sarah's arm a gentle squeeze. "But I want to know everything that happened."

Once in the parlor, Sarah lowered herself onto the settee, her legs still trembling. Danni sat on the chair across from her while Garrett tended to Brady in the entryway. No doubt, he'd put his military training to good use. Dallas curled up at Sarah's feet, looking up at her with sympathetic brown eyes.

Moments later, sirens screeched toward the house initiating a series of howls from Dallas.

EMT's bolted through the door and began tending to Brady's injuries amidst a series of static and comments buzzing from their radios. Shortly afterwards, the police arrived. One of the cops stopped to speak with Garrett before entering the parlor.

"I'm Captain McClure," he said. "I need to talk to you about what occurred here."

The captain sat down and pulled out a pad of paper and a pen. While Danni and Sarah relayed what had transpired, Garrett stood in the entryway watching the EMTs place Brady on a stretcher and load him into the ambulance. Dallas sat faithfully with Sarah the entire time. After their statements were recorded, the police left.

Once the authorities cleared out, Garrett slipped into the parlor and sat in the wing chair.

"I heard the story you gave the police. Tell me what really happened." he said, leaning forward with his elbows resting on his knees. "I suspect there's more to this than what you told Captain McClure."

Sarah filled him in on their discovery and the confrontation with Brady. Garrett's expression altered from shock to disbelief at the recitation of the afternoon's events.

"So, you're saying Tara's ghost scared Brady down the stairs?" Garrett asked.

"Yup."

Danni looked at Sarah, her complexion sallow. "You actually saw her go after him?"

Sarah nodded. "If it hadn't been for Tara, we might be dead."

"That's incredible," Garrett said, walking to the bar to fix everyone a drink.

"There's something more," Sarah added.

"What do you mean?" Garrett asked, handing Sarah and Danni their drinks. "Brady killed Tara; the murder is solved. Thankfully, you two weren't hurt and Dusty will go free. Now that everything has been revealed, Tara should be able to move on."

"I don't think it's that simple. There were others with her. If this was only about Tara, why were the other ghosts there?"

"You're freaking me out," Danni said, her eyes darting around the room. "There's more than one ghost here?"

"Seriously? A ghost just saved our lives and you're afraid of a few more?" Sarah asked sarcastically, still a bit shaken by Brady's attempt to kill them.

"What did you see exactly?" Garrett asked, his eyes gleaming.

"Tara was standing with an older woman, a young man, and two younger women. The older woman and the young man looked familiar."

"How so?" he asked.

Sarah closed her eyes and concentrated.

"The photos!" she exclaimed. "It was Mrs. Anderson and Brady's brother!"

"And the others?"

Sarah shook her head. "Never seen them before."

"Maybe his mother and brother didn't like what Brady did to Tara, so they joined her?" Danni offered, the color beginning to return to her face.

"That's not the way it works," Garrett chuckled.

"Then what does it mean?" Danni asked.

"I'm not sure, but I remember Grams talking about ghosts finding each other when they shared a commonality."

"They were all related to Tara," Danni added.

"What about the other two women? They seemed awfully young to be dead. We know Brady's mom died of a heart condition and his brother disappeared. Now we know he's dead."

"I don't recall any other females in their family dying young. We could look into it," Garrett offered. "All of Tara's research is still at the library, right?"

"Actually, it's here," Sarah replied.

"Let's check it out."

Danni stood, her eyes rimmed in red. "I need to change clothes and go to the courthouse to start the paperwork for Dusty's release. Text me if you figure out the identities of the two women."

"Are you up to it?" Garrett asked. "You've been through a lot."

Danni straightened her shoulders and put on her best bravado. "I'm the daughter of a Marine. I'm up to anything. I don't wither, I bloom."

"Ooh rah," he replied with a broad smile, squaring his shoulders.

Danni gave a nod and left the room to shower and change.

"Are you OK?" he asked. "We can do this later."

"I'm not the daughter of a Marine but I do see dead people, so I'm pretty tough myself," Sarah replied, standing.

"Maybe we should take the research to the library. We'll get Harry to help us. He's pretty good with this sort of thing. He's the one who usually finds the identity of the ghosts we film."

Sarah stopped. "We can't tell Harry about my dreamist skills."

"Don't have to. All we have to say is you saw some ghosts at the manor. He'll buy it without further inquiries."

AN HOUR LATER, Garrett and Sarah sat side by side with Harry peering over their shoulders as they looked for family members who matched the women Sarah had seen at the house. However, neither of the women showed up in their searches.

Sarah slumped back in her chair. "If they aren't relatives, who are they and why are they with Tara at Edgefield Manor?"

"Can you describe them?" Harry asked. "Maybe I can sketch them out."

"You're an artist?"

"I'm a man of many talents," he said with a sly grin as he grabbed paper and pencil from his desk.

Sarah described the first woman and watched him outline and make modifications like a police sketch artist. As soon as he completed the image, Sarah watched Garrett and Harry's face pale.

"What's the matter?" Sarah asked.

"That's Brady's ex-wife, Sofia," Garrett replied.

"She's dead?"

"Not to our knowledge," Garrett said. "According to Brady, after the divorce she moved out west, Arizona or something like that."

Harry moved to the computer, his fingers flying across the keyboard. "Um guys, we might have a problem."

They glanced at the screen to see what he'd found.

"This lists her address as Columbia, not Arizona."

"Maybe she came back," Sarah replied, dread shadowing her expression.

"Looks like we're not done yet," Harry said.

"So, it would seem," Garrett sighed. "Let's sketch the other woman and see if we can figure out who she is."

After more than an hour, the three stared at two drawings, one of Brady's ex-wife and another of a lovely twenty-something woman with dark eyes and latte colored skin.

"You guys don't recognize her?" Sarah asked.

"Never seen her before," Harry responded, shaking his head. "How about you Garrett? Do you know her?"

"Nope," he replied.

"How do we figure out this woman's identity and why she's haunting the manor?"

"That may take some wizardry from a technologically gifted individual," Harry said, a smile raising his cheeks. "I'll get Sheila to come in and watch the library. You call Ralph."

Harry went to his desk to phone Sheila, leaving Sarah and Garrett at the table.

"Ralph is your technological wizard?"

"No, but his brother is," Garrett winked.

AN HOUR LATER, they were gathered around a laminate topped dining table at Ralph's house. He and his brother, Walter, confirmed bachelors, shared the home which appeared to be exactly as it had been in the 1970s. The brick ranch was replete with shag carpeting, paneled walls, and olive-green appliances.

"What exactly do you need me to do?" Walter asked, steepling his hands over the keyboard. He wore a black t-shirt with *Geek Commander* in bold white letters and khaki shorts. His silver-streaked brown hair was thinning at the top.

"We need to find the identity of this woman," Harry said, handing him the drawing he'd done earlier.

Walter snorted. "You don't want much, do you? What do you know about her?"

"We believe she's affiliated with Brady Anderson."

"Heaven help her," Walter grunted. Popping his knuckles, he started typing with the fluid intensity of a bee pollinating flowers in spring.

"Why do you say that?" Sarah asked, surprised by his bitter response.

"Never liked Brady. Always thought he was shady. Turns out I was right. Can't say

I was surprised when Ralph called and said he'd murdered Tara. And for what? The man's a menace."

Sarah looked at Harry and Garrett. "You guys never suspected him of being capable of something like this?"

The two men exchanged glances.

"Not really. He could be presumptuous at times and a bit arrogant about his family line, but it never occurred to me he'd be capable of hurting one of us, especially Tara," Garrett said, shrugging one shoulder.

"Ha! Presumptuous, arrogant? The man was a miscreant. Used to torment me every opportunity he got," Walter grumbled as his fingers glided across the keyboard.

His ability to chat while typing impressed Sarah. On a good day she could hunt and peck on the keyboard, and that was *without* the distraction of conversation.

"In Brady's defense, Walter didn't get along with most people growing up," Ralph added.

Walter shot his brother a menacing glance. "I don't recall you being part of his crowd."

"I played with him a couple of times. He was too bossy for me. Always wanted to control everything. And he boasted about his family name at every opportunity," Ralph said. "It got kinda old after a while."

Garrett's brows furrowed. "It never occurred to me that you didn't like him. I figured you guys had other things to do."

"Well, now you know why. The guy's a twit," Walter sneered. "Got a hit."

They all drew closer to the screen. The image was undeniable. The photo matched the sketch Harry had created.

"Who is she?" Harry asked.

"Angela Combs. Says she's a paralegal at the law firm of Brady Anderson in Columbia, SC." Walter leaned back in his chair and crossed his arms over his chest. "Care to explain why we're looking at Brady's paralegal?"

Sarah swallowed hard. "According to Danni, Brady's paralegal ran off a few weeks ago. He's been going back and forth between here and Columbia to handle his cases because she left him in a bind."

"This is getting creepier by the minute," Harry said, straightening up. "And I hunt ghosts for a hobby."

"Creepy isn't the phrase I'd choose. Demented psychopath is more appropriate," Walter blurted.

Sarah shifted on her feet. Hopefully, Walter wouldn't start asking too many questions about where she saw the young woman. She doubted she could convince him it was nothing more than a ghost sighting in a purportedly haunted house.

"At least we know who she is. Let's go back to the manor," Sarah suggested. She needed to talk to Garrett about this in private. Something sinister was going on, she knew that now. And it sounded like Walter and Ralph weren't the least bit surprised.

Thankfully, Garrett picked up on her innuendo.

"Sounds like a plan. Thanks for helping us out, Walter," Garrett said, jiggling the keys in his pants pocket.

Harry followed them to the front porch along with Ralph.

"Thanks for getting Walter to help us out. I know he's got a lot to do," Harry said.

Ralph waved his hand in the air. "If having a lot to do means trying to figure out how to infiltrate the toughest fire-walls on the Net, then yes, he's inundated with work. Most of the time he's playing video games or searching websites for the most outrageous paranormal sightings."

Harry laughed. "That's why Walter's so good at what he does, he lives on the computer. Been that way since we were young."

"Which is why he was a target for bullies like Brady," Ralph said.

"How did we not know about this?" Garrett asked.

"Because people see what they want to see in others," Ralph replied, scrunching his lips. "When you've accepted someone as a friend, it's difficult to see the unscrupulous aspects of their personality. If you think back on it, you'll find clues of his meanness that your mind naturally covered up so you could accept him as a friend and not view him as the predator he was."

"I feel terrible for not seeing it before now," Harry said, shaking his head.

"We should probably go," Sarah offered. "I think Danni wants to meet us for dinner and I don't want to be late. This is kind of a big day for her. It's not often you get charges dismissed against a client while discovering one of your closest friends is a murderer."

AFTER DROPPING Harry at the library, Garrett and Sarah headed back to the manor.

"We need to figure this out," Sarah huffed as she sat in the parlor. "We have two women who supposedly left on their own and are now hanging out with dead people. I don't think it's a coincidence."

Garrett exhaled. "I don't think it is either. Let's dig a little deeper into your dreams and see what we discover. Somehow, I don't think it's going to end favorably for Brady, or these women."

Moments later, Danni rushed through the front door and stood in the doorway of the parlor.

"Find anything?" she asked breathlessly.

"We found a few things," Sarah said with a sigh. She dreaded sharing the information Walter had found. Danni wasn't going to take the news about Brady's ex-wife and his paralegal well. She'd already suffered so much.

"We've been able to identify the two women," Sarah stated matter-of-factly. "One was Brady's ex-wife and the other was his paralegal."

Danni wrinkled her brow. "How could that be? His ex-wife lives somewhere out west and his paralegal ran off."

"Nevertheless, they were the ones with Tara."

Danni stared at Sarah. "What are you saying?"

"These two women appeared in ghostly form with Tara, and one of them happens to be missing. The truth isn't much of a stretch. I think we know the answer."

Danni started shaking her head. "No, I don't believe it. Brady would never do such a thing."

"And yet he killed Tara," Sarah said. She could tell this was crushing her friend and wanted to help her face the facts as gently as possible. Despite what happened earlier, Danni still seemed reluctant to see Brady for the monster he was.

"There's no way he did this. He and his ex were at odds, but their divorce was amicable. They split everything 50/50 and she moved away."

"Do you have proof of that?" Sarah asked.

Silence clung to the air like moss on the side of a tree.

"I don't believe what you're insinuating. Brady made a mistake with Tara. He was scared and desperate when he threatened us. But I know he wouldn't have gone through with it. I'm not saying he doesn't deserve punishment. He lost control and committed a heinous crime. But what you're suggesting is the sign of a sociopath. I've known Brady for years. I would have noticed if..." Danni swiped a tear from her cheek. "I would've known if he was a monster."

Sarah's hand rested on Danni's shoulder. She chose her words carefully. The last thing she wanted to do was reveal the depth of Danni's relationship with Brady while Garrett looked on.

"He tried to kill us. Even the most intelligent people have been fooled by friendship."

"Like Sarah said, Brady fooled all of us, especially those

closest to him," Garrett said. "You need to talk to Ralph and Walter. They have a much different perspective on Brady."

It sounded as if Garrett was beginning to accept the idea that someone he'd held in high esteem for most of his life was a murderer. Sadly, Danni was nowhere near that point. Then again, her relationship with Brady had morphed into one of a romantic nature, complicating things.

Another tear trickled across Danni's cheek. "Let's do a background check on these women. If we find them, we can dismiss the notion that Brady runs around killing people on a whim."

She sat down at her computer and started typing, her jaw set with determination. Sarah couldn't believe her friend was still supporting Brady after he'd threatened to shoot them. Moments later, the stern expression melted from Danni's face. Sitting back in the chair, she squeezed her eyes shut and took in a deep breath.

"What is it?" Sarah asked, leaning over to read the screen. "Oh no."

"What?" Garrett said.

"According to this, the former Mrs. Anderson still lives in Columbia at Brady's address," Sarah replied.

"Walter found similar results."

Danni exhaled slowly, tears puddling in her eyes. "She wouldn't have divorced him, moved out west, and then moved back in with him."

"Maybe this database is old and hasn't been updated," Sarah offered, looking for something to cheer her friend, even though she knew Sofia Anderson was deceased. Danni just needed a little time to work through everything and Sarah was determined to give her the space to do so.

Danni's fingers flew across the keyboard again, desperation creasing her forehead. "No credit card activity either."

"Could she have remarried?" Garrett asked. "Perhaps she's using a different name."

Taking a deep breath, Danni tried again. "Nothing in the court records."

"What about the paralegal, Angela Combs?" Sarah noticed Danni's fingers quivering which was a telltale sign she was about to lose it. Although rare, it wasn't a pretty sight.

After several more searches, Danni gasped. "Got something!"

"What?" Sarah and Garrett said at the same time.

"Someone filed a missing person's report on Angela Combs. It says her brother, Jonathon Combs, contacted police when he wasn't able to locate his sister after several days of trying to reach her by phone. He called her place of business and was told she hadn't shown up for work. Reportedly, her boss, Brady Anderson, had been frantically trying to reach her as well, but to no avail. To date, there have been no leads as to her whereabouts."

"Which aligns with Brady's story that she took off without saying anything," Garrett said.

"Then why not tell me about the missing person's report?" Danni queried, her eyes pleading for someone to contradict the facts before her.

"This is all speculation," Sarah replied, hoping to ease Danni into the reality of the situation. She knew her friend well enough to know she needed to work this out in her own way.

An icy chill skidded down Sarah's back as if someone had opened a freezer door behind her. Instinctively, she turned. A scream rushed across her lips at the sight of Tara with four others in varying stages of decay.

Taking a step back, Sarah stumbled against Garrett who steadied her.

"What did you see?" he asked.

Danni rose from the chair, panic stewing in her gaze.

Sarah's voice shook as she whispered. "It was Tara, except she looked like she did when she was alive. She was standing with four others who were...rotting. It was the same group that went after Brady, except now they seem to have deteriorated."

Garrett placed a hand on Sarah's shoulder. "It seems there are more in need of your help. Their stories have yet to be solved. I'm afraid this is looking worse for Brady."

"How do you mean?" Danni asked.

"The spirits clustered with Tara probably share a connection. As we suspected, Brady may have killed others."

Danni shook her head. "I still can't accept that."

"He tried to kill us Danni! How can you defend him?" Sarah's patience was running thin. Dead people haunting her, her friend's college buddy and lover trying to kill them, and not being able to figure out the answers to the ghostly appearances were making it more difficult to remain calm for Danni's sake.

Danni buried her face in her hands, her silence more crushing than anything she could have said.

"I recognized the older woman and the young man. They're the same ones from the photo albums upstairs, Mrs. Anderson and Brady's brother, Thomas," Sarah said calmly. "It would seem they want to help the other spirits move on."

"Or he killed them too!" Danni screeched. "How could Brady have been offing people and no one suspected?"

Sarah wrapped her arm around Danni's shoulder and spoke softly. "We don't have proof of anything at this point, only some unexplainable circumstances. Keep in mind, we're basing this theory on visits from ghosts and the guidance of a very old book about haunted dreams."

"Do you hear yourself?" Danni exclaimed, red splotches tinting her face. "The ghosts haven't misled you yet. Why would they start now?" Taking in a deep breath, she looked at Garrett. "Is there any chance we're mistaken about the reason for the entities appearing with Tara?"

"I'm sorry this is so difficult for you, but my grandmother

was pretty knowledgeable about this stuff. I'm going by what she taught me, and the guidance from the *Dreamist* book."

A long breath blew across Danni's lips. "We need to investigate this further."

"You mean contact the police?" Sarah asked.

"No, you need to get some sleep."

"What?" Sarah declared, her eyes widening.

"Most of the dreams have taken place at the library and the farmhouse, correct?"

"Yeah, so?"

"Tara was the only one killed at the library. The others must be connected to the farmhouse."

Sarah looked at Garrett, hoping he'd disagree. With brows raised, he shrugged his shoulders. "I'm afraid she's right. Somehow, the farmhouse is affiliated with this. Houses hold memories that don't fade away, they just stay buried until the opportune moment. Chapter nineteen in the *Dreamist* book."

"Are you saying I can be haunted by a house?" Sarah asked, practically shouting.

"A house, property, anything that contains a spirit."

"Good gracious, this is getting worse," she muttered. "Just when I thought I was getting used to the idea of being haunted by the undead, you throw houses and land into the mix. Is there anything else I should know?"

"Furniture and art can hold onto spirits too," he said apologetically.

"Ugh," Sarah replied.

"Honestly, I don't know how you made it this far in life working with antiques. I would've thought you'd be haunted every moment of the day in your line of work."

Sarah rolled her eyes. "In hindsight, I have been. I spent most of my life denying what was happening around me."

"Considering you had no guidance until a year ago, I'd say

you've handled it pretty well. Now it's time to broaden your skillset," Garrett said.

Confidence flowed from his stare, buoying Sarah from the waves of self-doubt.

"Let's try it," Sarah replied, nervous energy flowing through her limbs. "If Brady killed these women, we need to make sure he's punished for it."

With a sniffle, Danni swiped at her eyes. "I don't want to believe he did these things, yet I still can't reconcile the image of him trying to kill us either. I've faced a lot of people in court who refuse to acknowledge the facts before them because they care about the person who committed the crime. I don't want to be one of those people."

Sarah could see the internal battle raging between Danni's heart and her mind. But the Danni she knew and loved was slowly resurfacing. This was the woman who would stop at nothing to bring justice to any unresolved crime, even if it shattered her heart in the process.

26

E   ventide succumbed to nightfall in a dusky sunset of
        muted oranges and golds. The truck bounced over the
        rutted driveway leading to the Anderson farmhouse,
the headlights reflecting from the darkened windows in an
eerie dance. As soon as Garrett put the truck in park and
opened his door, Dallas darted out and up to the front porch
where he sniffed every board. Sarah, Danni, and Garrett
stepped onto the porch, retrieved the key from under the mat,
and opened the front door.

The stale odor of the house felt oppressive in light of
Brady's involvement with Tara's death. Now they needed the
house to act as a conduit to help them solve the mysteries
behind the grouping of ghosts from Sarah's dreams. Her
stomach knotted at the thought of the haunted visions that
would seek her out. At least she had Danni, Garrett, and Dallas
by her side. After a lifetime of facing ghosts alone, she now had
a team of people, and an intuitive dog, to help her maneuver
the hauntings.

A shiver raced through Sarah's body as she scanned the

shadowy front parlor, the clock on the mantel a reminder of their discovery identifying Brady as Tara's killer.

"Are you alright?" Garrett asked, resting his hand on Sarah's shoulder, her skin tingling beneath his touch.

"Just want to get this over with," she replied. Something in her gut suggested the ghosts would reveal more than she was prepared to accept.

"Are you even tired?" Danni asked.

"Actually, I'm exhausted but I'm also wired."

"Thought you might say that," she said, pulling a silver flask from her bag. "Brought a little bourbon to escort you to dreamland."

"You know me so well," Sarah said, accepting the container.

She walked over to the sofa and sat. Opening the flask, she took a long draw before lying down. With her head propped against the arm of the sofa, she took another swig and closed her eyes.

"Can't sleep with you guys staring at me," she said.

"We'll look around the rest of the house. Maybe we can find something explaining the presence of Brady's ex and his paralegal in your dreams," Garrett replied.

Sarah leaned up on her elbow. "What could you possibly find about his paralegal here? She lived in Columbia. I doubt she ever traveled with him to Edgefield. Based on the layers of dirt and the road map of cobwebs in this place, it doesn't look like he came here often."

"Unless he was having an affair with her. Maybe he killed his wife so he could continue his relationship with his paralegal," Danni declared, her expression paling. "He seems to have a knack for seducing women." Her voice trailed off as she rubbed her eyes.

Seeing her friend in a state of confusion and disbelief yanked at Sarah's heart. Danni was the stalwart, logical part of their friendship. Rarely did she show pain or emotional reactions. It's what made her such a good attorney. Now she seemed conflicted between what she'd always believed about Brady and the reality of who he turned out to be.

"Let's not jump to conclusions. Hopefully, the ghosts will reveal their secrets and we can get to the truth," Sarah said gently.

Danni took in a deep breath and nodded.

"Now let me get some sleep or we'll never know what's going on."

Sarah leaned back on the sofa and listened as Garrett and Danni left the room. Moments later, she heard the clicking of Dallas's paws against the floorboards right before he leapt onto the sofa and snuggled at her feet. She opened her eyes and saw him watching the room. Smiling, she took another drink, screwed on the cap, and waited for sleep to find her.

WIND SWEPT across the cornfields behind the farmhouse, dislodging branches from trees. Thunder shook the ground as the rain came down in torrents, making it difficult for Sarah to see clearly. A bolt of lightning illuminated the area, revealing two women, Sofia and Angela, standing amongst wilted and dried cornstalks, their empty eyes staring in her direction. As she started to walk, the mud beneath her feet suctioned her in place. An eerie feeling niggled at her nerves making her want to turn back, yet she couldn't get her feet free from the muck. Sarah trembled in the frigid downpour, her hair clinging to her neck as water trickled across her shoulders and down her back.

Lightning ripped through the rain, its electric tendrils reaching across the sky. When the light show ceased, the two women stood directly in front of Sarah. Gasping, she steadied her racing pulse with a few deep breaths.

Their faces were pallid and bits of flesh were missing where decay had nibbled at their corpses. Despite the terror rippling through her chest and the chill of the rain, Sarah found her voice.

"Why are you here?" she muttered between chattering teeth.

Brady's ex-wife waved a decaying hand across the cornfields, erasing the withering stalks as she and the paralegal dissipated. All of a sudden, Sarah was able to move her feet. She walked across the empty field to mounds of dirt. Kneeling down, she ran her fingers across the soggy earth when a putrefying hand poked from the ground, wrapping its fingers around Sarah's wrist. She tried to yank free but only succeeded in pulling the corpse up from the spongy soil.

Tumbling backwards, Sarah hit the ground with a slimy splash as mud adhered to her clothes. The cadaver landed on top of her, its lipless mouth trying to speak. Sarah gulped down the fear strangling her words when another set of hands popped up from the ground and grabbed her ankles. A scream materialized from deep within as she bolted upright in the darkened parlor of the farmhouse.

Gasping, Sarah sucked in dry air as Danni and Garrett ran into the room.

"What happened?" Danni asked.

"Are you alright?" Garrett said at the same time.

Sarah exhaled; her shoulders still taut. Dallas licked her cheek, comforting her. She leaned over and nuzzled his soft head before speaking.

"Brady's ex-wife and paralegal were in the cornfield out back during a terrible storm. His ex-wife waved her hand in the air, making the cornstalks disappear and exposing two mounds of dirt. When I approached, a decomposing hand grabbed hold of me and then another," she paused. "That's when I woke up."

Danni grimaced. "Eww, that's disgusting."

"Terrifying is more like it."

"We need to figure out what they were trying to tell you,"

Garrett added. His matter-of-fact tone along with Dallas's furry body snuggling against her, helped to sooth Sarah's racing pulse.

"I'm not sure what any of it means," she said, shaking her head.

Garrett sat on the chair across from the sofa and leaned forward, his elbows resting on his knees.

"All we need to do is follow the clues. You said the two women were in the cornfield?"

"Yeah."

"And then Brady's ex-wife waved her hand and the corn stalks disappeared."

"After that the corpses started coming for me," Sarah said, rubbing her upper arms.

"Sounds kinda cryptic to me," Danni snorted.

"Very funny," Sarah replied, rolling her eyes. She could always count on Danni's demented sense of humor to lighten a tense moment.

"Actually, it's pretty straight forward," Garrett said.

"It is?" Danni and Sarah said in unison.

"You saw the two missing women, the corn disappeared, revealing two mounds of dirt from which the bodies emerged."

"Exactly," Sarah replied.

"It sounds like the women are definitely deceased and are somehow connected with the cornfields."

"As in buried back there?" Danni said, her upper lip scrunching in disgust.

"It's the most logical interpretation," he responded.

"You're actually suggesting their bodies are in the cornfield out back?" Danni said.

"Got any other theories?" he asked.

"I got nothing," Danni replied, throwing her hands in the air.

"What are we going to do?" Sarah asked. "It's too dark to start digging."

"Let's go home and get some sleep. First thing in the morning we can come back and check this out. I've got a friend who does archeological digs. Maybe he can help us."

Sarah nodded. "I'm more than ready to go. Let's get out of here."

Hopping up from the sofa, Sarah led the way with Dallas on her heels.

They locked the door behind them, piled into Garrett's truck, and rode in silence back to town. The sight of Edgefield Manor was a welcome relief after the harrowing dreams at the farmhouse. Sarah and Danni bid Garrett goodnight and went inside.

"This has been one heck of a day," Danni said, trudging up the stairs with Sarah behind her.

"Absolutely," Sarah replied. "I have to admit, it's nice having Garrett's input. He's good at interpreting this stuff."

Danni stopped at the upstairs landing and turned to Sarah. "Agreed. With his knowledge and experience, I think you're going to make a lot of progress with your dreamist skills."

"*We're* going to make a lot of progress. You and I are in this together," Sarah said with a slight smile.

Danni grinned back at her. "Looks like our duo has grown into a trio."

"You mean quartet."

Danni cocked her head and furrowed her brows.

"Dallas is an integral member too."

"That he is," Danni replied as they walked into the bedroom.

After washing up and changing into their night clothes, it didn't take long before Sarah and Danni drifted off to dreamland where Sarah's dreams were far from finished.

. . .

A TEN-YEAR-OLD BRADY ran through the farmhouse with his brother chasing him. Their laughter bounced off the walls, saturating the space in the joy of childhood antics. They bolted out the back door, the screen door bouncing in its frame, as their mother called for them to stop running in the house. The scent of jasmine and roses intermingled with the freshly cut grass as the boys sprinted toward the pond.

The scene altered. A much older Brady stood at the edge of the same pond, staring at the murky water, watching bubbles percolating in one spot, Brady's brother, Thomas, bobbed up from the water, his skin sallow and bloated. He pointed toward Brady who grinned mischievously, his empty stare suggesting a soulless man without a conscience. Thomas's swollen corpse started toward Sarah, its hands reaching out as if begging for help.

Sitting upright in bed, Sarah buried her face in her hands. The nightmares were vivid and nauseating. She engaged in her deep breathing exercises which quieted her quivering limbs; however, they did little to calm her mind. She glanced at the glowing numbers on the bedside clock which read 4:10 a.m. She'd only been asleep for two hours, yet it felt like she'd been awake for days.

Sarah scratched a few notes in the journal on the bedside table, so she'd remember the details in the morning. Deep down she knew what the dreams were trying to reveal but couldn't bring herself to accept it. Between Danni and Garrett, she was confident they'd unravel the meaning of the haunted visions. Resting her head on the pillow, she desperately wanted to go back to sleep but feared what grisly scene would appear next.

GARRETT ARRIVED EARLY the next morning. They gathered around the kitchen table over steaming cups of coffee and tea.

"I had another dream," Sarah said, sipping her tea.

"About the two women?" Danni asked.

She shook her head. "This was about Brady's brother. Based on his recurring appearances with Tara and the others, I think we can safely assume he's dead."

"What did you dream?" Garrett asked, leaning forward.

"Brady and his brother were children. They were running through the house and down to the pond. Then the scene shifted and Brady was a grown man. He stood at the edge of the pond as his brother's corpse rose from the water. It scared me awake," she said, taking in a breath.

"Thomas was in the pond?"

"Yes. Looked like he'd drowned. His skin was gray and puffy."

Silence blanketed the room. Finally, Garrett spoke.

"We need to go back to the farmhouse and look through the cornfield for any mounds. I'll call Harry and get him to bring his scuba gear. Maybe he can search the pond for any signs of Thomas's remains."

"Harry scuba dives?" Danni asked.

"Harry does a little bit of everything. Don't let his down-to-earth demeanor fool you into thinking he's a simple guy."

"If we do find something, how do we explain it to the police? We can't tell them that ghosts sent us." Sarah slumped back in the chair.

"First, we need to find out if there are actually bodies on the farm. Then we can figure out a way to let the police know without implicating ourselves or telling them about Sarah's secret," Garrett responded.

The confidence in his voice gave Sarah the courage to go through with this crazy scheme. The thought of searching for bodies was unnerving; however, it wasn't the first time she'd dug for bones after a dream.

. . .

AN HOUR LATER, Danni, Sarah, and Garrett arrived at the farmhouse. They hopped from the truck and grabbed shovels from the bed while Dallas zig-zagged across the yard with nose to the ground tracking the scent of some woodland animal.

"Let's search for Team Dead," Danni said, holding her shovel like the farmer in the painting American Gothic.

"Team Dead?" Sarah asked with a sideways glance.

"If your dreams and visions are correct, then it was a team of ghosts that lead you to the truth. Instead of the walking dead, they're team dead."

Garrett laughed and Sarah shook her head as they walked to the back of the house to comb the old cornfield in search of possible burial sites. Dallas continued tracking the area, his nose skimming the dirt and his tail bobbing in rhythm with his gate. Harry was going to meet them later in the morning.

Divots and weeds covered the once fertile soil. They ambled along, staring at the ground for any evidence of newly shifted earth. Moments later, Dallas started barking and pawing at a patch of dirt. They raced over with shovels in hand. Garrett commanded Dallas to stop which he did, his snout speckled with dirt.

"This seems like a good place to start," Garrett said, sweat sparkling across his forehead.

Danni rested one hand on top of the shovel handle and propped the other on her hip as she looked at Sarah. "This feels a bit like déjà vu."

Garrett paused. "Huh?"

"This isn't our first experience digging for bodies in a garden," Sarah said with an eye roll.

"Now, that's a story I want to hear," he chuckled, stabbing the shovel into the ground.

"Are you sure we should do this?" Sarah asked, looking at Danni. "The last time we dug for a body, the victim had been dead for more than a hundred years. If there are remains here, this is a crime scene, isn't it?"

"We could always tell them you're a dreamist and the ghosts led us here," Danni said.

"Are you nuts?" Sarah declared.

"I'm joking," Danni snorted. "Just trying to lighten the mood."

"She's right. We were so fixated on discovering the truth, we didn't think this all the way through. There's no viable reason for us being on Brady's property, more or less digging on the land," Garrett said.

"Perhaps we don't need to involve the police yet," Danni suggested, a wicked grin lifting her cheeks. "I could try to get a confession from Brady."

"Do you really believe he'd confess?" Garrett queried, wiping the sweat from his brow. "He didn't exactly admit to killing Tara."

"I have my ways," she replied. "Keep in mind, I know Brady intimately. His weaknesses are few, but he's got them. Not to mention, I can be extremely persuasive at times." Her eyes twinkled at the prospect of taking on a challenge. Thankfully, Garrett didn't question how *intimately* Danni knew Brady.

"I can attest to her persuasive skills," Sarah added. "I've seen her negotiate with her father dozens of times."

"And she won every time?" Garrett asked.

"Actually, no, but she was very persuasive."

Danni smacked Sarah's arm. "Dad was immoveable. Brady's freedom is on the line. Another body could land him on death row. If he confesses, I can offer to get a life sentence instead of the needle. He's a self-centered twit who will jump at the chance to save his own neck."

"Let's try it. If he doesn't confess, then we come up with another way to lure the police out here," Garrett said.

"Sounds like a plan," Sarah agreed as they headed for the truck.

A flash of sorrow dissolved the momentary spark from Danni's face, as she trudged along. Sarah touched her friend's arm. "I'm sorry Brady turned out to be a sociopath."

"Apparently, the Brady I knew never existed."

"Maybe he can redeem himself with a confession," Sarah suggested.

Danni straightened. "He'll never redeem himself with me, but I *will* get that confession."

Garrett dropped them off at the house and went home. After showering, Danni hopped in her Mercedes and headed for the hospital where Brady was being held until his injuries allowed for transport to the jail. Sarah's nerves prickled with electricity and her stomach churned. She knew how hard this was for her friend. Danni had always been there for her, even after learning about her haunted dreams. More than ever, she wanted to repay her by being with her when she confronted Brady. Sadly, under the circumstances, it wasn't possible.

In an effort to occupy her time, Sarah started removing tags from the items for the estate sale. Now that Dusty had been cleared, his mother no longer needed to raise funds for his defense.

Thunder shook the floor and rattled windowpanes. Looking out, Sarah watched storm clouds parade across the sky, leaving a trail of pewter in its wake. A bolt of lightning sliced through the steel gray canopy followed by a roaring boom. Her limbs twitched at the atmospheric show as droplets splattered against the windows. The moment was interrupted when the grandfather clock in the front hall began to chime.

Glancing that direction, Sarah swallowed hard. Something had to be in the house since the clock couldn't possibly chime after smashing to the floor the previous day. A shudder rankled her frame when a gentle touch rested on her forearm, sending a sense of peace flooding through her limbs. She glanced up to see Ola's smiling face, making her feel safe, regardless of what waited.

When Sarah turned, she saw the group of ghosts standing with Tara. On one side, was Brady's ex-wife and former paralegal, and on the other his mother and brother.

"I don't understand," Sarah muttered. "We're pretty sure Brady had a hand in the disappearance of his ex-wife and paralegal, but why are his mother and brother here?"

Mrs. Anderson stepped forward, the pallor of her skin the same shade as the storm clouds. She held out her hand and dropped something to the floor, sending Sarah skittering backwards as it rolled toward her. A small glass container rotated several times until it came to rest at Sarah's feet. Ola's translucent visage gave a quick nod before Sarah reached down, picked up the small bottle, and studied the label.

Cocking her head, Sarah looked at Mrs. Anderson's wavering image.

"Poison?" she whispered. "Is this how you died?"

Her head bobbed in slow motion. Her son, Thomas, stood at her side. His clothes were soaked and water dripped from his hair and hands.

"And his brother drowned in the pond?" Sarah queried.

She nodded.

"Did Brady have something to do with all of this?"

The soggy apparition nodded again. How had Brady been able to cover up the nature of his mother's death and the fact his brother hadn't run off but was decaying at the bottom of the pond only yards from the farmhouse?

Danni's previous statement about small town citizens protecting prominent residents flashed through her mind. If Brady had persuaded the judge to move Dusty's court date forward, it wouldn't be impossible to cover up the murder of his mother and brother. When Brady had held her and Danni at gunpoint, he'd mentioned getting the coroner to alter their cause of death. It wouldn't be improbable for him to have done the same for his mother. With his brother's alleged disappearance, there was no need to cover it up. Sarah swallowed hard. Brady truly was a serial killer.

Danni's heart was already shattered over Brady murdering Tara, his ex-wife, and his paralegal, but his own family members? It was almost too much. He'd seemed like such a great guy.

Sarah glanced at her phone. Danni was probably meeting with Brady right now, which meant she'd have her phone on mute. The best she could do would be to leave a message, but she'd not leave this kind of news in a voice mail.

"Sorry, but there's no way for me to reach her," Sarah said to the translucent entities hovering before her.

Sarah's phone buzzed in her pocket, making her jump. She pulled it out and stared in disbelief. *Call hospital* scrolled across the screen.

She remembered seeing a phone book in the kitchen and hurried to find the number for the hospital. With any luck, they'd let her speak to Danni. She found the number and dialed, her heart thrumming against her ribcage as she waited.

"Edgefield Hospital, how may I direct your call?"

"This is Sarah Holden. I need to speak with Danni Cook. She's meeting with Brady Anderson who was brought in with a head injury. He's probably in police custody."

The woman's tone cooled. Obviously, news had already spread through the hospital. "Not permitted to connect you."

"Then could you please get a message to her? It pertains to her meeting."

The woman on the other end sighed. "What's the message?"

Sarah hesitated. She couldn't blurt out that Brady may have

killed his mother and brother. "Tell her they're all on the same team. She'll understand." *Hopefully*, she thought.

"Right," she replied. "Anything else?"

"That's all. Thank you."

Hanging up, she dialed Garrett's number. He answered on the first ring.

"Did she get the confession?" he asked.

"Don't know; however, I had a visit from Ola and the others," Sarah said.

"And?"

Sarah relayed the broken clock chiming from the entryway followed by his grandmother standing beside her as the others revealed the poisoning and drowning.

"There's actually a bottle of poison?"

"I'm not sure how the ghost was able to produce a physical item, but it's right here," Sarah said, looking at the container in her hand.

"You've got me on that one. I don't remember Grams mentioning a ghost making something materialize in solid form."

"Looks like we've got some more reading to do," she chuckled.

"I've read that book numerous times and never come across anything like this," he replied. "Then again, this could be a play from your personal *Dreamist* book. You do deal in antiquities."

Sarah's stomach flopped. Ever since she'd learned of Garrett's connections to and knowledge of dreamists, she'd felt more secure. Yet, this revelation dismantled her confidence a bit.

Silence charged the air.

"You still there?" Garrett asked.

"Yeah, I'm just trying to process all the things I still have to learn. It's a bit overwhelming."

"There are some things in the book that might allow you to ask another dreamist for guidance."

"Living or dead?" Sarah queried.

"Probably dead. Other than familial associations, it's rare that living dreamists connect. As you know, it's not something they usually make public. I'll look for the answer later this evening. Do you want me to come over while we wait to hear from Danni?"

Yes, Sarah thought, her heart rate accelerating. Except this wasn't the time to get caught up in her growing attraction to a man who lived three hours away. Now that Dusty's name had been cleared, she and Danni would be going home soon. Inhaling, Sarah closed her eyes.

"I appreciate the offer, but I've got a ton of stuff to do. Since there won't be an estate sale, I'm trying to put everything back in order. Melinda's been through enough and doesn't need to worry about cleaning up this place."

"If you change your mind, text me," he said, his voice steeped in disappointment.

"Thanks for understanding," Sarah replied, hoping to diffuse the awkwardness of the moment.

She hung up with a promise to text as soon as she heard from Danni. Too nervous to sit still, Sarah resumed removing tags from items as thunder rumbled and rain beat against the roof in a cadenced cantata.

THE RAIN MOVED ON, leaving behind glittering droplets on tree leaves and flower petals. Sarah was working upstairs when she heard the crunching of tires over gravel. Running to the window, she watched Danni park and emerge from the car. Her face was sullen and her step subdued as she climbed the porch stairs.

Sarah texted Garrett before racing to the front parlor where Danni was filling a highball glass with scotch.

"That bad?" Sarah asked, taking a seat on the settee.

Danni slumped onto the wing chair and kicked off her heels. Her eyes were puffy, letting Sarah know the news must be pretty awful. Danni rarely cried.

"Depends on what you consider bad," she responded before taking a long sip from the glass.

"What happened?" Sarah asked, checking her phone as it dinged.

"Want to wait for your boyfriend to get here first?" Danni asked, a silly smile curling her lips.

Sarah leaned over and shoved Danni's arm. "He's *not* my boyfriend! He's involved in this too and wanted me to let him know when you got here."

"The old *I promised I'd text* excuse. Good one," she said, scrunching her lips.

"Stop it," Sarah blustered. "If he hadn't helped me understand this dreamist stuff, Dusty would still be sitting in jail. He deserves to hear what happened."

Danni downed the rest of her drink and got up to pour another. "Want something?" she asked.

"Not right now."

Moments later, Garrett and Dallas came through the front door, the small dog leaping onto Sarah's lap.

"Got here as fast as I could," he said, sitting on the other chair while Sarah cuddled Dallas. "Did Brady tell you anything?"

"You could say that," she replied, clearly disturbed by the afternoon's events. "Although I wasn't expecting what I learned. Want something?"

"No, thanks," Garrett said, leaning forward with his elbows resting on his knees. Sarah snuggled with Dallas as Danni began the sordid tale.

"It's so much worse than we thought. I told him we'd found multiple bodies at the farmhouse and demanded to know who they were." Danni took another sip of her drink. "He gave me some sob story about being sorry for threatening to kill us and begged for my forgiveness. Then he tried to convince me the bodies were probably civil war soldiers. Can't believe he thought I was that stupid."

"He's desperate," Sarah said.

"Anyway, I told him that wasn't possible because the bodies were in the old cornfield and would have been discovered years ago if they were soldiers. His expression wilted and I knew at that moment he was guilty of killing his ex-wife and probably his paralegal. I said I'd investigated and discovered they hadn't run away as he'd claimed. His face reddened and I thought he was going to break the cuffs holding him to the bed and come after me. Then he did the personality switch and pulled himself together. Tried the sympathy tactic. He said, 'You know me, Danni. I'd never do something like that. Tara was just an accident. I didn't mean to kill her. I only wanted to keep her from telling everyone I wasn't biologically related to the Andersons'.'" Danni slumped back in the chair. "Before I could go on, the nurse brought me your message."

"You understood it?" Sarah said.

"Of course, I did. Pretty clever by the way."

"Someone want to catch me up?" Garrett asked, sitting straighter.

"I left a message with one of the nurses asking her to tell Danni that they were all on the same team."

"In other words, he killed all of the people who've been haunting Sarah," Danni added. "Once the nurse left, I confronted him about his mother. It was like watching Jekyll and Hyde. His entire demeanor shifted and he spoke in a low growl. Said they all deserved what they got. Told me his mother had no right to hide the letters revealing his true birth history and that his brother was a spoiled, entitled kid who'd only cause heartache and disappointment if he'd been allowed to live. I thought I was going to be sick."

Danni paused and sipped her drink.

"His face contorted when he explained how he strangled his wife because she said she was leaving and demanded half of his inheritance. When his paralegal stumbled upon some inconsistencies in his records and started asking questions, he had no choice but to get rid of her too. Not a shred of remorse for what he did. His eyes were as empty as a swimming pool after Labor Day.

"I told him he was going down for all of it. That's when he threw his head back and laughed. Said I couldn't say a word because of attorney-client privilege."

"Oh my gosh, I hadn't thought of that," Sarah gasped.

"His mistake. I reminded him no contractual agreement had been made, thus no attorney-client anything. I said I'd be willing to represent him for sentencing if he confessed to the crimes and I'd do my best to arrange a lighter punishment, such as life without parole instead of death row."

"Did he accept?" Garrett asked.

Danni nodded as she swirled the liquid in her glass. Everyone sat quietly for a moment.

"So, he's confessed to killing his ex-wife, paralegal, mother, and brother?" Sarah queried.

"His brother was his first victim. Said he knocked him over the head with a hammer, tied weights to his body, and dumped him in the pond. When his mother shared the secret about his birth, he poisoned her coffee. Since she had a heart condition no one questioned her untimely death. She's the only one who received a proper burial.

"When his ex-wife filed for divorce and demanded part of his inheritance, he was afraid her lawyers would discover the truth about his lineage. He strangled her and took her body to the farmhouse where he buried her in the old cornfield. Then his paralegal stumbled on the discrepancies with his ex-wife's address, so he strangled her and disposed of her body in the same way.

"Poor Tara came across the letters and his birth certificate during her genealogical research and made the connections about his paternal ancestry. She called him to the library that night to discuss it privately. He panicked. Said he started out the back door when he saw the fireplace poker in the basement. It had been part of a display at the library showcasing local artists. He went back upstairs, snuck up on Tara, and smashed her in the head. He set up Dusty and played the concerned cousin by hiring me. And you know the rest."

"He did all this so he could inherit the estate?" Sarah grimaced.

"Yeah," Danni replied.

Garrett shook his head. "I can't believe this is the same person I grew up with. Brady was always a bit arrogant, but that was his nature. No one thought much of it."

"But there's more. When he was whining about being sorry and trying to play on my sympathies, he alluded to Dusty's financial difficulties. It seems Dusty borrowed money from some lowlife who gives loans at an exorbitant rate. Apparently, Dusty wasn't able to make his payment and went to Brady for help. Brady didn't want anything to do with it. Dusty was scared this guy might have him killed so he took out the insurance policies. That way Tara would be taken care of in the event he was killed."

"Brady refused to help him?" Sarah asked incredulously.

"Probably hoped the loan guy killed Dusty so he'd inherit everything."

"Except Melinda is still alive," Garrett said.

"Her life may have been cut short if Brady hadn't been stopped," Danni sighed. "Anyway, I went by Melinda's house on my way here. I wanted her to hear everything from me since the news will spread like wildfire through a town this small. She said we could stay here as long as we needed since I'll need to work on Brady's sentencing."

"You're really going to defend him?" Sarah asked.

"I made a deal. If he confessed, I'd represent him for the sentencing. If I hadn't, we might not know about all the victims, not to mention trying to prove he murdered them. All he would've needed was a good attorney to create reasonable doubt and Brady could've gotten away with the other murders, especially with his connections here."

"I'm sorry, Danni," Sarah said.

"Me too," she replied. "All my memories of Brady are nothing more than illusions. How could I not see who he was? What does that say about me as a lawyer?"

Garrett reached over and grasped Danni's hand.

"I can relate to that. All of the good times at the farmhouse seem tainted now. None of us could have suspected he was a murderer."

"The Brady you both knew never existed," Sarah said. "Your friendship shows you're both loyal friends who see the best in people. There's nothing wrong with that."

Dallas gazed up at Sarah with his deep brown eyes and licked her chin. She kissed the top of his head and snuggled him close.

They sat for several minutes without saying a word when Danni finally spoke.

"Don't know about you two, but I'm hungry."

And just like that, the old Danni was back, or at least she was pretending to be. Sarah knew it would take time for her to heal from her emotional wounds, but it wouldn't prevent her from moving on and living her life. It was one of the things Sarah loved best about her closest friend.

27

A fter dinner, Garrett and Dallas dropped Sarah and Danni off at Edgefield Manor and went home. They were all exhausted from the day's events. Danni went straight to the dining room and plunked behind her computer to work on a sentencing recommendation for Brady. Even though Sarah knew her friend was emotionally drained, she also knew Danni needed to see this through to the end.

"If it's OK with you, I'm going to bed. I'm beat," Sarah yawned.

"Goodnight. At least now you can have peaceful dreams," Danni said with a weak smile before returning to her typing.

Sarah readied herself for bed and opened the bedroom window, taking in the sweet fragrances of a sultry summer night. She crawled into bed and rested her head against the pillow, thankful the hauntings would be over. The shock of all that had been revealed in the past twenty-four hours weighted Sarah's limbs as her eyelids fluttered shut.

. . .

THE SHIMMERING BLUE light of the heart monitor bathed the hospital room in an eerie glow. Brady slumbered as the bleeping of machines kept time with the ticking of the circular clock on the wall behind his bed. The glint of the handcuff sparkled in the darkness.

Brady stirred, his eyes blinking open. Licking his lips, he glanced about the room when his gaze fixated on the curtain surrounding his bed. The fabric wavered as a fog formed. Brady's eyes grew larger as he tried to sit up, but the handcuff prevented it. He yanked on the shackle several times as the misty cloud began to shift into five forms. Tara, Sofia, Angela, Mrs. Anderson, and Thomas appeared, their zombie-like bodies cloaked in decay.

Opening his mouth, Brady tried to scream but it was muffled by the sudden convergence of the apparitions as they descended upon him. The beeping of the heart monitor increased as the blue line spiked uncontrollably. Brady's body shuttered and convulsed as the rotting hands of the corpses wrapped around his neck and clawed at his face. With one final convulsion, the beeping stopped, and the line went flat.

Sarah gasped as she jolted awake. Sitting up, she rubbed her eyes and took in a deep breath. Footsteps pounded up the stairs followed by Danni bolting into the room. Her breathing was labored as tears streamed across her cheeks.

"What's wrong?" Sarah asked.

"The hospital called," she croaked. "Brady is..."

"Dead." Sarah finished her sentence.

"Huh? How do you know that?"

"I just dreamed it."

Danni moved to the bedside and sat down, her expression one of bewilderment.

"I don't understand," she mumbled.

"In the dream, Brady was asleep but woke up when a group of ghosts materialized. He tried to get away, but he was cuffed to the bed. Before he could call for help, they surrounded him, clawing at his face and choking him. He must have had a heart attack because the monitors went quiet."

Danni gulped.

"What is it?" Sarah asked.

"They said the cause of death was a massive heart attack."

Wrapping her arms around Danni, Sarah patted her back as her friend sobbed into her shoulder. She knew Danni was torn between the Brady she loved and the degenerate he turned out to be. Regardless, his death was a shock.

Sarah pulled back and looked at her friend. "I'm so sorry."

"Don't be. Saved me the trouble of having to keep him off death row." She wiped at her cheeks. "Looks like he got death by ghost instead."

Squeezing Danni's hand, Sarah nodded. "So, it would seem."

NEWS OF BRADY'S death and his killing spree spread across town like a cool breeze in autumn. Shock, sorrow, and speculation filtered through restaurants, social gatherings, and the press. An autopsy revealed Brady had a genetic heart condition which led to his heart attack. The only people who knew the truth were Sarah, Danni, and Garrett.

Brady's body was cremated and his ashes scattered at the farmhouse. Despite all he'd done, Dusty and Melinda felt it was the right thing to do. No services were held. He was tossed to the wind without so much as a tear. A fitting end for a sociopathic monster.

Thomas Anderson's remains were recovered from the pond and given a proper burial next to his parents in the family plot. Brady's ex-wife Sofia, and his paralegal Angela, were transported to their respective families for burial. Finally, Brady's victims were at rest.

Danni, Sarah, Garrett, and the ghost hunting team gathered at Corner Pocket. Dusty declined the invitation, claiming he needed time to get his affairs in order and to grieve for his wife. Turned out, the secret Harry had been talking about during the phone conversation Sarah overheard at the library, was about Dusty's perilous interaction with a loan shark. Harry was aware of the situation but sworn to secrecy by Dusty. Fortunately, the life insurance policy on Tara paid off the nefarious character, allowing Dusty to escape any unpleasant collection tactics.

With the legal aspects over, there was no reason for Danni and Sarah to stay. They were scheduled to travel back to Beaufort on Sunday. Sarah rocked in one of the wooden rockers on the front porch of the manor, surrounded by the chirping of birds and the playful antics of squirrels as they scurried about the yard. She startled when her cell phone rang.

"Hello."

"Hey Sarah, it's Garrett."

"What's up?"

"Since you guys are going home on Sunday, I wanted to know if you'd like to join me at the club on Saturday night. Danni is welcome to come with us."

Sarah snickered. "No need to invite her, she hates any music before the 80s."

"So, you'll join me?"

She could hear the eagerness in his voice and it made her smile.

"Sure," she replied more confidently than she felt. The battle between her heart and her head continued. "I like that place."

"Pick you up at 7:00."

"See you then." She hung up and gazed out over the landscape at the heirloom rose bushes and blooming hydrangeas. In the far corner something moved. She stopped rocking and sat straighter. A smile lifted Sarah's lips as she watched Tara, her head injury no longer visible, give a slight nod and a wave before dissipating into nothingness.

Another mystery solved and another ghost free to cross over. Sarah felt a pang of sorrow over the fact she'd never see Tara again. She'd felt the same way about Nora after the mystery at Monroe Manse was solved. After experiencing so much of their lives through her dreams, she found herself missing the ghosts when they were gone. Then again, Tara was a dreamist. Maybe she'd reappear sometime in the future like Garrett's grandmother, Ola. The rungs of the rocker resumed their creaking as Sarah rocked back and forth. There was nothing better than relaxing on the front porch of an old house amidst summer's splendor.

GARRETT PICKED up Sarah at seven o'clock and drove out of town to Fitzgerald's. The feel of his hand warmed hers as he helped her from the truck. The sound of Benny Goodman roared as they stepped into the building where dancers were swinging and jiving in the darkened space.

They took a seat at the same table they'd occupied on their previous visit and ordered drinks. *In the Mood* started playing. Garrett hopped up from his seat, offered his hand, and led Sarah onto the dance floor where they danced the Lindy Hop until Sarah was breathless and glistening with sweat. Before they could catch their breath, the lilting tune of *La Vie en Rose* drifted across the room.

Garrett swept Sarah into his arms, his deep green gaze penetrating her heart as they swayed to and fro amongst the other couples. As the music cascaded over her, Sarah let go of the fear and trepidation that had held her captive for so long. For the first time in her life, she gave herself permission to have a good time without overthinking or analyzing the possible outcome. Tonight, she was a regular woman dancing with a handsome man who happened to share a love of ghosts, haunted houses, and big band music.

HER FEET THROBBED and her ears buzzed at the end of the evening as she climbed into the truck. She and Garrett chatted all the way back to the manor as if they'd always known each other. It was the most memorable evening of her life. As he pulled down the drive and put the truck in park, a pang of sorrow rifled Sarah's chest. She'd grown more attached to him than she wanted to admit. The reality of her departure the next morning hung over them like rainclouds in spring. They sat in silence for a few moments as the sound of croaking frogs and trilling crickets filled the air.

"I had a good time tonight," Garrett said, his gaze locked onto hers.

"Me too," she replied, her mouth dry and her eyes glistening.

Garrett blew out a long breath. "I'm not sure what to say. I've grown fond of you, Sarah."

"I like you too but..." her words fell away when she saw regret flicker in his eyes. "You live three hours from me."

He nodded as he ran his hand over the steering wheel like a lovesick teenager getting ready to be dumped. "It is a long distance in terms of a relationship. I've never met anyone like you. Most of the women I know are only interested in getting their nails done or having kids."

"I don't exactly have a long record of boyfriends considering my *abilities*," she said. "Doesn't mean we can't hang out every so often. I'd love to come back and go dancing at Fitzgerald's. We don't have anything like that in Beaufort."

"I happen to know an adorable, yet stubborn, Jack Russell who will sink into a deep depression once you leave. Perhaps you could come back to visit him. Wouldn't want the poor little guy to lose his spark."

"I couldn't live with myself knowing I'd caused Dallas any distress. And since I'm addicted to the burgers at Corner Pocket, it makes sense I should visit as often as possible."

A smile crept across his face, creasing his eyes. "I can live with that."

He opened his door, walked around to Sarah's side of the truck, and helped her out. They strolled to the front porch where a host of moths danced around the light. Garrett glanced around while Sarah chewed her lower lip. If the night had been the most memorable of her life, this was definitely the most awkward moment.

As they stood there, a humming buzzed through the atmosphere. It grew louder until the low sound of *Our Love is Here to Stay* materialized from the sticky night air.

They looked around trying to identify the source of the music when Sarah caught a glimpse of a snowy-haired woman near the edge of the woods. Ola gave a sly smile and a wink before vanishing into the night.

"Where is the music coming from?" Garrett asked.

"The love of a wise woman," Sarah replied.

Without further hesitation, Garrett leaned down, his soft lips meeting Sarah's. Her knees went weak as the world around them quieted. For that moment, it was only the two of them and Sarah wondered how she'd ever be able to go back to being on her own. But now wasn't the time to think of such things, now was the time to live.

SARAH ROLLED DOWN THE WINDOW, as Danni's Mercedes swept across the Whale Branch Bridge on the way back to Beaufort. The pungent scent of pluff mud and oyster beds was like a fragrant sachet to her crestfallen mood. Garrett's kiss lingered on her lips, soft yet purposeful. Danni seemed to have picked up on her turmoil, keeping the conversation on pleasant, inconsequential topics. Still, the sting of saying goodbye had left a welt on her heart.

The oyster shell drive crackled beneath the car tires as they parked at Monroe Manse. Sarah took in the rose scented air and smiled. Home. It felt good to be back, even with memories of Garrett haunting her mind. The idea of ever finding someone else so closely matched to herself seemed unlikely.

"Want me to spend the night?" Danni offered, concern veiling her expression.

"We've just finished an extended slumber party," Sarah responded, arching her brows. "I appreciate the offer, but I'm fine. What about you?"

"It'll take some time to reconcile the fact I allowed myself to fall for a sociopath. Nevertheless, I will survive."

"I know you will."

Sarah grabbed her bags from the trunk and waved as Danni backed down the drive and sped off. Meandering across the garden path, Sarah jiggled the key in the brass lock and stepped into the comforting embrace of home. The house seemed to sense her melancholy. It's one of the things she loved about old homes. They carried all the emotions of those who'd lived within their walls over the years. To her, they were living entities with memories tattooed within the plaster and wood at the core of their existence. Her house had witnessed so much, including a war and a murder, yet it exuded a sense of family and warmth. She loved the feeling of being cocooned in the shelter of its walls.

Unpacking her things, she drew a hot bath, and soaked in a sea of frothy bubbles until her skin was pruned and her eyelids were heavy. Slipping between the cottony sheets of her own bed, the soft marsh breezes billowed through open windows, caressing her cheek until she drifted off to dreamland.

28

S ix Months Later

SARAH'S PHONE buzzed in her pocket as she walked along the waterfront after a three-mile run. Running always helped clear her head and avoid any discomfort in her life. The screen showed Garrett's number.

Taking a seat on one of the park swings, Sarah answered, her heart fluttering.

"Hey Garrett."

"Did I catch you at a bad time?"

"Just finished a run. What's up?"

"Harry called me a few minutes ago. The team entered a contest a few months back and we won! We've been invited to Massachusetts to film for one of the cable channel ghost hunting shows."

"Congratulations! Sounds like fun," Sarah replied.

"We'd like you to go with us. With your abilities we may be

KIM POOVEY

able to solve a case that has haunted America for more than a century."

Sarah hesitated. Surely, Garrett hadn't revealed her gift to the guys.

"Do Harry and Ralph know about me?"

"I haven't said anything about your dreamist abilities; however, they know you've got a good eye for the spiritual world. This is a pretty big deal. We could really use your skillset."

"What exactly can I do to help?"

"A little imprinting could lead us to answers."

"Imprinting?"

"You and Danni haven't covered that chapter yet?" Garrett asked. "Sorry, I didn't mean to assume. It's one of the earlier chapters."

"Explain it to me," Sarah replied, curious about learning a new skill.

"Any time you touch a personal item of the deceased, it creates a connection with the ghost."

"We have read that chapter," Sarah declared, happy she already knew something. "I've never heard it referred to as imprinting."

"It's not actually in the book but Grams always used the phrase. Guess it stuck with me."

"That's a good way to describe it. I used that technique when I was trying to figure out the mystery behind the disappearance of one of my ancestors at Monroe Manse. I was able to decipher some of her messages, but it was a struggle. Granted, that was just after I'd learned of my dreamist abilities."

"So, you'd be willing to help us out?" he said, excitement tinting his words.

"What's so special about this case?" Sarah asked.

"The place is fairly famous, which could lead to bigger projects for us."

"What's the location?" she asked, her heart palpitating.

"Fall River, Massachusetts. Home of the infamous Lizzie Borden."

"We're going to a residence where two people were butchered?" Sarah queried, her gut churning. "I'm not sure about this, Garrett. It could be dangerous."

"We're only there to film some ghosts. It's not like they'll come to life or possess us."

Sarah envisioned gruesome scenes of forty whacks with an ax and blood-soaked visions. Thus far, she'd survived a series of haunted dreams that had led to the discovery of a century old mystery and the identification of a serial killer. How much worse could this be? It's not like she hadn't seen movies about the grisly hatchet murders. As frightening as it seemed, the idea of spending time with Garrett won the battle.

"Sure. After all, they're only dreams, not realities. What could possibly happen?" Even as she said it, a knot formed in her stomach and a chill traced her spine. Something told her this wouldn't be as easy as it seemed.

AUTHOR'S NOTES

Let me begin by expressing my thanks to the Edgefield County Historical Society for their kindness in allowing me to use Magnolia Dale on the cover of this book, especially Beth Francis and Bettis Rainsford. Magnolia Dale is an 1843 plantation home-turned-museum that houses portraits, artifacts, and furnishings affiliated with Edgefield County's rich history.

I also want to mention that this book is a work of fiction. While I researched many of the historical aspects for the storyline, everything else is a figment of my imagination. I know nothing of legal endeavors, court proceedings, or ghost hunting. Those features of the book are nothing more than storytelling on my part and in no way reflects actual events in the town. I also took artistic liberties with a few of the buildings (hotel, farmhouse, club) as well as some of the property locations in order to make the storyline flow. Research for the book included a trip to Edgefield to sample food in many of the restaurants, and thus I can attest to the quality of Edgefield's delicious cuisine.

The people of Edgefield are some of the friendliest you'll ever meet. I've been privileged to participate in many of their events over the years including the annual history showcase and the Prohibition shootout several years ago. Edgefield is a kind and gracious community.

A special thanks to Justin and Tonya Guy for sharing their in-depth knowledge of the town's colorful history and for their years of friendship.

I highly recommend visiting Edgefield! Make sure to tour their museums, enjoy their many eateries, and attend some of their annual events. It's a wonderfully historic, welcoming town with the best burgers I've ever eaten!

ACKNOWLEDGMENTS

To my husband, Darryl, thank you for listening to my stories (again and again), cooking and doing the dishes when I'm in an editing frenzy, calming me when technological aspects overwhelm me, and for supporting this crazy writing habit! I love you!

To my mom, thanks for editing, re-editing, and editing again and for always cheering me on! Love you!

To my other mother, Millie Boyce, thanks for the chats and encouragement! Love you!

To Charlotte Raines Dixon, the best writing coach ever! Thanks for helping me enhance and polish my stories!

To Rena Violet, cover designer extraordinaire, thanks for sharing your artistry and creating the most beautiful covers for my books!

To Alyssa Krob at Wildscriber Marketing, thanks for your friendship and for creating beautiful ads and marketing graphics for my books!

To all my family and friends, your support means the world to me! Thank you, Joan Jones, Gina McNeill, Darlene Stokes, Lynn Bristow, Diane Morrison, Michelle Dufour, Madison

Wilbanks, Janet McCauley, Kay Keeler, Peggy Callahan, Jo Beaver, Janell McClure, Sarah Hetzler, Kelly Taylor, Bernie Ladd, and Jonathon Haupt.

Special thanks to my pre-readers, Britainy Lewis and Dady Blake.

Thanks to all my readers! I truly appreciate every one of you!

Thank you Nevermore Books, Beaufort Bookstore, MacIntosh Books, Lowcountry Living Room, and Lowcountry Store for carrying my books and hosting my signings!

Most importantly, thanks be to God! With Him all things are possible!

In Memorium:

Thanks to all those who supported me over the years and have gone on to Heaven. Harvey and Catherine Oates, Michael Wiegel, David Clark, Sam Poovey, Rachell Poovey Navratil, Mark Navratil, Tom Boyce, Phyllis Sooy, Cathy Benson, and Becky Baldwin. Love you always!

ALSO BY KIM POOVEY

The Haunting of Monroe Manse

Shadows of the Moss

Truer Words

Dickens Mice; the Tails Behind the Tale

Through Button Eyes; Memoir of an Edwardian Teddy Bear (out of print).

Kim Poovey's books are available from Amazon, Barnes & Noble, Kindle, and kimpoovey.com. Books can also be ordered through your local bookstore or library.

CPSIA information can be obtained
at www.ICGtesting.com
Printed in the USA
BVHW031555030223
657817BV00004B/713